The Four Sworn:
Spring Equinox

LENORE SAGASKIE

ISBN: 0-9882716-2-1
ISBN-13: 978-0-9882716-2-3

DEDICATION

for Denise, always

ACKNOWLEDGMENTS

I would like to thank Jan and Kenny Dunbar who helped me in my early days of story development, the readers of the Emmett Village News who read my stories and encouraged me to continue writing. Special thanks to Don Bentley, Jr, Marguerite Fisher, and Audrey Desrosiers for their continued support. I want to thank Amy Foster for helping me with my cover art. My uncles Peter Roberts and Bill Roberts gave me my love of books; their bookstore gave me a safe place to escape to when I needed it most. Thanks to my husband, Dan and my sons, Hunter and Archer for putting up with my chaos and joining in when necessary. I still maintain the highest gratitude for my sister Denise Podhorsky who encouraged me to publish my books. I will always love her for that. Extra special thanks to Taylor Coe whose editing made the story so much better.

"Be who God meant you to be and you will set the world on fire." – St. Catherine of Sienna

CHAPTER 1

Abby picked up a piece of silver and dabbed some flux onto its surface before placing it onto a fire brick on the work bench. Starting her acetylene torch with a flick of her spark lighter, she adjusted the valves until she got the flame just right. Once she approved of the intensity of the flame, she moved it methodically back and forth over the piece of silver until the flux bubbled and hissed. The solder flowed into place exactly where Abby intended it to go. Satisfied, she shut off the valves with one hand, grabbed the hot silver with copper tweezers clasped in her other hand, and then dropped the piece into a pot of pickling solution on the far side of her work bench.

Abby always held the power of fire with awe and respect. As a metal-smithing artist, she loved being able to create beautiful things while harnessing its power, and she prided herself on her ability to utilize and control such a dangerous force.

Fire good....

(Yes, it is)

What?

Abby shrugged as she replaced the lid on the pickling solution with a satisfied smile and pushed a rogue lock of her brown hair off her face with the back of her hand.

That was strange, she thought to herself. A sound behind her broke her concentration.

"Hey, are you still working?" Her husband, Dan, called up the stairs as he ascended, his head peeking through the worn oak rails. His dark eyes fixed on hers as he smiled affectionately at her.

"Normally when artists go to shows they tend to take finished work with them. Aren't you going to be late?"

"I just needed to blow off some steam and relax." Abby replied, wiping her hands on a towel.

"Aren't you supposed to pick up Sara?" Dan questioned. "I thought it was your turn to drive."

Damn. She almost forgot Sara.

"Thanks for reminding me."

Abby cast one last glance at the bench. She felt the draw of the flame, a pull similar to that of a moth to a porch light. It was easier for her to succumb to that pull because she knew she wouldn't suffer the same fate as a moth. The draw of the torch was satisfying, as was the creation of an object with it. *It would be so easy to stay here, stay and work and play...*

Play with fire...

Abby shook her head. *Where is that coming from? Everything here can wait until later.* She would just have to resist the draw to the flame for now.

Dan stepped aside as Abby bolted past him and descended the stairs at break-neck speed.

"Slow down, don't kill yourself," he scolded as he trailed after her. "You still have some time. The van is already loaded, and I made you a lunch. I even made one for Sara. I bet she'll forget."

Abby had to smile. Sara probably wouldn't even be ready when she got to her place to pick her up. That would seriously cut into their time to set up their booth at the art show.

"I'd better head out." Abby glanced at her watch. "Thanks for the reminder. I don't know what I'd do without you."

Turning to face him she took a few steps forward and softly slid her arms around his waist and gently pressed her lips to his.

"Have a good day, sweetie." Dan smiled as her steered her towards the door. "Sell lots, have fun, and get going." He handed her a cooler bag and her key ring as she swung her backpack over her arm.

"Bye, sweetie." Abby waved as she walked through the doorway and through the door of her studio. Striding down the path to the driveway, she made her way to the van, tossed her stuff in, and drove to Sara's house.

Abby smiled as she recalled the first time she had met Sara. Abby had been a freelance metal artist for several years and always did her own thing—outdoor shows, some gallery work, and even private showings at her studio, but never belonged to an artists' guild or association. One day she encountered an ad in the Harmon Review—the Harmon Art Guild was looking for members, and the meeting was that evening.

What the hell? She thought. Abby had always avoided membership in clubs and associations. Didn't someone famous once say that they wouldn't join any club that would have them as a member? Abby thought it was Mark Twain, but it could have been someone equally as memorable. Besides, weren't artists who belonged to clubs a bunch of artsy-fartsy snobs? Abby was relieved that that perception was only a myth in the case of the Harmon Art Guild. Sara was not only the least artsy-fartsy person she knew, but she was probably the most interesting person Abby had ever met in her entire life.

Sara was a strikingly attractive woman with platinum blonde hair and prominent sapphire-blue eyes. She was dressed as she was always dressed—in jeans and a button up shirt with a leather jacket. Abby thought she looked as if she had just ridden a horse into town. *Or a Harley.* Sara had made Abby feel welcome as a part of the group with her easy conversation and bubbly laughter. It wasn't long before they got into a regular routine of getting together to talk about art over coffee at each other's homes. Abby felt comfortably familiar with Sara and appreciated Sara's penchant for black cowboy boots and bulky turquoise and silver jewelry. She even enjoyed some of Sara's more unconventional topics of interest, particularly the unexplained or paranormal. While Sara didn't always have an opinion, she seemed eager to learn as much as she could about any subject that piqued her interest so that she could form her own opinions. Abby admired that quality very much, even though she had ambivalent feelings about many of the topics that Sara delved into.

"What do you think about aliens?" Sara had inquired of her during one of their afternoon discussions. "Do you believe in the existence of other beings in the universe?"

"Well," Abby had answered, "I think the universe is vast, and I believe that there could be more than just humans in it, but I don't know if I believe that aliens have visited here. I guess I would have to see it to believe it." Abby added.

"Well, I'm sure that they have better things to do than anal probing, don't you?" Sara replied, laughing.

That had been the topic of discussion their first afternoon together, three years ago. *Wow, had it really been three years?*

Abby wondered what topics they would be delving into today. Abby thought about mentioning a disturbing dream she had a couple of nights ago, but quickly dismissed the idea. Abby never felt comfortable talking about her dreams. She always hated hearing about other people's dreams, and she also worried that all dreams could be interpreted in a Freudian manner. Anyone who told her she wanted to have sex with her father or kill her mother would definitely be in for a serious ass-kicking.

Besides, what would people make of a metal-smith dreaming of fire? They would probably say she was working much too hard.

Abby felt the familiar crunch under her tires as the road changed from pavement to gravel and began to slow down and turn into Sara's long, gravel driveway. As she pulled her van up to the front of the house, Sara came bounding out of the front door carrying a wooden easel under her arm.

"Guess what?" Sara called out to Abby. "I'm all packed and ready to go! I just have to haul it all out and load it up!" Sara plunked the easel down on the grass and headed back to the house to bring out more artwork and equipment.

Abby got out of the van and began to load it with Sara's artwork, bins and structures. In no time, the two of them got it all in the van and ready to go.

A small miracle happened today, Abby thought. *We're actually going to be early.*

Abby got into the van and turned the ignition as Sara plopped into the passenger seat.

"So," Sara turned toward Abby inquisitively. "Do you believe in past lives?"

"What?"

"Past lives. Reincarnation. The '*déjà vu*' feeling that you've done something before in a previous life. That sorta thing," Sara explained as she pulled her seat belt across her shoulder.

Abby shrugged noncommittally and pulled the van down Sara's driveway. She wasn't sure she believed, but the idea of remembering a past life left Abby with a bad taste in her mouth and an even worse feeling in the pit of her stomach.

Once they arrived at the park, Abby and Sara quickly found their spot and set to the familiar work of unloading the van and setting up their booths and artwork displays. This was Abby's third year setting up at the Harmon Art in the Park show and Sara's second.

At least they put us next to each other, Abby thought.

Though the sky was clear, they still opted to put up their display tents. While the weather was fairly comfortable and moderately cool for late August, the sun was still too hot to be standing directly under all day. While Sara was an avid sun worshipper, Abby didn't share her enthusiasm. "I shun the sun," she would say, retreating under a large floppy hat, long shirts, and SPF 50 sun block.

The morning passed relatively quickly. It appeared the majority of the residents of Harmon were taking advantage of the weather, strolling

4

through the park, pulling carts with their children, and eating an assortment of foods that came off the various carts.

"All that food is making me hungry!" Sara announced loudly. Her voice jolted Abby out of her musings.

"Oh yeah, I forgot. Dan made us both lunch." Abby fumbled inside the bag and produced two sandwiches, two apples, and two bottles of water. "He figured you probably wouldn't have had time to make something," Abby added.

"No, he probably knew I'd forget." Sara replied with a sigh. "I know I get distracted easily—," she broke off in mid-sentence as she looked out across the artists and vendors.

"There are a lot of artists we know here," she gave a little wave across the park. "Sharon is here, Steve, Tim, Tallulah — look," she indicated toward a brown-haired man across the park, "there's that potter you were interested in. What's his name again? Joe something?"

"Joe Asine," Abby corrected, pronouncing it Ah-see-nay. "And I'm not interested in *him*. I was hoping to get a deal on one of his stoneware bowls - you think maybe he'd do a trade?" Abby looked to Sara for a response. She was staring dreamily across the park at Joe, with a half-smile on her face.

"He is kinda cute, isn't he?" she breathed. "I wonder if he's married or something?"

Abby followed her gaze. Joe was placing a tissue wrapped bowl into a box. His shoulder-length brown hair was very shiny and the sun gave it the appearance of having red highlights. His broad shoulders and trim waist revealed that he had a good physique hidden underneath his denim jeans and a long-sleeved button front shirt.

"You know, for a Native man, he isn't really tuned in," Sara added. "I talked to him once. He's not into traditional Native beliefs." She leaned in closer to Abby and added, "in fact, he's very *conservative*." She intoned, as if uttering a swear word.

Abby gave a laugh and took a bite of her sandwich. She leaned her chair back and delved into her lunch.

The afternoon dragged as the crowds dwindled down to a trickle of people and the occasional family strolling through the park. As fewer patrons came through the show and sales started to slow, the artists themselves began to flit back and forth visiting, catching up on news, sharing show information, and doing the occasional trade. It was one of the better perks of being a "starving artist". You may not always have the big sales or get the ribbon and cash prize award for *Best in Show*, but you could always get a decent collection of good art through trading and bartering, or, at the very least, get a head start on your Christmas shopping.

Abby jumped up out of her chair, "Sara, do me a favor? Please watch my booth while I go see if Joe is interested in a trade."

Sara nodded and Abby strolled nonchalantly away from her display. She ambled slowly up each row, stopping at the odd table to pick up a piece to examine or just say hello.

"Hi." Abby said shyly when she finally approached Joe's space.

"Hi," he replied quietly smiling in return. "You're Abby, right? I remember you from the Art in the Street show in Coppertown."

"Didn't you get *Best in Show*?"

"Yeah," his smiled thinned. "The prize money helped to make up for the slow sales. Have they given out the show awards yet?" his eyes widened. "I wonder who'll place."

"I dunno." Abby scrutinized his table and the metal structure behind him outfitted with various shelves all featuring his many clay creations.

His pots were perfect; the clay was smooth, and the glaze was perfectly applied and gleamed brightly in the sun. He had several sculptures, some of people, some of animals, and several freeform pieces hanging on the structure. Her eyes moved along each piece appreciatively. Her hand came to rest on a five-inch pot painted in many hues of green and finished with a clear glaze.

"I was wondering whether you would consider a trade," Abby blurted out. "Are you interested?"

"You like that piece?"

Abby nodded as she picked up the pot and gazed at it appreciatively.

"Let's see what you've got," Joe replied.

He spoke briefly with the artist in the space next to him, and after arranging for him to watch his booth, he followed Abby back to her space. Abby caught Sara's eye and gave her a quick wink as she led Joe over. Sara jumped up so quickly she knocked her chair over and almost fell backward over it.

After casting a smile in Sara's direction, Joe began picking up and examining objects on Abby's table. He seemed to be particularly interested in the jewelry. He picked up a very feminine silver and turquoise brooch and turned it over and over in his hands.

"Looking for something for your wife?" Abby probed cautiously.

"Oh no, I'm not married." Joe stated (Sara covered her smile with her hand), "but my Mom's birthday is next week, and she wanted a new piece of turquoise for protection–not that I personally believe it. You're Sara Taylor, aren't you?" he said as if finally realizing she was there. "I really admire your work. Your mixed media sculptures are so interesting."

Sara beamed at him. It seemed she was also at a loss for words, but she finally managed to squeak out a shy "thanks."

"Abby, how about this brooch? Can we do this trade for the bowl? I'll throw in something else too. Meet me back at my booth, okay?"

Abby nodded in assent as Joe strode over to his booth.

As Abby boxed the brooch and placed it in a small organza gift bag, a group of show officials stopped at Sara's space.

"Congratulations, Sara Taylor! You have won the *Best in Show First Place Award*. Here's your ribbon," said the short, officious-looking judge. Both show officials in turn shook her hand. The short, officious-looking woman placed the ribbon on her table while the tall bald man pressed an envelope containing the cash award into her palm. Sara squealed with delight.

The two judges turned to face Abby. "Abby Fabrica, you have earned an *Honorable Mention*," the officious woman spoke again, setting down her clipboard, placing a ribbon on Abby's table with one hand and shaking her hand with the other. Sara spied the unawarded second and third place ribbons on the judge's clipboard.

"Hey, who got the second and third for *Best in Show*?" Sara inquired enthusiastically. She could hardly stand still behind her table.

"*Second Place* will be awarded to Joe Asine for pottery and *Third Place* to Sharon Janish for her pen and ink drawings." The officious looking judge picked up her clipboard and strode in the direction of Joe's booth.

"You better hurry and finish that trade," Sara urged, "in case Joe doesn't like the idea of second place."

Abby grabbed the gift bag and raced ahead of the judge to Joe's table. He had the bowl already boxed.

"I put a surprise in there." He added, "Oh yeah, say congrats to Sara. I heard she won first place."

Abby smiled and backed away as the judges reached his table. "Thanks, and congrats to you, too," she spoke over her shoulder as she headed back to Sara. A crowd had already gathered around her as she showed off the first place ribbon.

"First place, I can't believe it!" Sara was almost in shock with excitement.

"You earned it." Abby said sincerely.

"Yeah," echoed another artist.

"You don't give yourself enough credit," said another.

Abby looked at her ribbon too. Dan would be pleased when she got home. Something to celebrate.

After the awards were completely given out and the crowds of people had gone, everyone began to pack their wares and tear down their booths.

"Thanks for coming out to Art in the Park," a loud speaker boomed. "We hope that your participation will help to make next year's event a success as well."

Abby began packing her jewelry away into cushioned boxes. *At least I sold a few pieces*, she thought. *Maybe even enough to cover my booth fees.* After she finished packing her sculptures, she collapsed her tables and display panels. She loaded them into the van as she waited for Sara to get packed so she could help take down the tents. After getting the tables and panels into the van, Abby left the van's back door open and sat on the bumper to catch her breath. She pulled her water out of the bag and took a long swallow. She felt drained, but in a good way. She ran her hand through her hair and sighed. It was almost seven o'clock and she was more than ready to head home.

Sara was still packing and chatting. Abby stood and walked to a copse of trees in the park. The soft breeze was rustling the leaves gently, and the crickets were adding their night song as the melody.

Suddenly, Abby felt a prickling sensation begin at the base of her neck. It crept up the back of her head while simultaneously racing down her spine. She felt her body stiffen and become rigid. She was being watched. And she was alone in the trees.

What did all those women's self-defense classes teach? Her mind raced to remember. *Yes, that's it. Face your attacker.*

She whirled around quickly hoping to catch whoever it was off guard. But no one was there. She looked down to the ground to detect any signs of someone running away, and to her surprise she saw a man. A small man. A very diminutive man, to say the least. He couldn't have stood any taller than two feet unless he was standing on tip-toe. He was shaped like a beer keg and had no discernible waist. He appeared to be wearing moleskin pants and a sheepskin vest over a leather shirt. His face seemed to be entirely covered by a semi-long, wiry gray beard. His eyes were small grayish-blue buttons surrounded by crow's feet. Abby thought that he looked like a cross between Popeye and Danny DeVito, but he was wearing a hat any self-respecting New York cab driver would be jealous of.

Abby's jaw dropped. She couldn't help but stare, but she couldn't speak either. His eyes narrowed as he raised an arm up and waggled a finger in her direction.

"What the feck you lookin' at?" he growled.

"Abby, where are you?" Sara's voice sang through the trees. Abby was jolted by the sound of Sara's voice. She turned toward it and then turned back to the little man.

He was gone.

CHAPTER 2

Sara gazed out the window of Abby's van as it meandered along the road. She had a half-smile on her face and was humming softly to herself as she unconsciously wound and unwound her necklace with her left forefinger.

"Are you sure you didn't see anything unusual back there in the park?" Abby inquired, breaking the silence between them.

"Huh? No, I didn't see anything. What did you see?" Sara turned to look at Abby, straightening up and placing her hands in her lap.

Abby fell silent. Should she tell Sara about what she saw and her brief encounter with whatever or whomever that was? Either Sara would think she was starting to lose it or she would go on one of her rants. Not that Abby didn't think past lives and reincarnation were interesting, she just didn't want to "go there" this evening.

"I don't know," Abby muttered, staring straight ahead both hands clenched tightly on the steering wheel.

Sara went back to her window gazing and necklace twiddling.

"He really liked my work," she breathed. *"And* I won *Best in Show,"* she whispered. Her smile broadened.

They continued up the road to Sara's place, and Abby helped unload her displays and artwork.

"Thanks a lot!" Sara called out as she waved to Abby who was getting in the van. "Give me a call tomorrow, okay?"

Abby nodded and gave a return wave as she turned the key in the ignition and pulled out of her driveway. She drove a little slower than usual down the dusty road, watching the orange sun begin its descent into the horizon. *It looks like it's on fire,* Abby thought.

(Fire! Burn!)

A fire would be nice, she thought. *Maybe I'll do a little work when I get home tonight.*

(Burn! Fire!)
No, maybe a bonfire, she sighed, *that would be lovely.*
(Yes!)

Abby increased her speed to hurry home. She was in her driveway in no time and hauling her set-up and displays into her studio.

"Hey," Dan said as he came running out of the house. "You should've come in and let me know you were back. I can help unload your stuff." He grabbed a box out of the van and followed her into the studio.

"Yeah, I know you would've helped, but I just wanted to get the van unloaded before it gets dark. How about we have a fire tonight?" Abby turned to face him, waiting for his answer.

"Umm . . . okay . . . sure. That would be fine with me." Dan walked past her to set down the box he was holding.

"Great!" she said, bouncing over to him and giving him a kiss on the forehead. "Do you mind finishing unloading?" she added quickly, "I'll get everything ready for the fire."

"It'll cost you." Dan said, waggling his eyebrows.

Abby gave him a quick kiss on the lips.

"Well, that's a start," Dan countered as she threw a smile over her shoulder and bounded outside.

Abby headed directly to the back of the garden shed. Beside their black composter was a huge pile of brush and tree limbs. Most of the large limbs had been hidden behind the shed in the mid-summer when a huge thunderstorm had torn through the state. The smaller limbs were just from cleaning up the yard. They stored them behind the shed for use as kindling for their fireplace. Abby grabbed a few medium-sized long branches under her arm and dragged them to the back of the house where the fire pit was located, surrounded by a circle of neatly placed stones. She dropped the branches and went back for an armload of small branches and twigs mixed with dried leaves and pine needles.

(Burn! Fire! Quickly!)

She immediately set to work setting up the kindling and leaves. In no time (with the help of her trusty lighter), the kindling caught and she began breaking up the larger limbs and getting them ready to feed the fire.

Abby continued to make trips to gather more limbs, break them into manageable pieces, and pile them beside the fire pit. Every now and then she'd feed the fire a couple limbs to get the flames up.

(Fire! Burn! Burn!)

There was something satisfying about watching a fire burn, watching the flames lick at a piece of wood, and then watching it transform as the wood was devoured before turning to hot coals as it began to die. Then the fire would spring back to life as she added a new piece of wood, and the flames leapt back to life as their endless appetite for wood was fed. Abby watched, staring transfixed into the fire and breathing in its smoky aroma. She tossed another piece onto the fire, prodded the embers with a stick, and sank down into a nearby lawn chair. Abby had been so exhausted after the show, but now it was as if she was being revitalized with every log she fed to the fire. She stood up.

I need to get more wood, she thought.

(More! More! Burn More!)

Abby began hauling as much wood as she could carry and began tossing even larger and dryer pieces straight on the fire.

"Hey, Ab, I thought I'd bring our dinner out – HOLY SHIT!" Dan yelled, almost dropping the tray he was carrying out onto the back deck. He scrambled to place it on the table and then leapt down the steps to Abby's side.

The flames had risen substantially above both their heads, and the heat that was emanating from the fire was so intense that Dan stepped back a few feet immediately, grasping Abby gently by the shoulders and guiding her back from the fire with him.

"Why don't we let the flames die down some while we eat dinner?" Dan suggested. "I don't think the neighbors would like it if we burned down our house."

Abby opened her mouth to protest, but Dan was already leading her deftly by her elbow and up onto the deck, pulling out a chair and guiding her into it. The food smelled good and her stomach rumbled enthusiastically. *I can watch the fire from here,* she thought, picking up her fork and spearing a piece of chicken. Her eyes continued to observe the flames as she devoured her chicken Caesar salad.

"How's dinner?" Dan inquired after observing a few more bites.

"What?" Abby turned to look at him for a moment. "Oh, sorry, it's very good. Yeah . . . very . . . good."

Dan watched the reflection of the flames dancing in her eyes as they once again became riveted by the fire and its every movement.

"Well, I'm glad you're enjoying it as much as my company." Dan pushed slightly back from the table and crossed his arms over his chest.

Abby gazed at the fire, oblivious to his remarks, while absently stuffing a forkful of salad into her mouth. What would Dan think of her encounter today? Would he think she was crazy? If she questioned her own sanity, why would he be any different? Looking across the table at him, she set her fork gently back down on her plate. He met her gaze, his eyes slightly narrow and his lips a pale line across his face.

"Have you ever seen any unusual things?" Abby began. "I mean... things that you wouldn't normally expect to see?"

Dan looked puzzled. "Like what?" his brow furrowed and he uncrossed his arms and reached his hands across the table to clasp hers. "Are you okay? Is something wrong?" He asked, his voice full of concern. Abby recounted her encounter in the park to Dan, feeling a wave of relief wash over her as she let it pour out. She didn't care if he thought her crazy. She wanted, no, *needed* to tell it to someone. Dan listened intently, not taking his eyes off Abby for a moment.

". . . and when I turned back around he was gone." Abby finished. She looked up at him sheepishly. "Do I sound stupid?"

"No, I don't think you're stupid." Dan said quietly.

"Do you think I was imagining things?"

"Well, there are two possible explanations here: the first is that you may have been imagining things, and the second is that you really did see a small man in the clearing." Dan caught her eye and held her gaze for a moment. "I believe that you did see someone in the clearing. And I don't believe you were seeing things." He gave her a reassuring smile. He continued. "Many old stories, fables, myths, what-have-you, have included gnomes or dwarves in them. Who's to say they don't exist?"

He let go of her hand and stood up from the table. "But the question is then, why did you see him? I think perhaps it was an accident; that maybe he wasn't supposed to let you see him and he got outta there quick." He walked toward her and put a reassuring hand on her shoulder. "I don't think you'll see him again. Come on. Let's sit by your fire again." He offered her his hand and helped her up out of her chair.

The fire was glowing orange-red in the darkness of the night. The sky was clear with small stars twinkling around a pale, glowing half moon in the sky. The air was cool, but still enjoyable to be sitting out in their faded, green plastic Adirondack chairs sipping a glass of wine. The fire was burning steadily now, and the flames were much more controlled under Dan's gentle tending and stoking. Abby took a deep breath, inhaling the cool air and the smoky scent of the fire. She was feeling more relaxed; although the fire was a pleasant distraction, her manic enthusiasm seemed to have left her.

"Do you believe those creatures exist? You know, fairy tale creatures?" she looked at Dan, who had just plopped down in his chair and took a sip from his wine glass. He set down his glass and stretched his legs out.

"Well, I don't know if I believe all the stories and myths, but I do believe in possibilities."

"Possibilities?" Abby looked at him quizzically.

"Yes. Possibilities. I believe that anything is possible. Even Sherlock Holmes said—"

"Sherlock Holmes?" Abby snorted into her wine glass. "Here we go."

"Yes," he continued. "Sherlock Holmes said once you eliminate the probable, then you must examine the impossible. That, to me, means that anything is *possible*." He leaned back in his chair, a smile across his face.

At that moment, she wanted to tell him that she was relieved that he believed her, and that his opinion, above all else, mattered the most to her. She could always talk to him, confide in him, and know he would always back her up or make the appropriate sympathetic noises.

"Thank you, Dan." Abby managed to say smiling at him through the darkness.

"Anytime, darling," he replied, lifting his wine glass in salute to her.

Together in silence they watched the shadows of the flames play across the trees in the darkness. And, for a fleeting moment, Abby felt a shiver run across her spine. It was a strange feeling, she mused, pushing the veil of paranoia from her mind. But she still glanced into the trees, maintaining her vigil, alert and watchful.

CHAPTER 3

Sara reached an arm out from under the blanket and flicked to the next page of her book before jamming her arm back under the goose down cover on her oversized bed. *A perfect mental health day*, she decided. No shows, just a day to herself to do whatever she wished. It was definitely one of the few benefits of living alone. She might even stay in her pajamas unless she had to venture outside for some reason. Her neighbors were far too nosy and very prone to gossip. Not a great idea to let them catch her in her jammies in broad daylight. But, in an act of silent rebellion, she would linger in them as long as she could. It was her day off.

She was enjoying her book, one of many that had resided in a very precariously stacked pile at the side of her bed. Beside the pile of books resembling a miniature model of the Leaning Tower of Pisa there was also the moving mass of magazines. Occasionally it would migrate across the floor, either by Sara's stepping on it or by one of her two cats launching off her bed and grazing the pile upon landing on the floor. She needed to either do some serious reading or cull the pile.

She hoped to make a dent in both piles today. She quickly skimmed the next page and snaked her arm out from under the blanket to move along to the next fascinating book. Its title: *Transcendental Meditation: Tranquility on the Next Plane*. Although she had been recently fascinated with past lives and reincarnation, she also found transcendental meditation very interesting. The topic had become especially interesting since she discovered that you could use it to achieve astral travel. She thought she had achieved astral travel once, but she had fallen asleep and thought afterwards that perhaps it had been just a dream. Who knows? Maybe she would succeed if she learned to meditate *properly*. Sara snuggled further under her blanket and tightened her grip on her book.

Sara was startled a moment later by a mewling cry and the head of her gray tabby cat, Frick, insistently butting against her arm.

"Ouch! Alright, I'm getting up to feed you," she winced as Frick gave her an attention-seeking love bite on the forearm. Sara quickly marked her page and set the book down. She threw her legs over the side of the bed as she tossed the blankets aside, hoisted herself up, and padded barefoot into the kitchen. The hum of the can opener caused both cats, Frick and Frack, to appear, entwining around her ankles in their customary figure eight patterns, purring, and tripping her as she reached to fill their bowls. They quickly forgot her presence as they dove hungrily into their food.

"Ingrates." She complained.

Sara filled her coffee pot from the tap and got her morning coffee ready. She glanced out the kitchen window while waiting for the coffee to finish brewing. It looked like a crisp fall day, an average day—no sun, but not too gray, with just a hint of a breeze playing through the brilliant orange and red leaves in the trees. She leaned forward and slipped open the window slightly. She took a deep breath and inhaled the cool fresh air, allowing it to mingle with the smell of the fresh brewing coffee in her kitchen.

Maybe I'll get dressed after all, she decided. *Maybe I'll go for a bit of a walk instead.* She padded back to her room and emerged a few moments later in her favorite jeans and a worn but equally comfortable blue flannel shirt. Sara quickly poured herself a cup of the brewed coffee and added lots of milk and sugar to it. Although she was very careful about what she ate or drank, she could never cut back on the milk and sugar in her morning coffee. The very *idea* was foreign to her. She patted her slightly snug waist band. At 5'9", she could carry a few extra pounds in the winter, she told herself. But whether she was dieting or not, she would never give up her coffee.

Taking her coffee mug with her, she walked over to the door, setting her mug down briefly to pull on her cowboy boots. She paused briefly before stepping out the door as she caught her own blue eyes staring at her from the mirror in the entranceway. She raised a hand up to smooth back a wispy lock of hair that escaped from her hastily-tied ponytail. Normally she didn't like to tie her hair back, thinking it made her look younger than the 30 she was. *No time to fight with my hair today, though. After all, it's my day off.* She gave her reflection a wink and strode out the door.

Sara loved her house. It was a rickety, 100-year-old farmhouse that she had been restoring for the last five years. She couldn't really take credit for all of the work, though. The previous owner had done the majority of the work. It was three-quarters completed when the old man died. The house had been vacant for two years before Sara came along. She immediately fell in love with the house and the property. There was a small barn with a finished, heated workshop which was ideal for her art studio. And the property was beautiful and idyllic; ten acres of woodland in the back, with a stream running through the length of it. There were even rumors that there were ruins of an Indian village on the property; one rumor even suggested a sacred burial ground. That, coupled with the fact that the previous owner had died in the house, were the reasons the place stayed on the market for so long. Sara didn't care. She had felt only good energy from this place. And she absolutely loved it.

Sara downed her coffee and set the empty cup on the front steps before setting off down the path swathed in the grass leading toward the forest. Even though it was getting close to 11 a.m., the dew was still glistening on the grass and she could see her breath as she exhaled, although the breeze in the air felt slightly warm on her cheeks. She felt calm and relaxed, yet somehow invigorated. It wasn't long before she was under the orange-red canopy of the trees. Although it was early fall and the trees still had full canopies, there were enough leaves on the ground to completely cover the forest floor in a patchwork quilt of red, orange, and gold. A light breeze wafted gently through the trees, picking up leaves and randomly spreading them about. As she reached the stream, she plopped down onto a large rock jutting out of the ground slightly over but at the edge of the stream. Sara watched with interest as the breeze gently lifted up individual leaves and placed them into the stream where they then became miniature boats sailing down the waterway and out of sight.

Sara watched with earnest, her eyes following each leaf. *This is strange*, Sara thought. *It's too orderly, almost synchronized.* There was a slight rhythm to it almost like a cadence as each leaf was picked up and deposited into the water. Sara stared and the strange parade of leaves stopped. So did the breeze.

No, it can't be. Sara gasped. She closed her eyes, took a deep breath and cleared her head of all thoughts. She opened her eyes and stared at the fallen leaves on the ground.

She closed her eyes once more, drew in another long, deep breath and whispered, "Begin." The soft breeze gently touched her cheek like a delicate kiss. She opened her eyes. The leaves had continued their rhythmic march into the river.

"Whoa!" Sara jumped quickly to her feet and began frantically looking in all directions.

Her head was spinning every which way as she attempted to look for some other reason, no, *cause*, for this strange phenomenon. She took a couple of steps backwards, but it was too late—she realized she was still atop the rock. As her left foot stepped back into the air, she lost her balance with her right foot. She flung her arms out to her sides, swinging them madly in all directions in a last attempt to regain her balance as she fell backwards into the water. The cold water was an instant shock and brought her immediately to her feet. She could feel the tightening of her lungs in her chest as she gulped in air. The water was only up to her waist, and she waded carefully out of the river, gingerly setting each foot down to assure she had a good footing on the rocky river bed. She was completely soaked to the bone. Her flannel shirt and jeans were soaked with the icy water and felt like they weighed twice her body weight. She could feel the water sloshing around in her boots.

She reached up and pulled several leaves out of her wet hair and tossed them to the ground.

"Some day off," she stated flatly out loud. Her voice seemed to echo in the trees. Sara turned and began plodding back up the path toward the house, her clothes and boots squishing and squelching along the way. Her teeth were chattering uncontrollably. Sara stopped and listened for a moment. There was only silence.

Nah, must be just be me. She shook her head. For a brief moment, she thought she could hear someone laughing.

***

"Keep your hands steadier." Joe cautioned the young girl on the stool in front of the pottery wheel.

"But I can't control it!" she wailed miserably. "It forces my hands away, and my clay will get wobbly again."

Joe smiled patiently at her. "This time, brace your elbows into your hip bones. Then press in on the clay with your hands. That should put you in a better position."

"It's working! It's working! Cool!" she shouted enthusiastically.

"Now once you've drawn the clay up and down a couple of times, it's time to make the well in the center. Use your thumb like I showed you earlier."

Joe backed away from the girl sitting at the pottery wheel. A small group of students gathered around her, watching her progress with quiet interest as she pushed her thumb down into the center of the clay mound still spinning around on the wheel. Her thumb left a quarter-sized indentation which soon became a deeper hole with the young girl's continued pressure. She then withdrew her thumb with a satisfied smile.

"Does anyone remember what Susan's next step should be?" Joe asked the students gathered around. He nodded at a tall slender boy whose hand was up in the air.

"She needs to widen the opening that she just made using her index finger to push out to the sides. Then once the opening is wide enough, she needs to draw the sides up."

"Correct!" Joe smiled at the boy. "Susan, continue your fine work on the wheel. Mark, Al, both of you get on the free wheels and begin turning. The rest of you, grab a ball of clay and do some hand building. You can do a bowl or whatever else you wish; just use your imagination." The small group immediately dispersed, and the room was soon filled with the soft hum of pottery wheels spinning and the slapping of hands on damp clay. Joe took a plastic bag off a pottery piece he was working on and began carving some detail into the leather-hard outside brim of the bowl with a small carving tool.

Joe never really thought he could teach. Not that he didn't think he was smart enough for it; he definitely knew that he had the brains to teach. After all, he managed to achieve a Master's Degree in Fine Arts. But he just figured he'd be too busy doing art to teach it. After a couple of years on the art circuit, doing shows, courting galleries, and entering competitions, he really started to miss having a steady source of income. And when his childhood friend, Tara, told him that there was a teaching position open for an art teacher at the school they both attended growing up, he didn't hesitate to put in an application. He didn't really think he would get an interview, let alone the position. But within two weeks of putting in his application he had been interviewed and hired. Joe smiled to himself. At first, he felt guilty teaching because his reason for doing so was basic survival—he needed a reliable, steady source of income. He wasn't someone who had chosen a career path to mold minds—to encourage kids to develop their talents and go as far as they could with them. But his guilt soon wore off. Those kids that ended up in his class were definitely eager and enthusiastic, and it was infectious. Joe found that their enthusiasm fed his creativity too. He was producing much more now than he ever had. He certainly didn't think he would enjoy teaching, and it had been a pleasant surprise.

Joe glanced up from the bowl he was etching. All three wheels were humming, each with a student seated and hunched over a spinning clump of clay. The young girl, Susan, had a small group still crowded around her, each uttering the odd murmur of encouragement over the now almost completed and very respectable-looking bowl sitting on the wheel.

Joe stood up and wrapped his piece back in plastic and returned it and his tools back to their place on the shelf. He glanced up at the clock on the wall and noted that it was 10 minutes to two.

I should call clean up, Joe thought. He opened his mouth, but stopped himself. He felt a strange sensation run through his body. Almost like a shiver, but not cold. More like a shudder, as if something momentarily ran through his entire body at once. A rumbly, creepy shudder that felt like it ran through him and into the ground. And again. It was almost like he could feel—,

"Earthquake," he whispered.

No sooner had the words come out of his mouth had it happened. The rumbling passed under his feet, the workbenches and stools shook simultaneously, and some fell to the ground in a clatter as the contents of the cupboards shook and rattled the glass doors. A couple of the girls screamed, and then the school fire alarm went off, jarring Joe back to what was happening in the classroom.

"Everyone, please. Do not panic," he said calmly. "Is anyone hurt?" A general murmuring and shaking of heads chorused in answer. "We need to form a line and exit the classroom, just like in the fire drills. Okay? Now, let's get going."

Joe opened the door and held it open as the class exited the room. As the last student exited, Joe turned off the light, closed the door, and followed his students out the door to the base of the hill on the school grounds outside. He quickly counted his students and determined all were accounted for and safely out of the building.

Joe sat cross-legged on the grass with his class and they watched the remaining junior and senior high school classes filtering out of the building. Another surge swept through him. He didn't know why, but he couldn't help but feel that this, whatever it was, was no fluke. It was only the beginning.

Then the aftershock hit.

***

Abby had just set down her torch and turned off the gas when the quake hit. At first she didn't know what was going on—an earthquake in Michigan? Sure, earthquakes happened in California, but none that she had ever heard of happened in Michigan. Yeah, you heard the odd gunshot out here; hunters on occasion, but it was usually farmers dispatching pesky ground hogs or rabbits. Out here they had the potential to damage thousands of dollars of crops or cause deadly livestock accidents from cattle or horses tripping in their holes. But *earthquakes*? Although nothing had broken, Abby noticed that quite a few tools and bit of debris had been shaken and scattered off their shelves and displaced to the floor. Resisting the urge to set her workshop back in order, Abby stepped over the bits on the floor and made her way down the stairs and back to the house.

A cup of tea would be a nice diversion, she thought. She opened the door and went into the kitchen to put the kettle on. She walked into the living room and moved the pillows around on the couch until she found the remote and clicked the television on, switching the channel immediately to a local news station.

Maybe it wasn't an earthquake, Abby thought to herself. *Maybe it was terrorists*, although the thought wasn't a reassuring one. Just then, the aftershock hit, tinkling the china in her cabinets and vibrating the old planks in the floor and ceiling of her house. Abby fought the urge to bolt outside. *What are you supposed to do again?* She tried to remember. *Go into a bathroom?* She walked back to the kitchen as she strained her memory and turned off the screaming teakettle, setting it down on a cool element. Suddenly, the shaking ceased.

I'll find out what you're supposed to do. Next time, I'll be prepared, she vowed.

Abby pulled her mug out of the cupboard and fixed a cup of tea. She went back into the living room with her steaming mug and settled on the couch, propping her feet up on the coffee table.

". . . I repeat, an earthquake of a magnitude of 4.7 on the Richter scale. The quake could be felt from Thunder Bay in Ontario, that's in *Canada*," the news anchor intoned authoritatively before continuing, "to as far away as the Ohio Valley. The quake was the strongest, however, in southeastern Michigan and has caused some damage in a few isolated communities. Power lines are down in some towns, and Detroit Edison is working as we speak to restore power as soon as possible. If you are in an area experiencing a power outage, call 1-800 . . ."

Abby picked up the remote and flipped to another local channel.
". . . the first earthquake of this magnitude to affect Michigan in almost 15 years," a baby-faced meteorologist stated matter-of-factly.
"Although one aftershock has already happened, be advised we may be subject to more. After the break, stay tuned for tips on what to do when an earthquake hits."

Abby changed the channel. *That guy's a dork*, Abby thought with a contemptuous look on her face. It was one thing to enjoy his moment in the sun, but he was acting like a Weather Channel meteorologist during hurricane season in the Florida Keys. *I'd like to see him face down a storm,* she thought, a half-smile on her lips. *He'd probably shit his pants.*

Abby idly flicked from one channel to another while alternately blowing on and taking sips of her tea. She paused at a channel when she thought she caught a sentence with the word "art" in it.

"These are beautiful water color paintings, and each is unique not only for the scene it depicts, but also for of the nature of the depiction." The narrator was an older, dapper English man in a very tweedy-looking jacket holding a microphone and talking into the camera with a serious tone and somber expression on his face. "For each scene it depicts," he went on, his tone lowering and his voice taking on an even more serious tone, "is a prophetic prediction by the man that lives here, a Mr. William Walker."

The man stepped toward the door and made a motion with his head, as if indicating that the television audience, or, at the very least, the cameraman, should follow him inside. The cameraman seemed to take the cue and they entered the man's house: a small brownstone row house on what appeared to be an average, humble, and quiet English town.

Abby sat upright as the camera and commentator entered the man's front room. It was completely filled with paintings. Some were on easels and some were on walls, but the majority of them were bunched together in piles that were precariously stacked together and propped against every inch of wall space. The commentator appeared to be both eager to take it all in and nervous about tripping over the piles. To the left of the front window there was a small table and two chairs at which an annoyed-looking man was sitting.

Abby jumped up from the couch and picked up the phone to call Sara.

"Come on, pick up," she said urgently. She thought Sara would get a kick out of this guy. After the third ring, Abby was about to give up and hang up before the machine took the call when Sara answered with a quiet,

"'Lo?"

"Sara, it's Abby. Turn your TV on to channel...," she flicked the remote to reveal the channel number, "channel 264. Check it out and call me later, okay?"

"Uh, sure. Got it. Channel 264. Okay, later." Sara hung up and Abby returned to the couch.

The commentator was now sitting at the small table with a man who looked to be in his early to mid-60s. Although he was sitting, the man looked to be of greater-than-average height with a thin and wiry build. His hair was gray and had a slightly wild look to it, emulating Albert Einstein and Don King simultaneously. His blue eyes were bright and alert as if he was steeling himself for some kind of personal attack. He had his hand on a photo album in front of him poised at the ready to flip to a page. Abby was intrigued. She scooted forward and leaned hunched over toward the television. The commentator had a small framed watercolor in his hand. It looked no bigger than an 8"x10".

"So, you painted this picture? What was the picture about?" The man held the painting up, and the cameraman zoomed in.

"Well, I don't set out to paint such and such or so and so," the man replied gruffly. "I just paints what comes out, understand? It just comes to me, I paint it, and only when I'm done does it make sense, or maybe later when the event happens, then I understand what it was."

"Oh," the commentator drawled out with feigned surprise. "So, you only find out afterwards? That doesn't seem too prophetic to me."

William Walker snatched the painting out of the man's hands. "You haven't let me finish, have you?" he roared at the commentator. "Why don't you let me finish before you decide I'm a phony or not?" The commentator lowered his head meekly as William glared at him.

"This painting here, I painted it and when I was done, I noticed there were flames and that it was looking like the ferry dock in Swansea. And it looked like there was a small fairy, you know, like a mythical creature in the picture. See it over here," he pointed to the left corner of the picture. "And see, here's a clock tower over there, just inland, see? The hands on the clock indicate its 3:30. I assume it is in the afternoon because it is during daylight, not the dark of night. See these?" William pointed to the clouds, "they look like two figure eights, don't they? Eight, eight. See the petrol pump on the dock? See the flames on the side of the pump?" The commentator was now looking even more attentively.

"I also noticed an ambulance in the painting, and a small cemetery with only two crosses," the commentator interrupted enthusiastically, "Is this what I think it depicts?"

William nodded his head vigorously. The commentator looked into the camera again, his tone becoming serious once again.

"For those viewers who weren't aware of it, on August 8th of this year, at 3:30 p.m. there was a petrol explosion at the Swansea ferry dock just as the ferry was arriving from Cork. There were numerous injuries and two fatalities as the result of this explosion."

"So, tell me," the commentator leaned over the table, his microphone still clenched in his hand, "when did you paint this picture?"

"August 7th. The morning of August 7th." William added assertively.

"And how do we know that you did that painting on that day and not afterwards?" the commentator almost sneered at him.

William Walker flipped through the photo album and stopped at a page, jabbing his finger at a photograph on the page.

"This." He lifted the album up so that the cameraman could zoom into it. It was a photo of William holding the painting. He was directly under a date/time clock which stated the day was the 7th of August and that the time was 1:36 p.m. A sign directly under the clock and the presence of officious looking people tucked behind counters and glass windows suggested it was a government office.

"I always take my paintings to the town hall the day I finish them and get the town clerk or one of the other clerks to take my picture under the clock. I'm hoping that it will be considered proof." William picked up the album and closed it, showing that the album itself was at least three inches thick.

"This whole album is full of pictures of me with my paintings."

"But why do you need proof?" the commentator pressed.

"So someday someone will believe me," he sighed. "Maybe someone will eventually realize that I can see these things happen, and maybe we can stop some o' them before they start." He dropped the book back on the table with a loud bang, making the commentator jump with a start.

"And you try to warn people when you can? What do you do when you figure out what the prediction is?"

"Well, o' course. I always try to warn of the outcome if I figure it out in time." William looked at the commentator with smoldering blue eyes, "but they always think I'm a nutter, don't they? Just a crazy old codger with nothin' better to do." He looked momentarily at the camera, and it took Abby momentarily aback. *He really does feel bad that he can't convince people*, she thought.

Abby took another sip of her tea while she watched the commentator flip through the voluminous photo album and jab his finger randomly to the photos on the pages, asking for a brief description of the painting.

"Have you deciphered all of these paintings?" the commentator asked into the microphone and leaned just a little too far over the table.

"O' course not! Don't be daft!" William barked gruffly. "Some o' them I have," he explained. "Some seem like jumbled bits of nonsense. They may not be easy for me to figure out now, but they might make sense to someone else, or when—,"

"When the event happens?" the commentator finished for him.

"Exactly," William leaned back in his chair, a thin smile on his face.

"I've an idea!" the commentator burst forth suddenly, "Why don't you hold up one of these pictures and see if our viewers can help you out?" The commentator shot the camera a triumphant smile.

"Sure, why not? It can't hurt, can it?" William strode over to the wall on the opposite side of the room and picked up a large piece, which appeared to be at least two feet in length and a foot and a half in diameter. It was turned away from the camera.

"Okay, this piece is a fairly recent piece," he offered as a way of explanation. "It's an unusual piece for me because it obviously lacks the symbolism that usually requires translation." He turned the piece toward the camera and the commentator beckoned to the cameraman to zoom in.

Abby sat up closer to take a look at the watercolor painting that now filled the entire screen of her 32" television. She let out a gasp as she registered the sight coming in to focus in front of her. It was a painting of her and the little man captured almost exactly as they both had been standing in the copse of trees during the Art in the Park show last month.

"Does anyone know who the hell these people are?" William Walker tapped his fingers into the watercolor.

"If you know the identity of these individuals, please contact me, Nigel Simon, at BBC2, Studio—"

Abby didn't hear the rest of the address, as her phone immediately trilled, causing her to jump back momentarily. She grabbed it as quickly as she could and shoved it to her ear.

"Hello?"

"It's Sara. I'm pretty sure, no, make that, *positive*," she emphasized, "that was your face I just saw on TV. So tell me: who's the guy?"

"I think you better come over. We'll talk about it over a cup of tea." Abby didn't even wait for a response from Sara before she hung up. She strode over to the counter and filled up the kettle.

She'll be here, Abby thought, putting the kettle on the stove and switching the burner on. *She'll be here.*

CHAPTER 4

William Walker grabbed his paint box, a container of brushes, and a large pad of watercolor paper and crammed them into a large folio bag that he shoved unceremoniously under his arm. He snatched his keys off the table as he strode out the door, locking it securely before striding toward his sky blue 1979 Vauxhall Viva that was sitting in the driveway. He opened the boot and carelessly tossed the bag inside, closing it with a soft click.

That pompous dandy, he thought to himself, remembering the parting words of Nigel Simon.

"If you get any leads about the people in the painting, call my office *immediately*. Of course, you will get some cranks, but not nearly as bad as the ones I get, what, with being a famous TV personality and all, I get over 200 calls from viewers a day. But I'm sure you won't have that big a problem."

Nigel pulled out a business card from his pocket and thrust it at William. "Don't forget, call the office and leave a message - we'll do a follow-up piece - it'll be FAN-TAS-TIC."

William had muttered his goodbyes, and Nigel and his team of cameramen, boom operators, a director, and a couple of guys running cables disappeared just as quickly as they had arrived. William felt like he needed to leave too. He needed to get out of there, find some peace. Do some painting. He had to see *her*. He sighed softly as he jammed his key into the ignition and slowly backed out of the driveway.

William drove down the road and continued until he reached a secluded dirt road. Not many people came out here; it was like having his own private retreat where he could paint without being bothered or distracted by anything or anyone. That was, of course, until he met her. William continued down the trail-like road until his car was hidden in the trees. He stopped his car at a foot path, got his things from the boot of the car, and set off, walking along the wooded path toward the lake just ahead.

William took a deep breath as he slowly ambled along the path. The fallen leaves from nearby trees crunched softly underfoot. He inhaled deeply, drawing in the sweet earthy smells of the forest. He loved this place at any time of year, but he especially loved it in the fall. It wasn't as damp, and his poor old joints didn't protest too much from the walking when he returned home.

Once he broke through the forest, William set down his folio and the small chair he was carrying on a familiar grassy area at the edge of the lake. He stood erect and stretched his already stiffening arms and back while he gazed out at the expanse of calm water. He could only just make out the shadowy outlines of forms that dotted the other edge of the lake. His eyes scanned the area as he breathed in the wonderful scent of the water with a sigh. He reached down and unfolded his chair, setting it down almost within a few centimeters of the edge of the water. He picked up his folio and started pulling items out and setting them gently down in a row on the grass to the side of the chair. He removed the lid from his paint box and scooped up some water from the lake.

She'll come, she'll come, he assured himself. *Just do your work first.*

William put his hands on the arms of his chair and gingerly lowered himself into it. He picked up a piece of watercolor paper and laid it on a piece of cardboard in his lap. He picked up a brush and set his paint box on one arm of the chair and the lid full of water on the other. William closed his eyes, drew in a deep breath, and as he exhaled he leaned forward and stared into the still water.

"Show me," he whispered.

The water grew slightly opaque and warped-looking, as if he was peering into a carnival mirror. He continued his unblinking stare at the still water oblivious to everything around him. Then, as the water started to swirl a shadowy image formed in front of him; it gradually became clearer, as if it had been brought into focus. It was a face. It disappeared for a moment, but then swirled around, the back of the head facing him. The head turned. It was a man, a man with short dark hair and deep brown eyes. William set to work with his brush, capturing an image of this man on paper, lifting his head up on occasion to check the space between the eyes, the shape of the face, and the fall of the hair. The head smiled and the lips were moving, as if he was in conversation with someone else outside his field of vision. Then, as if his curiosity willed it, the focus moved to the individual the mystery man was speaking to. It was *her*, that woman that he had painted in the piece he showed to Nigel

Simon and his viewers – the woman Nigel asked his viewers to help them find. She looked almost the same as before, but she now looked very serious; her brown eyes were bright, but her lips were firmly pressed together in almost a grimace. She had her arms crossed in front of her chest.

William didn't know why, but he was starting to really dislike her. Her presence just rubbed him the wrong way, and he was oddly puzzled by his feelings.

She's a lovely-looking lass, he thought. And yet that seemed to rankle him even more. He continued to stare at her image in the water. She uncrossed her arms and lifted them straight out in front of her, palms cupped as if she intended to clasp them together. Instead, a reddish orange glow materialized between her hands until it took the shape of what appeared to be a fireball. William was puzzled and fascinated. He began to paint faster. He could feel the water and paint soaking through sections of the paper and cardboard onto his trousers. He kept alternating his focus between the painting and the vision in the water as if watching a video, only it was one he could not forward, rewind, or stop. The mystery woman then pushed her hands back. For a brief moment the soccer-ball-sized fireball seemed to suspend in mid-air before it hurled forward with lightning fast speed.

Better get out of the way, you poor bastard, he thought to himself, thinking the dark-haired mystery man was being attacked. At that moment another man appeared, one with shoulder length brown hair and dark eyes. His face was round with high cheekbones, and his skin was the color of teak. His eyes were focused intently on something in front of him; his concentration was obvious as he bent down and laid a hand onto the ground. He spoke briefly, but William couldn't make out what he said. The earth started to shake, and a deep crack formed in the ground where the man had touched it. The crack ruptured the earth and traveled in the opposite direction of the fireball.

What kind of people are they? He wondered. The man and woman appeared together, walking toward a stone marker. William was confused. A headstone? It was more like a large rock that was rounded at the top. William painted more furiously, ignoring the pains in his joints as he attempted to capture as much detail as he could from the marker.

As they approached the marker, he noticed that there was a compass engraved into the top pointing to the four directions. The woman moved quickly to the south, and the man moved to the north. William noticed that he was looking down onto the west and that a figure was running from the easterly direction. He couldn't make out the figure: it was too far away. He strained harder to see, but he still couldn't manage to see who or what was running toward the marker. The vision swirled away as quickly as it came, but was replaced instantly with the face of the grizzled, short man he had drawn with the mystery woman. His eyes were so tightly drawn that his blue eyes looked like tiny chips of glass. His mouth was practically non-existent in his beard. He would have looked terrifying, but he was wearing a tiny cowboy hat: a rather bizarre accessory to the outfit he was wearing. He raised an arm and pointed his finger.

"You be ready, Walker." The tiny man growled with a bit of an accent. "You be ready when it's time." With that, the man disappeared.

William yelled and jumped out of his seat, knocking his paint and water to the ground. He leapt forward to catch his painting before it hit the water. He handled it carefully by the sides and set it flat on the ground to dry, picking up a small clean rock to hold it in case a sudden gust or breeze kicked up.

He couldn't have meant me. William chewed at his lip for a moment. Never before had he had visions that included him in them, and it wasn't for lack of trying either. More times than he could count he had tried to predict winning horses, lottery numbers, stock picks, and even women to date, although all attempts were met with abysmal failure. Why would it be any different now? He suddenly felt too alone, and, for the first time in his whole 64 years on Earth, he felt a little frightened by it.

I need her, he thought. *It's time.*

William knelt down on both knees at the edge of the water and submerged his hand into the cool water.

I'm here, he thought. *Please come to see me.* He closed his eyes to better focus his concentration and kept his open hand below the surface of the water.

Soon, he felt the cool touch of softly webbed fingers entwine with his. He opened his eyes, and his hand rose up out of the water still clasping a delicately-shaped small hand in his own. A female figure rose up out of the water as if raised on some kind of magical, hidden, underwater escalator. The pale skin of her slender arms shone with an iridescence; the light of the afternoon warmed it to a robin egg blue hue.

"I answer your call, my dearest friend." Her words were melodious and inviting as they left her full, iridescent coral-colored lips and fell upon William's ears. Her deep green eyes fixed upon his and shone with eager anticipation. Her lustrous smile quickly vanished and her brow furrowed as her eyes recognized the confusion on William's creased face.

"What is it? You are upset about something, yes?" Still holding William's hand, she moved, gliding effortlessly toward the edge on the lake and seated herself gracefully upon the bank beside William, her legs still submerged in the water. With her free hand she gently pushed a lock of her flame-red hair off her face and continued to stare at William.

William lifted his gaze up to her face, his blue eyes caught in the emerald brilliance of her eyes. He wanted to hold her gaze for an eternity, to lose himself in her eyes: eyes that held not only a promise of something more, but eyes that had the wisdom of centuries. He had waited so long to see her, and a part of him needed to keep her with him as long as time would allow.

So lovely, he thought. And then he instantly felt guilty. *I covet the attention of a young woman who is young enough to be my granddaughter.* He sighed.

"I'm a ruddy old fool," William blurted out, turning his eyes away from her and diverting his eyes out toward a random bank on the other side of the lake.

"You are not a fool," she said quietly, gripping his hand even tighter. "But you forget two things: first, I am the older of the two of us. My people simply age at a different rate than yours. Secondly, you also forget that your thoughts transmit easily to me even though we are out of the water."

William felt the color rise in his cheeks. Indeed, he had forgotten she could read his thoughts.

"Rhysdale, if my thoughts are so easily read, why are you asking me if I'm upset? Don't you already know?" William turned to face her with a bemused smile on his lips.

"I only know what you project, but the rest is clouded by confusion. And, perhaps, a little fear?" she released his hand and gently stroked her fingers along the curve of his jaw. He reached his hand up to touch her hand and press it gently to his face before releasing it. He gently brushed a stray lock of her hair away from her face. Her hair was beginning to dry and was gleaming with a shiny, reddish-gold hue. He drew his hand back quickly as if afraid he might interfere with her glowing brilliance.

"Do all your people hear others' thoughts?" William inquired.

"Not everyone, of course." Rhysdale answered promptly, "There are those who don't hear or feel other people's vibrations at all. And not everyone can hear everyone. You have to be able to hear them transmit. Does that make sense?" she asked hopefully.

"So, only a small number can hear the thoughts that others project? Does that include your own people?"

"No," she sighed. "Most of my people can communicate with each other. This is the most efficient way to speak underwater. However, some are exceptional in their abilities and some are not. A small number of my people cannot transmit or read at all, but they still have a place in our society. Very few have the ability to hear other species. I myself can understand whales," she straightened her back with pride, "and, of course, I can communicate with humans vocally." She smiled at him as she patted his hand gently.

William looked at her. "So, is it rare that your people come into contact with humans?"

"Of course it is." She tossed her head back and closed her eyes, lifting her face up into the sun. She continued. "Generally my people are xenophobic. We do not invite humans into our domain. It was not that long ago when humans would kill us and justify their actions with stories that we led them to their deaths in the water. But," she turned her head back to face him, her eyes twinkled mischievously, and a playful smile was on her lips, "some of us are very inquisitive. I am not the only one of my people who has a special friend."

He smiled shyly back at her. There were so many questions he still longed to ask her, but he knew that she would soon have to go.

"Yes, I have to return soon." Rhysdale broke into his thoughts. "What is so urgent? Tell me what it is that weighs so heavily on your mind." She clasped both his hands by the wrists with a firm but gentle grip.

For a moment William felt a surge of strength flow through him as if he could take on the world and conquer it with her at his side. But no, he was veering off track. He began to open his mouth to explain everything, but she leaned closer to him, her full lips brushing his ear as she whispered, "No words, just transmit it to me. Think it with your mind."

William drew in a deep breath and closed his eyes, picturing everything as it flashed in front of his eyes. The picture of the beautiful (but somehow disturbing) woman and the small man, the vision he had just painted, and the small man telling him to be ready. When he was done, he heaved a gentle sigh of relief and opened his eyes and looked at her.

William watched her intently trying to read her reaction. She sat motionless, her eyes looking straight ahead as if fixed on some object on the horizon. Her lips were slightly parted, as if she was going to speak but lost the ability to do so. Her lips finally drew together and she closed her eyes, drawing in a deep breath and nodding in a sort of silent resolution.

"William," she whispered. Her emerald eyes were dark with concern. "I don't have the answers you need," she reached a delicate hand up to his face once more. "But I think I may be able to locate someone who can help us solve this puzzle. May I share your confidence?"

"Of course," William smiled at her. *She is going to help. It's going to be alright.*

"I will take your leave, then, my dear friend." She leaned forward and pressed her warm lips firmly to his mouth. He reached a hand up to the small of her back, pressing her soft, cool flesh gently against his chest for the briefest of moments before releasing her.

"Until next time," he cleared his throat and let the rest trail off.

Rhysdale slid gently from his embrace and slipped quietly into the water. William watched as her shadowy blue form moved deeper into the murky depths of water and out of sight.

CHAPTER 5

Answering the loud but persistent call of the alarm, Joe reluctantly surrendered his last vestige of hope that he would sleep in this Saturday morning. He had every intention to get up and put a good day's work in, but it was hard to resist the lure of his warm bed on a cool autumn morning.

His feet hit the floor and quickly found the slippers at the side of the bed as he groped around on the comforter for his terrycloth robe. Once his fingertips located it on the other side of the bed and almost out of reach, he hefted it toward him, slipping it on as he stood. He made his way to the kitchen and turned on the radio hoping to get an earful of the news while waiting for his coffee to brew.

Maybe there will be an update on the earthquake, he mused. *Not that I need an update. Maybe I have a future as a seismologist*, he thought wryly. Instead, the radio greeted him with a muzak version of the Captain and Tennille song "Muskrat Love". Joe shuddered with revulsion.

The earthquakes were a serious and puzzling matter to Joe. He couldn't understand how he knew the quakes were happening. Maybe he had a gift like some of the medicine men in the community he grew up in. *But why now?* He never had these senses before. In fact, he hadn't practiced any of the traditional ways since he left home as a teenager. He didn't knock traditional beliefs; he was just a little more ambivalent about them as he got older, as he imagined some teenagers in devout Catholic homes would be. Once he struck out on his own, he was free to do as he chose. Now he felt somewhat attuned. The earthquakes. He could feel how they ripped and tore the earth open. *Pain.* As if the earth was being cut by a knife, except there was no blood. And it wasn't just the quakes: he could lay his hands on the ground and feel the pulse of the earth as if it had a heartbeat with a definite rhythm and a steady breath. The earth was alive, and he could sense when it was at peace and when it was restless. It bothered him because something just felt *wrong*, and he couldn't put his finger on why he came to that conclusion.

Joe poured a cup of fresh-brewed coffee and plopped two pieces of bread into the toaster on the counter. He sipped his coffee while he waited for the toast to pop, then he buttered the warm toast and dropped it onto a paper towel to take to the kitchen table. He grabbed his coffee and sat down on the straight-back kitchen chair. He washed down each bite of toast with a mouthful of coffee.

Maybe I'm just imagining things, he thought in a weak attempt at rationalizing. *Maybe I'm working too hard and reading into things too much.* He drained his cup quickly and wiped his mouth with the paper towel before rising from the table and walking back to his room.

Joe rummaged through a pile of clothes on the floor in his room and located a pair of grubby jeans and an old sweatshirt.

The room was in a state of utter chaos. Clothes littered the floor and almost completely buried an overstuffed, worn leather armchair next to an equally old oak bookcase. If someone had walked in from the street they would have thought the room had been ransacked during a robbery attempt.

I should clean this joint, he thought. *Maybe I'll have company someday. Maybe I'll ask out Sara. She's kinda cute, and she might not say no to a date.*

Joe quickly dressed and gathered an armful of the scattered clothes off the floor. He looked around the room a couple of times before dumping the clothes onto the pile already on the seat of the armchair. *At least they're off the floor.* He gave the sheet and blanket on the bed a half-hearted tug before he abandoned his less-than-enthusiastic attempt at cleaning his room.

Joe walked into the living room/rec room of his bungalow that also functioned as his art studio and laid out some three-mil sheet plastic on the floor directly in front of the work bench he had set up just in front of the far wall. Most artists he knew had their own separate studios to work in, but he preferred to work in his house. Besides, except for the workbench and a tool caddy full of an unusual collection of carving tools, a small electric potter's wheel, and a metal shelving unit heavily laden with a variety of plastic bags containing assorted clays, the room held little furniture. He did have a nice collection of art on the walls, mostly acquired through some good old-fashioned horse trading at art shows and fairs. Located somewhere near the vicinity of the patio door, he had a worn-out old floral loveseat left over from a previous (but doomed from the start) relationship. The loveseat was unceremoniously covered in an equally-ugly olive drab sheet, which was itself covered in flecks of dried clay that had obviously splattered from the wheel. The worn maple hardwood floor had the odd clump of dried clay attached to it and it crunched to dust under his feet as he adjusted the sheet of plastic. Joe looked down and surveyed the floor. *Perhaps I need more plastic. Hmm... later.*

Joe stepped over to the shelving unit and selected a 25-lb. bag of carving clay, hoisting it up to the workbench and dropping it with a soft thud. As he picked through the tools in his caddy and laid them out on the table, his thoughts returned once more to Sara while he began to prepare his work area. She seemed so flustered when he had complimented her work as if she was genuinely surprised that he had liked it, let alone thought it was good enough to win the *Best in Show* award. But the truth was that her art was brilliant. She could do so much better with her sales if she went to an area like Birmingham or Ann Arbor. Instead, a lot of her work seemed lost on most of the show patrons. He hoped she wouldn't fall into the trap that some artists do - cranking out the art that people are willing to buy to earn a living. Most artists do it at some point to survive, but a lot felt it was like sacrificing their souls. While it could be a double-edged sword, sometimes it became a necessity to make ends meet.

"Well, Sara Taylor, you are definitely in my thoughts today, and I think I will honor you by making you my muse. Let's see where that takes me." Joe opened the bag of clay and set the block of green sculpting clay on the table, examining it from several stances to see what form the clay would take.

***

Sara was grinding the gears in her small, blue GMC pickup truck looking for third gear. Although she hadn't really been focusing on the road, she wasn't worried that she would run into any other vehicles. The drive from her place to Abby's was normally quiet and short, occasionally interrupted by a farmer driving a tractor, but when encountered they would always pull off to the side of the road and wave her on.

Sara could have stepped on the gas and torn up the road to get to Abby's, setting land speed records in the process, but she wanted to maintain an air of calm, something Abby most likely needed right now. After Sara tuned into that TV show Abby suggested she watch, she was utterly stunned when the artist (*what was his name again?*) picked up that picture of Abby. Clear as day, it was Abby, and Sara would have bet money that Abby was wearing the same clothes she was wearing during the Art in the Park Show. But who was the guy? Sara called Abby as soon as the credits rolled, but Abby only told her to come over.

"Abby, are you okay? Do you need—," Sara broke off realizing that she was talking to no one. Abby had already hung up.

And so here she was driving her poor, dusty, rusty, but trusty old pick-up down the sparsely-populated country road to Abby's. But Sara still didn't step on the gas. Part of her was eager to find out what was going on, and part of her was dreading the explanation. Sara had the strangest feeling that something was going down - something big, not just the usual run-of-the-mill psychic stuff she only read about. Something - what was the word - yeah - *ominous*. Just thinking the word caused a chill to run down her back. Sara bit her lip as she tried to remember back to the Art in the Park show. It wasn't too far back for her memory. She smiled thinking about Joe. He looked so handsome, and he had complimented her work. Very few people had good comments about her art lately. *No, think!* Sara silently chided herself. *Didn't Abby try to tell you something on the way home?* Sara just couldn't remember.

Sara slowed her vehicle and nudged her truck carefully into the driveway, pulling in behind Abby's van and turning off the ignition. As was her custom, she left the keys in the ignition as she climbed out of the vehicle. Although walking the path from Abby's driveway to her house was second nature to Sara, she felt as though it took all her strength of will to propel her body forward.

After what felt like an eternity, Sara managed not only to walk the path, but also to climb the stairs to the front door. Taking a deep breath, she opened the screen door and then knocked on the heavy wooden door. Without waiting for a reply, she turned the brass knob and opened the door slightly, popping her head through the opening.

"Hello?" She called out tentatively.

"In here," came Abby's soft voice.

Something's wrong, Sara thought to herself. *No, stop that!*

Sara moved cautiously toward the living room where Abby sat stiffly on the sofa; her back was ramrod straight as she continued to stare ahead into space unmoving and appearing not even to blink. On the table directly in front of her was a coffee service with what appeared to be a full carafe steaming and awaiting her arrival.

"Please, help yourself." Abby gestured to the tray as if reading her mind.

Sara made Abby and herself each a coffee and thrust a cup toward Abby, whose hands automatically grasped it.

They sat together side by side and sipped their coffee; the silence only broken by the sound of Sara's occasional nervous slurp from her cup.

I can't take it, I can't stand this! Sara agonized internally.

"Abby, what the hell is going on?" Sara blurted loudly, her voice echoing through the large room. "Do you know the man in that picture? Are you having an affair?"

Abby turned to face Sara, her expression unreadable. Then in a split second her expression changed to a smirk, punctuated by peals of laughter. Tears rolled down her cheeks as she struggled to place her coffee mug back on the table without spilling it. After releasing the cup handle she wrapped her arms around her waist as if trying to prevent her sides from bursting. Sara continued to stare at her, completely dumbfounded by this new outburst of emotion.

"No, I'm not having an affair." Abby finally gasped out. "Don't you think I could do better than that? *I* think I could do a lot better than that!" she joked. "But I do know the man, well, not personally. I have met him, but only once. I have a feeling we'll be meeting again soon."

"Did you meet him after the Art in the Park Show?" Sara inquired. Abby regarded Sara, her smile disappearing, eyes narrowing in suspicion.

"How did you know that?"

"Well, I sorta remember you trying to talk to me on the way home, but I was so geeked up about the day, I dunno, I guess I should've paid more attention," Sara's voice faltered.

Abby visibly relaxed. "Well, I'm ready to tell you what little I know. Maybe it will shed some light on a few things for me."

"Yeah, and hopefully it will help me figure out a few things myself." Sara added casually, returning back to sipping her coffee. "I have a few questions I'd like answered myself."

"Like what?"

"Like why I now have the ability to fly." Sara set down her cup and turned full face to look at Abby.

"Fly? You're kidding, right?"

"No, I'm not." Sara added softly.

Abby clapped her hands together gleefully. "It's sure going to be an interesting day after all."

***

Joe deftly flicked the Japanese rifling tool in his hand to scrape away a small clump of clay marring the underside of a well-shaped breast. He ran a finger alongside the area, making sure the cool clay was smooth and unmarked. He stepped back a couple of feet to scrutinize his day's work from a distance.

The 18-inch clay statute, while not to scale, was a miniature model of Sara Taylor. Well, a mostly accurate model of her since Joe had no empirical data to draw on and had to rely more on his memory and imagination to perceive her form nude. He was pleased with his depiction of the line of her jaw, the turn of her smile, and the gentle curves of her neck, but blushed when his eyes swept lower than her shoulders and collarbone. She was poised with her chin proudly tilted up, her eyes to the sky, and her neck slightly turned to the right. Her hands were upturned, her arms slightly away from her body at the waist. He did allow the statue some modesty, as she was partially clothed in a Grecian-type short skirt that had a bit of draped material over the right breast and shoulder. The breasts were round and full, but not so full that they sagged under their own weight. Joe blushed, *I'm staring at the breasts again*, he thought. *At least they aren't too large or small or pornographic.* The hips were round yet narrow, demurely hidden by the drape of the skirt and the legs were long and slender, and ended with very petite bare feet.

Geez, she looks like a cross between the Venus de Milo and an Egyptian fertility goddess, he shuddered at the thought.

Joe started to doubt himself. *Maybe I shouldn't show this piece,* he agonized. *What if I do and Sara sees it?* He recoiled back even further. *What if she doesn't like it?* He thought harder for a moment. *What if she does?*

The strain of his full day of continuous work was starting to hit him. Suddenly his arms and legs felt rubbery, and his mind began to wander.

He grabbed another sheet of plastic and strode back to the table to cover his *Sara de Milo*. Yes, that is what he would call her. He laid a gentle hand upon the statue.

"I wish I could give you life, my dear," he said as he gave the statue one last pleased look before covering it with the sheet of plastic.

Joe left his tools on the bench, stumbled into the kitchen to wash his hands, and, after hastily wiping his hands on the nearest tea towel, stumbled to his room and flopped onto his bed. He folded his arms behind his head and stared up at the ceiling for the briefest of moments before he closed his eyes and drifted off to sleep.

***

"No, no, Sara, It's okay, I like being this close to it." Abby waved a reassuring hand at Sara, who had been trying to coax her to sit further away from the fire and in one of the plastic Adirondack chairs a few feet away. Abby felt the warmth surround her and warm her skin in the cool autumn air. But it needed more.

(Feed it more wood!)

She picked up a large log and heaved it into the fire.

"Abby! Abby!" Sara cried out frustrated. "Didn't you hear what I said?"

Abby looked at Sara sheepishly, a slight grin on her face. Pulling herself away from the draw of the fire, she settled into the chair beside Sara.

Sara passed a hand through her hair in frustration. She turned to face Abby, locking her eyes directly on her face.

"I see you have some difficulty concentrating." Sara observed quietly.

Abby laughed. "Actually, you could say I'm hyper-focusing on something else—," Abby let her gaze wander back to the fire.

"No, Abby."

Sara reached over and grabbed her hand, forcing Abby to return her gaze to Sara's face. She did so, rather stiffly.

Sara continued.

"Abby, you were going to explain, no, tell me about that man with you in the picture, that English artist's painting—"

"Well, I can't start just yet. There are some things I need to show you. Watch the fire."

Abby rose slowly and quietly out of her chair and moved to face the fire. She put a finger to her lips and motioned for Sara to move closer. Sara carefully moved out of her chair and crept slowly toward Abby.

Abby pointed down into the hot embers and whispered, "Do you see them?"

Sara peered carefully into the embers. Within a few minutes her eyes adjusted to the brightness and heat of the flames. She managed to make out the forms of some creatures running across the embers. Lizard-like creatures, some of which naturally emulated the orange glow of the live embers and others the coal darkness of the dead and dying ones. They were moving and flickering in the fire as if basking in the heat and flame. Sara was dumbfounded and awestruck at the same time. *Shouldn't they die from the heat?*

"What are they?" Sara asked, in a whispered voice.

"Salamanders." Abby replied. "Keep watching." Abby placed an open hand on the ground next to the stones surrounding the fire. She made a crackling, hissing noise and one of the salamanders shot out of the fire and into her hand, running quickly up her arm, across her chest, and down her other arm. Abby turned more to Sara to show her how friendly it was and hoped that it would go to Sara, but it only ran up and down her arms one more time before it leapt back into the flames and returned to the warmth of the embers. Abby's eyes were drawn to the fire, and she found herself staring once more as if slipping into a hypnotic trance. It felt so good to be caught in its warmth. . . She caught herself. *No, not now.*

Abby turned to Sara. "If I were you, I'd go back to my seat now."

Sara moved quickly to her seat, her eyes riveted on Abby.

"Now watch this." Abby took a deep breath in preparation.

Abby lifted her arms up, cupping her hands. She turned her hands inward, as if to clasp her hands together, but stopped short a few inches apart. Abby closed her eyes for a moment. Sara stared unabashedly at Abby now. She was quite a sight: she stood so close to the fire that she was almost standing in it. Her arms out and her head slightly lifted and raised, she tilted back slightly, and her hair blew gently back from her face by the heat of the fire. She looked beautiful. Like a beautiful earth mother goddess. Sara's mouth opened in shock when she realized what she was seeing. Between Abby's hands a small ball of fire began to form. Abby opened her eyes. She moved her hands apart slightly and the fireball grew in size. Abby continued to move and manipulate her hands like she was patting down and forming a snowball until she had a fireball the size of a softball suspended in the space between her two hands. With a flick of her wrist, she casually tossed the fireball straight up in to the air.

Sara shrieked in alarm. *She's gonna burn the place down!* Sara thought, horrified.

But before the fireball was even halfway between Abby and the ground, Abby flicked her wrists again. The fireball froze in mid-air as if awaiting her instruction. She pushed both arms outward, directing the fireball out into a region of the garden. The fireball went as she directed, not once deviating from any of her instructions, even when she finally hovered it over her small pond and directed it into the water, where it died with an angry sizzle.

"Wow," Sara whispered, "That was *too* cool!"

Abby smiled at Sara. Before returning to the seat beside Sara, she tossed a few more logs into the fire. The salamanders jumped out of the way, and then continued their running up and down the flame drenched logs, their bodies changing hue with each flicker of the flames.

Once seated, Abby picked up her coffee mug and drained it.

"And now I'll answer your question regarding that man." Abby spoke. "It's true that I did actually see him once. You know, the man in the painting that was on TV? I didn't actually *meet* him; it was more like

I stumbled upon him in the clearing of the park. It was just after I finished packing my stuff in the van after Art in the Park. I saw him, and he asked me why I was looking at him. It was at that moment when you called out to me and I turned in the direction of your voice. When I turned back, he was gone."

"Why didn't you tell me?" Sara asked quietly.

"Well, I did think about it. And I thought, well, maybe he was just a little person that I bumped into in the park—,"

"No, Abby, he's not a little person. I'll bet he's a gnome." Sara's tone became more serious. "In fact, I'd almost bet money on it."

Abby looked at Sara to see if she was joking. Somehow, judging from the expression on her face, she knew that Sara wasn't. Abby couldn't imagine how both Sara and Dan could believe that such creatures as gnomes really existed, but she was willing to go along with it for now until a better explanation presented itself.

"Well, I didn't really know what to think, but I did mention it to Dan. But then I could feel the fire, I dunno, I guess you could say it was calling out to me. It started out little at first, almost at a subconscious level, but then it intensified every day. Then I was able to direct fire with my hands, and then the next thing I know, I see my face and that little man, gnome, or whatever he is, on TV. Then I started to get a little worried. And what should I do about that anyway?"

Abby nudged Sara with her shoulder. "I'll bet we weren't the only people watching that show! What if someone already saw it and recognized me?" Abby shuddered at the thought of television reporters clambering across her lawn, their cameras pressing in on her private, little world, treating her like a real-life tabloid freak.

"This guy, this *artist*, what's his name?" Sara enquired.

"William. William Walker, I believe."

"Walker. Okay, isn't he some kind of a psychic or something? Maybe we should try to find him and see what he has to say. Maybe we can contact him without the media. If he's a true seer, I'm sure he will want to find out more about you, or tell you more if he knows it. Maybe," she thought for a moment, "maybe he will shed some light on your new little friend."

"But why would you say he's a gnome anyway?" Abby looked at Sara quizzically.

"Well, because gnomes have a good relationship with the Elements."

"Elements?"

"Yeah, you know, Water, Earth, Air, and Fire." Sara stood up and raised her arms high above her head in a stretch. "I read about it online."

"Well, for sure there is a Fire thing going on here."

Sara smiled at Abby.

"Let's bring on the Air, shall we?"

***

Joe woke with a start some time later. Someone had touched him, touched his arm and woke him up. *IMPOSSIBLE,* he told himself. The room was as dark as pitch. *What time is it?* His alarm clock flashed 7:18 p.m. He fumbled for the light switch. He heard a noise at the side of his bed, no wait . . . no. . .there it was again. His fingers touched the lamp switch and he sat up, looking directly down at the side of the bed.

And there was the statue of Sara looking up at him, the smile still as he carved it and frozen upon her face.

Joe screamed and leaped out of bed, vaulted over the statue, and bolted out of the bedroom fast as a shot. He didn't stop running until he was out of the house and standing on the front lawn, bent over and gasping for breath. He kept looking up at the front door, half expecting the statue to pursue him at the same break-neck speed.

Joe clutched his side. The pain of a stitch from his sudden burst of speed intensified with every deep breath he took. He tried to breathe more slowly and deeply, but each time he was close to calming himself a new wave of panic would take over, elevating his heart and causing him to take rapid breaths once again.

Joe bent deep at the waist, his hands on his legs just above his knees, propping himself up so he could take deeper breaths. He kept his eyes locked on his front door, waiting and watching.

The sound of movement from the direction of the house set him into panic mode again. He dropped to the ground laying in a prone position, while keeping his head up and his eyes watchful.

The noise did come from the house — and it kept coming. The *Sara de Milo* statue had eased itself out the front door, its tiny feet moving heavily down the stairs of the front entry making squelchy, wet sounds as it moved forward. Joe dropped his head down, lying completely flat against the grass as if willing himself embedded into the ground. As he pressed himself into the ground, he could feel the earth. Humming? Breathing? No, it's *rhythm* moved against his body like a heartbeat echoing in his ear. He could sense the sound of the statue traveling along the ground, and as the sound decreased in volume, he guessed it was moving further away from him. He lifted his head to take a tentative peek and caught a glimpse of the figure's petite bottom rounding the corner and disappearing into the darkness behind his house.

Joe sat upright and breathed a sigh of relief. Then terror struck. *What the hell am I going to do?* He thought. *Where is it going to go? I'd better follow it.*

Joe rose up into a crouch and crept into the darkness looking for the statue. It had continued to move forward, and it had begun to walk into the forest of the park at the back of his yard. Joe hesitated for a moment. *How far could it possibly go? Maybe it will just run out of steam in the forest. But what if it doesn't?* Joe cringed at the thought. What would happen if a half-naked clay statue of Sara was found marauding around town? That would be hard to explain, particularly to Sara. The day was just getting worse and worse. Joe was getting a stomach ache just playing out the various scenarios in his head.

Drawing in a deep breath, Joe quietly pushed back some of the underbrush and entered the forest. The moon was full in the clear, starry sky which helped to illuminate the trek through the brush. The mini-Sara continued to amble awkwardly ahead, plowing through the underbrush in its way, oblivious to the chill in the air. Joe, on the other hand, was beginning to feel the chill of the crisp fall evening. He had left his house rather quickly and had no jacket, although he was thankful he was still wearing his sweatshirt. His fingers were getting stiff from the cold, so he held his hands together and blew on them to ease the stiffness in his joints. Joe couldn't linger long; *Sara de Milo* was still moving forward, and he could not risk losing her from his line of sight.

Joe tripped over a tree root and landed hard against the cold ground, cursing aloud as he landed. The palms of his cold hands hurt where little pebbles and small bits of tree bark dug into his skin. He attempted to recover himself quickly, looking over to where *Sara de Milo* had last disappeared behind a bush, but she was nowhere in sight.

"Shit, Shit, SHIT!" Joe swore aloud.

What am I going to do? How the hell am I going to catch it now? Then a small pair of feet appeared in front of his hands. Joe could only stare at them in shock.

SHE CAME BACK.

Joe felt the fear well inside him again.

No, no, she obviously isn't going to hurt you, he rationalized. He raised his head to look upon its face. And there it stood wearing Sara's serene expression, her knowing little smile, and those twinkling eyes in their perpetual stare locked on him. And mini-Sara stood there and appeared to be waiting for something. And Joe returned the stare, mute and dumbfounded and completely and utterly at a loss as to what to do next.

"What the feck you doin'?" A voice bellowed from behind *Sara de Milo*.

Joe shrieked and jumped with shock. *Now what?* His eyes scanned the dark shadows of the trees and he saw no one.

"Now I'm imagining things," he muttered, shaking his head.

"Imagination! My hairy backside! I'm right here, you git!"

Joe squinted peering into the trees again. The voice seemed to come from the area in front of him. *Wait, one of the shrubs is moving!* But it wasn't a shrub. Upon closer inspection, Joe realized the form moving nearer was a man. The jacket he was wearing appeared to be made of sheepskin, making the man look like a bulky cedar shrub. As the man moved closer, it was easy to see why Joe had confused him for a shrub. In fact, the cedar shrubs were probably taller than the man himself. He was wearing a suit under the sheepskin jacket that appeared to be made of moleskin. On his feet he was wearing a type of hiking boot. The moonlight illuminated his face, which appeared to be, except for his eyes, almost completely covered with a gray beard. Perched on top of his head was a - Joe rubbed his eyes - a raspberry-colored beret. It was the strangest accessory to an outfit Joe had ever seen in his life, unless, of course, you were in a Prince video. If he hadn't been so absolutely freaked out he would have burst out laughing. Instead, he opened his mouth to speak but could not find any words, any explanations, any greetings, or any *anything* that would serve him in this situation.

The small man stared at Joe angrily, tugging at his beard and squinting like an old sailor. "Are yeh gonna do somethin' 'bout the innocent, or are yeh gonna let it wander off an' cause all kinds o' trouble? I don' think the real Sara would appreciate yeh letting this one loose."

Joe's eyes widened, remembering what he'd set into the forest for in the first place.

"And what would you have me do?" he uttered helplessly, looking at the small man with desperation in his eyes.

"Well, you can touch the creature and tell it to return to the earth. It's supposed to do your biddin'." The man looked at him, an odd smile upon his lips.

Joe laid a hand tentatively on the delicate toes of *Sara de Milo*. He looked upon its face and intoned, "Uh, return to the earth, uh, please."

The toes started to change their shape, slowly oozing into a puddle of soft, wet clay. Joe moved his hand out of the way and the face, neck, shoulders, breasts, hips, and legs began to sink slowly into a tiny hill of clay that shifted into the puddle that subsequently oozed slowly into the ground. And then it was gone. Not even one small speck of clay remained. Dumbfounded, Joe turned to face the small man.

"Excuse me, but, uh . . . who are you?" he finally managed.

"Me name's Gabe." He thrust his small leathery hand out in greeting, but pulled it back before Joe could even shake it.

"My name's—," Joe started, but Gabe cut him off.

"Yeah, yeah. I knows who y' are," Gabe announced gruffly. "What y' doin' letting' innocents loose in the forest?" his eyes narrowed distrustfully.

"I didn't . . . well, I," Joe stuttered. "I don't know what I did." Joe looked at Gabe for an answer.

"What yeh did was, yeh created a golem. Is this what you're supposed to be doin' with your gifts? I don't thin' so." Gabe started to move away.

"I don't understand." Joe continued to stare at Gabe. "What gifts? What are you talking about?"

Gabe continued to stomp noisily through the underbrush muttering, "I don' have the time to baby sit no bleedin' humans." He grumbled as he continued. "Jus' don' make anymore golems, alright? I'm sure we'll be seeing each other soon." And with a crack of a branch being snapped, Gabe disappeared into the underbrush and out of sight, leaving Joe shaking and alone on the cold ground in the moonlight, slightly relieved, but more full of questions than ever before.

CHAPTER 6

Sara's hands fluttered in the air, and if anyone had spied her from a distance, it would have looked as if she was conducting the song "Shambala" by Three Dog Night, which was resonating loudly from the speakers on Abby's deck. Abby was watching intently, her eyes sparkling with glee.

"Wicked." Abby whispered in awe.

Sara turned to smile her acknowledgement before turning back to her odd opus. She was, in fact, conducting, though it wasn't the music she was orchestrating, but instead the various objects she was manipulating in time to the rhythm of the music. Fallen leaves, twigs, and even a plastic bag that had managed to tumble by on a slight breeze all had been incorporated into her display; they all rose up and down upon the gusts of wind as she directed. A swirl of leaves was directed to the left as the twigs were suspended in air while the plastic bag cart wheeled above them both. Even the branches of the nearby trees swayed in the rhythm of the wind.

The song faded out, and Sara directed all the objects to the ground except for the twigs that Abby directed, "Into the fire with them please, Sara."

Sara gently settled the twigs on top of the burning logs already in place. Sara looked at Abby for a moment, watching how her eyes lit up as Sara fed the flames of the fire.

It's like the fire is feeding her too, Sara observed silently, noticing how much more animated Abby became when the flames grew.

"Abby?" Sara said tentatively.

"What?" As Abby snapped at her, her expression changed to one of irritation, and her smile turned to a grimace as she turned away from the fire to face Sara.

"Hey, don't bite my head off." Sara retorted sharply, "I was going to ask you if you wanted to go for a ride."

"A ride?"

Sara glanced around, a secretive smile on her face. "Come on, Abby, let's throw caution to the wind." Sara started laughing out loud, and her laughter grew louder as she slapped her hand on her knee.

Abby felt herself smile, and soon she too was overcome with laughter. Wiping a tear from her eye, she gasped, "Tell me what you want me to do." Abby stood up, readying and straightening herself up to her full height, squaring her shoulders, her head at a slight angle as she eyed Sara expectantly.

"Come on, let's go down here," Sara directed, beckoning Abby with her hand as she stepped quickly down the steps of Abby's back deck and out into the yard to stand beside the pond.

"Here, here. No one should see us here," Sara beckoned Abby.

She looked up into the sky. The clouds were passing back and forth across the sun, making it alternately sunny and overcast. For now the sun was tucked away behind a particularly large and fluffy white cloud. Sara didn't want to deal with the sun. *Too much of a distraction*, she thought. Not that she thought it was too warm in the sun. It was almost October and the day was cool, but not unusually so for this time of year.

"Good thing my name's not Icarus," Sara muttered giggling slightly at the thought.

"Sara, you're babbling," Abby admonished, her hand on her hip. "Are we ready or what?"

"Yes, of course."

Sara took a deep breath and cleared her mind as she exhaled. She focused for a moment on the slight breeze. She *knew* now: knew how to summon it. In fact, she practiced until she got it perfect. Later she would tell Abby all about it, if she could pay attention long enough.

Sara stared at the ground, focusing on a small patch of ground just in front of them. A few of the leaves lifted off the ground and began to rise into the air as if on cue; a small part of a choreographed dance just above the ground. Then, the leaves began to spin in the air, and a swirling vortex became visible, lifting slightly from the ground and moving slowly closer toward them. Abby could feel the breeze gently push her hair from her face.

I wish I'd thought to tie it back, she thought as she ran her hand through her hair in an off-handed manner.

"Now, when it gets stronger you'll want to lean forward onto the current, okay?" Sara looked at Abby waiting for acknowledgement. Abby just stared blankly back at her.

"Okay, I'll tell you when its time, alright?'

Abby nodded. The wind was getting more forceful. Her hair whipped into her face, and a lock hit her in the eye prompting tears and stinging pain. Abby raised a hand and attempted to calm her wildly-whipping hair while wiping the tears streaming from her eye.

"Now lift up onto your toes," Sara yelled at Abby, pushing her own blonde hair out of her face. "Ready, now lean into the current... NOW!"

Both Abby and Sara leaned forward. Sara pushed off from the ground with her toes. Abby followed Sara's lead. For a moment, the two of them were immobile and suspended three feet off the ground in mid-air as if caught on an invisible thread.

Sara looked at Abby, whose expression seemed to be one of mingled curiosity and surprise.

"Be a good girl, Abby, remember I'm driving." Sara smiled gleefully.

Sara lifted her arms out to her sides and directed Abby to follow suit. She then reached over and grasped Abby's left wrist with her right hand. Without warning or fanfare, they shot upward into the sky. Abby looked ahead, willing herself not to look down or behind her. She could have sworn she had seen tiny little creatures riding on the wind currents. At first, she thought they were dragonflies; they were the same size but twice as luminous. No, they were little people. Little *winged* people. Fairies?

"They're beautiful, aren't they?" Sara breathed.

Abby nodded absently. Whatever they were, they continued to pace them in the sky like dolphins in the ocean racing just a fraction ahead of boats but always looking back to ensure their presence. These creatures, or fairies, were keeping a respectful distance but appeared to be escorting them. Abby noted that they flew in a type of formation, zipping and weaving back and forth in front of them in an orderly fashion as if they served as a type of aerial security or honor guard. Abby's observation was interrupted by the sounding of Sara laughing loudly.

"What's so funny?" Abby demanded, irritated by this sudden disruption.

"Well, I was thinking this is great fun, Abby, but you ain't Superman." Abby turned her head toward Sara and lowered her eyebrow.

"Oh yeah?" she retorted, "I was thinking *I* am a lot better looking than Lois Lane." Her frown turned into a smile which broke into laughter that echoed as they soared higher into the cloudy horizon.

Gabe stepped out of the trees from the side of the pond and stared up at the rapidly-disappearing forms of the two women in the sky. He shook his head in disbelief as he trudged through the trees.

"Better be makin' play time short," he muttered. "T'isn't gonna get any easier." Gabe pulled his brown felt hat down over his eyebrows as he trudged off through the trees.

***

Joe awoke the following morning irritable and edgy and feeling as if he had spent the night waiting for someone or something to storm the house. After his strange encounter with *Sara de Milo* and the small man (*Did he say his name was Gabe?*) he sat on the cold forest floor amidst the dead grass and fallen leaves and tried to figure out what the hell had happened. *What did I do to deserve this? Gabe said something about doing things "with your gifts." What gifts was he referring to?* Joe felt a surge of anger rise up like a sort of foul bile inside him as he recalled Gabe's admonishing words. He slammed his fist into the ground and felt the vibration of the force moving through him; afterward, he opened his fist and gently set his open hand palm down on the ground. He could feel the vibration of his blow still reverberating, though much fainter, through the ground. *If I could just push*, he remembered thinking - and then he had felt it. The rumbling, staccato tremors of an earthquake. He could feel the difference, the change from the normal cadence of the earth's rhythm. The earth felt like it was screaming in torment as it rumbled and heaved underneath him. When he realized he was sitting on the ground in the dark all alone during an earthquake, he felt naked and vulnerable. Joe jumped to his feet and stumbled back to his house. He had run inside the slightly-ajar front door and bolted it behind him, something he had never, ever done before. He even latched the chain too, just in case and then made his way to the back door and did the same, ensuring that it too was firmly locked tight against any possible invaders.

After what felt like an eternity, the ground had stopped rumbling, and the windows, which had been rattling slightly, had gone silent and stilled. Joe had given in to his impulse to check all the windows, ensuring they too were unbroken, firmly locked, and secure. Only then did he feel secure enough to quietly retreat to his room. He got into bed fully dressed, and he pulled the covers completely over him and above his head in an attempt at putting himself in a cocoon of safety.

Joe had not felt safe, and he had not slept well. As his shaking hands raised a fresh brewed cup of coffee to his mouth, he felt tired and drained. He was still trying to sort out his role in last night's events.

Well, for one, you made that stupid Sara sculpture, you big dumb ass, he silently berated himself. *That's what you get for being a big pervert. No, I'm not a pervert.* Joe sighed. *I just want to get to know her.* Deep down, Joe somehow knew that accidentally unleashing a living statue on Harmon like Godzilla on Tokyo wasn't the way to get to know Sara better or get in her good graces. Even if it was just a mere 18 inches in height, it had the potential to wreak a considerable amount of havoc. Joe's brow furrowed with concentration, his eyes fixing on a ring his coffee mug had left on the table. Gabe had called the statue a golem. What did that mean?

Joe set down his coffee mug and strode into his bedroom. He scanned his bookcase until his eyes alighted upon *Webster's Ninth New Collegiate Dictionary*. Its red, dusty cloth cover looked as if it had seen better days. He pulled it off the shelf and strode back to the kitchen. He placed the book on the table and sat back down on his chair, pulling it closer to the table. He opened the dictionary, and after flipping through the pages, came to rest on what he was looking for:

"Golem - an artificial human being (in Hebrew) endowed with life." Joe reread the definition before gently shutting the dictionary and pushing it aside. He reached again for his coffee cup. An artificial human being? Joe felt more confused than ever. Why should he have the ability to create artificial people? *Well, not flesh and blood*, he thought. *Out of clay. Out of earth. Earth! Maybe that's it!*

Joe thought back to the day of the earthquakes at school. He had felt them, knew they were coming. And he could feel the rhythm of the earth; he could feel its pulse and its pain. *Why, last night I -* Joe paused in mid-thought. *That earthquake last night - I didn't feel it coming first.* Joe opened his mouth, his eyes widened with realization. *I didn't feel it coming because -* he took a deep breath and whispered, "I caused it."

CHAPTER 7

Joe could see the hills rising up from the horizon as he peered through the dusty windshield of his Chevy pick-up truck. His hands clenched the steering wheel in a vice-like grip, but not because he had fears that his truck wouldn't survive the journey. Actually, he had great confidence that his red Chevy pick-up was more than up for the trip even with its tail pipe hanging on by a piece of jury-rigged coat hanger and the passenger side mirror held on with the aid of some duct tape.

No, this truck is up for the drive, Joe affirmed silently. *But am I?* Joe tried to be like his mother when things, times, and life in general got difficult. She was always so tough, so resilient, even though she was a petite woman. She always wore her long, dark hair (although a few gray ones have slipped in over the years) in a thick and neat braid that ended at her waist. Her braid was so straight it appeared to align perfectly with her spine. Well-spoken and well-read, she always had the right advice or answers in any situation. On the rare occasion when she needed advice, she would pack up some groceries - tea, sugar, canned milk, canned beans, matches, cookies, some tobacco, and some cloth - into a box and load it into her beat up old Dodge Dart. "You kids mind your Aunt Mary," she would say, "I'll be back tomorrow."

Joe would always watch her as she left until the taillights of her car disappeared down the road and out of sight. The house never felt right when she was gone, and Joe remembered how time seemed to drag until she returned. Like clockwork, she would always return the following day just before supper.

"Did you go see Dad?" Joe would always ask hopefully.

"Oh, no, not this time," his mother would say. "It was time to see Floyd Thunder Cloud."

Within minutes of her return from a visit to Floyd Thunder Cloud, she would retrieve her abalone shell and sage from the shelf in the kitchen and light the sage stick, the smoke from the burning sage wafting in the air as she moved throughout the house carefully conducting a smudge of each room. Joe would watch her eagerly until one day she asked, "Do you want to help?" And he jumped at the opportunity. He would begin by smudging his room, then his brothers' room before moving on to the room his sisters shared. Joe would always smudge his stuff really well, keeping solemnly quiet, his back ramrod straight as he moved slowly room to room fanning the smoke from the sage stick into every corner of the room, just as his mother had always done. He even had permission to use her lighter to re-light the sage if it went out. When the task was complete his Mom always thanked him ("*Meegwetch*," she would say) for doing a good job before taking the abalone shell from him and placing it back in its place on the kitchen shelf.

I was the man of the house, he thought, as he drummed his fingers on the steering wheel as he drove. *It was only supposed to be until Dad could come home.*

Joe strained to remember what it was like before his Dad went away to work. Joe was about seven years old when his Dad left with a suitcase. *He didn't even say goodbye*, Joe thought, *or "see you soon". He didn't even kiss Mom.* It was a cold, quiet departure. Before Joe Sr. had left, Joe Jr. could remember the odd raised voice, mostly his Mom's, as he couldn't remember his Dad ever raising his voice or his hands to any of them. Joe struggled to recall any stray memory of his father. Even his earliest memories of sunrise ceremonies, pow wows, learning to ride a two wheeler without training wheels, even special events at school when he was growing up had his mother at the core. It was as if his father had never participated in his life whatsoever. Joe was at a loss to understand why. He wondered if his brothers and sisters felt the same sense of ambivalence about him too.

At least I don't have any bad memories of him, Joe thought.
Joe knew that his mother had no ill feelings toward him either. She would always announce when the money arrived every two weeks without fail. "Your father has sent some money, and Derrick need shoes. Who else needs new shoes?" And she would pay the bills and get the shoes, or books, or whatever little extra thing they needed. And that was the way it was. Sometimes, Joe wondered if his parents had quietly divorced, but the odd time a man would ask her out she would state firmly, "Thank you, but no, I am a married woman."

Joe sighed. Once, as a teenager, he had been brave enough to ask her, "Why is Dad gone?"

"He's away working to take care of his family," she had answered.

"Why can't he work closer? Why can't he come back home and live with us?"

"It's too complicated for you to understand," she had answered simply, and strode quietly out of the room. Two days later, she had left to see Floyd Thunder Cloud, and on her return Joe once again returned to his job of smudging the house, and as usual his mother once again slipped back into her daily routine.

But things never changed. Years went by. Joe and his brothers and sisters grew up, and things seemed to be static for them. He wondered if his siblings had any memory of their father at all; he had been absent from their lives so long. His mom took care of them and worked part-time while his father stayed away, always dutifully sending money home every two weeks. And when things got intolerable or she needed advice, Joe's mother went to see Floyd Thunder Cloud. Joe could feel the sense of peace instilled in her each time she returned.

"Things will be better now." She would say, her head high, her eyes twinkling brightly as she would move into the house and retrieve her abalone shell from the shelf to give to Joe to smudge the house once again. A sense of peace would prevail, and things would be simple again.

"Perhaps things are too complicated," Joe murmured. Joe hoped above anything else that he could rely on his mother's faith in Floyd Thunder Cloud.

CHAPTER 8

Sara and Abby were lounging in chairs on the back deck, each sipping a bottle of beer when Abby's husband, Dan, got home from work.

"I see having a bonfire is becoming a daily event," Dan smiled up at Abby. He had gotten out of his car and had walked around to the back instead of through the house.

"If it's a problem, tell me now," snapped Abby as she bolted upright in her chair.

"No, Ab, no problem," Dan smiled thinly, running a hand through his hair. "It's been a long time since the yard has looked so good."

Dan stepped up on the deck and plopped down into a deck chair across from Abby and Sara. He stretched out his legs.

"How ya doing, Sara?" Dan gave Sara a warm smile.

"I'm as good as it gets, I guess." Sara laughed awkwardly.

Abby rolled her eyes.

"So what should we do about supper? Should I pick up some pizzas? Sara, you staying for some 'za?"

Sara looked over at Abby for a moment. "Ah, no, I gotta fly, actually, I mean, I gotta head home." Sara stood up. "Thanks for the invite, though. See you tomorrow, Ab?"

"Yeah, sure, tomorrow. Toss another log on the fire before you go, okay? Thanks." Abby leaned back in her chair again and took a long draught from her beer bottle.

Sara picked up a large log and tossed it gently into the fire as she headed out of the yard and toward the front of the house.

Dan eyed Abby tentatively. "Are you angry at me?"

"What? No, don't be ridiculous."

"You seem upset."

Abby rose out of her chair, grabbed her beer bottle, and strode through the sliding glass door into the house. "Yeah? Well, you're the one that's looking for a fight," Abby shot back at him as he followed her through the glass door.

"What? No, I'm just concerned about you, that's all." Dan reached out and gently laid his hand on her arm. Instantly he withdrew it with a shriek of pain. "Abby, oh my... Geez! You're on fire!" Dan looked at his hand, holding it gingerly with his other hand. A large, water-filled blister was beginning to form under the raw red skin on his left palm and forefinger.

"Dan, I'm so sorry." She rushed over to examine his hand. "I'll get the first-aid kit." Bolting from the room, she returned in a short moment first-aid kit in hand.

"Hold out your hand," she commanded gently.

Dan hesitated. "Maybe I should take care of this while you take something for your fever, okay?" Dan liberally squeezed the tube of burn ointment she handed him and gingerly rubbed the ointment into the tips of his fingers and the palm of his hand.

Abby touched her forearm and then her forehead. Both were cool to the touch. Strangely, she was no longer angry either.

"Dan, no, I'm alright now, see?" she placed her hand gently on his thigh. "Whatever it was, it's gone. It's passed."

Abby picked up a roll of gauze bandage and began wrapping his hand. When she finished rolling and taping she placed a pillow from the couch upon his lap and placed his hand gently upon it.

"Thank you." Dan smiled at her, leaned forward, and pressed his lips to hers.

"I don't like to see you angry and hurting," Dan spoke quietly. "I wish I could help take your pain away."

Abby sat down next to him on the couch. "What makes you think I'm hurting and in pain?" She stared steadily at him with wide, clear eyes.

"Because I've seen you like this before, Ab. When Callie died." Dan sank back into the couch.

Abby closed her eyes. *Please don't let me forget her.* Their beautiful baby girl had dark blue eyes you could get lost in and a full head of glossy, jet-black hair. Such a good baby. So happy. So content. The memories came flooding back so strongly. Abby woke at 8:00 a.m. on the very day their daughter turned four months old. She was so pleased. Callie had slept through the night for the first time. She sailed into the baby's room with a smile on her face, fastening the tie to her bathrobe.

"Wake up, sleepy head!" she had crooned as she wrenched open the curtain, flooding the room with sunlight. But something was wrong. No happy squeal of surprise, no movement, no sound at all. Suddenly, Abby's heart had frozen. Her mouth went dry as she crept up on the crib. The silence had been deafening to her. She could see the tiny form of the baby laying on her side with her back toward Abby. Abby reached a tentative hand into the crib and laid it on her back. The cool feel of her little body startled Abby; she yanked back her hand, and she sank to the floor cradling her knees with her arms with silent tears running down her face. She didn't know how long she had been sitting there before Dan found her – before he found them both.

Sudden Infant Death Syndrome. SIDS death. *"There was nothing you could have done,"* they all said, all those medical professionals in white coats. *"Not your fault,"* they said. But Abby felt it was her fault. *She* was Callie's mother. *She* should have woken at the 4:00 a.m. feeding. *She* should have been able to save her. But she didn't. Couldn't. Dan watched Abby quietly and witnessed her emotions play out across her face.

"It's not your fault, Abby, we couldn't have saved her."

Abby looked up at him, tears streaming down her face. "I know," she said softly, "I just miss her so much."

Dan put his hand around her and gently pulled her toward him in an embrace. "Me too, Ab. Me too."

They sat there together in their grief surrounded by the silence of their empty home. For the first time in a long time, their grief brought them together.

***

William bent down and affixed a large label on the packing crate on the floor in front of him. Ever since he had been on that television show (*What was it called?*), he had been swamped with people calling about particular pieces they had seen during the show. The piece he had packed in the crate was one of them.

"It's the piece that had a piano falling out of a second storey flat window," the lady on the phone had described. Indeed, he remembered the piece: a mahogany-colored upright piano on its way to a crash landing on a gentleman on the sidewalk below.

"Same fate took my poor nephew," the woman intoned over the receiver. "Poor old Bruce. Bruce Jeffrey was his name. He always was a teensy bit paranoid. I suppose with good reason, given the way he died and all."

William made all the appropriate sympathetic noises and promised to ship the painting once payment was received. But for the life of him, he could not understand why someone would want to immortalize the tragic loss of a relative by hanging a painting of it to commemorate it.

"How bloody cracked is that?" he uttered aloud.

William struggled to his feet and hobbled stiffly to the kitchen. *Which is worse*, he thought, *purchasing a painting about a tragic event, or being the prat who painted it in the first place?*

William filled the kettle from the tap, plugged it in, and flicked on the switch. Finally his work was starting to get some serious attention. So why was he so bothered?

He grabbed a mug from the cupboard and set it on the counter before tossing in a tea bag. *Maybe I should be painting landscapes*, he mused. *Or puppies. Or puppies in landscapes. That's more normal, more mainstream.* He snorted aloud. Why all of a sudden was it so important to be normal? Was he ever?

The kettle began boiling and shut itself off with a loud click. William unplugged the kettle and poured the hot water over the tea bag in his mug. He mashed the tea bag until the water turned a murky brown. He then scooped up the tea bag with the spoon and flicked it into the garbage. He added a spoonful of sugar and a tiny splash of milk before settling down with his mug and a tin of biscuits at the kitchen table. William popped the lid off the tin and replaced it after selecting two chocolate-covered Digestive cookies and setting them on the table beside his mug.

Galleries had even called him up too. *No doubt eager to cash in on my new-found fame*, he thought wryly. When was the last time a gallery looked him up? He strained to remember. Ten, fifteen years ago? They generally treated his work with disdain. William reached across the table and picked up the envelope he had carelessly tossed there earlier. Imagine, a gallery in the States interested in giving him enough space to do a single artist show!

William removed the letter from the envelope and unfolded it gingerly as he read:

> Please respond as soon as possible so that we can make every effort to accommodate your structure and set-up requirements. The target dates for this show, should you accept, would be February 28th to April 3rd of next year. If you have any questions, feel free to call or email the Harmon Gallery.

Sincerely,

Amy Foster
Executive Director

William dunked his cookie into his tea, lingering for a moment before taking a bite and dunking it again. A foreign show; that might be a nice change, maybe even a chance to do some traveling. He popped the rest of his cookie into his mouth and chased it down with a sip of tea.

Yep, might be good to take a break. His thoughts went to Rhysdale. Would she miss his visits? She always came to see him when he went up to the lake to work, but only when he called for her. William sighed and chased down his other cookie with a gulp of hot tea. She never came on her own. Maybe she only spent time with him out of pity - pity for a pathetic, old man. Try as he may, he could never veil his feelings for her. It was as if she could not only read his thoughts, but also read his emotions, his mood. She always knew when he was in a bad mood or when he was feeling down. But he never really got to know how she felt. She was such a good listener, though it was difficult to get her to open up to him. William felt a pang of guilt. *She's like my best mate*, he thought, *and I don't know what she's really about.* He lifted his mug and drained the last of the tea from it before standing up and placing the mug in the sink.

His joints ached as he strode up the stairs, gripping the handrail as he went. *A nice soak in the tub: that'll fix me right as rain.* He started the water running and poured some Epsom salts under the running tap. When the tub was sufficiently full and the salts dissolved, he stripped off his clothes and slipped gently into the hot water.

The heat of the water spread warmth into his body, easing the arthritic throbbing in his knees, shoulders, and elbows. He felt the steam rising up against the skin on his face and felt the warm flush spread across his cheeks as sweat beaded up on his forehead and nose. Even sweating felt good. He let himself slip a little further down into the water, closing his eyes for a moment. His head and shoulders leaned against the back of the tub. William opened his eyes. He felt so relaxed. The water was so warm, so enveloping, so . . . safe. His gaze shifted to the glass-like clear surface of the water. The water was still except for the tiny fluctuations caused by his slightest movement - the twitch of his leg, the rise and fall of his chest as he breathed. Not like his lake: his special place. The water would roll in gentle waves that lapped at the shore and rhythmically rolled back again and again. He loved everything about it - the smell of the water in the crisp air, the sight of its open vastness and the sound of the water slapping at the land, he could almost hear it now. *Wait a minute.* William froze in mid-thought, letting his eyes focus on the bathwater. *Waves, in my bloody tub.* Waves rolled almost up to the bottom of his chin before rolling back towards his toes and back again. William kept his gaze upon the undulating water as a sense of calm began to follow his initial shock.

There's nothing to fear here, he silently reassured himself.

The motion of the water had its usual effect on him. Its gentle rhythm was always hypnotic to him, and with each wave slapping, splashing, and breaking upon his chest, he fell deeper into its trance. William continued to stare transfixed as the surface of the water began to change; becoming calmer and glassier before a swirling, cloudy form appeared that suddenly turned into an image of two women standing almost directly in front of him. One was the brunette woman. *Why does she keep popping up?* He wondered. He noted she didn't look too pleased with her arms crossed in front of her chest and her eyes dark and narrow. He had never seen the other woman before. She was a smiling and slightly taller blonde woman with wide blue eyes. This woman stood next to the brunette woman in a much more relaxed stance with her arms loose at her sides. Behind them in the background was a wall completely covered in artwork. *Hey! That's my artwork*, he observed. The blonde was speaking, but he couldn't hear her words. He leaned slightly forward and strained to hear when the realization of what he was doing sank in and broke his concentration.

"I'm doing it IN THE BLOODY BATHTUB!" William now sat bolt upright in the bath; his vision and the wave pool had instantly abated as if a switch had been turned to the OFF position.

William leaned further forward and pulled the plug before reaching for his towel and stepping out of the water. His knees felt weaker under the weight of his body as he slipped on his robe and padded barefoot down the hall to his room. Suddenly, he needed to lie down. His heart was racing as he lay on his back on the bed. He took long, deep breaths to calm his body down and quiet his mind. He needed to think. *Think!*

William raised his hand up and ran his right hand over his forehead and his hair. *She* would know. His eyes widened with a sudden realization. He smiled slightly. *Rhysdale will know why this is happening; she'll know what to do.*

William smiled and closed his eyes. He had faith that Rhysdale would help him even if only by providing comfort. Suddenly weary, he let himself drift off to sleep.

CHAPTER 9

Joe craned his head from side to side, his ears almost touching his shoulders in an effort to loosen up his increasingly stiff neck while his hands firmly grasped the steering wheel. *Just a few more miles*, he thought as he clutched a map book lying on the seat and propped it just under the steering wheel and in his lap. Holding the wheel still, he afforded himself a few cursory glances diverted from the road.

I don't know why I need directions, he thought, tossing the map book back on the passenger seat, *It's not like I don't know where I'm going*.

Joe eased off the highway and turned down the off-ramp to the first side road. "Still haven't paved it," he observed aloud.

He would have called before leaving home if Floyd had owned a phone. "Don't believe in 'em," he would say. Even though he was completely isolated from communication with the civilized world, he was never caught off guard by the arrival of guests. Ever. He always knew when to expect company, and he always had a hot tea waiting for his guest (or, in some cases, guests) when they arrived. He just had a way of knowing, and no one even dared to ask him how he knew. You just accepted it and that was that. Floyd Thunder Cloud did just fine in his self-imposed exile.

The drone of the engine was instantly overpowered by the sound of crunching under his tires. Joe slowed down to avoid bouncing through the ever-present pot holes of the dirt road.

After what seemed an eternity of doing the pothole slalom, Joe saw the familiar cedar rail fence adorned with a buffalo skull. He turned right down the dirt path, following it through a copse of cedar trees. Joe rolled down his window and took a deep breath of the fresh air scented with the smell of the cedar trees. It was a familiar scent, one that transported him back to fond memories of his childhood, playing outside, climbing trees, and running through the woods during summer vacation. Joe smiled at the reminiscence and pulled his truck around on the other side of the trees to park. He hopped out of his truck and grabbed a cardboard box from inside the cab.

A field stone-lined path led from where Joe had parked up the somewhat steep hill to where Floyd's house sat approximately halfway up the hill. The exterior of the rough-hewn logs was worn from its original brown to a washed grey color, and it blended in as if it were a part of the hillside itself. "Nothing too fancy", Floyd would say. "Just a roof over my head." Even its worn shingles had the presence of rich, green moss as if the was earth reclaiming the space as its own once again.

Joe ascended the steps to the front door, which opened before he even got a chance to raise his hand to knock.

"Come in and sit down; have a tea and something to eat," Floyd gestured casually with his arm toward the table. Joe followed his gesture and set the box down on the table as he sat down.

Floyd pushed a full tea cup at Joe and began rummaging through the box before extracting a bag of sugar.

"Good thing you brought some, I just ran out this morning." He smiled and quickly filled the canister and passed it to Joe.

Joe scooped two heaping teaspoons into his tea. *He hasn't changed at all*, Joe thought to himself as Floyd eased his tall, thin frame onto a bench on the opposite side of the table. He looked as if he had been frozen in time all these years. His neat silver braid may have been a little longer, and the lines around his eyes a bit more pronounced, but he hadn't changed at all. Not meaning to be disrespectful, Joe averted his eyes from Floyd and gazed over his mug at the room as Floyd pulled out a bag of cookies and placed some on a plate, offering one to Joe. He accepted one and followed Floyd's lead by first dunking it in his tea before taking a bite.

Joe looked around the room. The kitchen table he sat at was parallel to the kitchen counter, which had a sink set into the exact middle. At each end of the butcher block counter were the appliances, the refrigerator was on one end, and the gas stove was on the other. Above the counter were dark mahogany-brown cabinets that matched the ones below. The rest of the room was more of a living room area with a large woodstove at one end. In front of that a large, worn area rug and an equally worn plaid couch were flanked with end tables. The bare, exposed beams of logs on the ceiling had many hooks in them, some of which had dried herbs, antlers, and animal pelts hanging from them.

The room stayed silent until Joe took a final draught from his mug and pushed it away from him on the table. Floyd reached into the box again and pulled out some red cotton fabric. He opened it and found a pouch of tobacco inside.

"What's this for?" Floyd asked quietly.

"For you." Joe replied.

"Why?"

Joe stopped for a moment, unsure how to answer. "I need your help," he finally managed.

"For what?" Floyd pressed quietly.

"I need some advice. Some answers." Joe explained. "Something is going on, something that I'm not sure I understand, and I need help to figure out what I need to do, or even what is needed from me."

"I cannot give you advice or answers," Floyd stated. "But I can help you to figure out where the answers lie within yourself. You just have to be willing to hear them, Joe." His dark eyes fixed on Joe's. "Are you willing to listen?"

Joe met Floyd's intense stare. He knew what he meant. He knew the underlying meaning of what Floyd meant. He would have to have faith in a power he couldn't control, a power greater than himself. He would have to trust in that power, although he ultimately might not like what he discovered. He knew that before he arrived at Floyd's, and he had already accepted it as fact. He was ready, though he felt the compulsion to explain. The need for clarity welled up inside him.

"You are like a father to me. I trust you." Joe blurted out as he looked down at his hands.

"Thank you, but you must trust in yourself first." Floyd rose slowly from the table. "You have until after the sunrise ceremony tomorrow to decide what you will do. *You* choose your path, Joe Asine. I am honored you think of me as a father, but your father is still among us. Perhaps soon you will see him again. Yes, maybe soon."

Taking Floyd's words as his cue, Joe got up from the table, ready to get his gear out of his truck and get settled in for the night. They walked together down the path.

"How long do you think I'll be staying, Floyd?"

Floyd smiled broadly, and a knowing look was in his twinkling eyes. "Until it's time for you to leave, Joe."

***

Abby looked down at the molten pile of silver as if it were an object of revulsion. At some point it had been a delicate sterling silver ring, but the intensity of the hot flame was applied too rapidly and quickly reduced it to a molten pile of slag atop her fire brick. Instead of blaming her impatience, she threw her torch down and stormed out of her studio, knocking a small assembly table over with a crash as she stomped down the stairs and out of the studio.

I need to get out of here, she thought, panic suddenly welling up inside her as she suddenly felt the confines of the walls pressing in on her, making it hard for her to breathe or to think.

After running into the house and grabbing her purse and keys, she jumped into her van and peeled out of the driveway as fast as she could. She rolled down her window and let the sun warm her face, gulping in gasping breaths of air; she felt her panic begin to subside with each breath.

Where to go, where to go? Faced now with her sudden freedom and ability to go wherever she chose, Abby opted for the nearest Super Walmart store on the outskirts of Harmon. She frowned as she glanced around the parking lot. It didn't matter what time of day you shopped: the huge parking lot was always packed with vehicles. Abby pulled her van into an empty spot at the farthest end of the parking lot, opting for ease in finding a spot instead of circling the lot like a shark waiting to glimpse that one close spot and then seizing it before another shopper. That sort of thing wasted far too much time in her opinion. She strode briskly through the parking lot toward the store. She could feel the heat radiating off the asphalt and the warmth emanating from the engines of the newly-parked vehicles she passed, and she could hear the odd clicking and ticking sounds of recently-idled vehicles. The heat warmed her almost as if its energy were drawn to and surging through her. She increased her pace and strode through the automatic door, commandeering an empty cart in mid-stride as she passed through the entryway.

Abby had not thought to bring a list of any sort at all. *I'm in no particular hurry*, she thought happily as she proceeded methodically down each monolithic row of merchandise and foodstuffs in search of anything that might catch her eye. In no time, she had accumulated almost an entire cart full of various items of food and merchandise.

(!!!)

No.

That feeling *(!!!)* was returning, no, rising up inside her like a wave of heat trying to consume and then escape her body. She could feel it: warm and pleasant sensations alternated with hot and painful tingles throughout her body. She jerked her hands off the handle of the cart she was pushing, fearing the heat would find its way out of her body through her hands. *Get it together, Ab*, she chided herself. She took a deep breath and exhaled loudly, causing an elderly gentleman passing in the aisle to jump slightly.

"Pardon me." Abby managed to get out. The man nodded and continued on his way past Abby. Their eyes locked and she felt powerless to look away.

Suddenly, Abby was staring at this old man. He no longer seemed small or meek. He exuded power; it emanated from him like a brilliant aura. She was caught in it, swirling down into a vortex—transported to a place somewhere out of time. Her wrists felt heavy. Abby glanced down and saw that both her wrists and ankles were shackled. Large black iron bands connected with heavy links of black chain; her arms were trapped at her sides tightly, and they were pressed against the plain yellow pinafore she was wearing. She felt tears flowing down her face and realized she was crying and saying something, though she was unable to hear what words were coming out of her mouth. Judging from her growing sense of urgency and fear and from the tears streaming down her face, she felt that she was pleading for her life. All of this was in front of that innocuous-looking but powerful man whose terrible presence was suddenly larger than life. He appeared to be seated behind a judge's bench, his gray hair and blue eyes contrasting the stark black of his officious robe. He smiled and proclaimed loudly as he slammed down the gavel.

"Let the witch BURN!"

Abby felt her body go limp as darkness overcame her. She knew he meant her. Then she smelled fire. She could feel its heat, and the flames began to lick at her legs as she stood bound to a post by a thick rope. Staring wide-eyed through the flames she could see people surrounding her on all sides, separated from her by a wall of fire. She could hear their taunts as she fought to hold back her panic . . . her screams.

Then, just as suddenly as she had been transported away, she found herself back in the store, gripping the blue handle of her grocery cart, fighting back a scream and trying to breathe. She looked around her for the man, but he was gone.

I've got to get outta here. NOW! She panicked inside, taking more deep breaths.

I can do this, she thought as she brought her anxiety under control. She surveyed the row of checkouts carefully for one with little or no wait. *Ah, number six is opening.* Just as she veered her cart into the laneway to the checkout, a woman with an overflowing cart pushed past her and moved into the line ahead of her, blocking Abby with her large and ample hips and knocking Abby into the handle of her own cart.

"Excuse me," Abby started angrily, gripping her cart until her knuckles were white with the strain.

"I'm in a hurry," the large woman snapped back as she commenced unloading her heavily laden cart onto the checkout conveyor. The checkout clerk gave Abby a helpless glance and, with a shrug of her shoulders, began to push the groceries through the scanner.

How dare she! Abby screamed internally as she glared daggers at the obese woman's form in front of her. Abby felt the rage well up again. And then she spied something that caught her attention. Stuffed loosely into the pocket of the woman's jacket was a package of cigarettes half-hanging out, the tip of the lighter just sticking out of her pocket. The call of the flame began to beckon her, feeding the fire of her anger.

So you like smoke, do you? She thought, a sinister smile forming on her face. She looked at the lighter and flicked the tip of her finger ever so gently in its direction. A small ball of fire, no bigger than a marble (but smaller than an aggie) floated in the air for a moment before zeroing in on the lighter and disappearing into it. A small flame popped to life from the lighter, and within a few seconds the cigarettes and the package began to smolder. A flame erupted a moment later that began to devour the package of cigarettes. Abby was mesmerized, powerless to look away but still feeling too smug and indignant anyway to raise the alarm.

She didn't need to. The smell of smoke and burning plastic and now the cotton of her jacket caught the immediate attention of "The Nasty Woman" and the checkout clerk.

"Oh my God, I'M ON FIRE!" the woman screamed while frantically attempting to take off her jacket, but unable to work with zipper in her blind panic.

"Stop, drop, and roll!" the checkout clerk yelled. She too seemed rooted to the spot, however, unable, or perhaps subconsciously unwilling to move.

Suddenly, a lanky, acne-faced young man brandishing a fire extinguisher leapt out of nowhere and discharged the fire extinguisher on the poor woman's torso. It felt like an eternity passed while she stood there, her pocket still smoking, her jaw agape and covered in the white, chalky-looking powder that had spewed from the fire extinguisher. Even the contents of her cart and the checkout belt were covered with a thin haze of dust. The air surrounding them was filled with a fog of white motes, the remnants of the fire extinguisher discharge hung in the air.

"Uh, Miss?" Startled, Abby looked up at the clerk. "We can take you on aisle five." She forced out a thin smile.

While the white particles from the fire extinguisher were still floating in the air and settling on the floor and the conveyor belt, Abby pulled her cart out from behind the woman and into the next aisle, a huge smile forming on her lips, while she fought to hold back what would most likely be hysterical laughter. As she was checked out swiftly through aisle five, the clerk from aisle six cast Abby a glance, catching her smile.

A chill went down the young woman's spine. *Beautiful woman*, she thought, *but somehow dangerous.* Her eyes followed Abby as she pushed her cart out of the store.

"Now there goes one scary bitch," she thought aloud.

"Wha, what did you say?" the large woman in the checkout line stammered.

"Nothing," she replied as she returned her focus back to her cash register and began ringing up the next customer.

CHAPTER 10

Thaddeus shivered slightly and drew the collar of his wool overcoat up to his ears and level with where his silver hair just grazed them. He stood near the trunk of a large maple tree shielded by the dark of night and the girth of the tree. The cold chill that hung in the air after an icy gust of wind was a harbinger of a bitterly cold winter. The frigid wind felt as if it sunk into his aching bones before it carried the fog of exhaled warm breath away from his body like an icy mist.

A good location, he thought to himself. No one would notice him, why waste a good cloaking spell when you can hide out in the open? His eyes focused on the house in front of him. He could see her through the window dancing around and waving her arms in the air to some sort of strange music that blared loud and clear outside of the house. She was in the center of a swirling vortex of what looked like pots, pans, books, and papers moving along beside her — moving at her command.

"Who does she think she is, the Sorcerer's Apprentice?" he muttered under his breath. "Tidy up or do the dishes. Don't make the place a bigger mess." He smiled as he watched, secure in the knowledge that she was oblivious to his observation.

His surveillance was suddenly interrupted by the appearance of a large winged creature on the horizon. The creature at first glance looked strangely like a pterodactyl, but as it drew closer it looked more like a vulture in flight. The slow rhythm of its wings beating up and down in the air suggested it was quite a large creature, and being close revealed that it was bat-like in appearance. As it flew nearer, its wings had the look of a dark leather, but thinner, like crepe paper. The moonlight glowed through them, silvery and black. The creature passed over Sara's house and over the tree where Thaddeus stood. He turned toward it as it banked back in his direction and descended slowly, retracting its wings as it made its way toward the ground. It landed soundlessly a few feet away from Thaddeus and lopped on talon feet toward him, using the tiny claws on its wingtips as miniscule crutches to balance his gait.

"Report, Taekyr," Thaddeus ordered the creature, narrowing his cold blue eyes.

"All is quiet in the realm, my liege," the Taekyr croaked, bowing his head and then returning his liquid, lidless black eyes up to meet Thaddeus' gaze.

"And what of Gabe?" Thaddeus demanded. "Have his movements through the Veil been kept under surveillance?"

The Taekyr opened his large, lipless mouth to speak then closed it suddenly, reaching a wing claw up past his gray cheek to pensively scratch the top of his head.

"We understood that the surveillance of the Dueagar, Gabe, was to be conducted by your commander, Michael. We Taekyrs have only been observing the state of affairs in Feyland and watching for signs that the Queen has any forewarning or knowledge of what is to come. As to that, I report that nothing appears to be any different. Everything is as it was and has always been."

A muffled cry came from the Taekyr's midsection. The weak, muffled cry of a small baby. The Taekyr pulled open the grayish-black leathery pouch on its abdomen and the head of a human baby popped out; its mouth was moving in a slow cry, and its skin was tinted with a grayish pallor. It looked to be no more than four or five months old.

"Sleep," the Taekyr gruffly commanded. The baby closed its eyes and slipped back into the darkness of the Taekyr's membranous pouch.

"I must go, my liege." The Taekyr bowed apologetically. "I must take this changeling to its home and return to Feyland with the child it replaces before the sun rises."

"Yes, of course. I wouldn't want you to turn to stone." Thaddeus said sarcastically.

The creature shuddered slightly. "I will tell the commander you are looking for him."

"Please do." Thaddeus answered. "And please tell him I think I have found our weak link."

"I will."

The Taekyr spread his wings and with a great leap sprung up into the air. Thaddeus watched as he flew higher into the night sky and out of sight before returning his gaze to Sara's house.

***

The smell of sweetgrass and sage permeated the air, mingling with the smoke from the fire, forming a haze in the otherwise clear sky as the sun began to rise over the horizon.

"AH HO, all my relations," Floyd's voice gently intoned, as he put down his abalone shell and sat down on a blanket in front of the fire.

He patted his hand on the blanket beside him, and Joe crouched down instinctively to join him. They sat together and shared a silent moment in contemplation, their eyes upon the rising sun; the only sounds were the soft cry of the loons in the water, the lapping of the water against the shore, and the crackling of the still burning fire.

"What is on your mind, Joe?" Floyd inquired quietly, his eyes still fixed on the hazy horizon.

Joe looked down at the ground soundlessly and raised his eyes up to meet the horizon once again; his racing mind was at odds with the serene calm of the morning. He felt intensely anxious and apprehensive. What good could come of his being here? How long had it been since he had sweat? He had turned his back on tradition for so long – what made him feel that it was now the way to find the answers he sought? Joe sat there mute and unable to form a single thought into words.

His eyes moved back and forth, rapidly scanning the horizon before he finally blurted out, "Too much, Floyd. Too much is on my mind."

Floyd looked at Joe with a serious look that instantly turned into one of utter bemusement. This was quickly followed by a loud belly-busting sound of laughter that was so unrestrained it caused Floyd to gasp for air several times before wiping tears from his eyes. Once he regained his composure he looked intently back at Joe, whose expression remained puzzled as he continued his shocked stare at Floyd.

"Why do you think you are here?" Floyd blurted. He leaned back slightly on his elbows, a serious look on his face as he spoke again. "A field mouse that fills its day scurrying around in a field looking down and searching only for food does not see the shadow of the hawk upon him. Do not be like the field mouse and be distracted by all the thoughts that slip into your mind; you must be in balance. Once you achieve balance you will be in harmony; not only will this give you inner strength, it will connect you with all creation and the universe. Harmony and balance will help you to find and focus on what is truly important and where you need to be. You must remember at times when your mind is full to focus on what really matters." Floyd looked over in Joe's general direction. "Do you know what that is?"

Joe shook his head.

"The only thing that matters is *now*. You are here *now*. A moment ago, it doesn't matter. It's gone. But you must focus on the *now* when your mind is full. That alone will help you to find direction and achieve harmony. Then you choose where you need to be." Floyd smiled with a twinkle in his sharp eyes. "But once you figure out what you should be doing, chances are, you already are doing it. Sometimes we don't always see what is in front of us."

Floyd rose, gathering his things and packing them into a leather pouch as he rose to his feet. He held out his hand to Joe and helped pull him up from the ground.

"So, where you headin', Joe?" Floyd asked, a bemused smile spreading across his face.

"I guess I'm chopping wood and gathering rocks, right, Floyd?"

Floyd laughed. "Gather lots of rocks, you have lots to think about."

Floyd clapped Joe on the back and together they made their way up the path through the trees in the direction of Floyd's.

***

William was sitting at the edge of the lake, his pants rolled up to his knees, his lower legs and feet dangling in the water. Sitting on the bank beside him holding his hand was Rhysdale, her red hair shining brilliantly, her delicate blue skin glowing with an iridescent shimmer as it warmed in the sun.

William had shared with Rhysdale what had happened in his bathtub the day before. He was still shaken from learning that he could unconsciously start drifting into a vision. He knew that what he could do was called scrying and that many seers or psychics employed this method to predict the future. Heck, he even heard that Nostradamus used scrying to achieve his predictions, though William doubted that even Nostradamus had to worry about it happening in the bathtub. What would he do if it ever happened it a public place? He shuddered once more at the thought.

"Why do you fear it so?" Rhysdale asked quietly as they both stared across the lake.

William cleared his throat. "'Cause it's not normal," he paused as he searched for a way to explain himself.

"I don't understand what you mean." Rhysdale said. "Do you wish to be normal?"

William looked at her. If he was normal, would they be having this conversation? Would she even be in his life? He couldn't bear the thought of not being able to share time with her, share his thoughts and feelings.

Rhysdale smiled at him and drew his hand up to her lips. "I cherish our friendship too," she whispered as she gently kissed the back of his hand. "But I do not understand why you feel the way you do about your gift."

"My gift?" William was utterly confused. "How do you figger it's a gift now?"

"Because the water calls to you. In a way, I understand that, as it also calls to me - it is my home. But water shows you premonitory events. It allows you to see things others cannot. And you can call it to you. Do you realize that?"

William remembered the hypnotic waves in his bath and with it the sudden realization that he had caused them. But how?

"I have shared your confidence with a friend as you had permitted me to do. Do you remember?"

"Yeah, o' course." William replied. "But I thought that yer people weren't allowed to—"

Rhysdale straightened up and moved closer to him, holding her steady gaze into his eyes. "William, I value your friendship greatly, and I would never do anything to put it in jeopardy. Surely this is something you already know?"

"Yes, I do, Rhysdale, and I also value your friendship," William replied softly.

"I spoke of what was happening to you with another, as I said I would. And he believes—"

William interrupted abruptly, "Another man?"

"No, of course not," Rhysdale answered swiftly. "He is not of your world or of mine. He is someone that I trust implicitly just as I do you," Rhysdale answered smoothly. Her eyes narrowed as she stared back at William. "Perhaps you do not impart the same degree of trust in me?" she continued to stare hollowly at William, her lips pressed tightly together as she awaited his answer.

William was at a loss for words; his mind was racing to hide his thoughts from her. *I wonder if her race even understands jealousy*, he thought. He raised his eyes up to meet her penetrating stare, which was still fixed upon him.

"I do trust you, Rhysdale," he began, clearing his throat. "It's just that . . . that I wonder if perhaps someday you'll always come when I call for you. If you truly need my friendship." *As much as I need yours*, he finished to himself, not daring to say it aloud to her.

He glanced up to meet her pale olive green eyes, and was surprised to find them welled up with tears that began to slip down her cheeks.

"Why do you believe that I would treat our friendship in that manner?" Rhysdale looked wounded and vulnerable as she sat softly crying and clutching his hand.

"No, no," William spoke quickly. "I don't question your friendship. It's just…," he broke away before reaching a hand up to brush away the tears and to cup her cool cheek with his hand. "I'm sorry. I didn't want to hurt you. I guess I'm just…," he couldn't find the words.

"I'm sorry," he whispered.

She pulled her hand from his and placed her hand over his for a moment as they sat there silently looking out across the lake, gently moving their legs to and fro in the water.

"I know you have many questions, many that I cannot answer for you or find the answers for." Rhysdale spoke quietly. She continued, "One thing is certain. The water is calling you. For years it has shown you many events that you have captured with paint and paper. Now it calls to you, for whatever purpose, I do not know. But in time, it will be revealed to you. And whatever it is, you must answer its call."

"But how will I know when that will be? How will I know for sure?" William questioned her, running his hand through his hair.

"How do you call me to tell me you are at this spot? How do I know you are here?" Rhysdale patted his hand. "All you have to do is ask," she continued. "I believe you will have your answers as soon as you start asking the right questions."

Ask the water? William almost laughed out loud at the simplicity of the idea. *Could it really be that easy?*

"Don't forget," Rhysdale broke into his thoughts, speaking aloud, "there are also others that reside in the water too. Other creatures, some of which are much different than me."

Rhysdale slipped softly into the water and moved directly in from of William between his legs. She leaned in close, and wrapped her arms around his neck and embraced him gently.

"Unlike you," she whispered into his ear, "I do not fear I will lose our friendship if you gain another."

She brushed his cheek with her cool lips before she gently eased away from him and turned her back, slipping into the water and out of sight, leaving William alone with his thoughts, his head full of more frustration than it has been before.

CHAPTER 11

Sara stepped back from her easel, brush in hand, to examine what she hoped were the final brush strokes to her morning's work. She stood in contemplation for a few moments, a satisfied smile spreading across her face. Feeling quite pleased with herself, she immediately set to work cleaning her brushes, inhaling the combined smell of paint and turpentine.

"I should probably crack open a window," she mused, feeling slightly heady and wobbly from the fumes. "A little late, though."

After tossing a last admiring glance back at her work, she shut off the lights and stepped out the door of her studio, closing it behind her with a soft click.

She drew in a breath of air as she stretched her arms up into the sky. She could feel the cool autumn breeze and shivered slightly, but she wasn't going to go in and get her jacket just yet. *No, still too early*, she thought. The day was sunny, the sky a clear blue with only an occasional wispy cloud floating lazily past the sun, casting a web-like shadow here and there on the ground. Sara couldn't bear to be cooped up on a day like this. She felt so different, so *good*. No, not just good. Somehow better than good — she felt *exhilarated. Was that it?* Sara shrugged. She didn't need a reason or explanation for why she felt the way she did. Perhaps she was entitled, maybe it was her due. Whatever the case, the urge to get out was strongly compelling her to take flight.

"Ah, there you are!" Sara trilled happily.

Two little, winged creatures the same size and iridescence of dragonflies appeared, flitting about her head making bell-like tinkling noises. Sara was encouraged by their presence. They always appeared whenever she was going to fly, and they accompanied her on these flights, cresting the winds alongside her. She was always immensely grateful for their company, as they warned her of the presence of turbulence so she could take precautions to adjust her flight path to avoid a scary drop.

It's nice having company, she surmised. *At least I'm not alone.*

One of the little creatures darted toward her face, and she felt the tiniest little flutter against her cheek and a constant stream of the tinkling sound, as if someone was ringing several small bells.

"I know, and I enjoy your company, too." Sara replied to the tiny creature. "It's just sometimes I would like someone to share this with." The creature flew back to its position at her side and hovered, as if awaiting instruction.

"Ooh, I know!" Sara yelped excitedly. "Let's go visit Abby and see how she's been doing."

Sara leapt into the air, anticipating where the gust of wind would catch her. It lifted her into the air, and she quickly rose high above the trees, faster than ever before, flanked on either side by her two iridescent, diminutive companions. She felt so free, so alive!

It's all getting to be so easy now, she thought. *It's like I've always known those abilities*, she thought idly, as she reached down to brush the top of a tall pine tree with her fingertips as she sailed over top. From her vantage point she could see the roof peak of Abby's house and commenced her descent. Six feet from the ground she straightened up and gently stepped down from the air pockets as if quietly descending a flight of stairs, her feet soundlessly stepping down onto the ground.

I hope Abby is up for some company, she thought hopefully. Then she frowned slightly. Lately, determining Abby's mood was similar to gauging the weather in Michigan - if you didn't like it, you just had to wait five minutes and it would change.

Perhaps she will be different today, Sara posited optimistically. *After all, it's a beautiful day.* Sara's optimism was soon dashed as she heard a crash followed by a string of curse words, some of which Sara had never heard uttered by Abby before. She flinched, but steeled herself quickly before striding into Abby's workshop and ascending the staircase toward the commotion.

"Stupid, fu–"

"Hi, Abby!" Sara blurted, cutting Abby off in mid-swear, her chirpy voice a little too high and shrill in greeting. "I just thought I'd drop in for a quick visit. I hope that's okay?"

Abby just stared at Sara with huge red eyes that made her look, from Sara's point of view, slightly, no, make that *extremely*, deranged. Not only were her eyes and eyelids red as if she had been crying, but the dark rings under her eyes were proof that Abby was lacking sleep. Even though Abby was a jeans and T-shirt girl, she was always put together well; her hair was always tidy and she always wore just a touch of makeup. Today her face was bare, her hair was quite mussed, and she gave the overall impression of having slept in her clothes. Even more strangely, her studio was in total disarray. Sara noticed that there were what appeared to be piles of molten slag in many places on her work bench and littering the floor. Many of her tools, in fact, were lying on the floor at the opposite end of the studio, and one glowed cherry red with heat. It was only then when Sara looked back at Abby and realized that both of Abby's hands appeared to be on fire. No, not *on* fire— flames were emanating from the tips of her fingers. Sara stared wide-eyed for a moment. Abby stared back, as if rooted to the spot and powerless to speak.

Sara finally broke the silence. "Y' okay, Ab? What's going on?"

Abby closed her eyes for a moment and drew in a lungful of air, sighing deeply. The flames in her fingers flickered and then went out. "Things are turning to shit," she blurted tearfully. "I can't do any work without burning it, melting it, or turning it to charcoal."

"Sounds like you need a break." Sara intoned softly. "Let's go have a tea, shall we?"

"Yeah, okay, but first I better get the fire extinguisher and cool down that tool over there." Abby motioned to the one with the reddened handle, "Else I'll burn the place down."

"Ooh, I got this!" Sara directed a cold blast of air at the tools and within seconds it returned to a dull, blue-gray color.

"Wow, look what you can do." Abby sneered sarcastically.

Sara blushed. "I'm sorry. I should have let you get the extinguisher," she said sheepishly.

"Don't worry about it," Abby said casually. "I'd probably just screw it up anyway." She ran her hands through her hair quickly before stomping down the stairs. Sara followed Abby, ambling cautiously down the stairs and up the path toward the house in no particular hurry to catch up with her.

Wow, she's really touchy, Sara thought. She opened the front door and stepped inside the house just as Abby was filling the kettle with water and setting it on the stove.

"Why don't you just–," Sara stopped. *You idiot*, she chided herself. *Remember the workshop?*

"I could boil the water myself, but as you saw," she gestured carelessly at the window with her arm in the direction of her studio, "control and accuracy are not my forté right now."

Abby pulled up a stool in front of the counter and Sara followed suit, sitting on a stool on the opposite side across from Abby.

"What are you doin' here anyway?" Abby demanded as she scowled at Sara.

"Well, I thought I'd see how you were doing since I hadn't seen you for a while, I thought I'd drop in, and then you invited me in for tea." Sara replied in a cautious and soft voice.

"No, actually, *you* invited us in for tea." Abby corrected staring at Sara.

Sara held her gaze. "Do you want me to leave, Ab?"

Abby continued to stare at Sara. "No, yes, oh, I don't know." she responded with a sigh. She rose from her stool and poured the contents of the kettle into a teapot which she brought over to the counter. She passed Sara a mug.

"Do you think I'm crazy?" Abby spoke fast, as if she was forcing the words out.

"What?" Sara furrowed her brow. "No, Ab. No. But I do believe you are a little unsettled. What's going on?"

"Well, I've been having these dreams, see? Like I'm somebody else, in another time. And there's this man. It's always the same dream, always same man. And he, well, he scares me – and I think he is responsible for killing me."

Abby told Sara about the vision she had at Walmart, carefully omitting her angry outburst on the rude woman that cut in front of her in line. When she was done speaking she looked at Sara expectantly, awaiting her response.

"Wow, that's pretty powerful." Sara commented carefully. "Have you had this dream before?"

"Well, no, not since... no. It's a pretty recent development." Abby answered as she poured tea into their cups.

Sara nodded in understanding. *The dreams are part of the package*, she thought to herself. "They scare me, but they make me angry too, you know?" Abby continued. "And when I get angry, I just lose it– completely. I'm sorry to say I've done a few things I'm not proud of." She looked down into her mug, watching the stream rise up from her tea.

Abby suddenly burst into laughter. Sara smiled in response, but Abby didn't stop laughing. It grew louder and louder until it morphed into sobs that racked her entire body. Her hands started to glow red, as if the fire inside her was finally breaking to the surface and begging to be released.

"Ab, careful." Sara cautioned as Abby reached for a box of Kleenex on the counter.

Abby yelped and jerked her hand away from the box and settled for wiping her face on her sleeves as the color in her hands returned to normal.

"At first I thought this fire thing was a gift," Abby whispered. "But now it feels more like a curse. What am I gonna do? I'm like a walkin' stick of dynamite."

"You could control it before." Sara reminded her.

"Yeah, but it's stronger now." Abby stated flatly.

"If you could control it before, you can control it again," Sara reassured her. "You just have to work on it. Maybe once you learn how it works and exactly what you can and can't do, you will be able to harness and control it."

"I'm afraid, Sara." Abby looked at her with big tear-filled eyes. "For the first time in my life, I'm afraid of myself."

Sara looked at her softly and smiled. "I'll help you. Whatever it takes, Ab."

"Thanks," Abby whispered, taking a sip of her tea. "Thanks for being my friend, Sara."

"Anytime," Sara grinned, picking up her mug and raising it in a mock salute.

***

Joe's body ached. He arrived at this great epiphany the moment he had entered the lodge on his hands and knees and moved into his position to take a seat on the cool, dirt floor. His hands were rough and calloused from carrying pails of water up to the sweat lodge; his arms were stiff from picking rocks and pushing heavily laden wheelbarrows up to the clearing in the cedar grove. He had split so much wood his shoulders ached. *But it felt good, no, it felt right*, he thought as he sat in the lodge clad in a pair of shorts and holding a towel on his lap, breathing in the combined aroma of sage, cedar, and earth that hung in the air.

The lodge, he observed as he cast an eye around, seemed so huge and expansive once he was inside. Though it was dark, it felt much larger than it appeared from the outside.

Floyd pulled aside the blankets covering the doorway and directed in the shovel that held another hot rock. He guided it with two sticks and arranged it atop a pile of rocks that had already been placed into a shallow pit in the center of the ground. Floyd murmured something in greeting that Joe couldn't hear and sprinkled some powdery substance upon its glowing surface which immediately turned to smoke. Joe inhaled deeply; the pungent smell was familiar and pleasant.

Floyd murmured something to the Fire Keeper outside and then pulled closed the heavy woven blankets that comprised the door, sealing the entryway and immersing them into total darkness. Not one glimmer of light peeked in from anywhere. Joe looked down and could not even see any part of his body or discern where Floyd was sitting. Floyd spoke quietly again, and Joe heard the hiss of water against the hot rocks. Instantly the lodge filled with hotter, humid air, and Joe felt it hit him like he walked into a wall. It felt almost too hot and acrid to breathe in his nose and too humid to breath in his mouth. A wave of anxiety started to rise up inside him, but he pulled his towel over his face, breathed though the cotton, and calmed himself with deep, even breaths. Once his sense of panic subsided, he opted for alternating between breathing in his nose and his mouth. As he started to breathe more evenly, he felt his body relax as sweat began to bead up on his skin and trickle down his chest and back.

A drum. He heard a drum. It sounded like a heartbeat, strong and steady. As it began to get louder, Floyd started to sing. The timber of his voice was warm, strong, and steady, its rhythm in time with the drumbeat, both resonating clear and strong. With every word Floyd sang, Joe could feel the intonations flow through him, urging the strength inside him to awaken.

It's getting bigger in here, Joe thought. *Really big*. He raised his head up expecting to see more darkness, but he was surprised to see the stars in the clear night sky, twinkling and bright. There was no sign of the sweat lodge; it was as if it had simply melted away after transporting him to this place and time. As he looked around, he noted that he was surrounded by little people. They were dressed in regalia made of very fine hides and decorated with feathers and shells. The beadwork that adorned them was exquisite; the patterns and designs were intricate and breathtaking. Joe knew he had never seen workmanship like that before. They were oblivious to Joe's presence as they danced in a circle, jumping and twirling and swaying to the rhythm of Floyd's song. One of the dancers was a much taller woman with a long, straight, dark braid down her back dressed in clothing with the same patterns and colors as the little people. She left, accompanied by one of the men. The constellations in the night sky swirled away, and darkness gave way to the light of day. Joe could feel the sun beating down on his back and the sweat pouring down his brow and onto his face. It was starting to sting his eyes, and he swiped his towel across his face.

The woman he had seen was in a camp now, a child sitting beside her, as she picked up beads on a needle and worked them into a piece of beadwork.

"Always know, child, you are special," she told the child.

The child merely smiled and laughed and asked for a story. Then a herd of buffalo appeared atop a hill behind the camp. Joe watched as the largest one walked over to a large stone atop the hill and stood in front of it.

Everything swirled faster around Joe as if he was being pulled through day and night, day and night, and in the background he could hear the beat of the drum and the sound of Floyd's voice resonating slightly in the background.

Suddenly, the woman appeared again. She was much older, but she still carried herself gracefully; her head was tilted proudly, and her back was straight. The beadwork on her clothing bore the mysterious patterns of the little people. Standing in front of her was a young man who could have been no more than 18 years old, wearing jeans and no shirt, his hair in two braids, his arms folded in front of his bare chest in defiance.

"If it is what you wish to do, I will not stop you," the old woman spoke softly. "You have always known that you are special and always will be. But know this - what people do not understand, they will fear – and that which they fear they will attempt to destroy. Do not shame us by being destroyed. We are a proud people, and we have a destiny to fulfill."

"Yes, Kohkom," he replied. The young man turned, stepped into the forest, and slipped out of his jeans, setting them inside a hole in a fallen log. As he took two steps, he transformed into a red tail fox and set off at a trot into the woods.

The swirling began again.

It's getting hotter in here, Joe thought.

He wiped the stinging sweat once more from his eyes, and once again he was immersed into total darkness. His eyes looked in vain for any little speck of light, but none appeared. Floyd's song had changed, as had the beat of the drum. It fueled a sense of urgency in Joe.

I have to get out of here, he thought. *It's too, too hot.*

Eyes closed, Joe took in a deep breath of air, but the smell of the air was changing. It began to smell like... hmm... Joe tried to put a finger on it. It was an acrid smell, like. . .

BOOM!

Gun powder. Joe's eyes opened wide, the shock of the sound seemed to have pulled him out of a trance. It was sunrise, or just a little before from the looks of things. There were people running everywhere, screaming, crying. It was cold. He could feel the chill on his body; he could see the fug of his breath in the air. Chaos reigned everywhere he could see; panic and fear hung in the air and ran through him as he took in the horrific sight that greeted him. The boom of guns firing continued to ring through the air as Joe noticed that he was surrounded by wounded and dying people on the ground. People were bleeding, screaming and dying. Joe was crying now; the suffering around him was too much to bear.

A man ran by yelling.

"Black Kettle says to stay around the flag." He pointed at a United States flag being flown from a lodge. "Black Kettle says they will not fire on us if we do." With that he ran over to the lodge and huddled with the others that had already assembled there under Chief Black Kettle's assurances.

Joe went to follow the man with the sudden realization that he was no longer a spectator, but a participant in this scene of events. He could hear the gun shots ringing out, the boom of artillery pieces being fired in the distance, and children crying for their mothers before being struck down dead by bullets. Joe ran to one, suddenly realizing as he bent down that he was wearing skirts. He was a woman. Stunned, but unconcerned, he bent down over the child's body and turned her gently over onto her back. Her face was bloodied, and her small, fragile skull was shattered by the bullet. Joe felt rage and tears well up inside him. He rose up, hearing the approach of soldiers whooping and yelling in excitement.

Suddenly, his leg felt like it had been simultaneously kicked by a horse and burned with a poker. Losing his balance, he spun around and fell down hard, sliding down the sandy bank of the creek.

Cold, it's getting colder, I've got to get up. As he struggled to rise, a soldier appeared. The soldier raised his saber above his head and brought it down to strike. Joe the woman had lifted her arm up in defense, and it was broken by the blow, falling painfully to her side. The soldier raised his saber again, and Joe the woman rolled over and lifted her other arm in defense. It too was struck and broken by the blow. Joe the woman looked wordlessly up at the soldier, awaiting the final fatal blow. But it never came. The soldier, dressed in his crisp, blue uniform with shiny brass buttons, returned his saber to its sheath on his belt, staring with his steely blue eyes, a menacing smile on his face.

"The Four cannot be," he whispered as his cold blue eyes bore into her. "The Four cannot be." He turned on his boot heel, and left her lying there on the ground helpless, the life ebbing from her body, powerless to do anything but watch the slaughter and mutilation of those lying dead and dying around her. The soldier that struck her down continued to walk away off into the distance as the others continued to shoot, kill, and mutilate.

"I am ready, please take me," he heard her voice whisper as she turned her cheek to the ground. Joe felt the rumble of the earth in answer to her plea; as he felt her draw her last breath, he rose out of her body and the ground rumbled and enveloped her.

Suddenly, Joe felt the coolness of the ground against his cheek and the darkness of the sweat lodge envelope him again. Floyd's song had changed again, the beat of the drum sounding like his heart felt in the battle. Wiping his brow, Joe joined in the song, singing as strong and as clear as he could, and, most likely, clearer and stronger than he ever had before.

CHAPTER 12

Joe had looked up at the sky for what seemed an eternity. He lay on his back, his arms at his sides, and drew in deep breaths of air that he exhaled as a light fog into the chill autumn air. Somehow, it didn't feel cool at all. It was as if it was a gentle breeze on a warm summer day - a pleasant and welcome respite from the heat of the sweat lodge.

And it had been hot. Joe didn't know exactly how hot and didn't want to know either. He wasn't entirely sure when the ceremony ended; he just remembered that suddenly there was an opening of light and cool air in the darkness. He vaguely remembered following Floyd out and finding only the strength to crawl out on hands and knees before collapsing onto the cool ground. Somehow he had mustered the strength to turn onto his back and gaze wordlessly into the sky.

That was when he had heard Floyd's voice speaking to someone, but he couldn't wrap his brain around what Floyd's voice was actually saying. Joe had cocked his head toward the voices and saw that Floyd was speaking to a rather small man dressed in moleskin pants and a sheepskin vest. The red bandana headband he was wearing that stretched across his forehead and knotted at the back of his head was standard attire for a sweat, but seemed oddly out of place on this man.

No, it can't be! Joe remembered thinking. *What is he doing here? How does Floyd know this guy?*

Joe contemplated getting up and going over to speak with both men, but his body was still exhausted from the sweat. He did, however, manage to catch part of their conversation.

"Thank you for presiding as Fire Keeper, Gabe." Floyd had spoken gratefully. "Are you ready to feast now?"

"Can't stay, Floyd," he apologized gruffly. "This task o' mine, it's become a bloody full-time job."

"Ah," Floyd had murmured understandingly. "Those that guard the paths often must provide direction."

"Yeah, direction - if they don't get themselves killed."

"You must trust that the right ones have been chosen this time, Gabe," Floyd stated with reassurance. "The Elements would not have chosen their vessels unwisely."

"True 'nuff," Gabe had agreed in a somewhat irritated manner. "But he knows of two of 'em now. That I knows for sure. And I have a terrible feelin' one of them is in danger. Tonight. Which is why - I must go now. I have a terrible feelin' that the bastard is gonna attack Sara."

"Then you better go and protect your charge," Floyd said.

"Feels like friggin' babysittin'," Gabe retorted sourly.

"Good luck, Gabe." Floyd smiled as Gabe stomped into the forest. He muttered a last inaudible response before he disappeared out of sight.

Joe had continued to stare at Floyd. He was even more stunned into silence by what he had witnessed and heard. What was Gabe doing here? Why didn't Floyd tell him? Who was in danger? Joe felt a jolt of shock had run through him. Sara! Could it be the same Sara? *His* Sara? Joe had a sinking feeling of dread. *Is she going through what I am?*

At least we'll have something else in common, he thought wryly. *I wonder if Gabe told her about the clay statue.* His face turned red with embarrassment and guilt at the thought.

Joe shut his eyes with a groan. His vision in the sweat lodge left him with so many questions. What did it all mean? Why did he witness such a horrific massacre? He knew the name Black Kettle from somewhere, he just couldn't recall where. He opened his eyes with great effort only when he felt someone tread across the ground toward him. The ground had reflexively formed a small mound of earth and gently lifted him into a reclined sitting position as he opened his eyes to see Floyd in front of him.

"Impressive," he intoned softly. When you are ready, we will go feast and, perhaps, talk if you like." Floyd handed Joe a mug of water and turned to make his way back down the hill.

Yeah, talk, he thought. *I can hardly wait.*

So now he was sitting in Floyd's cabin, sitting at a table covered in food, feeling incredibly hungry but unsure if he could eat.

Floyd had already prepared a plate for the offering and had begun to reach for the fry bread, which he ate with a large bowl of venison stew.

"Eat, Joe. Eat. You'll need to keep your strength up," Floyd pushed the crock pot full of stew and the plate of fry bread in Joe's direction. The smells of the food tempted him, and he soon dug into the stew with the enthusiasm of a starving man. It warmed him inside, and for the first time in a few weeks he was actually able to completely relax. He felt as if the weight of the world was lifting off him and that, somehow, being in this place with Floyd he had a special place of sanctuary. He felt at peace. *Safe.*

***

It was shortly after sunset when Sara was confident it was safe enough to leave Abby. Abby had actually cracked a smile: a sign, Sara hoped, that Abby was starting to feel like herself and take control.

They had done some meditative exercises together, and while Abby originally balked at the idea (hence the singe marks on Sara's sleeve) she soon relented and finally admitted it was helping her to relax. If nothing else, it was helping her to improve her marksmanship, a point Sara would keep a mental note of in case she inadvertently pissed her off in the future. Otherwise, she had better be quick at dodging fireballs.

Dan had walked in just before Sara had prepared to leave. He entered the house like a man who was bracing himself for trench warfare. But his eyes lit up when he saw Sara, and he smiled warmly in greeting.

"Great to see you, Sara! I didn't know you were here." he raised a hand up to scratch his head as he glanced out the window. "I didn't see your truck outside."

Sara laughed nervously and glanced at Abby for help.

"Sara just popped over," Abby chimed in, smirking.

"Dan smiled at Abby, relief washing across his face. "You gonna join us for supper? I was gonna brave the elements and barbeque."

Sara giggled in response. *Little does he know he's already been braving the elements in more ways than one*, she thought drolly.

Abby raised her eyebrows. "You gonna stay for dinner? You know you're welcome to."

"I'd love to, but I really gotta fly - I mean, get home." she stated.

"Do you need a ride?" Dan offered.

"Ah, no, some, ah, friends are going to meet me." she stammered. *Not a lie*, she told herself.

"Maybe next time?"

"Sure, Sara, anytime." Dan said cheerfully.

Abby had risen up to stand beside him and slipped her hand into his. He looked down at her with amazement.

"Well," Sara stammered, feeling like she was encroaching on a "moment", "I'm going to wait outside. My, ah, friends should be along any minute."

"Okay, thanks, Sara." Abby replied. Abby strode over to her and gave her a hug. "Thanks for everything. Really," she whispered in Sara's ear.

"No probs." Sara replied. "I'll catch you later."

Sara gave a little wave as she stepped out the door and onto the driveway. She double-checked to make sure no one was watching, and crossed back toward the lawn as the two little iridescent, winged faeries appeared.

"Ready when you are," she announced quietly to them. They tinkled in response and took to the sky just as Sara had thrown herself into the gust of wind, sailed high over the trees, and flew out of sight.

It was a clear, cool night. She would have enjoyed a long trip, but the wind definitely had an autumn chill to it that quickly worked into her bones.

I just want to have a hot cup of tea in my pajamas, she shuddered.

As was her custom, she stopped six inches from the ground upon arriving at her property and stepped down from the air as if descending a staircase. Her two companions began buzzing around her head frantically like two scared hummingbirds. They were twittering away like birds, and for once Sara could not understand what they were saying. But their actions were clear. Something was wrong. As they continued to flit and buzz around, the level of panic they conveyed gave her the feeling that it was definitely not good.

Sara glanced casually around as she sauntered slowly up the drive toward the house. *Nothing out of the ordinary*, she observed. It was a particularly bright evening; the moon was out in all its harvest glory and illuminated her driveway and front yard. Nothing she could see was amiss, but she could sense that something was not quite right. As she got closer to the house, she slowed her pace down to a creep, trying to buy time, linger a little longer. Her two companions gave two little squeaks and then shot up into the air, their departure lit against the light of the moon.

"Hey, where you going?" she shouted as she reached her front door, jamming her hands into the front pockets of her jeans, searching for her keys. Before using the key she reached out and instinctively turned the doorknob. It turned freely and opened.

My house is unlocked, she thought. *I swear I locked it before I left.*

Sara began to feel even more strongly that something was very wrong. She desperately wanted to run into her house and lock the door and hide in the dark, but thought better of it. What if a burglar was in the house? She would just be trapped inside with them. She turned slightly, looking out toward her front yard and glanced quickly at the old maple tree in her front yard. Most of the leaves had fallen and left behind bare branches. On the branches she saw dark shadows sitting… *No, that can't be right.* Sara looked again. The dark shadows appeared to be perched on the branches in the tree. *Definitely not birds*, she decided as she looked away. They were too massive and too bulky in form to be birds. *Hmm*, she thought. They looked as if they were waiting for something.

Sara suddenly had an idea. She turned back toward the doorway and looked at the light switch just inside the door and the one against the far wall. She raised her left hand casually and sent a small breeze directly at the light switches at the front door. They both flickered on. She waited at the doorway for a moment. Nothing. Not a sound or motion anywhere. She sent another flicker of a breeze toward the next light switch across the room and it flickered on. She heard the crack of a branch and spun around quickly to face her front yard.

The creatures left the trees and were flying through the air straight toward her. At first glance, they looked to her like the flying monkeys from *The Wizard of Oz*, but as they approached, she recognized their dark, hulking forms. Gargoyles? She stared for a moment. *Why are gargoyles attacking me*? She was puzzled.

"She didn't enter the house, you fools!" A man's voice bellowed. "Surround her!"

Sara got angry. They intended to harm her; that much was clear. She stepped forward and rose slightly off the ground into the air. The gray forms were looming closer, at least four of them, she counted. She hovered in the air and waited.

Get closer, you ugly-ass bastards, she thought angrily. *Just a little closer.*

The nearest creature sprang forward with its talons spread in an attempt to grab her. She thrust her arm toward it and blasted it with a gust of wind that knocked it backward into one of its companions that had the misfortune of being directly behind it. They both dropped slightly in the sky but recovered quickly and rose back up to attack once again.

Sara summoned her energy, concentrating hard.

Tornado! She thought while pushing outward with as much energy as she could muster.

Sara felt a surge run through her as she became the center of a swirling vortex of wind. As she advanced, the wind swirled around her, catching the gargoyles in its momentum and spinning them around while she remained in the safety of its core. The creatures were tossed around, howls of distress emitting from their gray, frog-like mouths as they flailed their wings helplessly in the wind, careening into each other and powerless to escape. Sara continued to advance, allowing the tornado to increase in speed until she noticed that the creatures had gone limp. Unable to resist the force of the wind, the creatures had lost consciousness and were being flung around like rag dolls. Sara felt a stab of sympathy at their plight; she slowed then halted the gale. The tornado stopped, dissipating like someone pulling the plug on a drain; it just simply swirled into the ground, leaving a few leaves still floating in the air in its aftermath. She looked around for the creatures and saw them sprawled unconscious several hundred feet away on the ground.

They don't look so menacing now, she thought as she observed their limp forms. *I wonder why . . .*

Suddenly, Sara felt a horrible pain in her back. It spread to her head, causing her to see stars. She sank to her knees, weighed down by the terrible pain in her back.

"Well, well, well," a man's voice sneered.

Sara turned her head slowly to see a man approaching. He looked familiar to her somehow, his cold blue eyes boring into her, a twisted smile on his thin lips, as if he enjoyed seeking her in pain.

"I almost thought you could do it," he laughed. "You definitely put up a good fight."

He drew closer, the moonlight illuminating his steel gray hair. He was undoing his dark overcoat, reaching into a pocket. He drew out a large dagger.

Sara remained frozen on the ground, grimacing in pain. He drew even closer.

"Who are you?" she whispered with great effort. "Can I at least know that?"

The dead fall leaves crunched under his feet as he approached. He stopped just a few feet from her huddled form.

"Sure, sweetheart," he intoned sarcastically. "I'm Thaddeus, and I'm the last person to see you alive." He raised the dagger up above her.

"Don't be too sure of that," Sara retorted. She dropped flat to the ground and rolled onto her back. He was directly over her, the dagger ready to strike when she lifted both arms into the air and blasted him with a great gust of wind that sent him flying high into the air. He grunted as he landed with a thud against the maple tree in her yard. The dagger had flown from his hand and landed in the grass over by the front stoop of her house. She continued to hold him pinned against the tree, directing the wind at him as she casually walked toward him.

"Don't ever call me sweetheart!" Sara spat at him. "EVER!"

Suddenly, she didn't feel too bad, though her head and ears still rang dully with pain. She let the wind die again, and Thaddeus dropped to the ground, gasping for breath. Sara could see the glint of a red spot on the back of his head.

He's wounded too, she thought. *Good.*

He rose up quickly and fixed Sara with a look of hatred.

"All you are doing is prolonging the inevitable," he spat angrily at her. "The Four cannot be! You will not win! Not now, not ever!" And with those words, he disappeared without a sound right in front of her eyes.

Sara looked around for the gargoyles that had been lying on the grass. They too were gone; the only evidence left behind were the indentations in the dead leaves and grass where their bodies had lain. Sara searched around in the grass until she located the dagger that Thaddeus had tried to kill her with.

"At least I relieved him of this," she muttered aloud, turning it over in her hands as she examined it carefully.

Before she got the chance, her two diminutive fairy friends appeared tinkling to her in greeting.

"Yeah, I'm okay," she responded to them gently. "All is well."

"I guess I missed the action," a gruff voice sounded beside her.

Sara whirled around and looked intently down at the small man standing beside her. He was wearing moleskin pants, a sheepskin vest, and a red bandana. Sara immediately recognized him from the painting that British artist, William something-or-other, showed on television.

"I was wondering when you'd come," Sara replied casually. "Would you like to come in for a tea?" She gestured toward the front door of the house.

Gabe laughed heartily at this. "O' course, Sara."

"Well, you first, please," she said, holding open the door for him to enter. "In case I have any other unexpected company."

Sara smiled widely and gave him a wink. Gabe smiled back, his eyes almost disappearing in the folds of his weathered skin.

"You are full of friggin' surprises, aren't yeh?" he said in awe as he entered.

"You have no idea," she replied, closing the door behind them and retreating to the comfort of her home.

CHAPTER 13

The musty smell of old tomes and paperback books permeated the air of the office. Thaddeus sat in darkness. The back of his head throbbed with painful irritation. It irked him that he was bested by a mere mortal; indeed, the blow to his ego was more painful than the actual physical manifestation of pain. How long it had been since he had felt pain? He reached a finger to the wound on the back of his head and applied just a small amount of pressure until he could feel the sensation. Yes, it was pain, but, oh, to feel it! He smiled and leaned back in the oak high-back chair behind his equally heavy, aged leather-topped desk.

When was the last time he had felt pain? He strained to remember. It was during the war, during the campaign; that was it. Ironically, it was also the Air Vessel that dealt him damage. He had joined the Nazis, introduced himself to those in the Thule society, and presented himself as a man of mystical talents and abilities. He made a few predictions and helped them to acquire the Spear of Destiny: a small price, he had surmised, for what he had hoped to accomplish. In exchange, he was able to locate the Air Vessel who was, by birth, a Gypsy. It was advantageous to him that the Nazis reviled the Gypsies almost as much as the Jews. With his pressure and guidance, the Air Vessel's entire clan was lined up in front of a firing squad. The company of soldiers had raised their rifles to fire when she revealed her power, knocking some of the soldiers, including him, into the air. She directed a bayonet at him, slashing his arm and shoulder in the process, before she was gunned down and killed by one of the soldiers still standing. Her body was thrown into a mass grave with the rest of her clan, buried, and never found again. He managed to steer clear of the Nazis after that, though Hess was always pestering him for more prophesies and more powerful mystical items. Thaddeus finally told him that if he went to England, he would succeed in securing England's surrender in the war and would be rewarded by receiving the title of Emperor of the British Isles. Thaddeus snorted derisively. How unfortunate for him he actually believed it and parachuted into England to be captured by the British. How surprised and shocked he must have been! Thaddeus once again slipped quietly into anonymity to wait and bide his time.

Now he was tired of waiting. Everything was perfect now: his power was consolidating, there was unrest once again in Feyland, the veil was weakening, and this new Four - while at least one of them was a formidable opponent - looked to be ill-prepared for their undertaking. Thaddeus frowned slightly. *At least, the two of which I am aware of.*

A knock sounded at the open the door of his office.

"Enter." He commanded, sitting ramrod straight at his desk.

A small man, no taller than two and a half feet tall, entered the room. His straight back and long stride belied his confidence. He was garbed completely in a cocoa brown leathery material that appeared to be a uniform; its only embellishment was a laurel leaf-like pip on each collar tab. The man stepped directly in front of the desk to face Thaddeus, assuming an attention stance.

"I have your report, sir." The man spoke sharply.

Thaddeus smiled. "Of course, Commander," he gestured to a chair for him to sit. Please, Michael, must we be so formal?"

Michael sat obediently in the chair, which appeared to magically accommodate for his size, bringing him up to the same eye level as Thaddeus.

"Perhaps not, Thaddeus, but we must be quick." Michael looked around anxiously. "I cannot be gone too long. My, er, absences are becoming too numerous to explain away. It is too early in the planning to risk losing the Queen's confidence."

Thaddeus folded his hands together atop the leather top of the desk. "You are right, of course," he conceded. "Please continue on with your report."

"There is enough dissension in the military that at least half the force will join with us, of that I am sure. The Taekyrs, though, appear to have lost some confidence in the campaign due to the failure of their mission with the Air Vessel. Those that were bested," he rolled his eyes, "have passed their tales along to the others. It seems they are a bit concerned that another encounter would also meet with failure."

Thaddeus slammed his fist down hard on this desk. "Then they must bear full responsibility for the mission's failure! They did not wait for the command; they did not follow orders as they were set forth."

Thaddeus regained his composure. "Ensure these creatures are disciplined accordingly, and make sure their glaring omission of their failures is also made known to the others. Let the others know they have my fullest confidence in their success."

Michael cleared his throat. "Have we any idea of the location of the other two vessels?"

"Not yet, but we do have options to locate them. You could always follow Gabe—"

"DO NOT MENTION THAT NAME TO ME!" Michael intoned sharply. His face contorted with rage enough that his eyes could barely be seen amidst the redness of his cheeks.

"The next time I see Gabe will be in battle," Michael stated flatly. "What are our other options?"

Thaddeus smiled. "They will find each other." He stood up, clapped his hands behind his back, and strode over to the window in silence, rocking back and forth on his heels, staring out for a moment before saying, "All we have to do is wait. They will find each other. And before the prophecy takes place, we eliminate them as a threat."

Continuing to face the window, he added, "You are dismissed."

Michael opened his mouth to speak but quickly changed his mind. He slipped out of the chair, stood to attention, and, with a click of his heels, strode briskly from the room.

***

It was well after the sun had gone down and the chill of evening began to set in when Joe and Floyd moved from his kitchen table to the couch in front of the fire in Floyd's small cabin. They sat quietly drinking tea and listening to the crackling of the fire for what seemed an eternity before Joe blurted out, "Aren't you going to ask me, Floyd?"

Floyd looked over to Joe and glanced back to the fire. "Your vision in the sweat lodge is yours. It's a personal experience. I will not intrude on your privacy. If, however, there is something you wish to share, I will listen."

At first, Joe didn't know where to start. It all seemed so jumbled; there were so many things he had seen, and it was difficult to piece them together or put them into words.

"Perhaps it would be best to start at the beginning so that you know what happened that led me to you." Joe spoke carefully.

"The beginning is always a good place to start," Floyd murmured in agreement. "Whenever you're ready."

Joe spoke of the earthquakes, of knowing they were going to hit, how he could make statutes of clay and animate them (although he didn't mention the one he had created in Sara's form), and of how he had lain on the ground and felt the earth's breath and pulse - how he could sense when the earth was in pain.

"I knew there was something to this - I don't know - connection? But I have yet to know or begin to understand why I have it or what purpose I must serve. I still have to fully understand my connection and the abilities that come with it."

Floyd continued to listen while looking forward soundlessly, his fingertips pressed together in a steeple and his eyes transfixed on a spot on the wall. The only indication that he was listening were the occasional nods he would give between sips of tea.

Joe continued. "For years, my family has come to you for advice in all matters, not just those of a spiritual nature. So I came here, looking, I hope, in the right place for the right answers."

"Just because you are here does not mean you are in the right place for the right answers," Floyd stated simply. "Perspective, direction, guidance: these are things you need to achieve to find your answers, but no one place holds them all. Ultimately, you may find that the truth and the answers lie hidden inside you."

Joe nodded. He felt mentally drained. He couldn't find the right way or the right words to get out what he really wanted to say. He was a teacher! How could he lack the ability to articulate his thoughts and feelings, especially when he desperately needed to convey them?

"Because it was disturbing," Joe uttered before realizing he had spoke aloud.

"Pardon?" Floyd gazed at Joe for a moment, his head tilted to one side.

"Well, part of my vision was very disturbing." Joe blurted out. "I was somewhere else, some*one* else, actually. A woman, in fact. And there was an attack and all the people were running; the military was shooting and a man, I think his name was Black Kettle . . .,"

"Yes, Black Kettle," Floyd broke in, "Continue."

"Anyway, Black Kettle was urging all the people to gather around the U.S. flag, that they would be safe there. But they weren't safe . . . ,"

Joe trailed off, remembering the confusion and chaos, the panic and cries of women and children. The despair. The death and mutilation of bodies.

Joe drew in a deep breath. "I was shot in the leg and fell down. I could feel the fire of the bullet in my leg. And as I lay there, a soldier came and struck my arm with a saber and broke it. He struck again, and I lifted my other arm to defend myself, only to have it broken as well. He looked at me for a moment, his blue eyes cold and angry. And then he walked away, to leave me to die. I could feel the life leave my body, and I could see the other soldiers continue to slay and massacre the people as I lay dying. The man who struck me down did not participate in any further atrocities after that, as if he was there just to destroy the woman. He just kept walking. I rose out of her body, and then I saw the woman die there on the dry river bed and the earth rise up to claim her body."

He looked at Floyd, tears forming in his eyes, choking back the huge lump in his throat.

"She was like me, wasn't she?" he questioned Floyd. "She was connected to the earth too?"

Floyd hesitated before answering. "It seems likely that she was an Earth Vessel too. And she died during the Sand Creek Massacre, from your description of the event."

"Sand Creek Massacre?" Joe asked quizzically. "I think I remember a bit about it from school."

"It was one of the most, if not the most, horrific massacres of Native Americans. Mostly women and children were killed; families separated, lives taken, and others changed forever. It is not as well known as the Wounded Knee Massacre, but still infamous for the brutality shown to our people. Never forget what you saw, Joe."

"No, I can't say that I will, Floyd." Joe started shifting slightly, adjusting his position on the couch. "But there was more to my vision."

Joe began to describe the little people he saw in their regalia with their mysterious patterns and seeing the woman and young man.

"Ah, the Mae Mae Quay Shewok." Floyd smiled. "Long have our people had a respectful relationship with them. Some of our people could see their markings in the woods and be able to understand them, even speak with them. They would leave them supplies like tobacco, meat, corn, whatever they needed, in the woods for them. When our people would return to the spot the following day, there would be something waiting for them in exchange. Usually tools - axes, arrows, bows, sometimes items of clothing. All the items would be well-made and of the highest quality. It was always a great honor to receive something gifted by the Mae Mae Quay Shewok."

"Well," Joe looked at Floyd, who seemed to be quite enthusiastic about the appearance of the Mae Mae Quay Shewok in his vision. "I don't think I have ever seen them or encountered them before unless - is Gabe one?"

"No," Floyd answered, smiling. "His people are from another place. And I believe they are a much older people, but of that I cannot be certain."

"Well, I'm not sure how it all fits together, but I saw a young woman with them and then I saw her with a young boy: I believe he was her son. Then I saw her again as a much older woman with a young man. They spoke, and he went into the woods and he turned into," Joe looked sideways at Floyd to gauge his reaction, "a fox."

But Floyd's eyes were blank, his expression remained impassive as he stared into the fire.

"A shape shifter," Floyd surmised quietly.

"Isn't that usually . . .," Joe searched for a word.

"Bad medicine?" Floyd offered. "No, they don't necessarily start out that way. There are a few medicine men that have tried shape shifting once and have not done it again. But," he sighed deeply, "there is something compelling about taking on the form of an animal. Feeling wild, enjoying the freedom that could come with it. Can you imagine what it would feel like to be the Mighty Eagle, to fly high in the sky? To feel the wind on your wings, to soar high above but to see things miles below you with the clarity that you see with now? Those feelings can be very strong to a shape shifter - suddenly a need to feel it, like an addiction that needs to be fed. Some become so attached to those feelings that they become detached from humanity. Some," Floyd paused and looked at Joe for a moment, "choose to make the change complete and walk away from living a human life." He turned his gaze back to the fire.

"Well, what does it mean then, Floyd?" Joe looked at him, waiting for his response.

"Well, Joe," Floyd stood up from the couch and added a log to the fire. He picked up a poker and prodded the burning logs before gently adding another. He stood by the fire as he spoke again. "It is not my place to say what the meaning of your vision is. But if I were to give you any advice at all, it would be to be more aware of what is going on around you. You know that you have a special gift; Earth has chosen you to share its power with. You know that there are others that share similar abilities. But you need to walk on the earth with your eyes open to see things that you have never opened your eyes to before."

"And what if I can't, Floyd?"

"Can't or won't?"

"Maybe both."

"If you won't, you of course have that choice. But you may regret your inaction in the future. As to can't," Floyd stared Joe squarely in the eye, "you would not have been given such an honor if you were not capable. Remember, you are not in this alone. There are others that are in this too. I'm sure Gabe will help to guide you further should you need it."

Floyd stood straight, stretching his back. "I am very weary; it's been a full day. Good night, Joe."

"Good night, Floyd," Joe replied as Floyd ambled into the room off the living room and closed the door behind him.

Joe stretched out on the couch, yanking the folded blanket from the back of the couch over his body. Suddenly he too felt spent, too drained from the day's work. He hadn't mentioned the buffaloes to Floyd. Perhaps he would tell him in the morning.

***

Joe felt like he had only just shut his eyes when the alluring smell and sizzle of bacon frying and the scent of fresh-brewed coffee roused him from his sleep. The light of dawn was already filtering in the windows. Joe moved quickly to take his seat at the table and devoured the plate of food that Floyd set down in front of him.

"You have a good day's drive ahead of you today," Floyd remarked quietly as he sipped his coffee. Joe understood its implication: it was time for him to go.

"Yes, well, I should get back to work," Joe replied quietly.

He was actually beginning to miss his students. *I guess this is what it feels like to be a real teacher*, he thought.

He quietly packed up his things into his truck and turned to say goodbye to Floyd.

"Oh, one more thing before you go," Floyd pulled a bundle from the inside pocket of his jacket. "I was given this a long, long time ago. It was a gift from your grandmother. It now belongs with you."

Floyd handed him a bundle of red cloth. Joe opened it and found inside a medicine pouch of beautifully tanned hide beaded with the mysterious pattern he had seen in his vision. He stared at it in awe, speechless for a moment before whispering,

"Thank you. *Meegwetch*."

Floyd opened the door of Joe's truck and held it open while Joe stepped in and sat down on the seat, cradling the pouch and red cloth in his hands. Floyd slammed the door shut, and the sound pulled Joe out of his daze. He started the truck, but before he pulled away, Floyd popped his head into the open window, smiled, and spoke.

"Remember, Joe, this is important. If you find that you are looking for a particular path and it cannot be found, follow the buffalo!"

Floyd popped his head back out and waved at Joe as Joe drove down the driveway, and out of sight.

Follow the buffalo. How could he have known? Joe looked down at the medicine pouch that was now sitting on his lap. He felt like a piece of a huge puzzle that was slowly being put together by an unknown force. Even though he felt powerless and out of control for the first time in his life, he was ready to face the unknown. He knew he was, and he

95

knew he would always be okay. He could feel it. And this overwhelming sense of - *What would you call it*, he wondered? Fulfillment? Yes, that's what it was that filled him as he drove home. The drive suddenly didn't seem as long, and soon he was surprised to find himself pulling into his driveway. He shut off his truck and sat there in the cab for a moment to gaze at the medicine pouch, delicately tracing the intricate bead work with a fingertip.

'Beautiful,' he murmured aloud as he ran his fingers along the perfectly stitched beads.

"Thanks, yer not too bad yerself," a gruff voice replied.

Joe yelped and jumped up, banging the top of his head on the cabin roof. As he rubbed his head, he glanced around for the source of the voice. Seeing no one around, he swung the pick-up door open wide and stepped out of the cab, slamming the door shut behind him.

Gabe was lying sprawled on the grass apparently bowled over by the door.

"What you do that fer?" he muttered as he picked himself up and brushed off his clothes.

"Sorry," Joe stammered, "I guess I didn't see you."

"Ya, ya," Gabe replied.

"What are you doing here?" Joe asked.

"Well, I just wanted to tell yeh that yer friend," he snickered, "Sara, and her friend Abby may be able to help you. But yeh better hurry; things are getting dangerous."

CHAPTER 14

"Sara's in danger?" Joe looked at Gabe slightly confused. "Is it because of me?"

"No, ya silly git," Gabe growled angrily. "Yeh share a common enemy." Gabe glared at him, squinting, his eyes disappearing into the folds of his face. "Haven't yeh figured it all out yet?"

"What?"

Joe unloaded his gear out of his truck and tossed it carelessly inside his front door.

Gabe looked at him with wide eyes. His face resembled two blue buttons on a pad of steel wool. He gave Joe a stern look as he gesticulated wildly in the air with his hands.

"Don't cha know what yer supposed to do? Don't cha know your role? Geez, thought Floyd was helping out up there, helping ya to figure things out."

Joe stopped and sat on his front stoop. "Well, he did help me to understand some things, but he told me that you," he pointed at Gabe, "would help me find others in a similar situation who…," Joe stopped in mid-sentence. He looked at Gabe, "Sara," he whispered. "She's one too?"

"Finally!" Gabe's voice was so loud it was almost a yell. He slapped his hands on his thighs. "Now git over there and get to work." Gabe started to walk toward the woods in back of Joe's house.

"Wait!" Joe jumped up and started to trail behind him. "Aren't you gonna come with me?"

"No, I ain't," Gabe answered sternly. "I got other places I gotta be today." He turned and faced Joe. "Yeh needs to hurry, things are moving fast and time may run out. Yeh need to get to Sara. I will see yeh soon enough, I expect."

Gabe turned, still muttering under his breath, and trudged into the woods behind a copse of trees and disappeared from sight. Joe watched him leave until he could no longer see his form and then strode back up the stairs and into his house in search of a phone book. If something dangerous really was happening, he mused, it may be best to call instead of just dropping by unannounced.

***

Gabe tugged at his vest, pulling it farther around his body in an attempt to ward off the chill of the bitter wind. He quickened his step and the vapor of his breath became quicker and more frequent in the surrounding air.

He stomped deeper into the woods, the ground crisp underfoot. He could feel he was close to the guardians of the doorway long before he spied them on the horizon. The guardians held an old magic, one much older than he was in years. That kind of magic was like catnip to the Fey, and they were naturally drawn to it. Gabe quickened his pace. He was anxious to return home. He did not like this world; no, that was wrong, he did like this world and all its beauty and wonder. It was the people he had a hard time with.

All those years ago, he thought bitterly. *And now, I have to help them.* The very idea went against everything he believed, everything he had sworn to protect. How could he want to help humanity when they turned against his kind not so long ago?

Gabe broke through the trees and came out onto a clearing. The scraggly undergrowth and detritus of the forest floor gave way to lush green grass blanketing the ground in an idyllic pastoral setting. The sky had opened up too; gone was the canopy of the forest trees, it was as if they had simply melted away. Also gone were the scents of the forest; the smell of pine needles, the faintly pungent smell of decomposition, the earthy smell of moss on the trees. These scents were replaced with those of the green grass and the hint of delicate wildflowers whose perfume would be abundant in the late spring. In the center of the grassy clearing, three willow trees formed a perfect equilateral triangle directly in front of him, their long slender branches still green with leaves and they swayed in near perfect unison with each other.

A little too perfect — that was always the give-away, he mused to himself. Their supple branches continued to wave to and fro as each gentle breeze caught them and swept them back and forth inches from the ground. These were not mere trees. These three were Dryads, fey that inhabited and bonded with their host tree. These three were sisters, and together they acted as the guardians of the Doorway, the Ophalmos, back to Feyland.

"Ladies, if you'd be so kind," Gabe addressed the trees. A trio of giggles soon filled the air as the forms of three women appeared in the boughs of each tree.

"Ah, it is only you, Gabe," crooned the fair-haired Dryad seated on the tree closest to him. "We were hoping it was someone more . . . interesting." The other sisters, who were seated in the exact same place on their trees, clapped and laughed in agreement.

"Yeah, well, maybe next time you'll get lucky," Gabe muttered staring at her. "Show me the way home."

"Only if you promise to bring us some new friends," the Dryad with the long brown hair the color of teak, coaxed with a smile. "Perhaps some of your new human friends?" She wagged her eyebrows at him and laughed again, her sisters chiming in.

"And would you like me to inform the Queen of your interest in meetin' some humans now?" he stared back at her.

She cut her laughter short and her smile transformed into a pout. "Gabe, we meant no harm; we only wanted to have some fun, "she answered contritely.

"Ya, ya, just get me home, okay?" Gabe answered flatly. "It's been a long day."

"Very well," the fair-haired sister answered smiling, raising her arms out to the center of the clearing. "Reveal Omphalos."

Her two sisters mimicked her actions as they called out in unison. Immediately, as if a fog had cleared, a large stone object appeared within the triangle of the weeping willows and the three Dryad sisters disappeared back into the safety of their trees, slipping into their trees as if entering into a cocoon.

Gabe passed into the triangle and lifted up his arm to place his hand atop the large circular stone. He closed his eyes, drew in a deep breath and whispered,

"Feyland."

The cold chill of winter seemed to fall away slightly as he opened his eyes. He found himself standing in the forest close to the side of the royal palace, near the walls of the courtyard. Gabe breathed a sigh of relief. He was home.

***

The dry, crisp grass crunched underfoot as William strode toward the water's edge. A misty fog hovered just above the glassy surface, but it wasn't high enough to encompass the barren hills on the horizon where two wild ponies stood grazing, unfazed and ambivalent to his presence. He stood there for a moment, calmly surveying the area, drawing in a deep breath, savoring the slightly earthy smell, reminiscent of peat.

"Bodmin Moor," he uttered softly. He was unsure what had really driven him to come to this place - the push by Rhysdale to seek out other water creatures or his curiosity about the legend itself. *Today I'll find out if it's really a myth or not.* The Lady in the Lake. Old tales of the Lady in the Lake said that she was the guardian of Excalibur; the legendary sword of King Arthur. Some stories said that she was the one who bestowed the sword upon Arthur. Others said that Excalibur was returned to her, here at Dozmary Pool by one of the trusted Knights of the Round Table after the Battle of Camlann when Arthur was dying. William stepped closer to the edge of Dozmary Pool. *How do I call to her?* He mused excitedly for a moment and then bent down and gently slipped his hand into the icy water.

"I need your help, milady, and I seek your counsel," he whispered quietly, his eyes closed. "Please answer."

He kept his hand under the water until every joint in his fingers ached and burned from the cold. He opened his eyes and forced himself up onto his feet. He stood in anticipation at the water's edge, his breath shallow and quiet. As the fog gradually started to lift, the glimmer of hope he had renewed itself with a mighty spark. He drew in a deep breath, inhaling the musky, humid scent of the moor mixed with a floral scent that was reminiscent of heather. And then he caught sight of some movement under the surface of the water.

A stone path was rising slowly up out of the water and parting the fog in the center of Dozmary Pool. William tripped excitedly over his own feet, righting himself before he slipped into the frigid water. He moved excitedly toward the path, driven by his curiosity, moving briskly despite the ache in his knees and fingers. He stepped tentatively onto the path, into the fog that mysteriously parted in front of him and enveloped the path behind him.

Just move forward, just keep going, he urged himself. The path, though it appeared to rise out of the water and remain at the same level as the pool, was dry and smooth, his steps falling silently upon the stones as he moved forward. The path led straight to a small island, and directly ahead of him was a small grassy knoll. At the bottom of the knoll sat two large rectangular stones that stood upright. Another stone lay across the top of them, forming a large stone door frame, which stood, by his estimate, at least three meters tall. The doorframe was partially covered in some kind of vine that was heavily laden with flowers that had a pleasant, pungent smell. The air was much warmer on the island. William noticed the absence of the chill in the air and he wondered if the heavy fog and mist were magical constructs to cloak the island's appearance in the human realm. William stood there, transfixed by the sight, trying to take in every detail. *Is this the site that Arthur saw?* He wondered to himself.

In the doorway a woman appeared as if deposited there gently by the mist. She stood for a moment staring back at him, her silver eyes locked upon his as he stared at her, speechless. She glided down the slope toward him as if propelled by some ethereal force. She stood in front of him as she continued to stare at him, her eyes the color of cold steel, her snow-white hair falling in gentle waves to her waist. Her blue and silver gown was simple yet elegant, the hem floating like an autumn leaf drifting down a river. She smiled delicately as he struggled to remember why he was there in the first place.

"You are of the water," she spoke softly, a slight lilt in her voice. "You have come for my aid?"

William realized he was staring and blushed before he averted his eyes.

"Yes," he stammered searching for the right words. "I need—"

"I do not know what you seek," she cut in firmly. "I can only direct you to those who can guide you." She closed her eyes and sighed, frowning slightly as she again set her gaze upon William.

"I sense what is coming. All of us here in this place. We feel it. Change, whether it be transformation or destruction, we are not certain. But I do know that only those who are destined to may call upon me for help. And help I shall."

She lifted her closed fist in front of her. "Open your hand," she commanded.

William lifted his hand up as she gently pressed a heavy coin into the palm of his hand and firmly closed his hand around it with her tiny, cool fingers.

"The water sprites hold the answer to what you are seeking. But they will not answer unless you pay tribute. The coin I have placed in your palm dates back to a time when," she looked around, "when things were much different than they are now. Perhaps better, perhaps not. But we cannot return to those times, regardless of situation or circumstance."

She straightened up and began walking back up the hill, her white hair falling like a thick cloud down her back, swaying gently as she moved. She turned halfway up the hill and spoke again.

"Pay tribute to the water sprites with that coin. You will find them in places where your people draw water." She turned to stare at him once more. "That coin is a piece of the puzzle; place it where it fits."

She turned away and without another word glided through the stone archway and out of sight. William watched for a moment, waiting to see if she would reappear, but the reappearance of the path in the lake made it clear. The Lady had finished with him, and it was time for him to go. He followed the path toward the shore clutching the coin in his still-clenched fist; his arm was out in front of him as if guiding him through the mist. He didn't dare open his hand to look at the coin until he was back in his world, thinking that if he did open his hand to look at the coin it would disappear, just like the Lady did. He quickened his pace as he neared the shore.

She's real, he thought, awestruck as he turned on the shore's edge of the pool and gazed back out toward its center; the island, the hill, and the mist had vanished, leaving only a thin wisp of its memory behind. The ponies still grazed upon the hill on the other side, one surveying him now with only mild curiosity.

William felt compelled to place his hand in the water and call upon her again, but he knew it would be futile. He knew he didn't need to, anyway. He was buoyed with confidence. *Things are gonna be okay*, he reassured himself. *If Arthur took her advice and sword and became King, I can certainly take her coin to some water sprites, whatever they are.* His steps were lighter as he wended his way back toward his car.

***

Angry voices rose to a crescendo before the sounds of breaking glass and chairs chimed in, followed by the sound of flesh hitting flesh. Gabe watched warily from across the courtyard as the violent riot erupted, seemingly out of nowhere, in the tavern area. He signaled one of the soldiers nearby with a wave of his arm as the riot continued to build in strength and number. The fighting flowed into the street, and passers-by were suddenly confronted by men flowing from the tavern angrily throwing fists at any moving body. A woman's scream rang out, echoing in the courtyard before being cut off by the undulating mass of bodies gathering larger in the street. Hundreds of beings both fey and half-human in form now thronged the street.

"Where the hell are they all comin' from?" Gabe mused aloud. Chaotic wails and screaming grew even louder as more and more beings took to the streets.

Suddenly, the sound of a drum filled the air. The gentle beating of the drum resounded like a heartbeat into the panicked crowd. The crowd quieted slightly and turned almost as one as the drumbeat was joined with the harmonic sounds of guitars, lyres, and violins. And then the song began. Gabe turned and looked at the source of the music promenading up the street towards him: a parade of musicians playing and moving forward toward the querulous crowd.

The Bards have been dispatched. Gabe smiled.

The soldier he had spoken with had gotten the message through. The music was gentle, its beat pleasant and calm. The crowd had been captivated by their magic and stood in the streets, some beings even swaying to the rhythm of the music. The wave of fear abated, and in its wake the music began to instill a feeling of euphoria. Gabe felt it too: a warm feeling of calm happiness fell over him. He smiled and watched as the expression on the faces in the crowd became serene as smiles and laughter replaced anger and hostility. The Bards drew closer, encouraged now by applause and cheers from the crowd.

The danger had passed, at least, for now.

The Bards played three songs more, encouraged by a now eager audience. The crowd gradually diminished in number, dispersing as people began to resume the dealings of their everyday lives. There were still purchases to make, jobs to be done, meals to prepare, cleaning to be done.

The Bards finished playing and returned back to the palace just as another throng came up the street in passing. Gabe stood up straight, recognizing the figure in the center.

"It's her!" One man whispered.

"Aye, yeah, it's the Queen," another exclaimed breathlessly. The group of courtiers parted, as Queen Ezreanna walked through the street and into the curious crowd.

It's hard not to be impressed, Gabe thought as he observed her gliding easily through the crowd. She smiled warmly and easily at the people, nodding her head and answering their questions and touching their hands as they bowed and reached out to her. She moved well in the crowd, but the tilt of her head and her carriage set her distinctly apart.

Gabe waited patiently as she moved through the crowd and toward the place where he was standing. His eyes met her gaze and he quickly lowered his eyes and dropped to one knee murmuring, "Yer Majesty."

She placed her hand gently upon his shoulder, compelling him to rise. He looked up at her gentle smiling face and tried to smile in return; instead, a contorted grimace set upon his face. She laughed.

"Come now," she chided. "Have your recent duties been that bad?" Gabe struggled to find a suitable answer but she continued. "Speaking of which, you will return to the palace with us once I have finished here. We have much to discuss."

He lowered his eyes again as she strode toward a young girl to graciously accept a bouquet of flowers with a smile.

CHAPTER 15

Joe found himself once again behind the wheel of his truck heading down an unfamiliar road; he was armed with MapQuest directions and another map sprawled across the bench seat of his pick-up truck. As he watched the telephone poles pass on the side of the road, he felt anxious about going to meet Sara. He was unsure how to broach the subject of what was happening with him, and he was just as anxious to find out what was going on with her.

That is, if she wants to tell me, he thought, his brow furrowing pensively. It was quite a strange conversation they had on the phone when he finally plucked up enough courage to actually call her. Nervous as he was, there was a point before he picked up the phone to call her where he was almost hyperventilating. When he finally mustered the courage to call her he sensed that she was grateful to receive the call (at least he hoped), though she hesitated when he suggested that they meet for a coffee.

"I just need your advice, Sara," he had coaxed. "It's an extremely important matter." She did relent after a bit of going back and forth and consented to meet with him, but she didn't want him to come to her place, and a coffee shop was "much too public, too many people" as she so succinctly put it. Eventually, she relented and agreed to meet him in the Harmon City Recreational Park, a park nearest the one where they had last seen each other at the Art in the Park Show. They mutually agreed to meet at the park's center, and he would bring the coffee.

Joe shook his head. Sara sounded different somehow. Definitely not as bubbly as she had usually been before, but somehow more . . . Joe searched for the word, *guarded, yeah, that was it*. It was as if she was wary, watching out for some unknown *something*. *Kinda paranoid. But hadn't Gabe said she was in danger?* Joe flushed slightly. *Perhaps she thinks I'm dangerous*, he fretted, remembering back to the incident of making his *Sara de Milo* come to life. His expression changed to one of horror. What if she knew about his creation? Joe was turning into a parking spot on the edge of the park. *If Gabe had told her about that,* Joe shuddered. If Gabe had told her, Joe didn't know if he could actually look her in the eye. He dreaded to think what she would think of him or do to him. Would she think he was a pervert? Or a creeper? Or worse: a creepy pervert? Joe shuddered again and pulled the ignition key out of his truck as he grabbed the coffees in a carry tray, slamming the truck door and heading toward the fountain area at the center of the park.

As he moved through the park he noticed it was almost devoid of people. Of course, the time of year had an effect on that as well. A dedicated jogger in spandex running pants did lope past him on the winding asphalt path chugging fogs of air like a train expelling exhaust in its wake, and a lone mother wheeling a stroller with an enthusiastic toddler passed him on their way to the play structure, but with these few exceptions the air was far too crisp for all but those of unusual constitution.

Joe took a deep breath and drew his jacket collar up around his ears with one hand while balancing the coffee tray in his other hand. The smell of the coffee enticed him with its aroma, wafting up to his nose in a tendril of steam. He found a bench in front of the fountain and sat down, placing the tray beside him on the seat. Joe looked around. This part of the park was deserted. The gray, overcast day combined with the drab, empty park created a strangely eerie atmosphere.

Not even anyone walking a dog over here, he thought. The coffee was becoming more seductive. *Should I wait for her or drink mine now?* Joe looked around again. No sign of Sara anywhere. Joe looked at his watch. It was 4:02 p.m. *Maybe she's running late,* he thought. He picked up his coffee from the tray and had a sip, breathing in the aromatic, warm steam.

He sat there sipping his coffee, occasionally giving a cursory glance to the vacant, motionless fountain with a critical eye. Why do all these park fountains have to be Grecian-type women pouring water from urns? Not that he didn't like or appreciate Greek art or architecture, but he was in Michigan, for God's sake! His mind drifted back to his creation of *Sara de Milo*. He blushed and shook his head to banish the memory from his thoughts.

A cold gust of wind coming from out of nowhere blew at Joe's back, and he instantly ducked his head down to shelter his neck from the cold gust. It was so chilly and so sudden that he felt as if someone had spilled icy needles down his spine. And then it died down just as suddenly as it arrived. Joe turned and was surprised to see Sara, bouncing on her feet on the ground. *Where the hell did she come from? That's weird*, Joe thought, startled and confused by her sudden appearance.

Sara brushed idly at her blue coat and fur-trimmed hood with gloved hands before turning toward the bench where Joe was sitting.

She smiled warmly at Joe, and he quickly returned the smile. He couldn't believe how beautiful she looked. The cold had given her cheeks a rosy color, and her eyes sparkled like blue icicles. Her blonde hair just peeked out slightly in places from under the fur trim of her hood. Joe started to feel conscious of the fact that he might be staring at her, and he quickly averted his eyes.

"I brought you a coffee," he blurted out. "I hope it's still warm."

"Umm, yeah, me too. Thanks." She murmured as she accepted the coffee in gloved hands and plopped down next to him on the park bench. Sara took a few quick sips of coffee and then brought her attention to the park, her eyes darting side to side as she craned her neck to get a 360° view of her surroundings. "You see anybody here?" She questioned Joe anxiously.

"No, not really," Joe answered. "Why?"

"Oh, no reason." Sara replied in a forced casual manner. After a few minutes of silence, interspersed with the sounds of them both sipping coffee, Sara finally spoke first. "So," she started carefully, looking at the ground as if searching for words. "What is it that you need my advice on?"

Joe attempted to speak while simultaneously swallowing a mouthful of coffee. It didn't work. The result was that he started to choke and cough, and Sara set her coffee down and began to assist him by hammering on his back with an open hand. Joe sputtered and coughed before standing up and taking another sip of his coffee, which helped to get the coughing somewhat under control. Sara noticed the change and stopped hammering on his body. He looked up and was aware that she was standing at his side.

"You alright?" Sara asked, her blue eyes filled with concern. He held her gaze for a moment; then realized he was staring at her again and his face grew warm with embarrassment.

"Yeah, I'm okay," he nodded sheepishly as he looked away. "Thanks."

They both sat back down on the bench together and Joe's mind was racing. He hadn't really thought about what he was going to say to Sara or how he would find out what was going on with her without sounding all weird and creepy.

"Ah, Joe?" Sara cut into his thoughts. "What's up?"

Joe cleared his throat and turned sideways on the bench. "Well, Sara," he began, "I'm worried about you."

Sara sat back, wide-eyed with surprise by his statement. "Why would you be worried about me?" She laughed nervously, but her eyes continued to dart around the park, as they had when she first arrived.

"Well, a mutual friend of ours told me you were in danger," Joe answered quietly. "And that disturbs me."

"Who, Abby?" Sara asked, a look of confusion on her face. "Why would she say anything? I don't even think she knows—"

"No, not Abby." Joe replied quickly. "Another friend. His name is Gabe."

Sara spat out her coffee, spraying Joe in the face. Sara went red.

"Oh no! I'm sorry! I'm so sorry!" she blurted out, yanking a tissue out of her pocket and quickly dabbing the drips of coffee off his face. She grasped his chin with one hand and vigorously dabbed the tissue on his cheek, his forehead, his nose, and his lips. Sara suddenly stopped dabbing with the tissue and locked her eyes upon his. She leaned forward slightly and Joe thought that she was going to kiss him. But Sara merely realized she had a strong grip on his chin and let him go quickly. She leaned back and thrust the tissue back in her jacket pocket. She stared ahead for a moment and then asked,

"How do you know Gabe? No, wait, I mean, what has he told you?" Sara sat up straight, her eyes narrowing slightly. "Why would he tell you anything?"

Joe sensed Sara was confused and getting angry. And that wind was picking up again, sending shivers down his back. He shuddered slightly. He had only the best of intentions, but how could he get this across to Sara? She was suspicious, almost to the point of paranoia, in his opinion. Joe was beginning to question what really was going on; was he involved in something more than he was led to believe? He couldn't begin to allow doubt to take hold of him, not now. He squared his shoulders, took a deep breath, and looked Sara directly in the eyes.

"I will try to answer your questions as best as I can, Sara. How do I know Gabe? Well, he recently appeared when I was having some, ah, problems of my own." Joe sighed with relief. She obviously didn't know about his "problem" yet. He continued. "As to what Gabe told me, well, he told me that there were other people that had problems similar to mine. And he mentioned you, and that you were in danger. So here I am."

Joe looked at Sara trying to decipher her expression. She was focused intently on his words, and she didn't appear to be looking at him like he was an insane person either. Before she could answer Joe remembered another detail.

"I think he mentioned Abby, too. Is Abby in any danger?"

Sara snorted. "Maybe from herself, but I think she's doing better now. I think she's coping right now, which is better for her. She's gonna improve soon. I know she will."

Sara smiled and sat up eagerly. "So you have it too? Which one?"

"Pardon?"

"Which Element?" Sara pressed. "You figured it out, right?"

"What do you mean exactly?" Joe answered.

"You know, which Element is using you as a vessel." Sara looked at him, a confused look on her face. "Isn't that the problem Gabe helped you with?"

"Yes, it is. I'm sorry." Joe apologized.

"So . . . which one?" Sara asked again.

"Umm . . . it's Earth." Joe answered quietly, returning her smile.

"Really? Cool!" Sara exclaimed enthusiastically. "It makes sense though, you being into pottery and working with clay and stuff. What can you do?"

"Do?" Joe looked at Sara, his eyebrows raised quizzically.

"Yeah, do." Sara motioned with her hands. "You know, do with your Elemental power."

"Oh, well," Joe began, "well, a few things—"

"Okay, well, show me one," Sara interrupted.

"Right now?" Joe replied, a little uncomfortable.

"Yeah, right now. You show me yours and maybe I'll show you mine." Sara raised her eyebrows suggestively and laughed.

Joe laughed too. She seemed more like herself again when she laughed.

"Well, uh, okay." Joe crouched down to the ground in front of the bench. "Step back," he warned. Sara just laughed in response.

"Hurry up."

Joe smiled over his shoulder and then placed his hands on the ground in front of him. He closed his eyes, and listened to the earth. He could feel its movement under his hands. He felt it rising up to meet him and he felt a surge in his body as if he was reflexively sending energy to meet it. The ground started to shake and Joe opened his eyes, his hands still on the ground. The ground was shaking; an earthquake was definitely in progress. The ground in front of him cracked and heaved, the crack rumbling, opening, and continuing along the ground in front of him. He watched it move, like the path of an invisible earthworm. It was at that moment that he realized he had made a huge mistake. Joe had forgotten about the fountain. And just as the thought entered his head, the crack hit the side of the fountain, cracking its concrete side, turning part of it to rubble. It continued into the center of the fountain toward the large statue of a lounging woman in a Grecian tunic pouring water from an urn. The water was not running. At least, not until the crack hit the hidden underground water pipe.

Joe let go of the ground and stood up just as a plume of water began spraying wildly from the crack in the statue which was split into two, large, uneven pieces. The water sprayed in every direction wildly soaking both Joe and Sara.

"Oh shit!" was all he could say as Sara laughed hysterically, jumping up and down in the stream of frigid water.

"Sara, we need to get out of here, now!" Joe urged, tugging on her arm. He was getting drenched. "I'm parked over there," he motioned with a wave of his arm.

"Okay," Sara replied and she quickly stood beside him and slipped her soaked arm around his waist in a tight grasp.

"I'll get us there since it's my turn now." She smiled brightly at him. "If I were you, I'd hold on tight." Upon hearing those words Joe slipped his arm around her waist and tried to grip her waist tightly, hoping he didn't seem too clumsy.

"Here we go," she breathed into his ear as the breeze picked up again and lifted them up in to the air as two little dragonfly-sized creatures fluttered and buzzed around their heads. Joe would have yelled in surprise, but being lifted high into the air that rapidly had taken his breath away. Within a few seconds they were above the parking lot just to the left of his truck. As quick as they had risen they dropped, and Joe's stomach lurched as they came to a sudden stop only mere inches from the ground. Sara let him go and his feet touched the ground as she hopped lightly down to land soundlessly on her feet beside him in the parking lot.

Joe stood, soaked through to his skin, his teeth chattering. He opened the passenger door for Sara, closing it after she slipped onto the bench seat. Joe walked around the front of his truck and opened the driver's side door and climbed in.

"Wow, that was really cool, Sara. You really got it under control." Joe praised her skill as he started the ignition. He cranked up the heat, holding his hands in front of the vent for a moment.

"Thanks," Sara replied proudly. "I've been practicing."

"I guess I should too." Joe replied. "I only know of a few things I can do. And I could probably learn a little more control."

"You think?" Sara added, laughing. Joe laughed too as they pulled out of the parking lot.

"Where are we going, Sara?" Joe asked quizzically.

"Well, I think we better go to my place." She said decisively. "I need to dry off, and we still have a few things to discuss."

"Yeah," Joe finally recalled what he was told. "Aren't you in danger? Isn't that what Gabe said?"

Sara laughed again. "Well, actually, I kicked their asses." She said proudly, sitting up straighter. She mimed blowing on her nails and buffing them on her jacket. "Gabe missed all the action. He only saw the bastards retreat." Sara's smile turned into a frown. "But I think it is only a matter of time before they come back. And my only hope right now," she closed her eyes and breathed deeply, "is that they don't know about Abby."

"So Abby is one of us?" Joe asked.

"Yes, and she is Fire." Sara answered flatly. "She doesn't have enough control yet, though she is working hard to change that. I think she'll get it soon, I hope before it controls her."

Joe drove quietly for a moment and then said, "If I am Earth, Abby is Fire, then you are Air. That means that—"

Sara broke in, "Yes, that means there is one more and that person is Water."

Joe looked at Sara. "Do you know who that is?"

Sara looked out the window. "I have a reasonably good idea. Abby may have stumbled upon him. But let's figure things out first, just the three of us, okay? Then we'll find the fourth together."

"Then what?" Joe asked.

"We will do what we are supposed to do, right?" Sara answered confidently. "I'm sure when the time is right, we will find out. But let's go back to my place and make a plan. At the very least," Sara gave a shudder, "I can tell you about my attackers and the one who led them. I don't think we've seen the last of them. I can draw you a picture." She laughed again. "Remember: above all else I'm still an artist." They exchanged smiles as Joe felt the road turn from asphalt to gravel and continued through town as Sara gave him directions to her place.

***

Gabe felt out of place perched on the large-seated, high-backed mahogany chair in the Elthynne Council Chamber. It was a climb for him just to sit in it, and the dark, ornate furniture and courtly atmosphere made him feel small and out of place. The room was used to hold council sessions attended by the highborn nobles of Feyland. They would be accustomed to such rich furniture and crystal chandeliers.

Gabe was much more comfortable in his sparsely-furnished room in his barracks, but it would be inappropriate to suggest meeting in such a place simply because the room was too luxurious for the likes of him. The room served another purpose, however: it was quiet and had the necessary magical wards in place to prohibit anyone from eavesdropping on conversations or meetings held within.

Queen Ezreanna looked at him intently, her finger tips pressed together as she leaned her elbows on the arms of her even more elaborate chair, her lips pressed so tightly together that they appeared bloodless.

"Are you positive this woman—Sara? Was she certain the attacker said his name was Thaddeus?"

Gabe nodded expressionless, "Yes, Yer Majesty. I guess he figgered he was gonna kill her, but she fought back hard." Gabe chuckled slightly at the idea then caught himself. He patted the front of his vest. "Oh yeah, she managed to relieve him o' this." Gabe drew out the dagger from inside his vest and placed it on the council table in front of him.

Queen Ezreanna jumped up from her chair, pushing aside the ample skirt of her ice blue and silver gown aside as she reached over and grasped the dagger. She eyed it with a mixture of reverence and revulsion. She held it gingerly in both hands, inspecting it carefully in an upturned palm, occasionally running a delicate fingertip down the blade and hilt, and then holding it up to the light and scrutinizing it further as she held it in her hands once again. She placed it soundlessly back onto the table and gathered up her silken skirts to return once more to her chair. She sat in silence for a long moment staring at the knife, her mouth twisted in revulsion.

"Ya recognize it, then?" Gabe rasped.

"Yes, you know very well that I do." she answered stiffly. "I'm shocked. I can't believe he would resort to—"

"Excuse me, Yer Highness, but I think he's done worse things than this. And we know he has, and is prepared to do even worse things."

"Yes, I know, Gabe." She answered softly.

"She must be quite remarkable, this Sara of yours." The Queen remarked.

"She's not mine," Gabe retorted.

"She is your charge, Gabe. It is your duty to provide direction to The Four."

"Yeah, we . . . I got there late."

The Queen shifted slightly, smiling at him. "Still, she is the first member to ever survive one of his attacks, Gabe. For that reason alone she must be remarkable."

Gabe looked down at his hands. *Bloody hell*, he thought. How many had died? How many did Thaddeus succeed in killing?

"He had the one burned, remember?" The Queen interrupted his thoughts as if reading them. "Burned her as a witch during the time the humans refer to as the 'Burning Times.'" The Queen shuddered and brought her hand up to touch the large blue agate at the center of her necklace before continuing. "Thaddeus is a master of manipulation. How could he not take advantage of the hysteria over witches? The Fire Element is so unpredictable and at times unstable . . .," she paused to wipe a tear from her eye. "That poor girl, she probably believed she was indeed cursed to be a witch. Not that they all go bad, but certainly her inability to control the fire must have driven her to madness. I'm sure Thaddeus loved the irony that she was consumed by the very element she embodied."

"Don't forget, Yer Majesty, he burned many more before he found her." Gabe added angrily.

"Yes, as he did with the Earth Vessel in November 1858. He took advantage of the greed of men to possess gold and land and helped them to massacre over a hundred women, children, and men of a proud nation of peaceful people at Sandcreek. He didn't care that he aided in the displacement and humiliation of these people. It was only a means to achieve his goal." The Queen moved her hands to her lap and balled them into fists.

"Aye, that he did, but the Native people of North America are still strong, they have their pride. They'll be strong again," Gabe reassured her. "But I can't say the same for the Gypsies during the human Second World War. How many o' them were wiped out? The Gypsies were so hated by the Nazis they didn't even bother to keep track o' how many they murdered. But the Air Vessel fought back that time too, remember?"

"Yes," the Queen sighed, "but it didn't save her from destruction."

"No, it didn't—I wonder if Air conveyed that experience to Sara. She defended herself well against his attack," Gabe surmised. He smiled broadly. "I thought she'd be, well, less *feisty* than she is."

"You like her, don't you?" The Queen teased smiling.

"Yeah, but not like yer gettin'at. She's just . . . I dunno . . . just . . . likeable."

The Queen sat quietly, her fingers pressed together in front of her lips, a contemplative look upon her face.

"Majesty?" Gabe spoke, breaking the silence.

She looked over her fingers at him in acknowledgement. "I know what you are going to ask, Gabe, and I will tell you in a moment. But first, I need your opinion. Do you think he is going to attempt it this time? Do you believe that he will attempt to breech the Veil and return from banishment?"

Gabe returned her stare. It all led to the conclusion that Thaddeus was going to return. The Veil was in a cycle and the Elemental Vessels had been called. Yet this was the first time he had used a force greater than himself to attack a vessel since, well, since the Veil between the worlds was constructed. The Queen was looking impatient. He wanted to give her the answer she wanted, but wasn't sure what that answer would be. Gabe could only give her his observations and hope that they would be enough.

"Your Majesty, I think we shouldn't overlook the fact that he seems to have some support, and he is using it now. I think we should prepare in anticipation that it will happen again. We don't wanna get caught with our pants down, if yeh know what I mean."

"Should I alert the Elthynne Council that there may be traitors in our midst?" The Queen questioned.

"Nah, just in case he has some hidden support in the Council. We must wait a little longer; keep our eyes on those that were suspected or proven traitors before. At least this time we're aware of the possibility of treason."

As the Queen looked over to Gabe her eyes filled with tears that threatened to slip down her cheeks. Her jaw trembled slightly as she fought to hold them back.

"Do you think I was wrong, Gabe?" She spoke softly. "Do you think I made the right choice all those many years ago?"

"Yeah, yeah, I do." He spoke quickly looking her in the eyes. "And seeing the brutality humans have wreaked upon each other, I don't question yer choice at all."

"So many died, Gabe. Many of our people on both sides of the war suffered."

"Yeh protect us all with your actions, Yer Majesty. Thaddeus only wishes to gain power and damn all those that come between him and his pursuit of it."

"And for that, Gabe, he will pay. Yes, this time my dear brother will pay — with his life, if necessary." The Queen stood, and Gabe clamored down from his seat to bow deeply as she gathered her skirts and swept from the room.

CHAPTER 16

Abby threw her acetylene torch across the room with a howl of rage and frustration. She could feel it well up inside her: the desire, no, *need*, to *burn*! The fire was calling to her, heating her up, ringing in her ears, and dulling her senses to everything except the sound of flames.

Running her hands rapidly through her hair, she struggled to remember how to focus, how to quell the drive inside. *God! I'm burning up*!

(Burn! Fire! Burn!)

"Leave me alone!" she screamed, her voice echoing in the empty room. She could feel the heat in the core of her body increase and quickly yanked her hands out of her hair. She didn't want to singe her hair - again.

Think calmly, she told herself. *Just take deep breaths and slowly walk down the stairs out of here. You can do it.*

She moved slowly and mechanically down the stairs, repeating inside her head, *You can do it, you can do it, you can do it,* as if it were her mantra as she avoided direct contact between her hand and the staircase railing.

They are so hot! She looked down at her hands. They were glowing a pale cherry red.

I'm not going to make it, she fretted. *Just get outside*, she told herself. *You can do it. Last step. You can do it. Closer to the door, you can do it.*

(Burn!)

She looked down at her hands. They were now a bright scarlet red. "I gotta get out of here," Abby spoke aloud, panic rising in her voice. "NOW!"

Waves of heat rose up in front of her and rolled off her body. It was building up inside her; she needed to release it before it blew her apart or roasted her alive. Abby placed her hands a few inches apart and a small fireball the size of a marble began to form. She rapidly moved her cupped hands apart as if packing snow into a ball to throw. The ball of flame increased to the size of a baseball. With one hand she hurled it full force at the door of her studio. The fireball hit the door and sent it crashing off its hinges covered in flames as it flew (by Abby's estimation) twenty feet into the air out onto the lawn. Abby ran outside into the cool air gulping it in like she'd been holding her breath. Usually bleeding off a little of the Fire helped her get back into control and cool down. The control she sought wasn't coming.

(Burn! Burn!)

"QUIET!" she screamed.

I need to cool down...breathe...calm breaths...you can do it. She flung herself down onto the cool ground flat on her stomach. She breathed in the cool smell of the earth and felt its chill against her body as she planted her hands, fingers splayed, on the ground hoping to transfer some of the cool of the earth to her burning hands. She was starting to feel better as the contact with the ground began to dissipate the heat and put the Fire out. She turned over onto her side, her cheek tickled by blades of grass. Tears flowed down her face, leaving cold trails as they slid down her face.

Why is this happening to me? She couldn't get the thought out of her head. *How can Sara be so together while I'm completely falling apart?*

As she lay there on the ground, she hazarded a glance up and noticed that Dan was watching her from the house through the picture window.

Poor Dan, she thought sadly. *I wonder what he thinks, me lying here on the grass with the door of my studio on fire a few feet away.* Fearing he would think there was a gas explosion, Abby quickly rose to her feet, grabbed a bucket, and dipped it into the pond, tossing the water abruptly onto the flaming door to quench the fire. The remaining flames winked out with a hiss. Once the door was just a smoldering chunk of charcoal, she returned the bucket to the shed and strode slowly over to the house. She noticed, out of the corner of her eye, that Dan darted away from the window in an attempt at nonchalance.

I wonder why he didn't come running out here to see if I was okay? Abby tried to put herself in his place. *I have been moody lately; it's no wonder that he didn't come out,* she thought ruefully as she strode slowly toward the house. *I guess I'd be afraid of getting my head bitten off too.*

Had she really been that bad? It was so hard to think, her mind was so full all the time. Her desire to be herself and the burning drive inside polarized her. *Maybe that's not even the right way to say it; I don't know*, she thought.

Ever since Dan had burned himself touching her he had been reluctant to come in close contact with her. The night Sara had helped her he had held her hand, and for a little while it felt like things between them were going to be normal again. But then the desire for the Fire would overpower her tenuous control and she would erupt in a fury of rage over the smallest things, often lashing out in anger at Dan. Small items of inconsequential importance left in the wrong place were unceremoniously sacrificed to the Flame. Abby still didn't have it in her to tell Dan that she melted the soles of his favorite running shoes in a fit of anger merely because she tripped over them in the living room when he knew damn well shoes belonged in the entryway on the rack. And now she felt guilty and remorseful realizing that it was crazy to get so bent out of shape over a stupid pair of shoes.

"Dammit, I miss him," she muttered softly. They were always so close, always sitting beside each other, holding hands, constant companions. She missed being able to talk to him about anything, or just being comfortable in sitting and saying nothing and that being okay too. Sara had said this was a gift, but right now Abby could only see it as a curse.

Abby opened the door and stepped inside the house, kicking off her shoes and tossing her dirt-covered, smoke-scented jacket into the laundry room as she passed by the doorway.

Dan craned his neck over the couch to look at her as she entered. "Would you like a cup of tea? I'll make it." He offered.

"Ah, yeah, please, that would be nice. Thanks." She smiled at him, grateful he had not mentioned what had occurred outside. "I'm just going to change out of my work clothes."

"Sure thing. By the time you're done, the tea will be ready."

Dan rose slowly off the couch and made his way to the kitchen as Abby darted upstairs to their bedroom. She peeled off her jeans and t-shirt and tossed them into the hamper. She quickly donned a velour pair of track pants and a white tank top and returned downstairs where Dan had the tea poured, and a steaming mug of tea was waiting for her at the table in her spot. Dan sat there waiting for her just across the table.

Abby smiled and sat down. She picked up her tea with both hands and took a sip. Two sugars: just the way she liked it. She smiled across the table again. "It's good. Thank you. "

"You're welcome," Dan smiled back while holding his mug on the table in both hands. His eyes went to her shirt and he began to say, "Aren't you a little cold . . .," and quickly broke off.

"What?" Abby answered absently.

"Uh, nothing. Never mind." Dan said quickly. He took a sip of his tea.

Abby gazed at him across the table. *He's afraid of me*, she thought sadly. *How on Earth did this get so bad?*

"Abby, are you okay?" Dan quietly cut into her thoughts.

"What? Why do you ask?" She blurted out.

"Well, just now you looked so sad. Is there something I can do?" Dan looked at her across the table, his eyes intently locked upon hers.

Abby shrugged and looked down at her tea. "I don't know, Dan. I wish there was something you could do."

"Maybe there is, Ab. Tell me what's wrong. Tell me what I can do. Please." He pleaded.

She could tell just by the desperate look in his eyes that the offer wasn't just idle words or a knee-jerk reaction to offer to fix a bad situation in the hopes of avoiding a worse one (not that he was one of *those* people anyway). He had never been one of those people before, so why would he start now? Abby looked at her husband. She wanted to tell him everything, but she was torn.

"Well, all I can tell you right now is that I've not been feeling like myself lately. And I am trying to deal with a few changes I've been going through. It's going to take some work, but I think I can get through it and return to being my old self. I just need a little time." She forced a weak smile at Dan. "I'm sorry it has been so hard on you, and I am trying very hard to change things. Sara has been helping me to—"

"Sara knows what is going on with you?" Dan blurted out.

"Yes, and she's trying to help me figure a few things out—"

"Like what?" Dan cut in again.

"Well, I can't really say right now," Abby stated.

"Why not?"

"Well, because Sara is going through something too, and I'm not sure whether she wants me to tell anyone yet."

"So . . .," Dan began, his voice wavering. "You can confide in Sara, but not in me? Abby, I thought we could talk about anything, no matter what. What has changed?"

Abby looked at Dan, surprised by the sad expression on his face.

"Dan, no, nothing has changed. It's just that, Sara, is well . . . it's just complicated right now. I'm not sure I fully understand it myself." She said simply, looking at Dan to gauge his reaction. Dan just continued to stare at her, looking like a wounded animal in pain.

"I want you to understand something, Abby," Dan stated as he reached across the table and grasped her hands in his. He lifted her right hand up to his lips planted a soft kiss on the back of her hand before placing them back on the table. "I love you." Dan stated. "I love you very much, with every fiber of my being. When you are hurting, I feel your pain. I want to share it and help you heal. Together, we will grow stronger. Your reluctance to share this, to talk to me about it, hurts deeply. Just think about that, and let me know when you are ready to talk." Dan stood up, taking his cup with him as he strode toward the staircase.

"You know where to find me," he called over his shoulder as he ascended the staircase.

Abby turned around in her chair to face to stairs. "Wait!" she yelled at Dan's back.

Dan stopped and turned to face her, still standing on the step. "Yes, Ab?"

Abby knew that now was the time to tell Dan everything. If Sara was upset, then Abby would willingly deal with the consequences. She couldn't bear to deal with the burden any longer, feeling like she was going crazy or about to spontaneously combust at the drop of a hat.

"Do you think I'm crazy?" she asked loudly, her voice slightly stilted.

"Pardon?"

"DO YOU THINK I'M CRAZY?" she yelled, her voice breaking.

"No, Ab." he answered calmly.

"No matter what?"

"No matter what, Ab."

"Do you remember the day I told you about that man I saw in the park after the Art in the Park Show?"

"Yes, of course I remember," Dan sat down on the step.

"There was an earthquake around the same time, maybe even a few days or weeks after the show, I don't exactly remember when. But shortly after that I found that I could control fire. Well, sort of, anyway." She looked at Dan, trying to gauge his reaction. But he sat there on the step, expressionless, listening intently. She continued. "Well, it got stronger. Really strong. And it is still there, this power inside me. But I can't control it for very long periods of time. It makes me feel like I'm going crazy." Abby laughed and felt tears running down her cheeks. She raised her hands and swiped them away.

"I know you saw what happened outside," she said flatly.

"Well, I heard a noise and saw you lying on the grass and the door on fire," Dan confessed. "But I wasn't exactly sure how the door caught on fire."

Abby looked at him, tears in her eyes. "I can make fireballs, you know. I felt so hot and closed in, and the door was in my way, and I just wanted . . . I just wanted...," Abby broke off with a sob as she put her head on the table.

Dan stepped off the stairs and walked over to Abby, stroking her head as she sat sobbing at the table.

"It's okay, Ab, it's gonna be okay." Dan crooned softly over her stifled sobs.

Abby looked up at him with red eyes and her face wet with tears.

"I wanted to tell you, but I was so afraid of what you would think. I don't know why this is happening, but it is. I need to learn to control this ability. And I don't want to hurt you again, Dan." Abby looked at Dan.

"That's a heavy load to be carrying around alone, Abby." Dan put his hands on her shoulders. "You don't have to do it alone. You know that, don't you?"

"How can you help me?" Abby asked.

"Well, the best way I can help right now is to support you. I can listen, and you can talk." Dan gathered her up in his arms, "You don't have to worry, Abby. I will always be here."

Abby hugged him back. The voices were quiet inside her, and she was content that they were subdued, even if only for a moment.

***

William stood in the doorway of his brownstone watching the last of his art crates being rolled up a ramp on a hand truck and stacked carefully into the back of a lorry. Once the final crate was secure he watched the man stow the cart, fold up the ramp, and latch the large doors shut. The driver, whose neat uniform jacket bore a fabric nametag ("Dave") stitched to the left front, shoved a clipboard and a pen under his nose with a quick, "sign here, please, sir." William obliged and signed the appropriate places as Dave pointed them out. "And don't forget here too," he added as he tapped another place on the form. William dutifully scribbled his name on the bottom of the officious-looking form. Dave quickly tore out the yellow copies of each and thrust them at William, reminding him to "keep these forms for your records and also in case you need to make a claim if some objects are damaged in transit." Dave smiled and tipped his hand in farewell as he strode to the vehicle. Dave climbed in the cab and drove away.

William stared at the papers in his hand then registered what had been said to him. "Nothing had better be damaged!" he yelled at the truck as it continued down the drive, down the road and out of sight. Grumbling and muttering under his breath, he slammed his front door behind him with effort.

William stood still for a moment and took stock of his living room. For once in his life it actually looked like a room where one could really sit down and receive visitors. He was visualizing having people over for tea (as if he was actually the sort of person who enjoyed entertaining and socializing). *Yeah, a person who actually has friends,* he thought ruefully. *Well, at least I have one friend,* he remembered, his thoughts perking up.

Rhysdale. Somehow, she didn't seem like the type who would just pop around for tea. William didn't even think she could leave her lake. He sat down on the now empty settee. Even when they sat together on the bank at the water's edge she always had her lower legs and feet dangling in the water. He wondered if she did that as a comfort thing or because she had to. William frowned and his brow furrowed. All this time and yet he still barely knew her. She was such an enigma to him; was he an open book to her?

A look of realization crossed his face as he jammed his hand into his pocket and retrieved the coin that the Lady of the Lake had given him. He pulled his reading glasses from the side table and jammed them up onto the bridge of his nose then peered through them to examine the silver coin in his hand. It was about the size of a one-pound coin and just as thick with smooth sides, but not nearly as hefty in his hand. He sensed that it was very old even though it lacked the patina of tarnish that was indicative of old silver coins. He had seen some once after it was unearthed from deep in the soil in his cousin's field after a spring plough excavated some long-buried Roman hoard. Those coins were black with tarnish. This coin, however, was unique. One side bore the image of a beautifully-crowned woman (*a queen?* he mused), the other bore the outline of a horse. *Looks like the chalk horse at White Horse,* he speculated. The coin bore no other markings, no year of minting, no country of origin. *A very special coin indeed,* he thought as he turned it over and over again in his hand.

The advice of the Lady kept running through his mind. "A place where your people draw water from," she had stated. *Hmm.* William was trying to imagine what life was like during her time, during the time of Arthur. If she existed, was it possible that Merlin existed too? *Wizards and witches could exist after all,* he thought. Well, if beings like Rhysdale existed....his mind could open to a world of other possibilities.

Perhaps Rhysdale could offer some advice. It had been a while since he had seen her. Three, four weeks maybe? He had been so busy with meeting the Lady and then getting his work prepped and ready to be shipped to America for the art gallery show that between the two he hadn't really had time to see her. He was lonely.

William rose stiffly from the settee and went to grab his watercolors before stopping himself. "I just need a bloody break," he murmured aloud to the room. He turned from the table, taking off his glasses and stuffing the coin deep into the farthest recess of his pocket. *It would be good to see her*, he thought, *if only to say farewell before going to America.* He donned his jacket, zipped it up, and set out of his house, keys in hand, his step a little lighter.

***

Abby had spent the morning, coffee in hand, sitting on her living room sofa gazing out the window; at least the part that wasn't encrusted with a layer of frost. Occasionally she spared a glance at the frosty film, marveling in its beautiful shapes and texture. It was its own art form, monochromatic in its coloring but magnificent in its free-flowing, simple grace. Abby felt good, really good about herself this morning. Even though she had divulged more to Dan than she wanted, she felt as if she had someone to share the load, if not necessarily the burden, of her powers. It felt good to have him stand at her side, her ally no matter what. *I wonder what I ever did to deserve him*, she thought, a smile spreading across her face.

So today, with the voices and the Fire under control and quiet, she was going to spend the day doing nothing. *Nothing extraordinary, at any rate*. Yes, today she was going to laze around, catch up on some reading, maybe take a nap in the afternoon, and then cook a fabulous meal that would be ready and waiting when Dan came in. Then they could actually eat together, a feat that had not been accomplished in quite some time. She curled her toes deeper into her warm, comfy slippers and lifted her legs up, tugging them up beside her on the couch. *Yes, today,* she thought, sipping her coffee, *today is going to be a great day*.

The ring of the phone jolted her out of her daydreaming. The loud ringing from phones strategically located around the house (*what, seven? A hundred?* She couldn't count) caused such a cacophony that it startled her into sitting up abruptly, spilling her hot coffee down the front of her pajamas. She lurched off the couch cursing a blue streak and lunged frantically for the phone before it could ring again, rubbing the burning trail down her chest and stomach.

Easy, take it easy, you don't want to get riled up, remember?

Abby took a deep breath, put the receiver to her ear, and between gritted teeth managed to force out, "Hello?"

"Hey, Ab. How ya doing?" Sara chirped in her ear.

"Ah, good, I guess. And you?" Abby straightened up into a sitting position.

"I'm good too," Sara answered with a giggle. Abby could hear a man's voice murmuring in the background and Sara's "Shh," followed by a muffled sound over the receiver. Abby strained to catch another bit of conversation, but Sara continued.

"Listen, can you come over here today?"

"Why?"

"Well, ah, I want you to meet someone," Sara answered.

"I knew it!" Abby said triumphantly, her voice louder. "You've got a new boyfriend."

Sara giggled again. "No, well, not really, or maybe I should say not *yet*. Can you just come over here anyway?"

Abby sat back on the couch and crossed her legs. She had to admit, she was curious about Sara's new boyfriend-not-quite-yet-boyfriend, whatever, but at the same time was looking forward to her mental health day.

"Sara, what's the rush?" Abby asked.

"What?" Sara was startling to sound confused.

"Well," Abby began, "If this guy isn't really your boyfriend, I mean, what's the rush to meet him? Can't it wait?"

Sara sighed. "It's got nothing to do with that, okay? It's got to do with something, you know, *bigger* than that."

Abby's eyes widened. Now she knew. "You found another?" She had whispered into the phone.

"You got it, Ab," Sara replied. "Just get over here, okay?" And don't worry," she added cheerfully. "You'll be pleasantly surprised."

Sara hung up. Abby held the phone to her ear long after the click before slowly turning the phone off and returning it carefully to the base. She settled back on the couch and picked up her coffee, took a huge gulp, and burned her tongue on the hot liquid.

Calm, calm, stay calm, she coaxed herself, but she could feel herself start to shake.

Pull it together! You can do it, she urged herself again.

Hmm, pleasantly surprised, Abby drew in a deep breath, exhaling slowly through pursed lips. Gradually, the shaking ceased. *She's your best friend. Just trust her judgment.*

Okay, she mentally answered. *Now get your shit together.*

Abby set her mug on the table and rose off the couch. She cast a longing look at the pile of books on the table. *Reading, it appears, will have to wait,* she thought ruefully as she headed up the stairs to shower and change.

***

Joe and Sara were sitting on the sofa in Sara's front room each holding a cup of coffee. They had gotten together a couple of times since meeting in the park, and Sara was glad to have someone to talk to that she felt comfortable with.

She had just retold the story of the night of the attack on her by Thaddeus and the winged creatures and from Joe's facial expressions, and he appeared to hang on her every word and make the appropriate sympathetic noises.

"So," Joe interjected, shifting his legs and re-crossing them, "What sort of creatures were those that attacked that night?"

"I dunno," Sara shrugged, "they just looked like gargoyles to me." She took a long sip of her coffee.

"Well," Joe continued, "did you ask Gabe? I remember you saying he arrived late. Did he help at all?"

Sara snorted, "No, he didn't need to. Besides, it was all over by the time he got here. But," she added, peering at him sideways, "Gabe did come in for a tea. We had a lovely chat."

Joe looked at her wide-eyed, his mouth open. He could scarcely imagine Gabe as a good guest, let alone be a party to what Sara considered a lovely chat. *It would probably be more enjoyable to have dinner with someone who dropped out of dental college*, he thought.

"Did he tell you anything?" Joe asked.

"Like what?" Sara countered.

"Like maybe why you were attacked, a hint of what the big picture is. You know, important stuff."

"Well," Sara dragged, pleased that she had his attention, "He did mention this guy Thaddeus tried to cause an uprising in his world quite a few centuries ago."

"I take it he wasn't successful?" Joe asked.

"No, not from what Gabe said. In fact, the guy was banished."
Joe's curiosity was getting the better of him.

"What world is Gabe from exactly?" Joe asked.

"The ethereal world, I guess we would call it. A fairy realm of sorts." Sara shrugged. "I didn't ask too much, and he didn't offer too much either. But he did tell me to be careful, that this Thaddeus guy may try to attack again." Sara straightened up and looked Joe in the eye. "So now I am. You know, careful now."

"Good." Joe smiled and she smiled in return, marveling at how white his teeth really were. *Wow, he must use a lot of floss*, she thought and she broke into laughter.

"What?" Joe looked at her, a bemused smile on his face.

"Oh, nothing." she smiled again, stifling the rising laughter in her throat. They looked at each other for a brief moment before simultaneously bursting into laughter and falling back on the couch.

Sara laughed a little longer and then quieted herself, resting her hands outward from her body upon the couch seat cushions. Joe did the same and placed his hand on top of hers. They both looked at each other, their eyes locked. Sara broke the silence.

"You're holding my hand," she announced loudly. They both burst out laughing again, but neither moved their hands.

A sharp rap on the door and the turning of the door knob caught both of their attention. Sara sat up, but soon eased back onto the couch when Abby walked into the room, closing the door behind her. She stamped her boots on the mat and unzipped her coat.

"Okay, I'm here now, Sara. What's so damned important?" she turned to the couch and froze as her eyes caught sight of Joe. She felt her face go flush for a moment before regaining her composure.

"Hey, Joe." She said as she made her way over to the couch, her hand thrust out in greeting. Joe lifted his hand off Sara's and shook Abby's. Abby noticed where his hand had been and threw a knowing glance at Sara, who feigned an innocent look and pretended not to notice. Abby grabbed a chair from the computer desk and turned it around, sitting on it backward, her elbows resting on the top of the backrest. She looked at Sara.

"So?"

Sara cleared her throat, looked at Abby, and then turned to Joe and announced, "And now there are three."

CHAPTER 17

"You summoned me, Your Highness?" Gabe stood in the doorway of the Queen's private chambers, which were guarded by two of Her Majesty's Guard Royale; their ice blue and silver regalia set them apart from the other guards in the castle. They alone had the honor of physically guarding the Queen. Not only were they the most loyal of her military, their unarmed combat skills were legendary.

"Indeed I did, Gabe," the Queen responded. "Please come in and sit down."
She turned to indicate the chair and Gabe instinctively followed her glance; with great relief he noted that the seat of the chair was lower to the floor so he would be able to sit with ease. He was grateful that she usually thought to accommodate his size, and he appreciated that she never made mention of it either.

"Gentlemen," she addressed her guard. They stiffened and stood to attention. "While I appreciate your presence, we require some privacy. You will both wait outside."

The guardsmen clicked their heels together, saluted and strode out of the room in unison. She waited until she heard their boots come to a halt outside the door and then with a broad wave of her hand uttered, "Activate Wards."

Gabe glanced around the room. Beautiful ice blue tapestries hung on every wall, and he strained to see if he could detect the presence of the warding devices among them. He glanced up at the silver ceiling, which had at its center a large chandelier comprised of hundreds of dangling quartz crystals. He suspected that some of them were disguising the devices.

"You will not see them," the Queen spoke, as if reading his mind. "They are hidden well, and are of the highest caliber, of course." She smiled.

"O' course, Yer Majesty," he replied.

The Queen adjusted her hands in her lap and then fixed a stare upon Gabe. "I suppose you are wondering why I have requested your presence here today."

Gabe's expression was, he hoped, decidedly neutral. He knew there were things happening, but he did not know if she was going to fill him in or ask his advice. He tried to answer.

"I think I have an idea." He answered simply.

"Do you?" she asked sharply, still fixing her eyes upon him.

"Well, I know there have been more incidents."

"Yes," she answered. "The Bards have been called out on at least five separate occasions in the past week. Two incidents have occurred in the last two days. Two." She emphasized.

Gabe sat motionless, his eyes intently upon her. As she rose out of her chair, he grasped the arms of his chair in an attempt to rise, but she motioned for him to continue sitting.

"No, I need to stand and walk to think." She clasped her hands behind her back as she began to pace the floor toward the doorway and back to her chair. "I fear that the Taekyrs are against us." she blurted out. "You said they were involved in the attack on the Air Vessel?"

"Aye, Yer Majesty," he answered.

"Well, I want some of them questioned," she ordered sharply. She stopped in mid-stride to face him. "There are others, Gabe, others that I do not trust. This is where you are to prove what a truly valuable resource you are to me."

"How do I do that?" Gabe answered, adjusting his vest.

The Queen picked a piece of paper off the table and thrust it toward him. "This is a list of individuals that have been acting unusual as of late. Some of their activities have been, how would you say it," she rolled her eyes, mentally searching for the word, "ah, yes, questionable." She continued. "I want you to have them followed, see if their loyalties have changed, or in the case of some," she tapped a few names on the list, "see if they have returned to their old ways."

"And what should I do with the information I gather, Yer Majesty?" Gabe asked.

"You will bring it to me as soon as you discover it." The Queen plopped down into her chair.

"What about those who may be on the opposing side? What yeh plan to do with them?" Gabe asked, the list clutched in his hands.

"Well, Gabe, a wise man one told me to 'keep your friends close, but your enemies closer.'" That is what I intend to do." The Queen kicked off her blue and silver slippers and rested her bare feet on a silk pouf on the floor.

"Ah, wise man that Merlin," Gabe nodded wistfully.

"Yes, he was," the Queen agreed. "I particularly miss his ability to make light of a bad situation. We are certainly going to need that skill soon enough."

"Don' worry, yer Majesty," he said. "We'll manage, don't ya worry."

"Gabe, I am counting on it." She smiled and shut her eyes, resting her head deep into the upholstered chair back. "You've no idea how much I am counting on it."

***

Michael strode briskly down the dim, dank corridor. The sounds of his footsteps against the stone floor echoed loudly within the corridor, the sound occasionally joined in chorus by the intermittent drip of water from the damp ceiling. There were no windows this far into the bowels of the castle, and although his strides were long, it felt as if the journey to the dimly lit room at the end would take hours.

The smell of the room hit him before he reached it, and he wrinkled his nose with distaste. Although they had the appearance of bat-like stone creatures, they definitely had a pungent smell akin to the vulture birds he had seen in the human world. They smelled like they subsisted on fetid meat. How ironic he had found it when he discovered that the creatures were vegetarian.

As he entered the door the room gave way to a light brighter than the hallway, but not by much. This room was devoid of windows; the only opening was a space in the wall where it appeared that four stones were missing. This was the sole entrance and exit for the Taekyrs and where they would leave the stable area and return to their nests.

Michael surveyed the nests within the stables. The great majority of them were roosting, as was their habit during daylight hours. As the sun began to set they would stir and he would send a few out to complete their missions of bringing back the marked children. Some would nest and manage their own broods. Only a select few would be singled out for other purposes.

Michael sighed, waiting for the sun to sink lower in the sky, watching darkness fall as the light entering the room became dimmer. Thaddeus was so confident this time. Michael shook his head. The attack on the Air Element had failed, casualties had resulted, and yet Thaddeus remained pleased about it.

Can't help but feel the man has been in exile too long. Michael chewed his lip pensively. He had hoped that this time would be

127

different. He wanted victory so badly he could taste it. With Thaddeus as ruler he would finally gain the position as Chief Military Advisor. After all his years of service, the Queen had given it to Gabe, not him. And after she had found that he had helped to form the force against her at the uprising she demoted him to Commander of the Taekyrs. "Glorified Stable Boy" would have been a more appropriate title. He kicked a piece of dried Taekyr dung with the toe of his highly polished boot. Still, he had to be thankful. Many of those who stood against the Queen had been executed or banished, and, Goddess knows, he was lucky to escape both, though he knew that neither Gabe nor the Queen would ever forget.

He had to be careful now, he reminded himself. The time was coming, and he could read the signs; he could see the dissension clamoring in the streets and the Bards coming in to calm the situation. The time was coming. Yes, he definitely had to be careful.

"Don't reveal our intention until the plan is fully underway," Thaddeus had warned him. "By then it will be too late to stop it." Michael heeded Thaddeus' warning and guarded his every move; he acted like everything he did every moment of the day was conducted under the greatest scrutiny. As far as he knew, they did not suspect him of anything.

The sun made its final descent into the horizon, and soon all light was gone except for dim light emanating from a small candle burning in a wooden sconce upon the stable wall. The Taekyrs were awake and alert now and ready for their orders.

"Section A, you will be out searching for the marked children in the mapped section," he pointed to the folded paper in his hand. "Ensure you have the changelings before you depart." He turned to his left and continued, "Section B, you will complete domicile assignments this evening. Please complete them in an orderly and timely manner." He turned to the group as a whole. "Questions, anyone?"

The whole group stared back at him, their dark lidless eyes fixed upon him, shaking their heads, their thin lips pressed together in an emotionless manner. "None?" Good. Dismissed," he dispatched them curtly. As they lurched by on their talons and wing tips, Michael spoke with one off to the side. "I need you to complete a special task tonight. A matter of great importance. Can you handle it?" Michael asked.

"An attack, Commander?" it seemed to croak weakly.

"No," he answered flatly. "More like a surveillance and reconnaissance mission."

"Yes, Commander," the creature almost whispered.

"Come down to my office after Section A has left so I may brief you on the details."

"As you wish, Commander," he nodded agreeably.

Michael turned on his heels and strode back down the hallway. *I don't care what Thaddeus thinks*, Michael thought angrily. *I just can't trust these creatures.* He picked up his pace and hurried back down the long tunnel back into the castle basement.

***

Abby was pacing back and forth across the floor of Sara's living room, her hands clasped behind her back in an imposing posture that any Sergeant-Major would be proud of. Joe and Sara, however, observed her motions with guarded expressions as they sat on the sofa; their eyes followed her like she was a ping-pong ball volleying between two opponents.

Abby drew in a sharp breath, paused in front of the table, and clasped her hands in front of her with such force it made a clapping sound that caused Joe and Sara to jump slightly. Sara started to giggle nervously but stopped when a sharp glare from Abby cut her short.

I feel like I'm waiting for a bomb to drop, Joe thought.

"So," Abby blurted out, staring at Sara, "you were attacked by a man and a bunch of flying monkeys?" Abby's glance made Sara redden slightly.

"No, Abby," She corrected, "I said they *looked* like flying monkeys *at first*. When I got closer to them, they looked like gargoyles. They were big too." Sara added giving Joe a sideways glance.

"Are you okay?" Abby asked.

"Huh?"

"Are you alright?" Abby pressed. "Were you injured?"

"Oh," Sara had to think about it. It seemed a lifetime ago. "Well, I remember getting hit in the back and some pain in my head, but no major injuries."

"Had you ever seen this guy before?" Abby inquired.

Sara had to think. Now that she thought about it, she had seen him before. "Actually, yes, I have, but not in real life," Sara said.

"What do you mean, not in real life?" Abby pressed.

"Well, I've been having these dreams, daydreams sometimes, where I've been someone else and this man is there and the other me, you know, the 'dream me' dies, and this man is there. Now that I think about it, it's him. It's definitely this Thaddeus guy."

Abby felt a jolt of realization run through her. She looked over at Joe and noticed he had a look of shock on his face too.

"Joe," Abby spoke sharply. Joe looked up at her quickly, his face a pallid color. "You've had dreams too, haven't you?" Abby asked softly. "You've seen this man in your dreams?"

Joe nodded. "Well, sort of. Not in dreams, but one time for sure during a sweat lodge—"

"You were in a sweat lodge?" Sara interrupted excitedly. "I've always wanted to participate in one - what is it like? Did you have —,"

One look from Abby silenced her. "Sorry, Joe," Sara apologized quietly. "I didn't mean to interrupt."

Joe smiled at Sara and patted her hand gently. "S' okay, Sara. We'll talk more, later." Joe looked back to Abby. "Yeah, I've seen a man in my vision, and like Sara I was someone else and saw this guy kill me. Sounds like the same guy to me."

Abby sank back onto the computer chair. "I think I have too," Abby spoke quietly. "And he sentenced me to death." Abby shuddered, and then fixed Sara with a look of admiration. "Sara, you survived him, and you kicked his ass." Sara smiled, uncomfortable with this sudden praise. "How'd you do it?"

"Well," Sara started slowly, "I just ... I just used my powers."

"Easy for you." Abby snorted.

"Why?" Sara asked innocently.

"Well, because you know how to use them," Abby admitted. Joe looked at both women attempting to figure out what he should say.

"Well, I don't know the full extent of what I can do," Joe admitted sheepishly. "I haven't really tried to do very much."

"And I can't get mine under control too well," Abby admitted, forming her hands into fists.

"But you're doing better!" Sara said with an encouraging smile. "You haven't burned anything or lost your cool in a while."

"The day's still young," Abby replied through gritted teeth.

"Well, maybe that's where I can help," Sara offered. "I can help you two learn what you can do, and we can figure out a defensive strategy."

"Good idea, Sara," Abby stated, her expression grim. "We know this guy is gonna come back; we'd all better be prepared."

"What about this fourth guy?" Joe asked Abby. "Sara said you may know where to find him."

Abby looked nervously at Sara. "Well, I have an idea who he is," she admitted. "But why don't we wait until the three of us are more skilled before we find him? It doesn't make sense for the four of us to be sitting around unprepared. It would be like shooting ducks in a barrel for this Thaddeus guy."

Joe and Sara nodded in agreement. It's probably not him that Thaddeus knows about. He definitely knew about Sara. *It will probably be better to keep the other guy safe for now*, Joe thought, remembering what he had overheard Gabe telling Floyd.

"Well, let's head out to the barn then," Sara said rising of the couch. "At least we won't burn down the house.

"Hey!" Abby protested.

"Just kidding!" Sara giggled.

Sara looped her arm through Joe's and opened the door to go outside to the barn. Abby lingered back following at a discrete distance watching Sara and Joe talk arm-in-arm with their heads bent close together in intimate conversation. Abby smiled and then frowned slightly. *I'm happy for her*, she thought, *but the timing sure sucks. I hope they both know what they're doing. And maybe we should do some research on these flying-monkey-looking gargoyle creatures too*, she thought. *Wouldn't hurt to know the enemy before it returns for another fight.* Abby smiled. For the first time in a long time she was really looking forward to a good fight.

***

William sat down at the edge of the lake, pulling his collar up to his ears to shield them against the bitter winter wind. He could feel the cold against his legs and was grateful he was wearing thermals under his trousers.

Although it was for all intents and purposes winter, the lake wasn't frozen. In fact, it didn't have a film of frost except at its lowest point directly in front of him. He had to look hard to see it, like a ring of icing at the edge of a chocolate cake.

He hadn't called her yet. He was afraid to in a way. He knew that the sooner he called to her, the quicker their visit would be over. And he knew that soon the coming months would bring the film of frost and nature would keep them apart until the spring thaw, just as it always had throughout the years. Yes, this would be the last time he saw her, at least, until he returned home from America.

William sighed as his hand went to his trouser pocket and sought the lump that was the coin given to him by the Lady. *Should I tell her?* He thought. He had never kept any secrets from her before, and now he felt he had been, in some strange way, traitorous, or, at the very least, unfaithful. To him, it did not matter that it was *she* that had suggested he seek out other water creatures. *Was it perhaps a test of my loyalty?* He mused. *Did I fail her, or did I do right by her advice?* His self-doubt was rising further, making him feel less than sure she would welcome his visit.

If she tells me to go, he thought sadly, *I'll never forgive myself.*

He could bear it no more. He moved forward on bent knee and placed his hand in the frigid water. He ignored the burning cold creeping into his knuckles and fingers, closed his eyes, and whispered, "Rhysdale, I need you."

Immediately, the water churned and began to warm as he felt her presence in the water as she drew ever closer. Her hand clasped his and he gently guided her up, as always, until she found a seat upon the bank. As she sat, she pulled him toward her with her hand and kissed him gently on the lips. Although her fingers felt cool, her lips were warm against his. He let go of her hand and embraced her in his arms. For a brief moment they held each other, Rhysdale resting her cool blue cheek upon his shoulder.

"I've missed you so, William," She whispered.

"Aye, I've missed yeh too," he murmured.

Rhysdale gently pulled away and grasped both her hands in his. "Did you do as I suggested?" she asked.

William looked at her. Her eyes looked red-rimmed, as if she had been crying. *Something's wrong*, he thought.

"Are yeh upset with me then?" William asked.

"What? No." she replied. Her eyes met his, and they moved back and forth rapidly, as if she was memorizing lines in a book.

She's reading me, he thought. *She's reading my mind.* Relieved that he wouldn't have to speak, he surrendered his thoughts to her.

She smiled at him, relief seemingly washing over her face. "Good!" she spoke, "I'm glad you saw the Lady. What an honor that must have been!"

"But what did she mean to 'go where your people draw water from'?" William asked.

"I believe those places are what your people call wells. Wells are inhabited by sprites. I believe you are to pay tribute to a sprite. Sprites hold many answers, but they will tell nothing without a tribute." She smiled, her skin a dark shade of blue, her green eyes sparkling with realization.

"So," William looked down, fearing to stare at her while trying hard to focus, "I just drop this coin into the nearest well and I'll get my answer then?"

"No, no, it has to be the right well," Rhysdale sighed.

"Well, how'll I know which is the right well?" He was starting to get frustrated, feeling like he was the bait in a cat and mouse game.

"William, you are embodying the powers of the Water Element. You will know when you find the right well. You will just have to trust your instincts," she smiled at him again, patting his hand gently.

"But how am I embodying the Water Element?" William asked impatiently. "All I've ever done is paint bloody pictures of visions I've seen in the water." He pulled his hands back and crossed his arms over his chest.

"Yes, you have." Rhysdale answered, pulling her hands back and placing them in her lap. "But you can do more now. You've done a few things, and you are capable of much more. You just haven't realized your potential yet...," her voice trailed off as she looked down into the depth of the water.

Her expression changed and William sensed she was afraid. "Oh no," she whispered. "They've noticed I've gone." She began to lift off the bank. "I must go, William. Please remember not to use the coin until you've found the right well. Perhaps while you are away in America?"

"How'd ya—," William muttered.

She cut him off. "Many new things and people will await you. But be careful," she leaned forward and kissed him on the lips, "I will not rest easy until I set my eyes upon your face once again." She looked into the water where an eerie green glow was emitting from below.

"I must go! Safe journey, my beloved friend." With those parting words she dove into the water and disappeared. William watched as the ripples of water moved away until all that was left was a motionless pool. He eased himself up with creaky knees and hobbled up the path toward his car. His head felt full of information, and his heart weighed heavy with sorrow. Spring felt like it was an eternity away. For once in his life, time seemed to move slower than him.

CHAPTER 18

Positioning himself behind the largest tree he could find at the back of the castle, Gabe reveled in how fortuitous it was that he could see the Taekyrs' exit from the castle without being discovered himself.

Gabe stood, leaning slightly against the tree, staring at the castle's impressive stone architecture. Though he had been inside it many times and knew the place like the back of his hand, he still marveled at its immense stature and its beauty. He watched as lights flickered in some of the upper windows as servants bustled through the rooms completing their duties. As the sun went down in the sky, he saw the silver and blue glimmer from the uniforms of two Guard Royale as they appeared on the roof and lowered the flags for the night, their movement smooth and orderly. The sun continued to sink in the horizon, and as the moon rose in the darkening sky he saw the orange glow of light emanating from within the Taekyrs' stable, the glow periodically interrupted by the shadows of the activities of the Taekyrs inside.

Although he was several meters away, Gabe could hear the murmur of a familiar voice. He knew that voice. Michael. He felt his upper lip rise as if he were holding back a snarl. "Traitorous bastard," he whispered. No wonder the Queen had her doubts. *She shoulda banished him a long time ago*, he thought. *We both were betrayed*, he shuddered. *I don't know which one was worse.*

The shadows in the orange glow began to darken even more and Gabe crouched further down and closer to the tree, his cheek resting on the cool moss-covered bark. Several of the creatures were lining up in the entryway until suddenly, as if they had choreographed the move, they leapt from the edge and soared into the sky like a cloud of large bats. And then, as quickly as they appeared, they disappeared as a group into the night.

Gabe waited. He knew by sight that the full flock had not left the castle. *Be patient, just wait*, he told himself.

He waited. Ten minutes, then 20 more. He knew to expect something else, he could feel it inside. And so he waited another 20 minutes. A small man, no bigger than Gabe, appeared in the orange glow of the doorframe flanked by a smaller Taekyr. *Michael,* he guessed correctly. Michael waved his hands in the air and the lone Taekyr ducked as if dodging an anticipated blow before nodding meekly, its head bowed in submission. It ascended alone into the sky, and Michael watched from the doorway as the creature disappeared into the night. He turned slowly on his heels before his dark figure disappeared back into the castle.

Gabe watched the opening for a minute more before quietly extricating himself from his place of surveillance and silently moving through the trees and into the forest.

This lone Taekyr was definitely not performing his regular duties. *Curious, though. I wonder where he's going?*

Gabe's eyes widened as the realization sunk in. *Sara! I'd better go and warn her!* He headed through the forest, barreling through the brush, hoping like hell he wouldn't be too late a second time. *It just might be the last*, he thought as he stomped toward the stone marker that would transport him to the human world.

***

The sound of Sara's giggles resonated through the air. Joe was suppressing a laugh, mostly because Abby stood firmly with her arms across her chest and an expression of grim frustration on her face that made her look dangerously close to screaming. Sara followed Joe's uncomfortable glance at Abby and the giggles instantly caught in her throat. Abby continued to glare at them, the silence making them squirm nervously.

"Are you two finished, then?" Abby asked, her arms still crossed, her foot tapping against the cold ground. Joe and Sara nodded mutely.

"Good." Abby stated flatly. "We really have to get it together, alright?"

Joe and Sara nodded again in unison.

"Now, Joe," Abby continued. "What exactly have you tried to do?"

"Don't show her that ground-splitting thing," Sara pleaded. "I've got underground pipes and a well out here." Sara smiled. "It would be hard to explain that kind of damage to a plumber, and it would be difficult and expensive to repair in winter."

"What 'ground-splitting thing'?" Abby looked demandingly at Joe.

"Well, I can touch the ground, you know, really feel the earth." Joe answered quietly. "Sometimes, the earth heaves up to me, sometimes the ground splits, and sometimes it causes, you know, earthquakes." Abby looked at Joe intently, absorbing everything he said.

"Did you say you can cause earthquakes?" Abby asked.

"Yes." Joe answered simply.

Abby looked at him accusingly. "Did you cause that big one that happened in September?"

Joe's brow furrowed pensively. He did cause an earthquake in September, but he had to think. Did he cause the first one? "No, Ab," Joe answered. "The first one I felt coming. It was like I knew it was coming. The aftershock I thought I had caused. But it's strange, you know? I never had these abilities before that earthquake. It's almost like it was the start of all of this."

Sara and Abby exchanged looks, their faces sharing the same look of shock and realization.

"You know, Ab," Sara began, "It seems that it was the starting point for all three of us."

Abby looked at her somewhat annoyed. "Yeah, Sara, I just figured that out too."

Abby leaned against the fence, staring at the back of Sara's barn for a moment. Her dark eyes narrowed as she searched her memory. Yes, it did seem like that moment was the beginning. Unless, of course, she counted the moment that she glimpsed Gabe in the copse of trees after the Art in the Park show. *But he didn't actually speak to me or even make his presence known, really. He just disappeared after I glimpsed him, leaving me to wonder if I was imagining a bizarre apparition or something.* Abby started to feel annoyed at Gabe. How come he had spoken to Sara and Joe and not her?

"Hey, Ab," Sara broke into her thoughts. "You still with us?"

Abby turned sharply toward Sara. Sara stepped back abruptly. Abby could feel Fire rising up once inside her, blurring her vision, filling her up with its fiery ferocity. Abby sensed Sara felt intimidated and fought to keep Fire banked. *What the hell is wrong with me?* Abby forced a smile. *Hope I toned it down enough,* she thought.

"Yeah, I'm still here." Abby replied. "Thanks, Sara." Abby turned her attention back to Joe. "So is there anything else you know you can do?" She looked at him expectantly.

Joe started to feel uncomfortable under her gaze. He didn't want to tell her because he feared she would ask questions he just wasn't ready to answer, especially with Sara sitting right beside him. He thought that things were going great, and he feared that if he revealed too much she might change her mind about him. On the other hand, though, Abby's mood was so unpredictable. He feared that by not revealing all he was aware of Abby would explode at him and unleash the force of a volcano on him. He didn't really know the extent of her powers, but he was respectful of fire and did not want to feel its warmth searing his skin.

"Well," Joe started, squirming a little under Abby's continued gaze, "I can animate beings I create out of clay." There, he said it. He returned Abby's gaze smiling slightly.

"Wow! Really?" Sara said enthusiastically. "That is so cool!" Sara nodded her head and smiled her approval as she glanced toward Joe and Abby.

Abby frowned slightly. "How did you figure that one out?"

He started to feel warm under her penetrating stare. Was she turning up the heat, or was it just him?

Joe sighed and looked back at Abby, a look of resignation on his face. "Abby, I work with clay, remember? It just happened one day when I was working, that's all."

"Oh," Abby's eyebrows relaxed, and her glare began to fade.

"Abby," Joe asked, "You work with fire, making your jewelry and sculptures, right?"

Abby nodded.

"Haven't you found any part of your abilities through your work?"

Abby smiled at Joe. "Well, I can light my torch without using a spark lighter, but apart from that, I turn everything I set the flame to into piles of slag. So I guess it would be safe to say that my ability is impeding, not aiding my work." Abby shrugged her shoulders. She ran a hand through her dark hair and turned away as her eyes began to brim with tears.

Sara stepped forward and placed her hand on Abby's shoulder and gave her a reassuring squeeze. "It's okay, Ab. We'll figure it out. It's just that control thing again. You'll be able to work soon; don't you worry, alright?"

Abby smiled and placed her hand over Sara's, giving her a gentle squeeze back.

"I know, Sara, it'll be fine. It's just sometimes," Abby sighed and turned back toward Sara and Joe, "sometimes it just seems like too much all at once. Sometimes, I feel like they picked the wrong person."

"Nah," Sara replied, "You're just not ready yet. You'll be ready soon enough."

"Speaking of which," Abby straightened, her voice getting stronger, "we should start figuring out how we can use our powers, maybe even figure out how to combine them together, in case of another attack."

"Sounds good to me," Joe replied.

"Me too," Sara agreed.

"Good," said Abby. "Let's get to work."

Sara, Joe, and Abby spent the better part of the day behind Sara's barn showing each other what they could do, encouraging each other, and giving gentle advice on how to improve their abilities. Although Abby did require a great deal more practice in using control, Joe found that she was not particularly fond of criticism. Sara was the only one she seemed to take criticism from, but Sara proved that she could soften her words to the point that Abby would respond well to her.

Joe smiled as he watched Sara shriek with delight as the snowballs she threw at Abby were quickly intercepted and melted midair by her friend's fireballs. It was when Joe saw Abby's smiles in response to Sara's squeals that he recognized what a great friendship they had. He watched Sara flick a lock of her blonde hair off her face and cup and blow on her mitten-clad hands.

"Brr!" Sara exclaimed, stomping her feet, "I'm getting cold! Let's take a break, shall we?"

Sara beckoned Abby over to an old barrel filled with leaves, twigs, and paper and coaxed Abby to light it. Soon the two women were standing around the barrel and warming themselves by the gentle, radiant fire that had been produced within.

"Come on, Joe," Abby urged, waving her arm, "come get warm."

Joe walked slowly over to the barrel and stood between the two women, holding his hands out to gain the warmth of the fire. It felt good, really good to get warm. He hadn't realized just how cold it was getting. But, it was to be expected at this time of year, especially in Michigan. They stood for a few moments idly chatting by the fire. Abby was more human and less fire-like when they were just talking, especially when she spoke of her husband, Dan. Joe listened quietly as she talked.

"I had to tell him something, Sara. I mean, I blew the damn door off my studio! And he saw it, can you imagine?" Abby's eyes lost their crazed look, and her dark eyes looked even deeper. "I've never kept a secret from him in my whole life, not once. *Ever.*" Abby looked over to Joe. "I know I've changed, and I know at times I've acted, well, erratic. But if something is happening with me, well, he needs to know. I love him and I couldn't bear to lose him. No secret is worth keeping if I lose him." Abby looked at Sara. "He knows that something is going on with you, too. But that is all I've told him. I hope you aren't angry with me for telling him that much."

Sara smiled at Abby. "No, Ab, I'm not angry. In fact, I think it would be a good idea for Dan to know what's going on. Perhaps we can benefit from having advice from someone who isn't directly involved. You know, a different perspective. What do you think, Joe?"

Joe looked at Abby, who was looking at him expectantly. He turned his gaze back to the fire. Joe had never met Abby's husband. *The guy must have the patience of a saint to deal with her right now*, he mused to himself. But Joe trusted Sara's instincts above all else. So far she had been right about everything and proven she was a lot more capable than most people gave her credit for. Joe looked over to Sara.

"Sure, I think it's a good idea too. " Joe agreed. "When do I get to meet him?"

Both women smiled, and Abby nudged him gently with her elbow. "You and Sara can come over for dinner sometime, okay?" I'll let you both know when it is a good time."

"Okay."

"Hey, Joe?"

"Yeah, Ab?"

"Thanks."

"No probs, Ab."

A light snow began to fall as darkness enveloped the world around them and the light from the fire and the moon gently illuminated the area they were working in behind Sara's barn. Joe had been able to make defensive hills rise in front of the three of them, Sara was able to surround them all within a protective whirlwind, and Abby alternated throwing fireballs and shooting snowflakes with tiny pinpricks of flames. The day had been long, but it had served its purpose. They were able to work together, regardless of how difficult it had seemed. Joe smiled. It had been a long time since he had felt like he belonged somewhere. It felt good, but he felt a pang of regret.

I should go home and visit my family for the holidays, he thought. *If only for a few days.* Joe's thoughts were interrupted as a snowball impacted with the back of his neck, sending chunks of snow and frozen ice down the back of his jacket and down his shirt.

"Hey!" he yelled, jumping up and whirling around to see Sara giggling and retreating behind one of the hills he had created, a second snowball in her hand, ready to be thrown.

Joe bent down and scooped up some snow, packing it into a ball. Abby retreated behind one of the other hills in an attempt to avoid presenting herself as a viable target to either of them.

Joe packed the snow into a ball and slowly approached the hill. With a wave of his hand the hill flattened.

"Hey! No fair!" Sara yelled as Joe tossed the snowball at her, catching in the shoulder. Sara caught a gust of wind and rose up into the sky above Joe, throwing her snowball at him and dropping it squarely on top of his head.

"Hah!" Sara yelled triumphantly as she glided back down and hopped to the ground. Joe grabbed an armload of snow and dumped it on Sara.

"Yah! That's cold!" Sara yelled, "I'm gonna get you!" Sara threw herself at Joe, laughing and giggling as they tussled on the snow-covered ground. Joe was laughing hysterically, unable to stop long enough to prevent her from pinning him to the ground. She sat on his chest, her hands on his wrists, her face hovering over his. She bent down to kiss him, and at that moment they both heard a commotion in the bushes like the squawking of two birds fighting. Abby came running over alert and excited.

"Hey, you two," she whispered loudly, "Something's going on over there. Hurry!"

Abby darted toward the location of the scuffling, her body crouched liked a cat, her hands already beginning to glow red.

"Get up!" Sara rolled off Joe and pulled him up with one hand. "We'd better follow in case she ends up frying two geese or something."

Sara kept a hold of his hand as they followed Abby at a discrete distance, her hands two beacons against the dark of night.

Abby moved swiftly into the woods at the edge of the field, darting crouched behind trees as she moved closer to the sound in the woods. *Yeah, it sounds somewhat bird-like, but it definitely isn't two birds fighting*, Abby surmised.

She moved behind another tree. She was getting closer. She strained to decipher all the sounds. Abby moved swiftly behind another tree. She could hear Joe and Sara crashing through the forest behind her.

"Shh!" She whispered loudly over her shoulder. She could just about make out the outline of *something* up ahead.

Abby moved closer using another tree for cover, crouching behind it while surveying the area in front of her. *Two creatures*, she could definitely make out the dark outlines of two creatures. One looked like a bird, the other, like a man. Maybe... maybe a small man. They were definitely fighting, and one of the creatures was shrieking like a wounded bird. It was high and piercing, and Abby found herself wincing as the shrill sound filled her head, vibrating all her nerves. *If only I could see better*, she thought.

Joe and Sara crouched down behind her. "What is it?" Sara whispered.

"I'm not sure yet," Abby answered quietly. "But I've got an idea. When it gets bright, Sara, you trap that creature. Joe, you trap the other, got it?"

Sara and Joe exchanged glances. Before they had a chance to respond, Abby had stood up and stepped away from the tree and held her hands out from her body, her palms facing the sky, sending two sparks of light high into the air, illuminating the night sky and the area in front of her. Both creatures stopped moving, frozen in place by the appearance of such bright light.

(*Burn! Burn!*) The voice in her head screamed at her. Abby fought to stay in control, falling to her knees on the snow-covered ground. *Stay here, stay focused*, she commanded herself.

Sara and Joe darted past her. Sara surrounded the dark creature in a vortex of wind as Joe approached the other figure.

"Don't cha dare try anythin', Joe, I'm doing ya a favor," a familiar voice snapped at him. Joe looked closer. He recognized the moleskin jacket and the craggy, beard-covered face peeping out from under a fur hat that a Bolshevik would be proud of.

"Gabe, is that you?" Joe stepped forward to see more clearly.

"Aye, it's me, ya idiot," Gabe grumbled. "I came to warn Sara that she was being spied on when I caught the bugger in the act."

Sara shrieked with delight. "I caught it! I caught it!" The Taekyr was trapped helpless in the vortex, squealing in frustration.

Gabe walked over to her, a smile on his face. "Lady Sara, don't cha think I helped a little?"

Sara smiled down at him and touched his shoulder gently with one hand. "Well, of course you did! Bravo!"

Abby rose and stepped forward, a grim look on her face. "So, how long do you think it's been watching us?" she asked Gabe.

"Long enough to get a good idea of who ya are and what ya were doin'," Gabe answered flatly.

"So what do we do with him now?" Abby asked impatiently. "Should we kill him?" Her right hand started to glow.

The Taekyr started to squeal and shriek even louder as it thrashed powerless in the vortex.

"No!" Sara cried out. "We can't hurt it! Poor creature! Can't you see how scared it is?"

Abby looked at Sara, her mouth slightly open. "Isn't this one of your flying monkey creatures that tried to attack you?"

"Well, yes," Sara admitted.

"He's obviously seen too much. Now he can be a threat to our," Abby searched for a word, "mission."

"Aye, the hot-head's got a point," Gabe agreed.

"Hey, I have a name you know. It's Abby," Abby spat at him angrily.

"Sorry," Gabe replied quickly, looking down at his boot. He looked over at Sara. "So what do ya propose we do with him then? If he goes back, I have to report him as a traitor and he could be sentenced to death. If he returns to his master and passes on what he's seen, then we're all in for it. If his master discovers he's been captured, he may kill him anyway. The pitiful creature may be just as good as dead."

The Taekyr folded his papery wings down and hung his head, whimpering softly. His large eyes appeared even moister. Could such a creature cry with self-pity? Sara couldn't guess. She just felt confused and torn between protecting the creature and protecting them. It looked very sad and vulnerable to her.

"Well, I have a barn," Sara suggested. "It used to have horses, but now it's empty. Can't I keep him here tied up or something?"

Gabe looked at her with astonishment, amazed that she could take pity on one of the creatures that could have killed her not so long ago. *Perhaps she senses this one's youth and its reluctance to fight. Or maybe she is just too trusting. Still . . .*

The creature's wings had been punctured in the scuffle. One wing bore two holes in its papery membrane. That would render it unable to fly.

"Sara, drop the wind for a moment," Gabe asked.

Sara opened her mouth to say something but quickly closed it and did as Gabe requested. Gabe walked closer to the creature. It whimpered and cowered as he drew closer.

"Taekyr!" Gabe spoke sternly. "You've been working as a spy for a traitor."

The Taekyr nodded mutely.

"Your actions are punishable by death, but this Lady has spoken to spare yer worthless life. You now owe her yer life. Understand?"

"Yes." The Taekyr croaked meekly.

Gabe continued, "Yeh will stay here with Lady Sara and do as she says 'til she releases yeh from her debt. Do yeh agree to this?"

The Taekyr looked at Gabe and then to Sara. He did not want to be involved in a battle; he just wanted to return to his brood. He couldn't do that if he were dead. He nodded.

"I give my word that I will stay with Lady Sara until I am released from my debt." The Taekyr bowed low to Sara, spreading its damaged wings prostrate on the ground.

Gabe looked over to Abby. "If he tries to escape, yeh can kill him."

"Gee, thanks," Abby replied tartly.

Sara was hopping up and down with excitement. "Let's go back to the barn so I can show our new guest where he'll be staying. You are a 'he' aren't you?"

"Yes," the creature answered flatly.

"I knew it!" Sara exclaimed. "Come on, everybody, let's go!" she shouted as she guided the creature on a wisp of wind back toward the barn.

"I can't believe it," Abby said, shaking her head as she followed. "Sara's got a new pet."

Taekyr's don't make fer good pets," Gabe interjected, rubbing his hand through his beard. "They are used fer other tasks generally."

"Like what?" Abby asked.

Gabe looked at Abby. *Now's not the time to tell her*, he thought. Abby looked at him awaiting an answer.

"They're not very bright," Gabe finally answered.

"I hope not," Abby replied, "or we're in some deep shit if it does escape."

"Don't worry," Gabe reassured. "I think it will like Sara much better than its master."

Abby smiled. "Sara is good with pets."

Gabe smiled back. "I'm not at all surprised at that." Laughing, they followed Sara, the Taekyr, and Joe through the trees as the moonlight sparkling off the lightly falling snow illuminated their way.

CHAPTER 19

As the tapping of his toes against the stone floor reverberated throughout the long corridor a cacophony of sound invaded the stillness with its endless echo. His very presence in the hallway caused the torchlight to flicker and cast shadows upon the walls. Michael repressed the urge to pace the floor like an agitated animal. He forced his heels together in a feeble attempt to remain at a stock-still attention stance, though his frustration and impatience increased as he continued to stand his watchful vigil. He stood silently alone just inside the stone entryway that the Taekyrs used to exit the castle at sunset and return through just before sunrise. A few of the creatures flit into the doorway, returning with pouches full of food for their broods. Some of them carried marked children in their pouches, as was their task. The Taekyrs' main purpose was to take human children that were marked and replace them with changelings: near exact replicas of the human children they were to replace, the only difference between them being that the changelings were fragile and would not thrive. The changelings would soon wither, leaving their human parents to believe that their own children had died. Michael didn't really understand or question how the Taekyrs knew which children were marked or how they received the changelings. He accepted that his duty was to command them, even if he didn't understand all there was about them. He continued to silently observe their activity while he maintained his guard.

As it drew nearer to sunrise, fewer Taekyrs entered, and there was still no sign of the one he had singled out for surveillance of the Air Element. Where could it have been? It had not returned for two days now. Occasionally they wouldn't make it back in time for sunset and would roost in the human realm. If they were trapped in the sunlight they would turn to stone and remain frozen until the sun dipped down again. Though it didn't hurt or cause them pain, it would render them vulnerable if an enemy chose to trap or destroy them. Taekyrs were also creatures of habit, and they had strong bonds with their brood mates. Michael noticed that the creatures usually bonded with a mate for life. It wasn't likely that the creature would willingly absent itself for two nights in a row. He did not know what would cause the creature to be gone for such a long period of time. *Perhaps she killed it*, he speculated. When the sun rose on the horizon, the stables went silent as the flock of Taekyrs succumbed to their daily slumber. If the creature was to return, it definitely would have been back long before now.

Michael turned from the opening and strode down the stone corridor and wended his way to his quarters on the far side of the castle. He was quartered close enough to the Taekyrs to care for them but far enough that he would not be overwhelmed by their scent and bird-like chatter.

Michael opened the door to his cell and strode through, quickly closing it behind him. He sat down on the lone chair placed next to his tightly-made bed in his spartanly furnished room and wiped the dust from his boots so that the bright, high-gloss polish reappeared. He stood in front of his mirror, adjusted the front of his steel gray uniform jacket, and quickly exited the room again.

Thaddeus will not be pleased, he thought grimly as he clasped his hands behind him and strode out the east exit. He stood outside the doorway surveying the area, and once he was satisfied there was no one observing him, he strode quietly into the forest and toward the stone Omphalos that would transport him to the human world.

Michael stood in front of the stone Omphalos. Even though it was made for individuals taller than he, it was not difficult for him to touch the stone or even to see the strange markings and symbols carved into the top of it. The markings were not familiar to him, but the symbols were known to those whose magic had woven the Veil that separated his world from the human one. Michael placed his hand on the marker, closed his eyes, and focused his thoughts on his destination. When he opened his eyes he found himself in a wooded area only slightly different than the one he left. If he hadn't known any better, he might have been apt to believe that he had not traveled at all: there was no sensation of change that came with passing through the Veil.

Michael moved his hands to his side and navigated quietly through the trees, careful to discreetly scan the area around him. The disappearance of the Taekyr made him wary that he could also be under surveillance, and he did not wish to face the wrath of Thaddeus if his location and involvement were revealed before he was ready to implement his plans.

Michael stepped out of the forest at the side of a narrow asphalt road. He walked parallel to it at the edge of the tree line, following it as it snaked its way toward the small town that was visible just a few miles down the road. It was colder here, he observed, much colder than the land he just left. Michael could feel the chill of the air beginning to nip at his hands, and he deftly pulled his leather gloves out from a uniform pocket and tugged them on. He began to move quicker now, his body motivated by the cold, but when he was hit with the sudden realization that he may have looked like he was marching, he forced himself to slow his pace to that of a casual stride. His less than average height and uniform would set him apart from the humans he was trying to blend in with, but he was confident he would not draw undue attention to himself if he continued forward with purpose.

Michael reached the strip of stores that seemed to appear from nowhere as the road instantly turned into Main Street. *Typical small human town*, he noted as he walked past a bar, a convenience store, a Mega Dollar store, and a dress shop. A lawyer's office, hardware store, and insurance office with nearly identical brick facades mirrored them on the opposite side of the street. Michael paused in front of the next store. "Ye Olde Bookstore," the sign proclaimed. "New, used, and rare books bought and sold here," another sign in the window advertised. Above it, a sign that read, "Visit Our eBay Store Online!" Michael grasped the brass knob and turned it while simultaneously pushing the heavy wooden door open. The tinkling of bells being disturbed on the back of the door announced his entrance, and he quickly shut the door to silence them. He stood for a moment behind the door waiting and listening to see if anyone was alerted to his presence, his eyes scanning the room for anything or anyone out of the ordinary.

Michael could hear voices in conversation in the next room.

"*Tales of the Arabian Nights?*"

Thaddeus' voice echoed in the room as Michael stood in the entryway and peered into the main store room. It was an immense space with old, dusty bookcases lining every wall, complemented by the worn mahogany-stained and varnished wooden floor and the over-sized rectangular wooden table in the center, piled high with neatly stacked books. A small, average-looking bald man with large eyeglasses was perusing a two-volume set, turning the leather-clad covers over in his hands. He murmured an appreciative response.

"Do you have a preference for the translation or print edition?" Thaddeus inquired politely.

The man nodded and replied something inaudible that Michael could not catch. As he bent down to pick up another tome, Thaddeus spied Michael standing in the alcove. He moved quickly and said to the man,

"Please take your time and browse our selections. I shall return in just a moment."

Without waiting for a response, he slipped into the alcove to join Michael and proceeded to lead him down the hall to the rear of the store, opening his office door and motioning him inside.

"Wait here," he whispered. "I shall have this transaction wrapped up in a few minutes. Do not leave my office." Thaddeus turned on his heel and closed the door swiftly and quietly behind him.

Michael stood inside the dark, gloomy room and eyed the familiar furniture. He chose to stand next to the chair instead of sitting in the hopes that this visit would not be very long if he remained standing. Michael's eyes dropped to the large wooden desk in front of him. The top was covered with papers mostly dealing with the day-to-day operation of the bookstore. He had to admit that Thaddeus was quite good at being a bookseller; he appeared to enjoy himself immensely while conducting his business. At least, that was the impression Michael got when he observed Thaddeus in action.

After a few moments, Michael could hear Thaddeus talking in the alcove and the murmur of the customer's voice in reply. He heard the tinkling sound of the bells heralding the departure of the gentleman through the front door and then the sound of Thaddeus' footsteps down the hall. Michael turned to face the door as Thaddeus turned the knob and entered the room. "Another satisfied customer," Thaddeus said a hint of pride in his voice. "That's the third one today."

He strode behind his desk and sat down in the large chair behind it. Sitting up straight, he placed his hands atop his desk and folded them together. His blue eyes focused on Michael's form and he asked, "So, what have you to report?"

"I sent a lone Taekyr on a surveillance mission to watch the actions of the Air Element," Michael began, "in the hopes that it could secretly gather more information on her tactical strengths and weaknesses, and also to find out if she has made contact with any of the other vessels."

"And what did you find out?" Thaddeus asked a sinister smile on his face.

"Well, actually, nothing, sir."

"Nothing?"

"No, sir. The Taekyr has not returned at all. That was two days ago."

Thaddeus pressed his fingertips together, and his eyes grew darker. He stared at Michael, his eyes almost boring holes in him before he spoke.

"Do you believe our friend has been discovered?"

Michael stepped forward, his back straight, his head held high as he looked over the top of the desk. "I don't believe so, otherwise there would be guards awaiting me at my duty station."

"Yes, true." Thaddeus agreed, leaning back in his chair, placing his arms on the arm rests, his hands curling around the round wooden ends.

"But still, perhaps the Taekyr, what was his name?"

"Oogan, sir."

"This Oogan, perhaps he has been captured," Thaddeus speculated. "How much does he know about our operations?"

"Very little," Michael replied curtly. "He was informed that he was only to observe and report back with the information he gathered. But the creatures do talk amongst their broods. Perhaps he was made aware of the failure of the previous mission."

"Well," Thaddeus rose. "I think we should make finding this creature a priority. Had he been born in the castle?"

"Yes, sir," Michael answered, "and he was banded at that time."

"Excellent." Thaddeus replied, moving to the front of his desk. "You will track him magically through his band and discover if he is alive or dead. If he is alive, we will take the necessary steps to recover him."

"Should that be done immediately?" Michael asked.

"No." Thaddeus was standing in front of him now, his size and proximity slightly intimidating to Michael. Thaddeus smiled as if sensing his discomfort. "We will wait a little while longer. Perhaps if he has survived, he can provide us with even more information that could aid us in our mission."

"Very well, sir." Michael agreed.

"Well, I will follow you out then," Thaddeus said as he strode over to the door. "I have an appointment with a few old friends that may need a little, how should I say it? Ah, yes, *coaxing*, to return to their old alliance."

"Anyone I know, sir?" Michael enquired as he strode into the hallway.

"I'll let you know when I am successful," Thaddeus replied smiling, "just in case things don't go as planned. The less you know at this point, the better." Thaddeus closed the office door behind him and they both made their way silently down the hall. Michael said goodbye, strode out the door, and made his way quickly down the street toward the tree line.

He looked back over his shoulder and saw Thaddeus at the store front door fumbling with a set of keys before locking the door.

Way too calm, Michael thought. *He is not at all as I expected.* He had never doubted Thaddeus' ability before, and yet he felt as if this attitude of his may lead to failure. He didn't know whether Thaddeus was just confident or if he was being arrogant. Sometimes it was difficult to tell the difference between the two.

I've got too much riding on this, Michael thought, his heart pounding in his chest. *I hope the bastard's right.* Michael slipped into the forest and made his way toward the stone Omphalos that would take him home.

***

A light snow was falling on the windshield of Joe's Chevy truck as he drove purposefully down the Michigan State Highway. It was really just an average road with two lanes flanked by the occasional farm house or a gas station. Periodically, it would run through the center of a small town and would be flanked by tightly-compacted storefronts. Some would advertise "Liquor, Wine, Lotto," while others would always be a mixture of mill stores, supermarkets, five and dime stores, and hardware stores. And in each town there would be at least one stoplight and a sign that the highway was now "Main Street", at least until you passed the 55mph speed limit sign where the state highway sign would miraculously appear, but both signs would always be preceded by a well-worn wooden one that said "Thanks for Visiting! Come Back Soon!"

How many of these little towns and road signs had he passed? Joe couldn't remember. He knew the way so well that he took it for granted that there were other places in between along the way. And he had a lot on his mind too. He had spent his last day at school attempting to get his class to do some serious work, but the students too were excited and distracted by the thought of having two whole weeks off school. They were busy talking excitedly about their holiday plans and whether they would be spending time with family or anticipating what they would get for Christmas. In the end he had surrendered to their desire to sit and talk and found that both individually and collectively they were a great bunch of kids. When the bell had rung he waved them out with a "have a happy holiday! See you next year!" But before they left one of his more outspoken and creative students, Mary, slid up to his desk with an envelope and thrust it toward him.

"We all pitched in to get you this, Mr. Asine," she said rapidly, a big smile on her face. "Merry Christmas!"

"Merry Christmas to you too, Mary." He said. "Thank you all. Merry Christmas!" he yelled toward the doorway to the backs of his retreating students.

Mary turned on her heel, her brown hair bouncing along her back as she had grabbed her book bag and strode from the room. Joe opened the envelope and was surprised to find a gift certificate for a local pottery supply store. He hadn't been expecting anything at all, but he was moved by the practical and thoughtful gift.

Joe had packed up his suitcases and loaded them into his truck as soon as he got home from school. Part of him wanted to stay and spend Christmas with Sara. Another part of him wanted to take her with him up to his mother's to spend Christmas with his family, but he knew it wouldn't have been a good idea to ask. Their relationship hadn't progressed to the really serious stage, and Joe felt that even making or suggesting sleeping arrangements would have been awkward. Their relationship was moving at a comfortably slow pace, and he was okay with that. Best that he tell his family about her first before springing her upon them. *At least we will spend New Year's Eve together*, he thought happily.

Joe's eyes moved from the windshield to the clock on the dash. Even when correcting for the hour he should have set the clock back in the fall, he calculated he had been on the road less than half an hour.

Must have passed fewer towns than I thought. He noticed that the sky darkened and the snow continued to fall steadily. Joe was wrapped up in so many thoughts, but time was at a premium. He had been working with Sara and Abby as much as he could to develop his abilities and defensive strategies in case, no, make that *when*, they were attacked again. So far there had been no attempts or signs of any surveillance on them since they helped Gabe capture the creature he called a Taekyr. They were lucky that there was only one creature and that it had only been watching them rather than a group of them ready to attack the Vessels as they had Sara. The capture of the creature served as a wake-up call for the three of them. They would have to exercise more caution in how they conducted their training, and afterward they had moved their activities to inside Sara's barn. Sara had only agreed to using the barn for training after insisting each of them provide a fire extinguisher and to keep it near them at all times. Abby had rolled her eyes at the suggestion, but she acquiesced after the first indoor session. They had been training daily, and the rest of his time comprised of working on his lesson plans for school, getting some pieces built and fired for upcoming summer shows, and trying to find free time to spend with Sara.

Joe sighed and relaxed his grip on the steering wheel. Perhaps it was good that he was coming home alone. It would be a good time to unwind; he didn't realize how much he missed his mother and siblings. Everyone was so scattered around now; it would be good to see everyone and catch up.

After what felt like an eternity of driving through the ever-increasing snow and the dark of nightfall, Joe turned off the highway and down the side road. The snow was much deeper here, he noticed, and the road hadn't been plowed or sanded yet. Joe edged his truck along, following in the tire tracks of a vehicle that had been down the road previously, the center lines and the shoulders of the road obscured by the blanket of snow.

Joe crept his truck along slowly, following in the tracks ahead even though they were beginning to fill with snow and become somewhat obscured. *Good thing it's not too much farther*, Joe thought with relief as he sat straighter in the seat, his eyes riveted ahead into darkness of the snowy night.

The entrance to the driveway was so full of snow that Joe almost passed it. Judging from the amount of cars in the driveway and the lack of fresh tire tracks, Joe assumed that everyone else had arrived much earlier in the day.

Hope I'm not the last, he thought grimacing. As he pulled up alongside his sister Anne's station wagon, he caught a glimpse of the front window. The faces of two petite, dark-haired women and two aesthetically similar males were pressed against the glass, peering out the window expectantly.

"Oh yeah, I'm last all right." As Joe looked at their faces he cut the ignition. He grabbed his bags out of the cab and strode up the snow covered path to the front door. His mother, Mary, had already opened the door and smiled at him in greeting.

"Hi, Mom," Joe said as he put down his bags and bent down to give her a hug.

"Hey, Joe," she replied, hugging him back and patting him on the back before releasing him. "Let's get you in out of the snow and settled. Have you eaten yet?" Mary moved to the kitchen and opened the fridge. "We've already eaten, but we saved you some stew and bannock."

"Yeah, Mom, that'd be great," Joe replied, his stomach rumbling.

"Hey, Joe," his brother Derrick called as he came over and held his hand out for Joe to shake and dragged him into a bear hug.

"Hey, good to see you," Joe replied.

"Hey, no hogging!" His sister Anne protested as she pushed past Derrick to give Joe a hug too.

"You look like shit," his sister Rose declared scowling. "You need to eat. I'll help Mom get your dinner ready." And she disappeared into the kitchen.

"Hey, bro." His brother John greeted casually. "It's been a while, hasn't it?"

"Yeah, I guess so," Joe replied as John wandered back into the family room and sat down on the couch. He picked up the remote, and after he turned the television on he started flipping rapidly through channels.

"Geez, do you gotta do that, John? You know it drives me nuts!" Rose yelled from the kitchen in protest.

"Okay, okay," John replied. "I'll go slower." John deliberately slowed to flipping channels at a snail's pace. Rose seemed even more irritated as she stomped into the living room crossing her arms across her chest and tossing her head back.

"You kids settle down, okay?" Mary intoned quietly looking at John and Rose in turn. "Everyone's here now, and I want all of you to get along over the holiday, okay? I want us all to have a good time, alright? Even if it kills you." Mary stared, waiting for the two of them to reply. After they both grudgingly mumbled their assent, Mary turned her attention back to the kitchen. "Now, where was I? Oh yeah. Joe, sit down at the table, we'll fix you up."

Joe ambled into the kitchen and pulled up chairs at the well-worn wooden kitchen table. Anne had placed a spoon and a plate of bannock on the table in front of him, and Rose placed a large steaming bowl of stew directly in front of him. The smell reminded him that he hadn't eaten since lunch, and his stomach grumbled loudly.

"Eat while it's hot, Joe," Rose insisted as his two sisters sat down at the table on opposite sides of him. His mother filled a kettle and set it on the stove, flicking on the burner.

Joe dipped chunks of bannock in his stew and listened as his sisters caught him up on the details of their daily lives.

"David has the kids on his own tonight," Rose had answered brightly when Joe had asked where his niece and nephew were. "He's going to bring them up tomorrow morning. He offered to do that so I could spend a little quality time with Mom and you guys. Personally, I think it's good for him. It'll make him appreciate me all the more."

Rose smiled and pushed the plate of bannock closer to Joe. He took up another piece and tore it before dipping it in his stew. Mary set down a pot of tea and some mugs on the table and sat at the opposite end of the table directly across from Joe, pouring her own cup of tea and sipping at it while listening to the conversation.

"Well, I'm done with exams now," Anne offered excitedly. "New semester starts in January. Who knows? Maybe I'll end up teaching too!"

Mary smiled at her proudly. "As long as that's what you want to do. Just finish your degree and then decide."

"Yeah, Ma," Anne replied, winking at Joe.

Once he had eaten his fill, Joe sat at the table with his Mom and sisters idly chatting and emptying the tea pot. Eventually, his brothers grew bored with the TV.

"How come she's got cable now after we've all moved out?" John declared indignantly. He also migrated into the kitchen to join them and add to the lively conversation.

Joe watched as his sisters, brothers, and mother chatted animatedly about nothing in particular. *It's just like old times*, he thought. The faces may have changed, but the characters have still managed to stay the same. Age, time, and distance influenced his family in much the same way they do for all families. Looking around the room at everyone, he marveled at how much his family changed and how little it mattered. They still were able to get together for holidays and pick up where they left off. How was that possible? He smiled, grateful that he had come, grateful that he had such a great family. *If only Dad....*

"Hey, Joe, ya alright?" his brother Derrick looked over at him, his brow furrowed, his voice deep.

"Huh? Oh yeah, I'm fine," Joe yawned and rubbed his eyes. "I guess I'm just driftin' off a bit."

"Look at the time!" Mary declared, pointing at the tea pot-shaped kitchen clock perched on the wall over the sink. "We should all be getting to bed. It's nearly tomorrow." Everyone rose from the table and the chairs scraped across the floor in unison.

"You all know where you're staying tonight. Same as always," Mary declared. "Last one to bed turns out the lights. Goodnight." They all murmured their goodnights as she strode down the hall to her room. Joe moved into his old room, pulled off his clothes, threw on a set of sweatpants, and climbed into his old bed, pulling the covers up to his chin.

Safe. He felt safe and relaxed. Joe smiled; he knew the reason. It just felt damn good to be home again. He closed his eyes, turned on his side, and let sleep take hold of him.

CHAPTER 20

Joe rose to the smell of coffee and the clatter of pots and pans being pulled out and set back reorganized into the cupboards.

"Shh, Rose! You'll wake the rest of the house up!" Mary scolded her daughter in a loud whisper.

"Ah, Ma, don't worry about it. They'll be getting up soon enough," Rose replied as she continued to pull pots out of the cupboard and bang them on the countertop. "Besides, we need to get cooking. Everyone else will be arriving today."

"What time are David and the kids heading over?"

"Not soon enough," Rose had replied, "Damn, I miss 'em, and it's only been one night."

Joe smiled listening to the two women through the door. He threw on his jeans and a t-shirt and stepped out of the bedroom and into the kitchen.

"Morning, Joe." Mary greeted him as he entered the kitchen and extracted a coffee mug from the cupboard. "Sugar's on the table," she motioned with a wave of her hand.

"Thanks, Mom." Joe poured himself some coffee and sat down at the table, heaping three large spoons of sugar into his coffee.

"Knew you'd be the first up," Rose grinned at him.

"Well, not really," Joe looked at his sister. "You and Mom are already up, right?"

"Well, I meant besides us moms," Rose clarified smugly.

"So, what's the plan today?" Joe asked his Mom, quickly changing the subject.

Mary smiled, "The usual, you know. Everyone will probably arrive this afternoon sometime. Lots of cooking to do, Joe."

"Need any help?" Joe offered.

Mary smiled. "Thanks, Joe, that's sweet of you to offer. You can smudge the place after the rest wake up but before everyone else arrives, okay?" Mary walked behind Rose and put her hand on her shoulder. "I think we got the cooking covered. Besides," she added, "everyone will bring something too, they always do."

"Yeah, I know, I remember," Joe added, even though he had for a brief second forgotten. He paused for a moment before asking, "Did you say everyone was coming?"

Mary looked at him with heavy eyes and sighed quietly. "Yes, I did, Joe, but I don't think *he's* coming."

Joe wanted to ask her how she knew. Did she speak with him? Did she ask him? Had she communicated with him at all in the past few years? None of them ever knew, and none of them even dared to ask the questions. And he could tell by her continued stare that now was not the time to start.

"Oh," was all he managed to get out and he sipped his coffee quietly. Soon his brother Derrick and sister Anne joined then at the table.

After a couple of pots of coffee, during which time Joe, his brothers, and his sister Anne took turns in the shower, the house became a hive of activity. Rose's husband David arrived at the house as Rose and Mary put a turkey into the oven.

Joe barely heard David say, "Hey, how ya doin'?" over the screams of the children running to their mom and then to their grandma to hug her. Suddenly the house wasn't so quiet with two children under ten careening around, saying hello to everyone, and chattering excitedly about Christmas.

After 15 minutes passed, Mary had them helping in the kitchen measuring flour and stirring ingredients together in a large plastic bowl.

"I'm a good helper, aren't I, Grandma?" Leena looked up at her grandma with her wide, dark eyes, mustering all the innocence that a four-year-old could.

"Yes, you are sweetie," Mary had replied smiling.

"Me too, Grandma! Me too!" echoed Silas.

"Of course, you are always a good helper too, Silas." Silas beamed with pride and stuck his chest out proudly as he vigorously stirred batter in another bowl.

Soon the younger cousins arrived and Leena and Silas hastily abandoned their posts in the kitchen to begin chasing their cousins screaming and laughing through the house. Suddenly, the house seemed much too small.

"Hey, you kids!" Rose yelled through the din. "Why don't you all get into your snow pants and coats and go play outside for little while?" Murmurs of agreement from the adults mingled with shouts of anticipation from the children, and suddenly it seemed everyone was at the doorway, children trying to find their coats and adults trying to get their children sufficiently dressed to go outside.

"Who's going outside with them?" Rose demanded, her eyes scanning the room, her expression as if she intended to delegate someone.

"I'll do it. I'll go with them," Joe volunteered, throwing on his coat.

Derrick rose from the recliner he was sitting in while watching TV. "I'll go too." Derrick said as he strode over to get his coat. He smiled at Joe. "Ya can't have all the fun." Joe opened the door and seven children flew out ahead of him.

"Keep an eye on them," Rose yelled behind him. "If their cheeks get too red, bring them back in, alright?"

"Sure, no probs, Rose," Joe replied agreeably as he held the door open for Derrick.

The kids had run down the driveway and into the backyard. The older children began immediate construction of a snow fort while the younger ones started rolling balls of snow bigger and bigger in the hopes of making a snowman. Derrick and Joe stood close to the house but kept a watchful eye as they chatted. Joe was surprised that Derrick was considering returning to school to get a degree, something he had always told Joe was a "waste of his time."

"The job's not goin' anywhere, you know?" Derrick said with frustration evident in his voice. "I just wanna get a good job, settle down, have a family," Derrick looked at Joe. "What about you, Joe? You ready to settle down yet?"

Joe looked at Derrick, a thin smile on his face. He paused for a moment before finally answering.

"Sure, I'm ready, it's just," Joe didn't want to mention Sara yet; he thought in some way it would jinx everything. "It's just . . . I don't know, I guess I'm gonna let things happen on their own. If it happens, great. If not, I think I could still be happy."

"You happy now, Joe?"

"Sure."

"You like what you're doing? You know, with your life?" Derrick pressed.

"Yeah, I like what I'm doing." Joe answered simply. He looked at his brother quizzically.

"I hope you don't think that I don't believe you or anything." Derrick added quickly. "It's just that you were supposed to be on a different path; remember what everyone used to say when we were kids?"

"Yeah, I was supposed to follow in Dad's footsteps. Learn the teachings, follow the traditional ways." Joe looked ahead into the forest that began at the edge of the yard. "But you can't learn from a teacher who isn't there," Joe said quietly.

"Floyd Thundercloud could have taught you," Derrick pressed. "You didn't have to turn your back on it completely."

Joe shrugged. He wasn't sure if his brother was trying to help him or provoke him. Either way he didn't feel like taking the conversation much further. Joe was especially grateful when Leena yelled, "We need some help putting on the head!"

Her little legs started to buckle as she clutched a ball of snow the size of a bowling ball against her legs and stomach, attempting to roll it into the snowman's body mid-section. Joe and Derrick hurried over and Joe relieved her of her burden while Derrick placed the head on top of the other snowballs. The other children smoothed it onto the body with packing snow.

"There!" Leena stated triumphantly as she placed her arms across her chest and stepped back to scrutinize her handiwork. "He needs a face," she declared loudly. "And arms, and maybe a hat too." She stared at Joe.

"Okay," answered Joe. "We'll get some sticks and rocks out of the forest, and you two keep working on his body."

"What about a hat?" Leena demanded.

"We'll get him one once he has a face and arms, don't you worry," Joe turned away from the snowman and ambled into the woods, wading through the occasional knee-deep snowdrifts. Joe bent down and picked up a dry twig lying on the snow.

Okay, I've got one arm covered, he thought.

"Hey! Wait for me!" Derrick yelled as he entered the woods.

Joe slowed his pace so Derrick could catch up as he slowly scanned the ground for sticks. He made his way to a copse of trees where only a thin layer of snow covered the ground. He bent down to pick up some small rocks and some acorns that he thought might serve as eyes. Joe halted in his tracks. He had a strange sensation, a feeling like there were eyes on him, as if he was being watched. He rose slowly and glanced around casually as if he was still searching the ground for more items. He caught a flash of movement up ahead and saw a dark shape dart behind a pine tree. Joe ignored it and pretended to examine the items in his hands. Then he looked up sharply. A red tail fox was standing just slightly behind the tree upon the rise, its head and forelegs just peeking out. Joe stared back at it as it continued to stare at him as if they were locked in each other's gaze. It obviously didn't believe he was a threat because it timidly edged out from behind the tree, moving closer to Joe and pausing tentatively every ten feet or so. Joe just stood there, immobile, waiting for the creature to approach him. And the fox crept closer, his feather duster tail just sweeping the surface of the snow, his head tilted slightly upward as he sniffed at the air as if trying to identify Joe's scent.

It was less than five feet away from Joe when it just halted in its tracks, sat down and continued to calmly scrutinize Joe. *It's not scared, not scared of me at all*, Joe thought. He wondered if he should be worried that the fox was diseased or ill despite its perfectly healthy appearance. It appeared to be as curious of him as he was of it.

"Wow! Look at that fox. It's beautiful!" Derrick said in awe as he stomped through the snow behind Joe, pausing in his tracks when he saw the fox.

Derrick's presence snapped Joe out of his daze. The fox appeared startled too, and it jumped in alarm, but instead of bolting out of sight, it started to make a yipping, growly noise before turning around and ambling back through the woods and out of sight.

"Hey, Joe, is your helper the red tail fox?" Derrick asked enthusiastically.

"No, I don't think so," Joe answered softly. If he had an animal helper, it definitely had never been revealed to him before.

"We better head back," Joe said firmly. "The kids will be waiting for these," he held out the assortment of twigs, rocks and nuts he had collected. Both men turned and began traipsing through the snow back to the yard.

"You know, Joe? I remember seeing a fox on occasion out here when we were kids. Think that one could be one of its family?"

"Yeah, sure, I don't see why not," Joe answered in a noncommittal way.

"It sure looked familiar though," Derrick pondered out loud. "It sure sounded like it was giving me shit, didn't it?"

Joe laughed and smiled at his brother. Now that he thought about it, it sure seemed like it was grumbling at Derrick's noisy intrusion. They continued to laugh about it as they moved away from the trees and returned back to the children and the snowman.

***

The rest of the day had passed in what had largely seemed like a blur of activity to Joe. His mother's small house was perpetually full of people, but not uncomfortably so, for most of the day. Aunts, uncles, and cousins arrived and left in a steady stream all day, and gifts were exchanged also, though most were given to the children, who always received and opened them with great anticipation and excitement.

Food was omnipresent too. His mother and sisters (though Rose was more obliging in the kitchen than Anne) had prepared the turkey, stuffing, bannock, and potatoes; relatives had also brought various dishes with them, adding an abundant quantity of food ranging from wild rice to gelatin to the already heavily-laden kitchen table. Everyone was well-fed, and extra plates were heaped with food to be taken home or to relatives that couldn't make it.

As daylight dwindled, so did the number of people in the house. By the time the sun had set in the sky, Joe, his brothers, his mother, his sister Anne, and Rose's family were the last left at the house. Leena was curled up on the couch asleep, her dark hair falling softly off her face and her tiny arm dangling over the side of the couch. Silas was lying on the floor beside the couch, a pillow under his head as Rose tried to gently slip an arm into his coat without waking him.

"They're so cute when they're sleeping," Mary cooed as she gazed adoringly at the two children while Rose successfully got Silas' arm into the other sleeve.

"Yeah, hopefully they'll sleep in the car. They had a busy day." Rose spoke quietly, scooping the still sleeping Silas into her arms.

David opened the front door and stepped in to the house. "I got the car warmed up and the gifts in the trunk. Anything else?"

"Yeah, take this one while I get Leena ready," Rose passed Silas to David. David pressed Silas close to his chest, resting his head on his shoulder. "I'll be out in a sec," Rose said as she fiddled with Leena's coat.

"Okay," David replied softly. He turned and motioned to the family. "Thanks for a great day. Merry Christmas, everyone." They all murmured their good-byes as David went out the door with Silas. Rose followed shortly behind with the half-asleep Leena cuddled into the crook of her neck and shoulder.

"See you soon, everyone," Rose said as she headed out the door.

The momentary silence was broken by the sound of the television turning on and Joe's brothers bickering back and forth about what they would watch as they vied for possession of the remote control. Mary did not allow it to go on for long and seized control of the remote before flicking the television off.

"Enough!" Mary announced loudly, her voice firm. "It would be nice to just enjoy each other's company for a little while, right?"

John and Derrick shot each other skeptical glances.

"Well, it won't kill you," Mary said flatly.

The boys knew better than to argue with their Mom. They shrugged and grudgingly turned their attention away from the television. They sat in the living room and chatted idly, and only the sound of their voices disrupted the silence of the room. But it wasn't long before Anne stood, her hand covering a wide yawn.

"I'm gonna hit the hay. I'm beat," she declared through her yawn. "See you all in the morning."

"Goodnight," Joe said as his mother and brothers murmured the same. But soon John and then Derrick filtered out of the room, the day's activities having caught up with them as well. And Joe found himself alone with his mother. He was about to rise, taking cue from his siblings that perhaps it was time to turn in, but, to his surprise, Mary stood up too, and before Joe could utter a word she said,

"Let's have a tea in the kitchen before we turn in."

Joe followed Mary into the kitchen and sat at the table as she boiled a kettle and fixed two cups of tea. She placed one on the table in front of Joe, and she cradled a mug in both her hands as she sat down across from him. As she blew into the mug, tendrils of steam rose up around her face while she took a tentative sip. Joe did the same and set his mug down on the table, his hands still curled around its warmth. He looked up and saw his mother staring out the kitchen window as if intently eyeing the crescent moon, but her eyes appeared more than a little far off and distant. She must have felt Joe's gaze on her, and she quickly lowered her eyes, returning her attention quickly to her cup before meeting Joe's stare.

"You doin' okay, Joe?" Mary asked softly.

"That seems to be the question of the day." Joe answered. "Don't I seem okay?"

"Yeah, I guess you do," Mary answered. "Just sometimes I need to hear it." She paused for a moment and then asked, "Was it because your father left?"

"What?" Joe asked, suddenly confused.

"When you stopped, you know, following our ways, falling off the path." She looked at him more intently. "Was that the reason?"

Joe's hands encircled his coffee mug a little tighter. To his surprise, he answered, "Yeah, I guess that was when I changed my heart. Suddenly, it didn't mean so much anymore."

"But you smudged the house today," Mary stated. "Have you changed your mind again?"

Joe smiled, mentally searching for an acceptable answer. He couldn't tell her everything, but he wasn't exactly sure what she wanted to hear. He knew that she had worried so much in the past; at one time about his father, and then about him.

"Well," Joe began slowly, "I've had my eyes opened in the last few months. Perhaps it is time for me to work on my spirit, get back in touch with what is important. After that, I don't know. I guess I'll see what happens," Joe took a gulp of his tea.

Mary smiled and spoke softly, her eyes once again on his.

"You are a good man, Joe. What happened with your father won't happen to you. As you walk your path alone, he walks his too. Someday your paths will cross again. And you will be ready. Just don't judge the type of man you will become by the type of man you think your father is, for you will find yourself two times wrong."

Joe watched as his mother picked up her mug and drained it as she rose out of her chair. She gave Joe's shoulder a gentle squeeze.

"Have faith in yourself and you will always know what to do. No matter what you do, I am proud of you and love you." Mary placed her cup on the counter and slowly walked out of the kitchen.

"I love you too, Ma," Joe said softly as she disappeared into the dark shadow of the hallway beyond.

Joe sat there, sipping his tea, thinking of all the questions he wanted to ask but couldn't put into words. *When the time is right*, he thought to himself. *I wonder when that will be.*

Outside the window a light snow was falling, illuminated by the light of the crescent moon. The sound of an animal yipping into the night jolted Joe out of his thoughts, and his eyes caught sight of a small but familiar shadow, its full tail low to the ground. It stopped and gave a yipping howl before it continued loping across the snow and out of sight.

***

A bright fire burned in the woodstove in Dan and Abby's living room. The flames flickered gently through the glass doors, giving a soft light to the room. Across the room, in front of the bay window, the lights on the Christmas tree glowed and flickered in time with some rhythmic electronic pattern. A small scented candle glowed on the table in front of the couch, casting shadows on the bottle of wine and tray of cheese and crackers laid out in front of them.

"Er, Abby," Dan said quietly, his eyes darting nervously from the fire to the candle. "You sure this is a good idea?" Abby took a gentle sip from her wine glass before answering.

"It's okay, Dan, really," She spoke quietly but with confidence. "I got it under control now." She took a last sip from her glass, leaned forward and placed the glass on the table. She leaned back into the couch slipping her arms around Dan and snuggling into this chest as she drew her feet up to rest on the couch beside her.

"You sure you really have it under wraps?" Dan insisted, his body tensing as she snuggled in closer.

"Well, I can feel it call me, you know? The fire calls out to me." She sat up and looked Dan in the eye, carefully holding his gaze. "But like a call, I don't always have to answer. I won't hurt you again, alright?"

Dan smiled at her, his body relaxed. He picked up his glass from the arm of the couch and sipped his wine.

"I know you wouldn't intentionally hurt me," he said placing his glass back on the arm of the couch.

"You're right about that," Abby agreed. She snuggled back into his chest, listening to the gentle beat of his heart, breathing in the musky scent of his cologne. "I love you," she murmured.

"I love you too, Ab," Dan added quietly, stroking her dark hair.

She felt good just sitting together with him. No flare ups, no yelling, no fighting. Indeed, it had been a great day. Abby smiled as she recalled squealing with surprise and delight at the new air compressor she unwrapped and how Dan had only sighed in resignation. "Why can't you get excited about gifts other than tools?" But Abby had laughed and he joined in. It was hard to believe that Christmas was over and soon she would have to start working on building up the stock that she would need to take to upcoming shows for the New Year. Boy, the year was almost over, the New Year was a week away . . .

Crap, New Year's Eve! She had forgotten all about it. Abby sat up. "Dan, you didn't have any plans for New Year's Eve, did you?"

Dan looked at her a little puzzled. "Was I supposed to make plans?"

"Well, no."

"Good," Dan smiled in obvious relief. "Then I'm not in any trouble. Why?"

"Well, I invited Sara and her boyfriend to join us here."

"Woo hoo! Sara's got a new boyfriend?" Dan asked a little salaciously, an evil smile surfacing across his face. "Do I get to grill him? Is it anyone I know?"

Abby smiled at Dan's response. He always did act like Sara's nosy older brother, but he had been very accurate in his assessments of a few of Sara's ex-boyfriends. *Actually scared one away*, Abby remembered.

Lucky for Dan he turned out to be a real jerk after all. *Wait, get back to the topic at hand*, Abby chided herself.

"Well, I think you've met him a few times at a couple gallery shows you've come to. His name is Joe Asine."

Dan's browed furrowed silently for a moment. His face lit up.

"Isn't he a potter?"

"Yes, that's right." Abby answered.

"Yeah, I remember him," Dan added. "He seems like a nice guy. Calm — not the type Sara usually seems to go for, though."

Abby nodded in agreement. "Well, I should add that I don't know how serious things are with them yet, so don't be too hard on him, okay?"

"Okay, okay," Dan said grudgingly.

"But that's not the only reason they are coming here," Abby added, casting a sidelong glance at Dan.

"Really?"

"Yeah. Remember when I told you about the problems I've been having?" Dan nodded mutely, his dark eyes locked on Abby. She continued. "Well, Sara and Joe and I have decided that we could use your advice and input, so we thought we'd all sit down and tell you what the deal is with all of us."

Dan continued to stare blankly at her.

"You okay, Dan?" Abby placed a gentle hand on his shoulder.

"So, this guy, Joe . . . Sara's not-sure-if-he's-serious boyfriend is involved in this too?"

Abby nodded.

"He . . . doesn't use fire . . . does he?" Dan asked cautiously.

"No," was all Abby was prepared to say.

Dan heaved a sigh of relief, and took another sip of his wine. "Good!" he said a little too enthusiastically, a strained smile on his face. "For a moment there, Ab, I had visions of New Year's Eve celebrations involving our house on fire and everyone standing around toasting marshmallows."

Abby almost laughed out loud, but she soon realized he was half-serious.

"Don't worry, Dan, I know you'll like him . . . everything will be fine, alright?"

Dan scooped her into his arms and kissed her deeply on the lips. Holding her close and gazing into her eyes, he whispered, "I trust you, Abby. No matter what."

Abby buried her head into the crook of his neck and shoulder and closed her eyes. Smelling his scent comforted her even more than the sound of the peaceful crackle of the flames still burning softly in the woodstove.

***

Abby reluctantly disentangled herself from the sleeping embrace of Dan and carefully slipped out of the bed so as not to wake him. Dan stirred, his eyes still closed, stretched, and turned onto his other side with a loud snort.

Abby put on a fresh pot of coffee and had a quick shower while it brewed. She managed to dress and down a cup of coffee before Dan stumbled sleepily down the stairs in his pajama bottoms.

"Why didn't you wake me?" he asked, as he simultaneously stretched and yawned.

"Thought you'd enjoy sleeping in a little today," Abby replied pushing a plate stacked with buttered toast onto the table and handing him a steaming mug of coffee.

"Thanks," Dan said, taking a sip from the mug before taking his seat at the table. Abby leaned across and snagged a piece of toast and stuffed it in her mouth.

"So, any plans today?" Dan said raising an eyebrow, indicating he noticed she was already dressed.

"Yeah, I thought I'd go pop in on Sara if that's alright with you." Abby looked at Dan. "You know she spent yesterday alone, right?"

"What about that sorta-boyfriend Joe? Oh yeah, not that serious, I forgot." Dan looked at Abby with surprise. "Why didn't you invite her over for supper?"

"Well, I did, you know. But she insisted on being alone," Abby sighed exasperated as she bit off another piece of toast. "But I thought I'd check on her today, take her the present I made, and see how she's doing."

Dan stood abruptly. "Do you want me to come too? I could throw on some clothes quick and be ready in ten minutes."

Abby waved him back down. "No, no, you stay here and relax. I won't be too long. Besides, Sara's got a new pet, and I don't know how it's going to react to new people yet."

"Really?" Dan asked enthusiastically. "Did she get a dog?"

"Let's just say it's a big dog-like animal for now." Abby evaded Dan's eyes as she gulped her coffee.

"Oh, a mixed breed," Dan said.

"Yeah, something like that." Abby replied vaguely.

Today was not the day for Dan to meet the Taekyr. He was accepting of a lot of things, but Abby had the distinct impression that the sight of the Taekyr would probably cause him to run for the hills. *Maybe I'll spring that on him another day*, she thought.

Abby stuffed the last piece of her toast into her mouth and chased it down with the last gulp of coffee. She unceremoniously wiped the crumbs off her hands onto her jeans and grabbed her coat while slipping into her boots. She walked back over to Dan and kissed him gently on the cheek.

"I promise not to be long. I'll be back before you miss me," she murmured.

"Too late." He replied with a smile. Abby smiled back as she grabbed her purse and keys off a chair before heading out of the door.

Even though it had been snowing off and on for the past two days, the roads were clear, and only a few extra inches of light, fluffy snow blanketed the countryside. The sun was peeking through the clouds and hitting the snow, causing it to sparkle like the sides of the road were sprinkled with tiny glittering crystals. Abby pulled into Sara's driveway and was greatly relieved that Sara had already shoveled the snow clear. Sara's driveway was treacherous to begin with, let alone when covered with a few inches of snow.

Abby was greeted at the door by an enthusiastic Sara, who was bouncing up and down on the pads of her feet.

"Hey, Abby! Happy Holidays, Merry Christmas and all that," Sara said exuberantly as she hugged Abby on her way through the door.

Sara looked at the beautifully-wrapped present Abby was holding out in her hand. "Ooh, a present!" Sara exclaimed excitedly, her blue eyes sparkling with anticipation. "Ooh! Wait, I got one for you too," Sara added bounding out of the living room and down the hall.

Abby could hear Sara rustling through stuff in another room. "It's here somewhere," Abby heard he mutter aloud to herself. "Aha! There it is!" Sara came down the hall draping a beach towel around a foot-long rectangle.

"Sorry," Sara said, smiling sheepishly. "I forgot to wrap it. I hope that's okay."

Abby smiled widely at Sara. She would have been surprised to find that Sara actually remembered to buy wrapping paper, let alone wrap a gift with it.

They swapped gifts and Sara eagerly tore the wrapping paper off the box, while Abby removed the towel to reveal a portrait of Abby and Dan that Sara painted.

"It's lovely," Abby said admiring the painting and its detail with awe.

"You like?" Sara asked.

"Yes. Yes, I do. Thank you," Abby replied and motioned for Sara to continue to open her present. Sara tore open the box and pushed aside the tissue paper inside to find a sterling silver and blue crystal necklace and matching earrings.

"These are great, Abby! I love them." You know, blue is my favorite color," Sara added while putting on the necklace.

"Yes, I know," Abby added. "I'm glad you like them."

Sara put the earrings on and admired them in the entryway mirror.

"Let's go show them to Oogan. I think he'll like them."

"Who?" Abby asked, racking her brain to see if she knew what that was.

"Oogan," Sara repeated. Abby looked at her blankly, blinking as her dark eyes searched Sara's for an answer.

"Oogan is the Taekyr that's staying with me," Sara added excitedly. "Come on, I'll take you down to see him. I was making him a sandwich when you arrived. He just loves peanut butter and honey sandwiches."

Sara bounded into the kitchen and grabbed a sandwich off the counter and then tossed on her coat and boots and strode out the front door, Abby following at her heals.

How lovely, Abby thought wryly. *We're going to meet Oogan, the friendly Taekyr.* Abby smiled wryly. Maybe Sara has taught it a few tricks - at least that way it would be an entertaining experience. Abby followed, her feet crunching in the snow as she tried to catch up with Sara's long strides and quick pace.

CHAPTER 21

Abby managed to catch up to Sara as she opened the side door of the barn. Sara politely held it open for Abby while she stepped inside with caution, halting just a few footsteps inside the doorway. The inside of the barn was almost completely black, and the darkness was quite a contrast to the brightness of the daylight against the stark snow-covered ground outdoors. Abby moved further inside as her eyes adjusted and she looked around warily. It felt strange and different, but it wasn't just the darkness that felt strange to Abby. There was an atmosphere of *wrongness* in the air, though Abby wasn't sure she could describe how that was possible. It was as if the barn pulsated with an aura of gloom, and the mood was the same as if she had just walked into a visitation at a funeral home: sad and creepy. Abby shuddered.

"This way," Sara's voice directed softly as her hand grasped Abby's wrist, guiding her slowly into the stable area. "Bright light bothers him, so I try to keep it dim in here," Sara offered by way of an explanation. "Plus," she added, casting Abby a sidelong glance as they passed a few enclosures, "I've learned that they're nocturnal creatures. Oogan has adapted himself so he has the ability to spend a little more time awake in the mornings. It has allowed us to spend some quality time together and get to know one another."

Quality time with Oogan, Abby thought sarcastically. *There's five minutes of my life I'd never get back.*

Sara smiled and moved to the center of the stable area. She grasped a handle on the wooden gate as she crooned, "Oogan, dear, it's just me. I've brought you a treat!"

Abby stared in wonder as she stood behind her, attempting to glance past Sara's side and through the gap in the gate rails. There was definitely some movement accompanied by an irregular shuffling sound on the dirt floor, but her eyes could only make out vague shadows in the inky darkness.

Sara pulled the gate back further, and Abby backed up behind her. Once Sara had the gate fully open, she moved slowly toward the shuffling sound. Abby stepped off to Sara's side and back far enough that she could watch.

Oogan shuffled forward on his talons, the hook-like protrusions from his wing tips both balancing him and propelling him forward. His gray-black head barely reached the mid-section of Sara's thigh as she squatted down onto her knees to give him the sandwich.

Oogan's lidless eyes widened as he caught sight of the sandwich.

"Here you go, sweetie. It's your favorite: peanut butter and honey."

Oogan smacked his lips, making an odd squelchy sound that made Abby wince with disgust. Sara patiently held the sandwich out and continued to smile like a doting aunt. Oogan reached out with a talon and grasped it gingerly, just as a parrot would grab a cookie. He got the sandwich into his mouth in two bites and made fast work of it. Abby silently wondered how he managed that, as it didn't appear that the creature had any teeth to speak of.

"Thank you, Lady Sara," Oogan spoke in his croaking, low voice.

Sara reached out and patted him on the head as if he were a dog.

"How's the wing?" Sara asked, her voice filled with concern. "Do you mind if I take a look?"

Oogan gave her a pitiful glance but slowly extended his right wing out. Abby had once owned a kite when she was a child that was her pride and joy. It was bright red and was over six feet long. Oogan's one wing was easily larger than that kite, measuring over six feet in length by her estimate. It was large and black, similar to a large bat wing. Evident on his wing was a hole, located in the membrane between the wing tip and the outer edge. It looked like an inner tube with a large puncture, Abby thought, as Sara placed her hand on the wing and examined it with carefully probing fingertips. Oogan cried out feebly when she touched a tender spot close to the hole and pulled his wing out of her grasp. He tucked his wing back into his side with deliberate care, and the membrane folded up in a manner similar to that of a collapsible umbrella.

"I'm really sorry, Oogan. I didn't mean to hurt you. Perhaps when you wake up I'll put some more salve on it. Did that help last time?"

Oogan looked at Sara and nodded.

Abby eyes began to water and she coughed as the musky smell of the Taekyr reached her nostrils. Oogan jumped, startled by the sound. He recognized Abby and tried to dart behind Sara.

"Oogan, this is my friend Abby." Sara said by way of introduction.

"She's the one who wanted to burn and kill me," he croaked, his dark eyes fixed on her as he pressed himself against Sara's leg.

"Yes, well that was before when we thought you were a threat. But she's here now to get to know you." Sara spoke very patiently like she was speaking to a small child and stroked his head in a reassuring manner.

"She doesn't like me," Oogan croaked flatly and he stared fixedly at Abby with his liquid, black eyes.

"Oh, yes she does, don't you, Abby?" Sara looked at Abby, her eyes darting from Abby to Oogan and back again. She stood there silently, waiting for Abby to answer, and motioned with her hand for Abby to enter the conversation.

Abby felt uncomfortable. How could she like this creature when it clearly worked for the enemy and was only at Sara's because it was being held against its will? Abby knew she didn't trust it. How could she? They caught the creature spying on them! Sara had obviously bonded with Oogan, but could she really believe it would to continue to stay with her after it was healed enough to fly? And what would it do if Sara did release it? Would it return to where ever it came from and report what it discovered about them to its master? Abby didn't want to see Sara's kindness be repaid with treachery.

Abby looked at Sara and shrugged her shoulders. "Yeah, I guess I like you," she offered hesitantly, hoping that humoring Sara would be enough for the moment.

Oogan's dark eyes narrowed, "She lies," he hissed accusingly.

Sara looked at Abby and folded her arms across her chest.

"Well," Abby stammered, trying to reach her brain for a more truthful and diplomatic answer. "It's . . . it's not that I don't like you, it's just that . . . I'm not ready to trust you yet, that's all." Abby forced out the words. "I haven't spent as much time with you as Sara. Maybe I just need to get to know you better." Abby forced a smile to her lips but stopped once she realized that the shallow breaths she was taking to inhibit the smell of the Taekyr were causing her to grimace more than smile. He continued to eye her with thinly-veiled suspicion.

Sara turned and bent down so that she was at eye-level with Oogan.

"Don't worry, sweetie," she crooned softly. "Once she gets to know you, she'll like you as much as I do and we'll all be great friends." Sara patted him once more on the head; his thin black lips looked as though they were curving into a sort of smile, or something close to it, Abby observed with revulsion. She adjusted her face to a more neutral expression and nodded mutely, as if in agreement with Sara.

"Now, you best get to bed and I'll take care of that wing once you wake up."

Oogan shuffled into the back of the pen. Abby, her eyes now accustomed to the dim light, could make out a form in the back corner that appeared to be a large nest constructed of straw and sticks.

Looks like Big Bird from Sesame Street has moved in, Abby thought wryly. *If only.*

Oogan hopped into the nest and stared accusingly at Abby as Sara grabbed the gate and began to swing it shut.

"Have a good sleep, Oogan," Sara chimed sweetly.

"Thank you, Lady Sara."

Sara nodded to Abby. "Don't you want to say good-bye, Ab?" she whispered.

"Uh, bye, Oogan. Nice to meet you, uh, again," Abby said quietly, but Oogan ignored her. He turned his back and tucked his head under his wing.

The gate closed with a soft click.

"Let's go," Sara whispered softly and she began to tip-toe back through the barn. Abby nodded and followed silently at her heels.

Abby quickened her step once Sara opened the door, and instantly the glint of sunlight appeared in the doorway. It wasn't as if she didn't like the dark, but she was eager to put the gloomy darkness of the barn behind her. And the smell of Oogan.

Abby stepped out of the barn, and Sara was there waiting for her. Sara pulled the door closed quietly and looked at Abby, her eyes narrowing as she moved her hand up to shield her eyes from the brightness of the sun.

"Abby, you didn't have to be so . . . so . . . ."

"Truthful?" Abby suggested.

"No, well . . . maybe," Sara stammered. "It's just that . . . he's so alone here. Why can't you try to be friendly with him?"

Abby looked at Sara. She could feel the anger well up inside her, the fire inside begging to be released in a flurry of anger. Abby took a deep breath and closed her eyes, extinguishing the flame of her frustration before she spoke.

"Sara, you've been around this creature for a little while and have gotten close to it," Abby began carefully.

"Him."

"Pardon?"

"Him," Sara corrected. "Not 'it'."

"Sorry," Abby continued, "You've been around *him* much longer than I have. My only experience with *him* was when Gabe caught it spying on us. I also recall you telling me you were attacked by a number of these creatures the night Thaddeus dropped by to visit." Abby ran her hand through her hair and moved closer to Sara.

"You are my closest friend. I trust you implicitly. But please allow me to make up my own mind with regard to this creature, okay?" Abby looked at Sara awaiting her response. Sara met Abby's gaze, her eyes a deep blue that seemed to hold a hint of sadness to them.

"I'm sorry, Abby," Sara said softly. "I shouldn't try to push my feelings on you. It's just . . . it's been nice to have the extra company, especially around the holidays." Sara leaned against Abby and put her arm around Abby's shoulders. A wide smirk quickly spread across her face. "Once you get to know him, I'm sure you will like him as much as I do."

Abby laughed at the notion and Sara joined in. They walked slowly up the path toward the house when a noise behind them alerted Abby's attention. Tensing up, she spun around sharply and raised her right hand as if ready to toss a baseball overhand, her palm glowing outwardly with the rapidly building heat.

"Hey! Don't you go throwin' fire at me!" Gabe muttered with gruff indignance.

He was wearing his usual trousers and vest, but completed his ensemble with a lime green toque atop his head. He looked like a rather hairy lollipop that had been excavated from behind a seat cushion of a frat house sofa. Abby bit her lip to stifle the smile already forming.

"Gabe!" Sara greeted him warmly, extending her hand and bowing down slightly. He shook it briefly.

"Fancy joining us for a cup of tea?" Sara offered excitedly as she gestured toward her house.

Abby saw Gabe's cheeks redden slightly. "Thanks much, Sara, but I got to speak with Abby here if ya don't mind." Gabe looked down at his boot and then back up at Sara's face.

"Perhaps next time then?" Sara offered smiling. Gabe nodded mutely and then looked over at Abby.

Abby nodded and returned the stare. *If he's got something to say*, she thought, *he can go first*.

Sara broke the silence. "I'll leave you to it and go in and put the kettle on. Take all the time you need and come in whenever you're ready, Abby." Sara strode back up the path, waving over her shoulder as she walked. "See you soon, Gabe."

Gabe muttered a brief reply to her retreating form and then fixed his attention back to Abby.

"Let's walk a bit," Gabe said gruffly as he turned toward the path that led to the forest. They walked slowly, Gabe reaching up periodically to scratch at his beard-covered chin. "So," Gabe began, "hear you're not keen on the Taekyr."

"Where'd you hear that?" Abby asked coyly, smiling sweetly at him.

Gabe cleared his throat. "Ya know damn well I overheard a bit of your talkin' with Sara." Gabe looked at her carefully, as if waiting for her to react. Abby remained emotionless and silent. "Personally, I agree with ya that Sara is too trustin' of the creature. But who knows? Perhaps they've bonded. Stranger things have been known to happen."

Abby shrugged indifferently. It felt good that someone agreed with her, though she wished he had backed up her apprehensions while Sara was present. Gabe probably didn't want to hurt Sara's feelings. Joe would probably not give an opinion on the Taekyr, regardless of how he felt, for the exact same reason.

"Was there something else you wanted?" Abby said abruptly, stopping on the path.

"Yeah, actually, there was," Gabe looked at her in surprise. "I just wanted to let ya know that you're doin' alright." He pulled a pipe and a pouch of tobacco from his pocket. "Fire is the hardest Element to handle. I guess you've figgered that out for yerself, haven't yeh?" Gabe said as he opened the pouch, pulled a wad of tobacco from within, and stuffed it into his pipe.

Abby nodded. She had felt the dreadful feeling of insanity and loss of control that the woman in her visions had felt. She too had felt the same way when she couldn't control the Fire inside her, felt it draw out and feed her emotions, like she was on some kind of crazy roller coaster with no brakes and no end in sight. She cringed at the memory, but she prided herself on her ability to exercise some control over the constant call of the flame. She watched Gabe pull the drawstring on his tobacco pouch and stuff it back into his pocket. He held his pipe up.

"Gotta light?"

Abby flicked the end of her finger and a tiny flicker of a flame danced from the end. She held it to the bowl of his pipe as he took a few draws on it. He nodded at her as the smoke began to draw through the mouthpiece and the tobacco in the bowl glowed with a warm orange light. Abby moved her finger away and held it up to her mouth, gently blowing out the flame.

"Ya got somethin' the others couldn't seem to master. Control. You've come farther than any of them has in hundreds o' years." Gabe continued to puff on his pipe, blowing rings of smoke into the cool air.

Abby swelled with pride. She had been worried she hadn't been the right choice; that someone would come up, tap her on the shoulder, and tell her a grave mistake had been made. Now she felt like the Element belonged with her, that she had found a part of her that she needed to feel whole. Gabe's praise lifted her spirits in a way she couldn't put into words. It felt good.

"Thanks." Abby smiled and put her hands deep into her coat pockets. They walked a little further down the path in silence, keeping a slow pace as they ambled forward.

"Well, I should get goin'," Gabe spoke, breaking the silence. He turned to look at Abby. "Ya just behave yourself when the Water Vessel comes along, got it?" He waggled a callused finger at her, a half-smirk visible under the bushy, gray beard.

"Why would you say that?" Abby asked, raising an eyebrow.

"Well, fire and water don't mix, ya know." Gabe muttered as he tapped his pipe to empty the ashes onto the ground. "Best be goin' now," Gabe turned and began to walk toward the forest.

"Wait!" Abby yelled.

Gabe paused and turned to face her.

"You mentioned the Water Vessel," Abby started. "Who is it exactly?"

Gabe looked at her with a twisted smile on his face. "I think you two have it figgered already. I can't help you that way: you have to find each other. But, if it's any consolation, you're on the right track." Gabe turned back, heading into the forest.

"Yeah, thanks," Abby said sarcastically as he continued through the trees. "You son of a bitch," she muttered under her breath.

"Can't do all your work for ya," Gabe chuckled as he disappeared into the thicket of trees.

Abby turned and headed back up the path, her breath a visible fog in front of her, leading the way to Sara's house. *What a curious day*, Abby thought. She smiled. And the best part of it was that it wasn't over yet.

***

"So what time are they arriving?" Dan yelled from the bedroom upstairs.

"Around eightish, I think," Abby replied loudly from the kitchen.

She was busy filling a bowl with tortilla chips and setting it on a platter on which she had already placed several bowls of chips. Abby had already placed a tray of hors d'oeuvres in the oven in preparation for the arrival of their guests.

"What time is it now?" Dan said loudly as he appeared in the staircase, buttoning the sleeves of a white collar shirt.

"It's ten to eight," Abby replied as she moved the platter to the dining table.

"Do you need any help?" Dan offered as he crossed the room.

"Yes, you can find the champagne and ginger ale and put them in the fridge." Abby took off her apron and grabbed a wine goblet from the counter. "I'm going to have a little break."

Abby went over to the CD player placed her MP3 player and dock on top of it. Abby had to laugh. They had spent a lot of money to purchase a decent stereo system just before MP3 players and iPods took over the market, rendering their expensive purchase obsolete almost overnight. Now Abby just used the CD player as a stand. After selecting a playlist that appealed to her, she pressed play and adjusted the volume accordingly. She strode over to the couch, humming softly along with the music, ignoring Dan's groan of protest from the kitchen as she settled on the couch and sipped her wine.

It was hard to believe a new year was almost here. And tonight would be the first time she had seen Sara since the day after Christmas. They had talked on the phone a few times since, but Joe had returned from his family get-together the day after that and Sara had been spending a lot of time with him. Not that Sara didn't want Abby around; she had been eager for the three of them to get together to work on—how had she put it? "Tactics and strategies". Abby smiled at the recollection. *You'd think we were soldiers or something.* Abby took another sip from her glass. *I guess in a strange way we are*, she realized.

In the end, it hadn't been too terribly difficult to convince Sara that the holiday season was time to take a break from all things and relax, especially to spend time with new friends. She was relieved that Sara took this to mean with Joe, not Oogan.

Abby had no doubt that Sara had been spending a great deal of time with Oogan too, but hopefully being with Joe would keep the gloomy atmosphere the creature emitted in the barn from casting a dark shadow over Sara. As happy as she appeared to be around Oogan, Abby couldn't help but feel that being in his presence was bringing Sara down. Abby could barely tolerate a few minutes cooped up in there without it affecting her mood. It was depressing.

I hope she doesn't bring Oogan here tonight. Abby cringed at the thought. *One thing at a time.*

A soft knock on the door roused Abby from her thoughts. As she rose to open the door, Dan yelled,

"Come on in!"

Abby shot Dan a dirty look as she strode across the room. She was half-way to the door when it opened and Sara walked in, followed by Joe.

"Hi, guys," Sara chirped as she set a bottle of wine on the counter and unzipped her coat. She hung it on the coat-tree and gave Dan a hug.

"Hey, Dan," Sara said as she hugged him. "I'd like you to meet my friend, Joe. Joe, this is Dan, Abby's husband."

Joe stepped forward and shook hands with Dan. "Hi, nice to meet you," he said. He was holding a bouquet of carnations in his other hand. "These are for your lovely wife." Joe said, holding the bouquet out.

"I'll take those," Abby moved forward and intercepted the bouquet. "You give flowers to Dan and you've pretty much sentenced them to death," she quipped. "I'll just put these in some water."

"Water? Is that your secret? No wonder they always die on me." Dan joked as Abby located a vase and filled it from the tap.

Everyone laughed as Abby playfully stuck her tongue out at Dan. She quickly had the bouquet arranged in the vase and placed it in the center of the table.

"Thank you, Joe, they're lovely," Abby said.

"You're welcome," Joe said, smiling at her as he placed his coat by Sara's.

"Please come in and sit down," Dan said, relaxing into his role as host. He led Sara and Joe into the living room.

"I think we've met before, haven't we?" Dan asked Joe as he sat down in a chair by the sofa where Joe sat.

"Yeah, I think we have," Joe agreed. "Probably at one of the gallery shows."

"Yeah, probably," Dan replied. "I try to get out to most of them when I can."

Abby quickly offered drinks and brought them out on a tray with the hors d'oeuvres she had pulled out of the oven. She was grateful Dan had stocked the fridge with juice and pop, as Joe didn't drink. When she asked Joe what kind of pop, she found that he certainly was easy to please.

"Whatever you have," he replied easily. "I'm not picky."

Abby brought another tray from the kitchen with a bottle of wine, three glasses, and a glass tumbler of cola and ice. She poured wine into the three glasses after passing Joe his cola. He and Dan were deep in conversation, and Sara was sitting patiently beside Joe waiting for Abby to quit flitting about and to take her seat.

Abby returned the drink tray to the kitchen and grasped her wine glass as she sat gently next to Sara. Sara moved her head closer to

Abby's in a conspiratorial manner and murmured in a low voice as not to be overheard by the men,

"Are we to do this tonight, then?"

Abby took a small sip of her wine, swallowing it carefully. "Yes," she answered in the same murmuring tone. "There's no going back now."

Abby turned and scrutinized Sara's expression. "Are you having second thoughts?" she queried.

Sara smiled widely. "No, not at all. I'm just . . . just anxious, I suppose. You know what I mean?"

Abby nodded. While she had told Dan what she could, she did have a nagging sense of guilt that she was keeping secrets from him, something she swore she would never do. Abby took another sip of her wine and set the glass on the table in front of her. Suddenly, the room seemed too quiet. She looked up and noticed that all conversation had ceased, and the attention of everyone was on her, their eyes all mirroring the same expectant look.

Abby cleared her throat and set her hands neatly in her lap. She took a deep breath. *It's time to begin.*

"Dan, I know that in the past few months that you have noticed a change in me—,"

Dan snorted and nodded. Abby rolled her eyes at him and with a smile continued.

"And I have changed somewhere along the way. I have been either gifted or cursed with the ability to harness the power of Fire. You could say I have become a Vessel for the Fire Element to work through."

"Yes, that's true," Dan agreed, his full attention on his wife.

"Well, Sara found out that she too has the capability to be a vessel for an Element. The Element that she works with is Air."

Dan looked at Sara. Although he had been told by Abby that Sara was in a similar situation to her, he had been unsure exactly what it was or what that meant. Dan looked at Sara. She nodded at him in acknowledgement before Abby continued again.

"Sara and I were very surprised that both of us had received such unusual abilities. But we soon found out that someone else had also developed abilities."

"Let me guess," Dan added excitedly, turning to Joe, "it's you, isn't it?"

Joe nodded mutely, a sort of half-smile on his face. Dan looked at him expectantly.

"It's the Earth Element," Joe added, then looked back to Abby.

Abby continued. "The three of us seemed to have been selected for these gifts. As of now, we are not sure why we were chosen. But there is obviously a reason for us to be given these abilities, although we still haven't quite worked that part out. We were told we would find each other and, so far, we have."

Dan leaned forward. "It's clear to me you are missing an Element, aren't you?" Dan took a sip from his glass and set it back on the table. "You are missing the Water Element."

"Yes," Abby replied smiling. She was pleased that Dan was following and seemed interested.

"Do you know who that person is?" Dan queried.

Sara and Abby exchanged nervous glances.

"Well, we thought of one person it could be," Sara began.

"But he may be too far away," Abby added quickly. "And we don't know the individual personally like we did Joe."

"We were told we would find each other when the time was right," Joe added, shifting slightly in the chair.

"Who told you that?" Dan asked quickly.

"Well, we have an advisor of a sort," Abby added quickly. "I think I mentioned to you when I saw him the first time?"

Dan sat back, deep in thought. A look of realization spread across his face.

"The little person you saw in the woods?"

"Yes," Abby stated. "His name is Gabe. I don't think he is a human little person, though."

"Well, can't he tell you who the other Element is and what you are supposed to be doing?" Dan asked curiously.

Abby thought back to their last conversation where Gabe had said he couldn't do all their work for them.

"Ah, no," Abby said. "I believe he can only advise us to a point. I think that finding each other and the task is like part of the test, or something like that."

Joe and Sara nodded in agreement.

Dan looked at the three of them. "So why are you confiding this in me?"

Abby smiled at him. "I don't want to keep secrets from you, as I've said before. I respect your opinion, and I need your help, just like I always do."

Sara looked at Dan. "You are a good friend of mine, too. I trust your judgment and value your input."

Joe spoke next. "I deeply admire both of these women. They respect you greatly, and I feel I could benefit from your insight too."

Dan looked touched. "Thank you all for your confidence. I'm glad you all feel I'm worthy of it, and I hope I can continue to keep it." Dan smiled and his eyes lit up. "Excuse me a moment," he said as he rose quickly out of his chair and leapt up the stairs two at a time.

Joe and Sara looked at Abby for an answer but she just shrugged as she strained to hear what he was doing. He had entered the office, they could hear him rummaging around; they heard the familiar rattle of file cabinet drawers being opened and then slammed shut, followed by the sound of paper rustling on the desk. Dan uttered a triumphant, "Aha!" before his footfalls thumped heavily down the staircase. Clutched in his hand was a folded piece of paper.

"Here," Dan said smugly as he handed her the folder paper. "Read this and tell me what you think."

Abby scanned the paper and silently handed it to Sara. She did the same and passed it wordlessly back to Abby.

"Well?" Dan asked impatiently.

Abby stood up and kissed Dan on the lips. "I think you've found our Water Vessel." Abby said with a mixture of pride and relief.

CHAPTER 22

Joe stared at Sara, hoping to catch her attention as Abby and Dan spoke excitedly beside him. Sara took a sip from her wineglass and set it down as she commenced chewing on her bottom lip, her eyes glazed as if transfixed on some far off object.

"Oh, Joe, I'm sorry. I didn't mean to be rude," Abby apologized swiftly. "Take a look at this."

Abby thrust the familiar-looking paper toward him. He immediately recognized it as a Harmon City Gallery press release. Grasping it carefully in one hand he read,

"Harmon Gallery is proud to present a collection of watercolors by renowned British artist William Walker. Walker, a self-taught painter, has had a unique career that has spanned three decades. He has combined art with a unique ability to predict future events by a method known as Scrying.

"Scrying is the ability to foretell future events that are channeled through another object, such as water, a method utilized most famously by Nostradamus. William Walker will be presenting a vast collection of his work in this country—his first show outside of the United Kingdom. His exhibit will be exclusive to the Harmon Gallery—a unique opportunity to see this once-in-a-lifetime exhibit of his beautiful and mystical work.

"The opening gala and reception will be held on Friday the 28th of February from 7 to 10 p.m., and the exhibit will continue during regular gallery hours in the main gallery until April 3rd."

"If you have any questions, feel free to call Amy Foster, Executive Director, for details."

Joe read the paper several times before looking up at the expectant faces of Abby and Dan. Sara, he noticed, was quick to look away as she continued to pensively chew on her lip.

"Eh? Whaddya think, Joe?" Dan asked, smiling at him eagerly.

"Uh, yeah," Joe said quietly. It sure sounds like the guy."

"It's the same guy, too!" Abby breathed excitedly, jabbing a finger at the photo on the flyer. "The same guy that we saw on TV, remember, Sara?"

"What guy on TV?" Dan and Joe asked simultaneously.

Sara looked at Abby nervously. She had stopped chewing on her lip and was now twisting a lock of blonde hair between her fingers as her eyes caught hold of Abby's. Abby hoped she read Sara right and continued.

"Well, it all goes back to that infamous day in the park..." Abby began.

And she retold the incident once again of seeing Gabe in the park and him disappearing, how she had been channel surfing at home and seen William Walker on a TV show featuring his work and how he held up a piece depicting Abby and her moment in the trees with Gabe, and how Sara had called her to say she saw Abby on TV.

"Is this the guy you two suspected of being the fourth?" Joe asked quietly, looking at Sara, his dark brown eyes fixated on her and awaiting her reply.

"Well, yes, we did suspect it might be him," Sara added. "But we had no idea that he would be coming here or if we should even contact him—not until Dan showed us that flyer."

Dan puffed up with pride at the mention of his name.

"So how come you didn't tell me?" Joe asked Sara directly.

Abby interrupted. "Well, we did agree that if we discovered who the fourth was, we would wait until the three of us were prepared to defend against another attack, remember? That way, we wouldn't be all sitting together unable to defend ourselves. You said that Thaddeus already knew of two of us."

Sara nodded and smiled in agreement with Abby. Joe knew this was what they all agreed on, of course, but if Sara knew...he couldn't understand why she hadn't mentioned something to him, they had been spending so much time together.

"Hold on a sec," Dan's voice rose slightly, causing everyone to jump. "Did you say *another* attack? When were you attacked? Who's attacking you?"

As Abby refilled wine glasses and got Joe some more pop, Sara regaled Dan with a condensed version of the thwarted ambush at her place.

"...not a single one was left standing," Sara said triumphantly, a satisfied smile played across her lips.

"But what does this guy want?" Dan asked Sara, his face full of concern.

"Apparently for us not to get involved," Abby interjected dryly, taking another sip of wine. She picked up an hors d'oeuvre, examining it briefly before popping it into her mouth.

"So....," Dan began, watching Abby carefully chew the hors d'oeuvre, "why do you have to get involved?"

"Cause we're supposed to," Sara added. She waved her arm in the air in a broad circle, motioning at Joe, Abby, and herself. "We're the good guys."

"I'm not saying you aren't," Dan added quickly. "I'm just concerned for your safety, that's all. Do you think there will be more attacks?"

Joe nodded. "Most likely. Yeah. But we've been preparing. Sara has been a good help with training."

Sara smiled and winked at Joe. He smiled slightly in return.

"Well, they definitely won't be sending any spies anytime soon either," Sara added. Dan looked at Sara.

"Is your new dog a very protective breed?" Dan asked excitedly. "I can hardly wait to see it."

Sara looked at Dan as if he had two heads and opened her mouth to speak, but Abby quickly interjected. "I hope you don't mind, Sara, I told Dan you got a new pet."

Abby cleared her throat loudly, hoping it would draw Dan's attention away from Joe choking on a mouthful of pop. Sara shot Abby a look of confusion but quickly recovered.

"Uh, of course I don't mind, Ab."

"So what have you named him then?" Dan asked.

"Oogan," Sara answered.

"Oogan? That's different," Dan said.

"Yeah, wait 'til you meet him," Abby said as she snorted into her wineglass.

"I can hardly wait," Dan said agreeably.

"Neither can I," Sara said smiling, holding out her plate as Abby piled a few more hors d'oeuvres onto it.

"So, are you sure you can handle this?" Abby asked Dan.

"I can if you can," Dan answered quickly, kissing the end of her nose.

"I love you," Abby said softly.

"I know. Now let's usher this New Year in properly, okay?"

"Hey, I'm all for it," Sara agreed.

Sara handed Joe a plate of hors d'oeuvres while Dan and Abby fiercely debated over whether playing a board game or charades was first on the agenda. Sara shrugged. It didn't matter. They had all night to have fun, and she was ready to relax and just enjoy the company.

The evening passed with no more reference to their abilities as they played a few board games, and then sat around and grazed on the copious amount of tempting snacks that Abby kept shoving in front of them.

"You have to try this, it's amazing," Abby said enthusiastically setting out another plate on the table. "I got the recipe off the internet. I played with the ingredients, and I think it's much better this way. What do you think?"

Joe picked up one and took a tentative bite, nodding his approval. He was positively stuffed, but she seemed pleased with his reaction.

"Come on, Sara," Abby coaxed. "You try one too."

"Geez, Ab, I don't think I can eat another bite."

"Come on, try it. They're only little," Abby coaxed once more.

"Dan, is she always like this?" Sara turned to him as she picked up an appetizer off the tray that Abby had thrust in her direction.

"You have no idea," Dan answered in a mock dry voice. He smiled as Abby shoved the tray in his direction. Dan picked an appetizer off the tray. "Thank you, sweetie."

"You're welcome." Abby smiled back.

Dan got up and turned the stereo off and the TV on.

"Won't be long now," Dan added, watching the New Years' Eve revelers on the first channel he clicked to. Dan stood and motioned to Abby to join him in the kitchen. He opened the fridge and grabbed the chilled champagne and a bottle of ginger ale while Abby grabbed the noise makers and party hats off the counter.

"So whaddya think?" Abby muttered softly to Dan cocking her head in the direction of Joe and Sara as they sat talking quietly in the living room.

"He's great that Joe. Really. " Dan answered quietly giving Abby a reassuring look. "He's really likeable. And, most importantly, he's nothing like the other guys she's dated."

"Yeah, you're right," Abby agreed. "Maybe he won't break her heart like the others did."

"Somehow I don't think he's that kinda guy."

"Oh really?" Abby said, raising an eyebrow skeptically. "And what gave you this insight?"

"Call it man's intuition," Dan replied. Without waiting for a retort, he swept past her into the living room with the champagne and ginger ale on a tray.

Abby laughed. As she brought out the party favors she urged everyone to get ready as Dan poured three glasses of champagne and a glass of ginger ale for Joe.

"Hurry, Dan, hurry!" Abby urged as the countdown began.

"10, 9, 8, 7, 6, 5, 4, 3, 2, 1, Happy New Year!" They all shouted in unison.

Sara and Abby blew their noisemakers and the men shook hands and everyone exchanged hugs. Dan kissed Abby and after Sara gave Joe a quick peck on the lips, Abby yelled,

"I propose a toast!"

"Here, here," agreed Sara, raising her glass.

"Here's to a fabulous new year and to victory."

"Victory!" The others murmured in unison as they all took a sip from their glasses.

The party soon wound down and as Joe noticed Sara try to conceal a wide yawn, he took it as a sign that it was time to leave.

"I'll go start the truck and get it warm," Joe said, putting on his shoes and coat. "We'll let it warm up, okay?"

Joe walked outside and climbed in his truck and started the ignition. He turned the heat on full blast and watched a light snowfall begin to dust the windshield. The snow hadn't accumulated, and there was no frost to scrape from the windows. Joe got out of his running truck and inhaled deeply. He loved the crisp smell of a cold winter's night. He stood for a moment, looking around, taking in the silent, peaceful surroundings before turning on his heel and heading back toward the house. He paused for a moment on the front landing to look out at the snow-covered ground and night sky again and was surprised to see a small figure huddled under a pine tree in the yard. Joe squinted in an effort to identify it. *Too small for a dog*, he thought. *But also much too large for a cat.*

Slowly, it crept out from under the branches of the tree, the white tip of its bushy tail almost dusting the snow-covered ground. Joe recognized it immediately: it was a red tail fox. It crept closer until it was less than ten feet from Joe, and then it calmly sat down on its haunches, observing him with patient curiosity. It sat that way for a couple of minutes as Joe returned its curious stare. He began to wonder if the red tail fox was his helper, or if the creature was sent to guide him. He thought about putting some tobacco down on the ground, but quickly realized he didn't have any tobacco in the jacket he was wearing.

"You followin' me?" Joe questioned the fox, thinking it couldn't hurt.

The fox made a yippy, yowly noise at him, then turned its back and trotted away down the driveway where it disappeared into the woods on the opposite side of the road. Unsure of whether he got his answer or not, Joe watched as it loped out of his sight before he returned inside the house to get Sara.

"Thanks for everything," Sara said as she pulled on her coat. "It was a lovely evening."

Joe engaged in idle chit-chat with Dan while he waited in the entryway for Sara. As he waited, his eyes roamed the large collection of family photos on the wall. A great many of small-framed pictures surrounded an 8" x 10" in the center of the wall. Joe was surprised to see it was Dan and Abby, huge smiles on their faces, and cradled in Abby's arms was a small baby dressed in a pink dress and white lace bonnet.

Joe hadn't heard a child, and neither of them had mentioned one either. *Not my business*, Joe reminded himself mentally.

"Thanks for coming tonight, Joe," Abby said, giving him a quick but gentle hug. "I'm really glad you came."

Joe smiled. "Me too. Thanks for a great evening."

"Well, I'm sure we'll all be seeing each other again soon," Dan added smiling broadly.

"Yeah, count on it," Sara chimed in.

Sara and Joe said their goodbyes and headed out to his truck. Joe opened the passenger side door for Sara and closed the door once she was sitting comfortably on the bench seat. As Joe walked around the truck to the driver's side, he couldn't help but look for his furry stalker. But the fox was nowhere in sight.

"Happy New Year to you, too." He said softly into the night sky as he climbed into his truck.

***

A huge blizzard was raging outside Joe's front door, and according to the radio weather man, the whipping wind dumping vast quantities of snow across most of the state was proving that the New Year had indeed started with much ado. At least two feet of snow blanketed the ground, and it looked as if the storm was in no hurry to cease its blustery rampage.

Joe turned from the window and pulled the quilt on his lap up to his chin and picked up the book he was only half-heartedly attempting to read. He had had no firm plans to go anywhere today, and for once he was grateful for some down time alone. Although he was a bachelor, Joe prided himself on being very prepared for any emergency and that included being snowed in. He had a pantry full of canned food, bottled water, instant coffee, candles, and wood for the fireplace in case of a power outage.

"No sense worrying about the weather," his mother used to say. "It's not like we have the power to change it."

So he decided it was okay to just have a quiet day sitting on his comfortable chair, listening to the radio blurt out the weather report every hour, and trying to read a book he had been looking forward to focus his full attention on. But it wasn't as easy as he thought it would be. Joe's thoughts kept drifting back to Sara.

Sara had sat snuggled up beside him, her head resting on his shoulder, on the bench seat of his truck when he drove her home last night. Joe drew in a deep breath, as if somehow it could bring back the memory of how good her hair had smelled as it had softly brushed up against his cheek. And when they arrived at Sara's, Joe dutifully got out of the truck and walked her to her door. She had opened the door and he had not asked her if he could come in. He bent toward her, gave her a kiss on the cheek and a brief hug before admonishing her to get inside from the cold and telling her he would call her tomorrow. She had smiled and whispered goodnight as Joe headed toward his truck and backed out of her driveway.

On the way home he had wondered why he didn't ask to come in for a coffee. But he also wondered if maybe Sara would have offered if he hadn't been so quick to speak. Joe shrugged to himself and gazed out the window at the raging snow outside.

"Well, I did call her today," Joe thought out loud. He had called her place at 10 am to see how she was braving the weather, but all he got was her voicemail. He left a brief message and asked her to call when she had a chance and quietly hung up. Joe looked over at the clock on the living room wall. The indigo blue digital numbers read 2:14 pm. He thought about calling again, maybe she hadn't gotten the first message, or maybe she was too busy. Since he didn't want to come off as needy or clingy he resisted the urge to call her again.

Joe frowned. He really liked Sara, but last night when Abby and Sara revealed the information they had kept from him on the fourth, the Water Element, he had noticed that Sara avoided making eye contact with him. He had to admit to himself he was more than a little hurt that Sara didn't share the information with him. Perhaps she didn't trust him enough to reveal that information to him before last night.

"Maybe I have been too trusting of her," Joe surmised aloud.

He had always been a little naïve when it came to women and relationships, and maybe this was just another example of his inexperience or poor judgment with regard to those topics. Whatever the case was, the information about the fourth was out and the damage was done. *Just to be on the safe side*, Joe thought, *it might be a good idea to back off a bit.* Joe knew that they certainly had bigger things to do—would this really be the right time for a relationship?

Joe looked at the phone. Well, time would certainly tell. And the ball was in Sara's court now. Joe gave one last look out the window before picking up his book and settling back into the chair.

***

Before any of them knew it, the first weeks of January had passed in a blur of activity. Joe had returned to teaching after the holiday season, and he was preparing not only his own work for summer shows, but also a student art show at the school. This would be the first year the kids had ever displayed their work, and they were becoming quickly aware of how much work and preparation was involved in organizing an exhibit.

Abby and Sara were both busy producing work that would be shown and hopefully sold at upcoming summer shows. They also spent their time filling out juried show applications and taking photographs of their works for consideration in the exhibits. They both managed to meet a couple times a week for a coffee and a chat, and they and Joe gathered once a week to practice at Sara's. Dan had been eager to go to Sara's too, but Abby convinced him that he would be bored at their little practice sessions. She explained that his talents were more brains than brawn, and that he would be the best person to keep track of William Walker in order to let them know when he had arrived. Dan appeared to enjoy being considered the "brains" of their little group, and he definitely enjoyed his role as their self-appointed detective.

Gabe had appeared briefly at one of their training sessions. He had come to tell them that, while Thaddeus' forces were lying low, Gabe's sources had told him that some of his supporters from the past were having difficulties accounting for their mysterious absences. Gabe figured they were safe from further attacks for a while and spared some time to hang around to observe their training with a minimum of grumbling. Although he would make the odd comment ("Watch each others' backs, cover yer flanks"), it was apparent he was satisfied with how well the three of them were able to use their abilities and how they managed to work as a team. It appeared to have instilled a fatherly sense of pride in him. The relationship that had developed between Sara and Oogan, however, had surprised him the most.

Indeed, it was a strange relationship. Sometimes it was as if Sara treated Oogan like a stray pet that had been neglected and followed her home. Other times it she treated him like a naïve or slow-learning child, teaching him what he needed to know to survive in her world. During his waking hours Oogan would follow Sara around the barn, his penguin-like waddle slightly offset by the use of his wing talons as canes to keep him upright out at the back area of her property. Sara had cautioned him to stay away from the main house and the road. Oogan was beginning to resemble, in action at least, the dog that Abby had told Dan he was. The only difference was that he would ask her many questions as he loped along behind her, and Sara always patiently answered every single one.

"How do humans get honey from bees?" he once asked. Oogan's affection for Sara was so obvious and genuine that both Abby and Joe wondered if Oogan would leave once he had been freed. Abby herself wondered if Sara would be ready to let him go when the time came.

Abby shuddered at the thought. Oogan had emitted such an aura of sadness that it was hard for her to be around him at all. The worst of it was that Oogan obviously noticed the effect he had on her, often using it to his advantage to get Abby to leave early. Abby shrugged. Although she had made efforts to get along with him, he apparently still held a grudge against her stemming from their first encounter.

"Well, I don't care what he thinks of me." Abby told Joe. "As long as he likes Sara and can't tell the bad guys about us we're doin' okay, right?"

Joe would merely nod wordlessly and offer no further insight regarding Oogan. Abby suspected that he did harbor some worries and speculation about Oogan, but he was discreet about his apprehension and kept it to himself. *Perhaps with good reason*, Abby had thought. Oogan treated Joe respectfully but kept at a distance. He exhibited a rather indifferent attitude to Joe in general, and did not show any open hostility toward him as he did with Abby. Abby did notice that Joe was very cognizant of all of Oogan's actions while he was at Sara's during Oogan's "waking times". On one notable occasion she had observed Joe cast a wary sidelong glance toward Oogan as he loped toward the copse of trees behind the barn. Oogan sighed and stared longingly into the woods, smacking his lips as he spied some type of vegetation that he desired to eat. But he remained loyal to his bond to Sara. Abby felt reassured by Joe's watchful gaze.

At least I'm not the only one with doubts of his loyalty, Abby thought.

As the month wore on, Abby, Joe and Sara cut their time together to one day a week. All three of them were busy making objets d'art and sending out slides and pictures for coveted places in various art shows. And it helped to keep their minds off the fact that maybe there would be no shows this summer, if at all for them. And things had been quiet. An unnerving type of stillness one experiences before a huge, devastating bomb was dropped. Was that what they were waiting for? None of them knew. But as each still, quiet day approached with no attacks or surveillance, they all speculated whether the appearance of William Walker would bring about instant change and herald the dropping of the bomb they were expecting. They were eager with anticipation. The arrival of Walker would mean that they all had to connect and then work together. All the training and their increased ability with their powers gave them confidence. They would conquer evil as long as they found it on their terms.

On the last Saturday of January, Abby and Joe found themselves outside the back of the barn staring up at the crisp, clear, blue sky, their eyes oblivious to the fog of their breath rising into the air around them. Simultaneously they both looked downward and met each other's gaze. They stared at each other for a long moment before Joe opened his mouth to speak. Abby held her hand up to stop him. She just looked at him and said quietly,

"I know."

Joe closed his mouth and nodded. And he looked back up at the sky, satisfied that in some bizarre way he was understood, and for the day he was content with that knowledge.

CHAPTER 23

"Report." Thaddeus' voice demanded from within the fog. Michael turned toward the voice. He had been summoned to report to Thaddeus, and he had responded to the urgent message immediately, leaving his second-in-command abruptly with a wave of the hand and no real explanation. It had been risky to leave, and he felt that Thaddeus should have had some idea, or at least the slightest inclination that his departure would look suspicious. Thaddeus was aware that Michael would be suspected of treason if the Queen was aware of any plots against her reign, so Thaddeus must believe that his presence was urgent and highly important. Why else would he jeopardize their mission now?

When Michael heard Thaddeus' voice resonate through the fog as he arrived at the Omphalos near Thaddeus' human world location, he felt his heightened sense of caution was somewhat validated. Thaddeus emerged quickly from the haze to meet Michael at the stone.

"We shall move into the fog for more cover," he announced brusquely as he strode toward Michael, his steel blue eyes scanning the area. "I hope you weren't followed," he added as he moved into the mist. Michael followed obediently as his heels.

"No, I don't believe so." Michael answered flatly as the cadence of his footfalls fell into time with Thaddeus' pace.

Once he was sure that they were safely within the concealment of the fog and that they would be unobservable from the stone Omphalos, Thaddeus stopped.

"Why have you chosen to meet here instead of at your store?" Michael enquired, lifting an eyebrow.

Thaddeus raised a hand into the air, making the fog surrounding them even thicker as if ice particles hung heavy in the air.

"I believe I am being watched," Thaddeus declared quietly. "Someone tripped a magical ward outside the bookstore the other night."

Thaddeus cleared his throat, his eyes narrowed as he spoke. "The alarm roused me from my slumber and summoned one of my personal security forces to the location of the breech. By the time we both arrived there was no one there."

Michael clasped his hands together behind his back and took a few pacing steps. "Do you know who it might have been?" Michael asked quickly.

Thaddeus crossed his arms over his chest. "Well, that's part of the reason why I have summoned you," he responded flatly. "Have we been found out?"

Michael's mind flashed back to the castle and the activity that had seemed to have increased lately. He had seen Gabe on more than one occasion lurking near the corridors and staircases that led down the Taekyrs' dungeon stables and training yard. And the guards in and around the castle had increased at least five-fold by his best estimate.

"I do not believe we have been found out yet, sir," Michael answered confidently. "Security in and around the castle has increased, yes, but with the Veil beginning to weaken, so have the constitutions of many of those that live in our land. I mean, Feyland," he quickly corrected himself before continuing. "The hysteria and emotional tension of the masses has increased, there have been many incidences—"

"There will be even more yet to come," Thaddeus interrupted, clasping his hands in front of him, his eyes lighting up, his mouth twisted into a toothy smile. "Change is coming. Yes, it is definitely coming soon."

Thaddeus raised a hand up to the air, his fingers splayed apart, his palms facing outwards as he closed his eyes, a serene expression on his face as he stood there silent for a brief moment. "Soon, soon," he murmured softly before opening his eyes. It seemed to Michael as if he snapped out of a trance and then quickly regained his composure. "Well then, if the Queen and her agents have not caught on to us, then I believe one of our allies may be testing our strengths." Thaddeus smiled again.

Michael thought he rather looked like the cat that got the bird.

"I believe I shall pay a short, unannounced visit to one of our allies in this world. Perhaps it will shake him up to find me standing on his doorstep." Thaddeus crossed his arms across his chest, a smug expression on his face.

"One last thing before you go, Michael."

"Yes, sir?"

"I want you to locate the Taekyr that has gone missing. Send out a locator spell on his leg band—you did say he was banded, that he was castle-born?"

Michael nodded.

"Very well. Locate the Taekyr. I think it's time we found out where he has been. Perhaps he will provide us with some useful information if he is found alive."

"Yes, sir." Michael replied, as he turned to walk toward the Omphalos. He spun around quickly on his heel to face Thaddeus once again.

"Sir, I also wanted to inform you that the Water Vessel is on the move." Michael added. "I believe that he will be making contact with the Air Vessel within a fortnight's time." Michael watched Thaddeus for a reaction. Thaddeus smiled triumphantly.

"Remember, he is to be observed *only*. He is not to be harmed. Understood?"

"Yes, sir." Michael answered quickly, snapping his heels together.

"That's all, you may go now," Thaddeus said with an indifferent wave of his hand.

Michael turned away and headed back toward the Omphalos. The fog was receding and as it moved away, it began to dissipate rapidly, no doubt due to Thaddeus' magical abilities.

"Don't forget," Thaddeus called quietly as Michael reached the stone. "Locate the Taekyr and report his location to me before you go retrieving him."

Michael acknowledged Thaddeus' parting words with a salute and then placed his hand on the cool stone surface. Thaddeus' face disappeared out of view and a strand of trees took his place in place in Michael's field of vision. He was relieved to be home, but he warily scanned the trees to ensure he was not being observed or followed. Spying no one, he slipped soundlessly away from the stone Omphalos and in the direction of the castle.

***

William Walker stood in the middle of the immense gallery room and just stared, taking in the absolute vastness of the empty space. Though he had been provided with dimensions and a "virtual video tour" through the internet, nothing could truly prepare him for the immense size of the room. His carefully packed crates had arrived two days before him, an accomplishment he hoped wouldn't come back to haunt him if any of his work had been damaged in transit.

William strode over to the large picture window at the front of the gallery and peered out into the street. The town was small, nowhere near the size of the village he was from, yet the sidewalks bustled with people walking along and tucking their heads down into their collars and pulling hats tighter over their ears as a gentle snow steadily fell. William stood in awe, watching the snow fall gently to the ground and settle on the walks and pathways like a perfect, soft powder. How long had it been since he had seen snow in his own country? William strained to recall. It was 1970-something, at least that was the best guess he could conjure. He turned away from the window and began to survey the room again, this time with an eye to where he would display his work.

"Is the space what you expected?" enquired Amy Foster, the gallery's Executive Director. The pretty, petite blonde strode over to William, a folder in one hand, her other extended as way of introduction.

William shook her hand, surprised at the firm grip of such a seemingly delicate hand.

"Aye, the room's fine," William said, glancing admiringly at the glossy hardwood floor and the upholstered display wall.

"Well, I thought I should bring the floor plan you sent us. It may aid you in your set up." Amy set the open folder face up in the window sill. "I have arranged for two interns to come in and help move and set up structure. If you want them to help hang your work too, that also can be arranged." Amy looked at him; her blue eyes were friendly but focused on the task at hand. "I know some artists are particular about others handling their work and prefer to hang it themselves." Amy shrugged, and continued. "Whatever the case, please do not hesitate to ask if you require anything, and if you have any problems, please call our attention to it immediately." Amy smiled again. "We are eagerly anticipating your first North American exhibit. My personal assistant, Gloria, is at your disposal, and she has my cell phone number, should you need me before the opening gala. Do you have any questions?" Amy looked at him carefully; her eyebrows rose, waiting for a response.

William stood mute for a moment; his brain seemed to be moving slower, a side effect, no doubt, from jet lag. "Thanks very much, Ms. Foster, for yer generosity. I meself am looking forward to the show. Bin awhile since I've bin this excited." William spoke carefully, forcing the words out.

"Well, I believe it's going to be wonderful," Amy enthused. "Anyway, I must go, can I get Gloria to bring you some coffee or tea and a sandwich? I have no doubt you're hungry."

William's stomach protested loudly at the mere mention of food. "Aye, a sandwich and a tea would be welcome indeed," William said, holding his hands over his groaning stomach in an attempt to stifle the noise.

Amy laughed and began walking toward the back of the building toward the exit.

"A sandwich and a tea it is then. I'll have those sent to you immediately." Amy halted briefly at the exit door and called out to William. "Oh, welcome to the United States, Mr. Walker, and on behalf of the community and gallery, welcome to Harmon."

"Thank you very much." William replied as she darted out the door. He felt humbled by such welcoming hospitality. William strode over to the layout plan that was open in the window and scrutinized it carefully before striding over to a crate and prying the top off with a crowbar. As if by magic, two young men appeared with a display rack stand and a frame stand in tow.

Blimey, they didn't waste any time, he thought as he pulled several pieces out of the crate and propping them up against the walls. *Work while ya got it, Wills*, he reminded himself as he motioned to various places the work was to be hung and displayed. At least with his helpers the work would come along quickly.

William was focused so intently on his work that he failed to notice the dark-haired man. His hands and face were pressed up against the window glass from the outside, taking in the sight of William and his paintings, his eyes the size of dinner plates. The man peered in the window for a moment before entering the gallery. He nodded in the direction of William and the two interns as he hurried past and knocked on the administrative office door.

A young, raven-haired woman, who William took to be Gloria, opened the door and beckoned the man in. He heard the low murmur of voices and paid it no further attention and continued to uncrate and set up his work. Another young man arrived carrying a tray bearing a small pot of tea, milk, sugar, and a roast beef sandwich. He set the tray down and quietly exited the room.

William sat down and wolfed down the sandwich, trying to remember when he had last eaten. *On the plane? Yeah*, he remembered. That was twelve hours ago. No wonder he was so damned hungry. William poured himself a cup of tea. It was good too, the best he had had since he left home. *Boy, these Americans sure are friendly and welcoming. I best not get used to this nobby treatment and enjoy meself too much*, he thought.

William was draining his cup and stood to commence set up when Gloria and the man entered the room.

"Hello, Mr. Walker," Gloria chirped. "I'm Gloria, Ms. Foster's assistant. If you require anything, I am here to help you. My office," she gestured over her shoulder, "is over there. So feel free to knock or scream if you need me."

"Thank you." William said. "So far, I'm doin' okay thanks to these two here." William waved in the direction of the two young men moving display racks. They acknowledge his praise with silent nods as they continued their work.

"Quite a bit of set up, isn't it?" the dark-haired man spoke. Gloria looked at the man beside her as if seeing him for the first time.

"Where are my manners?" Gloria chided herself. "William Walker, this is Dan Fabrica. Dan, this is William Walker. He is the featured artist and he will be exhibiting his work here for the next month."

"Yes, we received the announcement in the mail." Dan said. He shook William's hand in greeting.

William studied him carefully. "Are yeh an artist too?" William asked Dan.

"Oh no, my wife's the one with the talent," Dan smiled. "But I was in the neighborhood and my wife had arranged for me to pick up her commission check. I do have an interest in art, and I am very much looking forward to the opening of your show." Dan smiled widely at William and gave an appraising look around the room.

William didn't know what to say, it has been years since people acknowledged his work, let alone say they were actually looking forward to seeing it.

"Well, I must go," Dan spoke quickly, turning toward the door. "It was nice to meet you, and I look forward to seeing you at the opening."

Dan headed for the door with Gloria following in his wake. He gave one last wave before he disappeared out the door. William watched him walk down the snow-covered sidewalk and disappear out of sight before he returned to his set up.

What a nice bunch of people, William thought. He smiled to himself. *Perhaps this show is a better opportunity than I thought.*

Suddenly, his bones didn't ache so much and his step seemed lighter. He heard the sound of a jaunty tune being whistled and was pleasantly surprised to find that it was coming from him.

***

Sara sat on a blanket on the floor of the barn just outside the stall where Oogan had made his temporary nest. On the blanket beside her lay an open picnic basket, its contents had been removed and spread out neatly on the blanket. Sara had set up a plate of sandwiches and a plate of salad for Oogan as well as a shallow bowl of water. She had been surprised when she first observed him lap up water in much the same manner as a cat.

"Come, Oogan, I brought lunch down. Come have something to eat."

Sara set herself out a sandwich and poured a thermos cup of coffee for herself as she waited for Oogan to amble out from his stall and over to the blanket. He stood at the edge of the blanket as if awaiting instruction. Sara looked up at him with wide, bright eyes and a smile.

"Please, I made you your favorites. Eat."

Oogan shuffled forward. "Thank you, Lady Sara," he croaked as he snagged a sandwich in an extended talon and began to eat.

"You're quite welcome." Sara replied as she picked up her own sandwich and took a bite. Sara smiled as she wondered what Abby would think about her little picnics with Oogan. Sara noticed Abby crinkled her nose with distaste whenever Oogan entered the barn or whenever they passed his stall. In the beginning, Sara had also noticed the pungent, acrid smell that seemed to hang around him. Perhaps being around Taekyrs was akin to living on a farm. After a bit of time, you just got accustomed to the smell. It didn't really appear to bother Joe either. Sara frowned. Not that he had been around that much lately anyway. Still, although he was spending less time with her, she was comfortable that they were just going slowly. Although she would have liked to have spent more time with him, she wasn't about to try to change things and scare him away either. *Why do relationships have to be so complicated?* Sara sighed as she bit into her sandwich.

"You are sad." Oogan said in his deep, croaky voice.

"What?"

"You are sad." Oogan repeated with the same lack of inflection in his voice. "Why?"

"Why am I sad?" Sara was a little puzzled. "Do I really seem sad?"

"Sometimes," Oogan answered flatly. "Do you miss your brood?"

"My brood? You mean my family?"

"Yessss. Why do they not come to see you? You seem nice, for a human," he added as he reached for another sandwich.

"Well thanks, I guess," Sara replied. "But I have no brood, no family."

"Why?" Oogan asked, his black watery eyes fixed on her.

Sara squirmed slightly. "Well, my father abandoned my mother and I when I was a baby," Sara began slowly," so I never knew him. My mother became ill when I was ten, and she died soon afterward. I went to live with my widowed Aunt at that time. Just after I had started college, Aunt Alice passed away. Except for my father, who I've never known, she was my only family.

"You are alone." Oogan spoke quietly.

"Well, yes, I suppose," Sara replied, "but I have my friends, so I guess in my case, they are my family." Sara looked at Oogan and saw that he was gazing out the barn window, a far off look in his watery, dark eyes.

"I guess you must be missing your brood." Sara spoke as she nibbled on her sandwich.

"This is the longest I have been away from them." Oogan said.

"Do you miss your children? Your offspring?" Sara asked, a guilty pang clutched at her heart.

"No, I don't have a mate yet," Oogan answered. "I just miss their company, their smells, their sounds...." Oogan's voice trailed off and he looked at Sara. "But someday I will return to them, yesss?"

"Of course," Sara beamed at him as Oogan rocked back and forth from one talon to the other, something Sara noticed he tended to do when he was happy.

"Then I am glad I am able to spend time with you, Lady Sara. Then I don't feel so lonely."

Sara smiled widely and reached her one hand out to touch Oogan above his right wing.

"I'm glad," Sara replied. "I really enjoy your company too." Sara stood up and moved closer to Oogan.

"Let's take a closer look at that wing, shall we? If it has properly healed, perhaps you could get a bit of exercise outside tonight. Stretch your wings a bit. We could go for a little flight. Would you like that?"

Oogan nodded and gingerly unfolded his injured wing for her inspection. As Sara scrutinized the wing she had to suppress a smile. It was nice to have company, even if he was a bizarre companion. And it felt good to be needed. Perhaps Gabe would let him stay on a little longer. She could only hope.

***

The murmurs of voices mingled with the sound of soft Celtic music as Dan and Abby made their way into the main gallery room. The crowd was the biggest Abby had ever seen at any one time in the building. Amy Foster, the director, her assistant Gloria, and a myriad of staff were hastily moving throughout the crowd, encouraging patrons to "continue upstairs for refreshments" once they had taken in the exhibit. It looked as if a few pieces had already sold judging by the staff frantically packing at the main counter.

"Is he here?" Abby whispered into Dan's ear as he guided her through the mass of people by the hand.

"Yes," he replied in a loud whisper. "He's over there in the corner talking to some lady. Where's Sara?"

"She said she'd be here, that she'd meet us." Abby glanced around, but she saw no sign of Sara in the crowd.

"What about Joe?" Dan asked. "Is he coming?"

"Sara said she would call him. I don't know if she got in touch with him or not." Abby looked at Dan. "So....what's your plan?"

Dan raised an eyebrow mischievously. It was as if he was waiting for her to ask.

"My 'plan', as you put it, is for you and I to make our way over to where William is standing in the corner. We stand in front of one of those pieces, chat idly, and when he's freed from his conversation, I'll catch his attention and introduce you."

Abby looked at him, her left eyebrow raised. "Then what do we do?"

"I don't have a clue after that. Tell you what," Dan leaned over and kissed her on the cheek. "Let's burn that bridge when we're on it, okay?"

Abby smiled sweetly at him and gave his hand a hard squeeze. "Do you *really* want me to burn that bridge?"

"Figuratively, darling, just figuratively." Dan gave her hand a small tug in the direction of the corner where it appeared that William Walker was trapped in a long conversation with a group of people. He had only uttered a couple of words, from what Abby could see, and he appeared to be nodding his head a lot. As they inched closer to the group, they stopped in front of quite a few pieces. *The imagery in his work is very powerful*, Abby noted. While Abby had never painted with watercolors in her life, she was able to appreciate the beauty and feel the emotion that seemed to emanate from the work.

"So what do you think?" Dan asked quietly as they were almost on top of the group speaking to William Walker.

Abby grinned slyly at Dan. "Sweetie," she said in a much louder voice, "I heard they're serving those wonderful hors d'oeuvres in the upstairs lounge again. Remember how fast they went at the last opening?"

"Uh, yeah, I do," Dan replied a little too loudly as Abby shot him an exasperated look.

"Let's just finish taking a quick peek down here and head upstairs. I don't want to miss the food." Abby crossed her arms in front of her chest.

Dan smiled. "What do you think of this one?" He pointed to a painting to his side.

Out of the corner of her eye, Abby noticed the largest woman in the group surrounding William was tugging on her friend's sleeve as she whispered something hurriedly in her ear. The woman bustled past Abby and Dan, followed by her friends, the last of whom uttered,

"It was very nice to meet you, Mr. Walker, we will drop by again during your exhibit," as she hurried to catch up with the others.

Abby watched the women head for the stairs to the lounge.

"Works every time, doesn't it?" Dan said, giving her a satisfied look.

Abby looked at him and rolled her eyes, her arms still crossed over her chest. "Yeah, no thanks to your bad acting."

Dan's laughter cut away and Abby felt as if someone was standing directly behind her. The hairs on the nape of her neck were standing on edge.

"You're Dan Fabrica, aren't yeh?" A gruff voice with an English accent came from behind her. She couldn't help but stiffen her body in response to his voice. The voice was familiar to her ears from hearing it on TV, but the sound of it grated on her nerves.

"Yes, we met earlier," Dan said eagerly, extending his hand and shaking William's in greeting. "I see you've gotten everything set up. Looks great too." Dan gave a cursory glance around. "Oh, and I've brought my lovely wife to meet you." Abby turned around slowly to look at William. "Abby, this is William Walker. William Walker, this is my lovely wife, Abby."

William's eyes widened as he extended a slightly shaking hand to Abby. She gripped it, but felt slightly repulsed by the sensation of his hand in hers. Judging by how quickly he retracted his hand, Abby guessed that he might have felt the same sensation.

They continued to stare at each other until Abby finally forced out, "Nice to meet you, Mr. Walker."

He continued to stare at her wordlessly. "Call me William." He suddenly blurted out.

As they continued to silently scrutinize each other, Abby felt more awkward. She wanted to say something to him, but wasn't sure what to say.

"You must be thirsty, William, it seemed you were talking with that group for quite some time. Would you like a drink?" Dan offered. "I was going to get a glass of wine for my wife and me."

"Aye, yeah a glass o' wine. Sure." William spoke quietly.

"I'll get the wine and I'll be right back," Dan said cheerfully.

"Do you need any help?" Abby asked; a pleading don't-leave-us-alone look on her face.

Dan ignored it. "Nah, I got it," he replied. "Why don't you two chat until I get back?" Before William or Abby could protest, Dan was already heading up the stairs.

Coward, Abby silently seethed, staring daggers at his back as she watched him move up the stairs and out of sight. She was starting to feel really warm, and hoped that it was from being surrounded by so many people and not a reaction to being this close to the Water Vessel. Her hands were starting to heat up and she looked down at her palms, examining them for any sign of spontaneous combustion. Once she was satisfied she got the fire under control, she rubbed her palms onto her pants.

"Somethin' wrong with yer hands?" William inquired politely.

Abby looked up at him. He appeared a little younger than he did when he was on TV. *Still a lot older than me,* she surmised silent, taking in his gray hair and ruddy complexion. With a start, she realized he was still looking at her, waiting for an answer.

"I think you probably already know what's wrong with my hands," Abby spoke in a lower, menacing tone. William gasped, but said nothing.

"You recognized me, didn't you?" Abby persisted, her tone still low so that no one else could overhear them. William still said nothing, so Abby carried on.

"I saw that show on TV with that Nigel Simon guy," Abby said flatly. "I saw the picture." William continued to stare at her, an incredulous look frozen on his face. "I know it was me, William, because I also know the man in the painting too. His name is Gabe."

William started to shake slightly. It was at that precise moment that Dan appeared at his side, causing him to jump nervously.

"Here's the wine," Dan chirped as he brought over the glasses and handed one to William and one to Abby. Dan was stunned to see the pair of them simultaneously knock down their drinks in one big gulp.

"Another, please," Abby said handing him her glass. She grabbed William's and handed it to Dan also. "He needs a refill too." Dan looked at the pair of them incredulously, and without a word he returned to the lounge for refills.

"So," William began as he fidgeted with the collar of his shirt, as if his tie was shrinking and starting to choke him. "What exactly is going on?"

Abby smiled. "Well, William. We expect that we will find out soon, now that you have arrived."

CHAPTER 24

William Walker stared nervously at Abby, his blue eyes wide. Though she was very attractive, there was something about her that he found disturbing. She spoke so low and menacingly, as if she had the ability to harness a dark energy that could engulf and swallow you up. *There is something hidden there behind those deep brown eyes*, he told himself. He found her disturbing and compelling at the same time, which was probably why he felt obliged to listen to what she had to say. He had a sense that he could trust her; his instincts told him unequivocally that she would not lie or mislead him. But regardless of his instincts, he was wary of her — mostly because she still managed to piss him off.

"Whaddya mean you'll find out once I'm here?" William replied, his anger starting to rise (*where did that come from anyway?*) "Yeh think I got answers for yeh?" William crossed his arms over his chest too as he faced Abby, steadying himself for her response.

Abby looked at him, her nose wrinkled in distain as a frown appeared on her face. She sighed deeply and closed her eyes for a moment before speaking.

"No, William, I don't expect you to have the answers. I just expect you are merely a piece in a puzzle into which we all fit." Abby stared at him unrelentingly, hoping the answer would keep him from going off on her.

But before either of them could react, Dan re-entered the room carrying refilled wine glasses, and on his heels was Sara, clutching a small plate in one hand and a wine goblet in the other.

"I just got here and headed straight for the food," Sara explained as she smiled sheepishly at Abby. "They have those great hors d'oeuvres they served at the last exhibit. I wanted to get a few before they ran out." As Dan looked at Abby with a smirk, Sara set down her glass, took a bite of a hors d'oeuvre and through her mouthful of food muttered, "Did I miss anything good?"

Abby and William looked at each other and then at Sara. Sara looked up, in an attempt to decipher what was going on.

"I have a feeling I intruded on a 'moment'," Sara said, as she dabbed her hand into a napkin. "Start again?"

With a broad smile at William, Sara now offered her clean hand. "Hi, I'm Sara Taylor," she began, tossing her blonde hair as she shook his hand.

William grasped her hand in a firm grip and returned the smile.

"William Walker," he announced.

"Yeah, I know," Sara chirped casually as she turned her head, as if trying to take in all his work all at once.

"I saw you on TV, did Abby mention it?"

"Er, yeah, she did," William answered, fidgeting slightly.

"Where's Joe?" Abby broke in abruptly.

Sara set down her glass and swallowed her sip of wine. "Joe couldn't make it, he had some school thing he had to do that the students were counting on him for. He said he'd catch up with us maybe tomorrow." Sara shrugged, and looked over at Abby.

"Who's Joe now?" William asked, his gray eyebrows arched slightly.

Sara's mouth was pursed to reply, but Abby cut in.

"He's Sara's boyfriend."

Sara looked at Abby incredulously, but Abby didn't seem to notice. Her eyes were riveted on William's, as if she were gauging his response. He held her gaze for a moment, then turned away with a shrug. The three of them stood around shooting each other the occasional glance but shifting uncomfortably under the burden of the silence that seemed to have encompassed them.

"Hey, you two," Dan's voice broke the silence. Both Abby and Sara jumped at the sound of his voice. "I'm sure William here must 'work the room', as it were, as part of the opening so we really shouldn't hold him up. So, William, how about you join us for dinner tomorrow evening? Would that work for you?"

William nodded, and he told Dan where he was staying so Dan could arrange to pick him up. Abby leaned over to Sara and whispered, "What d' ya think?"

Sara leaned over and whispered back. "I think I'm glad Dan is handling this one."

Abby giggled slightly. "Yeah, me too."

Sara smiled at her and tipped her wineglass in Abby's direction as she drained it.

"Okay, so I will pick you up at the motel at 6 pm tomorrow then," Dan's voice carried.

Sara stuck out her hand. "It was nice to meet you," she said as he offered her hand.

"Likewise," he replied shaking her hand. He looked at Abby expectantly.

"Have a good evening," Abby spoke curtly, her body stiff.

"Thanks." William responded in a similar, guarded tone.

"Bye!" Sara almost yelled as they walked out of the room.

Almost instantly, William seemed overwhelmed by a crowd of people, all seemingly wanting a piece of him. Dan guided Abby out gently, his hand on the small of her back.

"Geez, Abby, could you seem any more like a cold bitch?" Dan said quietly as they walked out.

Abby was incredulous with the realization of what kind of first impression she must have made.

"I couldn't help myself!" Abby protested. "It just came out that way! I really didn't mean...,"

Abby broke off, remembering Gabe's warning about fire and water not getting along. *Was that a general operating principle or what?* She wondered. *Well, I'm going to try harder to remove that preconception,* Abby thought smugly. *If anyone can do it, it will definitely be me.*

* * *

Gabe stood at attention, his back to the stone wall of the royal courtyard. Queen Ezreanna was sitting in a wrought silver chair partially hidden by a canopy of billowing ice-blue fabric. Two members of the Guard Royale flanked her, and a few more were scattered in visible locations throughout the courtyard. It was astounding to note that there were at least three times as many Guardsmen present concealed in various locations and rooftops in the vicinity. Even with his training and sharp eyes Gabe had great difficulty in detecting their locations.

The Queen was in an animated discussion with the Bard Commander. At her side sat a Sage, no doubt the one who wove and placed the magical wards throughout the castle and its grounds. The wards must have been set very sensitive and high, as Gabe felt the hum and vibration as he passed through them. The Bard Commander stood at a nod from the Queen, saluted, and briskly marched out from under the canopy. He looked frazzled and weary, but nodded in polite acknowledgement to Gabe as he bustled past. Gabe nodded in return and noticed that the Queen was waving a dismissing hand at the Sage, and the Sage slowly drifted out as Queen Ezreanna motioned to Gabe to enter. He reached his hand up and removed his hat before entering the Queen's tent, standing at attention, awaiting her acknowledgement.

"Oh, Gabe, at ease please," she intoned, her voice cracking and sounding somewhat hoarse. "It's been a long day, and I have little patience for military formalities at the moment."

She raised her hands to her forehead and swiped her hair from her face. Motioning for a pitcher, she accepted a glass of lemonade and had a glass set in front of Gabe.

"Thank you, Yer Majesty," he murmured.

He waited, quietly sipping his drink. She obviously needed a moment to gather her thoughts, regain her composure and her voice. In a brief moment she sat up straighter, her eyes brighter and steely in their focus.

"What have you to report?" Queen Ezreanna demanded wearily.

Gabe riveted his gaze upon her and decided to get straight to the point.

"The Dryads have reported increases in activity in and around the area of the Omphalos." Gabe's face was grim. "They aren't willin' to divulge names or places. They claim neutrality if a war results."

"How can they possibly claim neutrality if war becomes us?" Queen Ezreanna asked; her eyebrows sank so low her eyelids almost disappeared. "They are the guardians of the gateways to our world. How can they not be on our side? They have always stood with us as allies."

Gabe cleared his throat. "Well, I believe that they've been intimidated."

"How so?" Queen Ezreanna's eyes narrowed suspiciously.

"Well, one of the sisters was murdered."

The Queen gasped, covering her mouth with her hand.

Grim faced, Gabe continued. "They found one of them pulled from her tree and stabbed to death, and what remained standing of her tree was black. It appeared to have been set on fire. The remaining sisters are grieving their loss, but are remaining silent. If they know who murdered their sister or if they have any information on the enemy, they aren't sayin' a word."

The Queen looked at Gabe, her emotions clearly playing across her face. Her eyes brimmed with tears as she struggled to keep them in check. Swallowing hard to maintain her composure, she asked,

"We have had our own people, including you, transported through the Omphalos on many occasions. How do we know the Dryads won't give out that information?"

Gabe looked at the Queen, his eyes peering out from amongst his wild, bristly beard. "I believe they won't. They wouldn't give information to aid those that murdered their kin."

The Queen's eyes darted around the courtyard, as if she was scanning every tiny space she could see.

"There have been attempts on my life," the Queen whispered in a barely audible voice, staring hollow eyed over his shoulder. "Several, in fact." She heaved a sigh. "All have been thwarted, with no casualties. But now this Dryad—do you know which one?"

Gabe thought for a moment. "I believe it was Delphia."

The Queen closed her eyes and swallowed hard, a few tears escaping down her cheeks. "I used to play amongst the Dryads as a child. Delphia was always good to me, always a good friend." The Queen took a long draught from her glass of lemonade and set it down hard on the table. She cleared her throat.

"The riots are getting worse and are becoming more frequent. The Bards are being dispatched almost constantly to quell the disturbances; the air is heavy with discord. You can feel the Veil weakening as each day passes, and the disturbances are furthering weakening the Veil. Please tell me that our champions will be ready when the time comes."

Gabe stood. "They are in place now and have found each other. The rest is up to fate and their actions."

The Queen rose also and steeped quickly to Gabe's side. "For Goddess' sake I hope they succeed," the Queen spoke softly. "Let's pray that Delphia's killers do not win."

Gabe nodded in agreement and escorted Queen Ezreanna back to safety within the castle walls.

***

Dan climbed out of the car and strode over to the motel, stopping in front of unit number four (*how ironic*, he mused) and gently knocked on the door. The door was immediately flung open by William, who was wearing a white undershirt, brown trousers, and suspenders.

"Dan," he almost yelled as he pulled him into the room and shut the door.

"I forgot teh ask what the dress was." William held up a shirt. "This alright, or should I wear this other one with a tie an' jacket?"

After Dan explained it was just a casual dress dinner, William selected a long sleeve shirt and wool vest.

"You may want a jacket, it's pretty cold out," Dan offered.

"Aye, yer not kiddin', are yeh?" William answered and gave a little shiver. "I've only ever imagined this much snow." William pulled on his jacket as he struggled to remember. "Nah, I probably read about it in a Dicken's story."

Dan laughed as they strode outside. He had to remind William that the passenger side of the vehicle was on the right as he unconsciously made his way over to the driver's side. William trudged around to the other side of the car, muttering under his breath.

Dan smiled. He knew it must be quite a transition for a man of his age, everything being so different than what he was accustomed to. Still, you had to respect that he was willing to do it; to step outside of his comfort zone.

Dan let William set the tone of the conversation on the drive to his house. William was busy looking around—asking questions about certain buildings, different places and what they were like. For each of his questions, Dan had a patient answer.

"If you like, I can take you around on a few day trips, you know, really see the sites," Dan offered with a smile.

"Well, I wouldn't want to be putting yeh out now," William answered as he continued to gaze out the window.

Dan pulled up to a stop sign, looked both ways, and turned right.

"You wouldn't be putting me out," Dan answered. "Besides," he gave William a sidelong glance, "you never really experience where you live until you show it to someone from out of town, right?"

William thought about it, thinking of all the things he hadn't really seen in England; Hadrian's Wall, Stonehenge, and the crown jewels in the Tower of London were only a few he could name off the top of his head. "Yeah, I guess you're right. And thanks."

Dan nodded in acknowledgement and continued driving. He had made it on to his road. It was covered in packed snow that appeared to be freshly plowed. *At least the potholes will be filled in*, Dan thought, appreciating the less-bumpy-than-usual drive.

"Not much further," Dan said as he turned down another road. "There's the driveway up ahead."

Dan pointed to the right as he approached and then turned into the driveway. As he followed the driveway he noticed that the trees around his home, as well as the surrounding air, seemed to be full of birds and small creatures. Squirrels, perhaps? Dan was puzzled. Too soon for that many birds to return. He pulled up behind Abby's vehicle and noticed that a pick-up truck was pulled in on the other side. Dan guessed it must be Joe's: it was much too beat up to be Sara's.

Dan cut the ignition and stepped out of the car. He stood for a moment looking at the birds in the sky. They seemed to be watching, waiting for something. Dan heard the passenger side door of his car open and heard William ease himself slowly out of the card. As he drew himself upright and slammed the door shut, he heard whispers, voices whispering from up in the sky.

Two of the birds drew closer to each other and twittered rapidly before ascending farther skyward and disappearing. Dan paused to observe them briefly before once again focusing his attention on William Walker.

"Coulda swore those were little people," William blurted out, his face reddening. "Now yeh probably think I'm a crazy old man."

Dan looked dumbstruck at the sky and then looked down at the fresh snow-covered ground. There were prints in the snow, but they definitely did not belong to a bird. More like tiny, Barbie-doll-sized footprints scattered all around.

Dan pointed at the footprints in the snow as he looked up at William. "You're not crazy...not unless we're sharing the same hallucination."

Dan's eyes caught sight of some movement in the tree line, and he jerked around to face the sound, but whatever it was had moved so quickly he was unable to catch another glimpse.

"So, it's not always like this, then?" William asked, a half-smile on his lips.

"Ah, no....not usually," Dan shrugged. "But who knows? Maybe things are about to change. Let's go on in, shall we?" Dan led the way as they entered the house. The smell of food instantly caught the attention of both men, and they inhaled the inviting aroma deeply.

Dan took William's coat as Abby stiffly offered him a cup of tea, which he gratefully accepted as he joined Sara and Joe, already sitting at the dining table and sipping tea from ceramic mugs. Sara beamed as she nodded in greeting to William. She gestured to Joe.

"William Walker, I'd like to introduce you to Joe Asine. Joe, this is William Walker."

The men reached out and shook hands.

"Joe is a fellow artist too," Sara added.

William's curiosity was piqued. He raised his eyebrows.

Joe smiled and looked down, shifting in his chair. "Yes, I am an artist, but right now teaching art is paying the bills."

William nodded and took a tentative sip of tea. William was pleasantly surprised. It was the first decent cup of tea he'd had since he arrived in America.

"Umm, that's a good cuppa tea," William raised his cup in recognition to Abby who was busy in the kitchen. Abby nodded back and returned her focus back to her preparations.

William turned his attention jack to Joe. "So, what's yer medium?" William asked politely, his blue eyes fixed upon Joe.

"I work mostly with clay," Joe answered. "Everyone calls me a potter, but I do sculptural work as well as pottery."

William nodded. This Joe looked familiar, so familiar to him. William strained to think. *I know I've seen him someplace....*

"Don't you think it's strange?" Sara's voice drifted into William's thoughts and he turned abruptly to look at her.

"What's strange?"

"Well, you know. That all four of us are artists. Don't you think that's strange?"

The four of us. William made the connection. Sara, Joe, Abby, and himself. *The four of us.* William took a large gulp of his tea, unsure of how to respond to Sara's question.

"I mean, out of all the jobs out there, how come we're all artists? It's just an odd coincidence, that's all." Sara seemed to be addressing everyone and no one at the same time.

Dan coughed loudly, causing Sara and William to jump slightly.

"Need any help, Abby?" Dan offered as he moved into the kitchen.

"As a matter of fact, I do," Abby said bluntly, handing Dan a bowl of mashed potatoes and a gravy boat. "Start setting the food at the table."

Dan smiled and winked as he grabbed the food and started setting it out on the table. Dan hoped the conversation would be light as they ate dinner. His hopes were scattered when William asked Sara,

"So what's the deal with the fairy folk outside here? Yeh'd almost think there was an infestation or something."

Sara laughed. "That's a good description," she replied as Dan set a platter of roast beef and Yorkshire puddings on the table.

At least the conversation promised to be lively. Dan pushed in Abby's chair and poured a glass of wine for her and one for him before taking his place at the table. Sara's laughter filled the air. Dan could see William and Joe in rapt attention as she chattered. Joe nodded occasionally at her responses to William's questions, a slight smile playing across his lips. Dan peered over the rim of his wineglass at Abby, her expression remained stony as she stabbed a piece of meat with her fork and jammed it forcefully into her mouth. Dan took a large gulp from his glass before setting it down on the table.

What is with her anyway? Dan deliberately attempted to keep his expression neutral while observing Abby. Her behavior was certainly not normal. At least, it wasn't normal behavior for her before she changed.

Dan caught Abby's eye. "Dinner is wonderful, Abby. You've really outdone yourself." Murmurs of assent drifted across the table.

William straightened up. "Thanks for invitin' me into your home," he began looking at Dan first and then to Abby. "This was the first decent meal I've 'ad since arriving here. And the Yorkshire puddings were perfect. Haven't had 'em in years. Thanks."

William tried his best to give her a warm smile but felt that he was merely gnashing his teeth in her direction. What was wrong with him? He meant what he said, but for some reason, just looking at her made him uncomfortable.

Abby smiled back, though she too seemed to almost growl at him in response. "You're welcome," she replied through her gritted, bared teeth. "There's more if you like."

William nodded in reply and the room went silent, the only sounds being those of forks and knives scraping across plates and the occasional swallowing sounds.

"So, when did you receive your gift?" Sara asked. "If you don't mind me asking," she added quickly.

William set down his fork and knife and motioned for the wine bottle. Dan quickly filled his glass. William took a sip before answering. "Well, I s'pose I've always had it."

William's expression was thoughtful as if he were searching his memory for a precise time.

"Always?" Joe asked, his curiosity peaked. "Since you were a child?"

"I dunno, maybe," William answered, staring out the window over Joe's shoulder. "Ever since I could paint, I could do it. Maybe since I was a teenager."

William thought back to his first time at the lake, sneaking away; how it had taken him half a day to get there just to paint in privacy. He remembered having a vision and painting it as it revealed itself before his eyes in the reflection of the water. It was so vivid and vibrant, lingering in his mind long after he had painted the image he had seen in the water. He remembered how he had bent down to touch the water, feeling that perhaps he could make a physical connection. How surprised he had been to feel a hand reach out of the water and grasp his. *Rhysdale*.

William slipped out of his memory and felt the eyes of everyone at the table upon him as if waiting for a more detailed explanation. *They have their secrets*, he thought. *And I'm damned well entitled to mine too.*

William cleared his throat. "Yeah, around when I was a teenager," he continued. "It's hard to remember, it was so long ago."

Sara cast Joe and Abby quick glances at this bit of information. William was quick to notice.

"How long have you three—"

"Not long," Sara cut him off mid-sentence as she pushed a pile of potatoes around on her plate. "We've only discovered our abilities within the past year."

"Figger yeh need a bit of advice from this old hat then? Words of wisdom from someone who's been doin' this awhile?" He glanced at each of the three in turn.

Abby snorted derisively into her wineglass. Dan shot her a look, but she remained silent.

Joe cleared his throat. "Well, I think we should get together over at Sara's and see what we can learn from each other. I don't think it could hurt any of us if you shared the wisdom of your experience with us." Joe smiled at William and took a sip from his soda.

"Why Sara's?" William asked quickly

"Well, I have a very private piece of property," Sara leaned closer to William. "Sometimes it's best that we not be seen," she added in a conspiratorial tone.

William smiled. He understood and felt relieved by the reassurance that they weren't just going to take him out to the country and dump him there, although, God knows, that Abby sure looks like she'd like to do just that. William looked up to catch her giving him a stony stare, but once she realized he was returning her stare, she gave him a weak smile before averting her eyes and returning her attention to her food. William shook his head. She sure looked like her eyes were red. Maybe it was a reflection of the light.

"Yeah, alright, I'm up for it," William agreed. "When we gonna do this?"

"I'm thinking tomorrow after five would be best," Sara said, looking around the table for consensus. Everyone nodded their heads in agreement.

"Dan will have to get his own supper tomorrow," Abby declared.

"Sure, I'll pick up pizza. I'll survive, don't worry," Dan answered brightly, a broad smile on his face. "You guys need me there too?"

Abby cast Sara a nervous look.

"Um, I don't think so yet, Dan," Sara said. Dan looked rather crestfallen. "Once we get it together it might be better."

"Perhaps it would be good to keep in cell phone contact or something," Joe added. "You know, Dan could be our headquarters. In case we have a problem or something."

"Good idea," William answered. He gazed out the window. "Are we going to have a crowd tomorrow too?"

Abby, Sara, and Joe stood to see what he was looking at. The movement in the trees was catching their attention, as was the activity on the ground. Instead of birds, there were what appeared to be a flock of small, winged people up in the canopy, some buzzing around in the air, some appeared like iridescent hummingbirds, others like multi-colored dragonflies. They glimmered and shimmered on every tree branch and shrub as they caught the last rays of dwindling sunlight. The ground was undulating with activity too, with tiny creatures ranging from small, odd-shaped animals to diminutive human-like creatures. As they stared out the window, all movement ceased and a silent reverence fell over the yard as all eyes moved as one to focus on the group within the house.

"They know something," Abby whispered. "They know something we don't."

Sara waved at two little dragonfly-like creatures as they hovered by the window. They waved in return before darting away.

"I've never seen so many before," Sara said in a hushed voice as she observed the crowd in Abby's yard.

"Yeh've seen them before?" William whispered as he continued to stare wide-eyed out the window.

Sara nodded.

"Then we'd best be gettin' down to it tomorrow, then," William added. "We may be needed soon."

Dan, Abby, Joe, and Sara nodded in agreement. Abby smiled wanly. *Hopefully this so-called wisdom of his will come in handy.*

CHAPTER 25

Sara and Abby were sitting on the couch in her living room when Joe arrived at the door with William Walker in tow. Sara glanced at the clock.

"You're late," she declared, tossing back her blonde hair as she pointed emphatically to a digital clock on the wall that read 5:25 pm.
Joe hunched over and gave her a sheepish grin. "Yeah, I know," Joe admitted, sticking his hands into his pockets. "It's third marking period and I had to get the students' grades in. I guess I just lost track of time."

"Did we miss anything?" William piped up, his gray hair visible just above Joe's shoulder. Joe stepped aside as not to block him.

Sara smiled at William, her face softened. "No, not really." She rose and started to put on her coat and shoes. "We, well, I, am eager to get started."

Abby rose too, and following Sara's lead, she put on her coat and tugged on her boots.

"Where we goin' then?" William asked nervously.

"Just out the back of the barn. I'll give you the grand tour. Follow me." Sara lifted her hair from inside the back of her coat as she walked out the front door. The air was crisp and cool and she could see her breath as she exhaled. The sun was beginning to set; darkness was falling as the moon began to rise in the sky.

Sara could hear William's shuddering and his breathing become faster, so she cut her stride in half. For a moment she had forgotten that he was not accustomed to the winters that they had in Michigan.

The sensor light at the back of her barn turned on as the four of them turned the corner. William and Abby both jumped, but Sara and Joe were accustomed to it. Sara heard Abby harrumph in annoyance, but Sara pretended not to hear it. *Abby is getting so.....* Sara had to search for a definition...*testy*...*yes that was it*. Sara was hopeful that it would go away and everything would go back to being sunshine and roses again.

"Ouch! Watch where you're going!" Abby's voice snapped.

Or maybe not, Sara sighed.

"Well yer the one who walked into me!" William responded in an irritated tone. He turned to face Abby, his blue eyes steely, his arms crossed over his chest. Abby merely stared at him, her eyes dark and stormy, her hands at her sides balled into tight fists.

"Uh, what's going on here?" Joe asked quietly. He lifted his hand out to touch Abby's shoulder, but Sara moved toward him and gently placed a hand on his arm, lowering it back down to his side.

"Let's stay out of this," Sara whispered in his ear.

Joe felt Sara's warm breath in his ear and he felt a little heady. It felt good to have her near; he forgot how much he missed her. He looked into her eyes for a moment, caught in their depth as her eyes locked on his.

"Good idea," Joe managed to quietly force out. When did his mouth get so dry anyway? He couldn't take his eyes off her. Sara finally looked away, breaking the trance he felt he was caught within.

"No, Abby, no!" Sara yelled as she waved her hands frantically out in front of her as she rushed to intercept Abby.

Joe could only hear the raised voices of Abby and William, but he was having difficulty hearing exactly what they were shouting at each other. Joe snapped out of his confused state when he saw Abby holding a blazing fireball between her hands.

"Thinks he knows everything, does he? Thinks he's better than us? How dare he come in here and think he's going to just take over!" Abby's eyes were blazing with the reflection of the fireball that she still held in her hand.

"Yer provin' you're a bit of a hothead, that's for sure," William replied loudly. "But how you gonna help things by throwin' fire at me? What's it gonna prove?" William stepped closer, his eyes level with Abby's.

"Do what ye gotta do, young lady. I'm gettin' older just standin' here." William stared at her calmly, waiting for her reaction.

Sara stood beside Joe and hooked her arm through his and gently pulled him back a couple of steps. Sara held her breath. Abby looked at William, rolled her eyes, and tossed the fireball into a snow bank at the side. Sara heaved a sigh of relief as the fireball was extinguished in the snow with a loud hiss, melting the snow pile into a considerable pool of water.

William smiled almost gleefully when he saw the water. He looked at the water and it began swirling upon the ground. As it gained momentum it swirled faster and faster. Within seconds it was a seven foot water spout swirling in their direction.

"Hey, hothead!" William yelled at Abby. "Wanna cool off?"

Abby jumped out of the way and dove for cover behind the nearest snow bank, but there was no need. With another chuckle, William directed the waterspout into a hill where it had abruptly stopped and became a puddle of water once more. Sara moved toward William tugging Joe by the sleeve.

"Wow, that was amazing, wasn't it, Abby?"

Sara was looking at Abby with a worried look. Abby scrutinized Sara and Joe's expressions and William's obviously defensive stance. For some strange reason she found it amusing; her shoulders started to shake as she erupted with laughter.

Sara smiled and nervously laughed too as Abby continued to laugh heartily.

"Yeah, not bad for an old, wet dish towel," Abby gasped as she wiped a tear from her eye.

"I'll take that as a complement coming from a young hothead like you," William answered smiling thinly at Abby.

"Yeah, okay, I can deal with that," Abby replied shrugging. "Truce?" She stuck out her hand.

William looked at her hand and raised a gray eyebrow. "I accept your truce, but there's no way in hell I'm shaking' yer hand. Especially after I've seen what you do with them."

"Can't fault him for that," Sara chimed in. "So, this is part of our training area. Joe made the hills for a bit of privacy." Sara motioned with her hand over her shoulder. "That's my studio and barn. Oogan's in the barn; he'll be getting' up soon. You can meet him last."

"What's an 'Oogan'?" William asked, his head cocked toward Abby and Joe.

"Oh, you'll see," Abby said nonchalantly, smug that she was in the know and he was not.

Sara fished around in her jacket pocket and pulled out a small flashlight. "I think you'll find this much more interesting. Follow me." Sara turned on the flashlight and headed toward the woods. It was still not completely dark, but the flashlight made the trip much easier to navigate than stumbling blindly in the snow through the woods as nightfall was nearing. The air was cool and refreshing and had a calming effect on them all as they followed Sara along the unmarked path.

Though the snow covering the frozen ground crunched underfoot, the river ahead of them flowed freely; only its edges glistened with shards of ice. The sound of running water was surprisingly pleasant to hear, and William was particularly delighted by the soothing sound.

"It has never frozen completely," Sara said aloud, almost as if she were reading their thoughts. "Not once since I've lived here."

The sound of the water running appeared to mesmerize William. He stepped forward calmly, drawn to its sound as if in a trance, as if the river called and awoke a part of him that slumbered since his arrival in Harmon. It thrilled and exhilarated him, and suddenly he was no longer cold, his joints no longer ached, and his mind was clear and sharp as he focused on his purpose. He eagerly moved forward, compelled to touch the body of water that lay in front of him. He bent down at the water's icy edge; his knees screamed in protest at the cold contact, but he managed to ignore the sensation in his legs. He could hear Sara's voice, as if in some far off place saying, "shhh!" in reply to some very faint whispers. He ignored that too. He knew what he had to do. William removed his left glove and put his fingers into the icy water at the river's edge. He could feel the cold like needles in his joints and knuckles, and he gasped. He blocked out the awareness of discomfort and plunged his hand into the water farther until it was wrist-deep. He closed his eyes, and for a moment he imagined Rhysdale at the pond back home. He pushed back the pang of homesickness and sent out a thought again. *What if no one hears my call?*

William felt a pressure squeeze his fingers. He opened his eyes and gently lifted. A small blue-green creature rose out of the water. William gazed at the creature for a moment. It was naked and appeared feminine, though he didn't really try to get a closer look. It was so lithe and delicate, with full lips and large, liquid, almond-shaped eyes that dilated to catlike slits when it blinked to focus on his face. He was unsure how he should greet this creature, but before he could speak, the nymph began to speak.

"Greetings, William Walker," it acknowledged in a silky feminine voice. "Rhysdale sends you her regards and a wish that you return home safely."

Sara nudged Abby and gave her a knowing look. Joe stood behind them, his hands inside his jacket pockets, doing his best to avert his eyes.

William blushed slightly at the mention of Rhysdale's name. He was thankful for the cover of darkness so the others couldn't see his face.

"What news have you for me?" William asked rather gruffly.

He slowly pulled back when he realized he was still holding the nymph by the hand. The nymph laughed.

"I can see by your trembling form that you are not used to this weather." The nymph reached out and grasped his shoulder gently before lifting up his chin with her other hand so that they were looking directly into each other's eyes. *Her eyes are green too*, William mused.

"You must do what you've come here to do." The nymph spoke softly, her voice both comforting him and commanding his full attention. "War is coming, William," she whispered. "Both our worlds will be affected. It's starting to change now; can't you feel it?"

William nodded.

"Alliances have already been formed. Armies are being gathered. But you and your companions cannot concern yourself with this. What you must do is follow the course that is intended for you. The tribute given to you by the Lady—it must be given soon. Time is something that we are quickly running out of."

"But where do I give the tribute? I don't want to lose it to the wrong choice." William stared pleadingly at the nymph, his heart racing, his blue eyes watering from the wind and cold.

The nymph smiled calmly and patted him gently on the head. "You are not far from the place, so have no worries. Come again tomorrow and use the river to show you the way. Just as your water shows you the future, our river will also aid you. Have faith, as we do in you." The nymph looked at the others.

"We have faith in all of you." The nymph smiled as her eyes fell upon Sara. "Perhaps now that you have mastered your abilities you will be less clumsy when you enter the water."

The nymph laughed gaily, her laughter sounded oddly like a fish flopping in the water.

Sara grinned sheepishly as Abby and Joe gave her quizzical looks.

"I'll be more careful," Sara said suppressing a giggle.

The river started to glow from below the nymph and she pulled gently away from William. "I must go," the nymph said. "I cannot allow my absence to be noticed. We are not to interfere with 'The Four'."

William nodded as she disappeared under the water. They all watched in silence as the glow dimmed and the river returned to its usual gurgling sound.

Joe was the first to speak as he walked over to William and extended his hand. "Need a hand?" Joe offered. William grunted in assent as he put his hand in Joe's much warmer one and allowed him to hoist him upright. His knees screamed in protest as he tried to straighten out while he stood.

Sara stuffed her hands into the back pockets of her jeans. "Shall we head back?" Sara looked around to see all of them nodding in agreement.

"Right, then." Sara pulled the flashlight from her jacket and turning the light on, she led the way down the path and through the forest.

***

The four of them sat in silence, sipping from steaming mugs of tea that Sara had made (with some extra help from Abby). Sara eyed Abby and William carefully. Both of them were more at ease, more relaxed, and generally *better*, appearing to have forgotten the raging animosity they exhibited toward each other only a scant few hours before. William was the first to break the silence as he turned toward Abby.

"So how old is yer daughter, Abby?" William asked casually as he sipped at his tea.

Abby's dark eyes widened. "Uh, what made you think I had a daughter?" Her eyes were still as big as marbles, her face an ashen color.

"Well, I saw loads of pictures on the wall at your place. There were some of a small toddler and a portrait of you and your husband and a baby...," William trailed off, realizing he may have made an error. "Perhaps a relative's child?"

God, he's really trying to be nice to me, Abby thought. *The poor man.*

"Well...the toddler picture is of me when I was a child," Abby began slowly, her eyes down, her hands cupping her mug carefully. "The, uh, portrait is a family one, but our daughter, well, she, she didn't survive. We were told it was Sudden Infant Death Syndrome, that there was nothing we could have done." Abby sipped from her mug and swallowed hard, her eyes misty as she looked away. "She died when she was only a few months old," Abby added softly.

A red flush crept into William's face as he squirmed uncomfortably. "I'm sorry, Abby. I didn't know," William said. "I didn't mean to upset you."

Sara reached over and gave Abby's shoulder a gentle squeeze. Abby nodded and looked away. "It's okay, William. You couldn't have known."

William set his mug on the table and ran his hand through his wild gray hair. He stifled a yawn with one hand and glanced up at the clock on the wall. The traveling, work at the gallery, opening of the show, and the array of activities over the past few days were beginning to catch up with him. He was surprised to see that it was just slightly past 10 pm. *Much too late for me*, he thought as he stifled another yawn. *These weary bones just wanna to go to bed.*

A loud rapping at the door made them all jump nervously. Sara bounded over to the door to open it.

"Don't you think it would be best to ask who it is first?" Joe asked her as he rose up off the couch.

Sara gave him an annoyed glance and flicked her hair off her shoulder.

"The bad guys don't knock, remember, Joe?" Sara flung open the door and squealed with delight at the sight of Gabe standing there, his gray hair wildly standing up straight on the top of his head; a tiny cowboy hat perched on top of his head.

"Gabe, you're just in time. Do join us." Sara motioned to the room as Gabe stepped reluctantly inside.

"I'll get you a cup of tea," Sara said as she moved quickly into the kitchen and returned with a steaming mug. "Cream and sugar on the table," she added. "Just help yourself."

"Thanks." Gabe muttered as he sat on the edge of the couch closest to Abby.

He added a couple of spoonfuls of sugar to his tea, stirred it rapidly and took a few tentative sips; all the while, William was staring at him in utter disbelief. Sara opened her mouth to speak, but a wave of Gabe's hand instantly silenced her. His mug disappeared into his beard for a moment as he took a sip.

"I suppose you've seen me before, William Walker."

William stared at him and nodded mutely. Gabe looked straight at him, his eyes barely visible under his big hairy beard and lined face.

"Well, ye best be ready, William Walker," Gabe said sternly. "Time is running out."

Just like in his vision. *It's like déjà vu all over again.* He would have laughed if he wasn't so damned tired. William just nodded in agreement. "What do we need to do exactly?" William spoke so quietly, it was almost a whisper. "How should I be ready?"

Gabe took another sip and swiped at his mouth and beard with the sleeve of his coat. "How the hell should I know?" Gabe said defiantly. "I'm just the poor bastard that's sent here to tell yeh that time is running out."

Gabe gave Abby and Joe acknowledging looks and they each nodded in return. Gabe turned to Sara, the gravelly undertone in his voice softening as he spoke to her.

"The tea is good, thanks."

"No problem," Sara responded smiling widely at him.

"Well, there's a problem, alright, I'm sorry to say, but not with yer tea, Sara."

Sara looked up through her hair, her blonde eyebrows lifted, eyes full of concern.

"What's wrong?"

"Well, it's that Taekyr of yers, Sara," Gabe said quietly. "Oogan has disappeared."

The silence was almost deafening as the severity of Gabe's words registered in their minds.

"No," Sara whispered, a tear streaming down her cheek as she stared into the murky depths of her mug.

Joe reached over and placed his hand on her shoulder. Sara looked up at him, her eyes brimming with tears she gave him a weak acknowledging smile. Sara turned to Gabe.

"How do you know he's not just foraging in the woods?" Sara asked quickly. "Just because you didn't see him doesn't mean that—,"

"Sara, he's gone," Gabe said flatly.

"Well, I'm going to check myself." Sara stood, set down her mug and grabbed her jacket. She quickly tossed her arms carelessly into the sleeves and pulled on her boots as the others stood in unison.

"You can wait here," Sara waved at the others. "Enjoy your tea. I'll be right back." Sara stepped out and quickly pulled the door shut behind her.

"Somebody had better follow her," Gabe said quickly. "He's definitely gone. An' it don' look right at all. I don't think he went willingly."

Abby and Joe looked at each other.

"Go ahead," they both said in unison. They both laughed nervously.

"You go, you're her best friend."

"No, no, no, you go, you can be more comfort to her."

William stood. "We're all goin'," he ordered. William cast a glance at Gabe and jabbed a finger in his direction. "You too."

Gabe shrugged and took a last gulp before setting his mug down on the coffee table with the others.

"Fine," Gabe sighed. "Let's go."

The four of them hurried out the door of Sara's house and down the path to the barn. Abby opened the side door and found the lights were on. The aura of gloom that hung around whenever Oogan was present seemed to have diminished, as did the pervasive, pungent aroma that clung to the air around him. Abby felt the hairs stand up on the back of her neck. The room felt like it was full of static electricity. The static seemed to encompass her entire body now, the hair and skin on her arms, even though sheathed by her coat, seemed to tingle like a greasy, electric current was being pulsed through her body.

"I feel......odd," she whispered to Gabe.

"Ya feel that, do ya?"

Abby nodded.

"It's like a form of magical residue. I'm tellin' ya—somethin' went on here tonight." Gabe scanned the area carefully.

William listened to their exchange. He had plenty of questions, but he sensed that this particular moment was not the right time.

"I feel it too," William also whispered, shuddering slightly.

"So do I," Joe said, crossing his arms and grasping his biceps as if he could wipe the feeling away.

Abby stepped ahead of the group as they moved deeper into the barn. The old horse tack still hung on its hooks, a blanket was spread out on the floor in front of the stable stalls. The tingling sensation was getting more intense—she stepped forward and toward the open stall where Oogan had been staying as Sara's "guest."

Sara was sitting on the floor next to the large nest in the far corner of the stall, her face in her hands. She was crying softly. Abby looked around and squatted down on the floor next to Sara.

"It's all my fault," Sara sobbed into her hands. "He was so lonely, he just wanted to see his family."

Abby reached into her pocket, extracted a tissue, and pushed it into Sara's hand.

"It's not your fault," Abby said calmly putting her arm around Sara. "You treated him very well, Sara. And you were a good friend to him."

Sara wiped her eyes and looked at Abby. "Really?"

"Yes, of course you were." Abby pushed a lock of hair from Sara's eyes.

"Yeah, an' I don't think he left willingly either," Gabe interjected gruffly. "Look at the ground here." Gabe pointed to some footsteps and some long furrows in the dirt and straw. "Looks to me like there was struggle," Gabe said flatly as he stroked his beard. "That, and the magical residue left behind, I'd say it's safe to say that Oogan's master located him and came to collect him."

William's voice burst in. "Who the hell is Oogan, an' what are ye talkin' about his 'master'?" William looked confused and angry.

Joe stepped forward. "I'll do the explaining," he offered as he led William to the other side of the barn, talking in his best "teacher" voice.

Sara began to sob quietly again, her face pressed into the palms of both hands. Abby ran a hand through her own hair and sighed. She rolled her eyes before looking at Gabe, her dark eyes drawn and her face pale.

"What are the implications of this to us?" She stared evenly at Gabe.

Gabe reached into his pocket and drew out his pipe and tobacco. "Well, it's safe to say that the enemy is aware that Sara had Oogan," he said as he loaded his pipe. He motioned to Abby as he lifted the pipe to his lips. She flicked a flame in his direction, lighting the tobacco in the bowl.

"Thanks for stating the obvious, Gabe," Abby replied irritably. "Is there any other helpful advice you'd like to impart on us?"

"Well, I think regardless of what Sara thinks she may know 'bout him, Oogan may reveal what he knows about the four of yeh. Willingly or not, he'll tell his master what he wants to know."

Abby watched Gabe smoke his pipe as Sara continued to cry quietly.

"What do you advise we do then?" Abby asked solemnly, watching the tendrils of smoke drift lazily into the air.

Gabe looked at her and laughed. "I'm not supposed to get involved, remember? I'm only supposed to provide yeh guidance and nothin' else."

Abby looked at Gabe, her eyes alight with the fire that burned inside her. *Calm, calm*, she told herself.

"Well, Gabe, what would you do in such a situation? Hypothetically, of course."

"O' course," Gabe smiled widely at her. He tugged on his beard. "Well, if I were you, I would be on guard from now on. Never be alone, always check in at intervals, an' always travel in pairs. Be cautious at all times. Act like I was under constant surveillance. And while I'd be doin' that, I'd also be finding out real quick what we're supposed to be doin' to change the balance in our favor."

Abby fixed her eyes upon him, her head cocked to one side.

"I'm not followin' you."

Gabe pulled her down closer to him and peered into her eyes, almost pressing his nose against hers.

"If Thaddeus gets his hands on Oogan, then he has a treasure trove of information on the four of ya. The faster ye move, the better chance ye have of success before he has a chance to use his new information." Gabe tapped his pipe against his boot, knocking the spent ashes out onto the barn floor.

"It's an old military tactic. If the battle yer fighting doesn't seem to be winning, then ye have to change the rules of engagement."

Abby raised an eyebrow, her upper lip raised in a slight sneer.

"That easy, is it?"

"No, but it can be," Gabe added, stuffing his pipe back into his pocket. "It's up to the four of yeh to figger out how to do it."

"But now that Oogan's gone we have to do it faster," Abby said, sitting on the barn floor.

"Right."

Sara looked up and wiped the tears from her face. "We'll do our best," Sara sniffled as she stood up. She held out a hand to Abby who pulled her to her feet.

"Well, there's no time to be wasted now," Gabe said, turning toward the door. "I'll send word if I hear anythin' else," Gabe said over his shoulder.

"Likewise," Sara said suppressing a sniffle.

Gabe stopped halfway to the door and turned toward Abby.

"Hey, Abby, you've really surprised me," Gabe added.

"Oh really? Why?" She eyed him suspiciously.

"Walker doesn't seem the least bit singed. You losing yer touch now?" Gabe grinned, his yellow teeth visible through his beard.

"Piss off!" Abby casually yelled back at him with a dismissive wave.

"That's my girl," Gabe said. Chuckling, he turned and walked out the door and into the night.

CHAPTER 26

Michael walked stiffly down the corridor; his boot falls echoing loudly with their staccato cadence on the stone floor. The hall to the Taekyr compound was as dark and dank as ever; the musty smell of it mingled with the cloying odor of the Taekyrs themselves. Michael wrinkled his nose in distaste as he went further down the passage. He paused 30 yards from the opening that led the way into the Taekyr domicile area. He cast a quick glance down each end of the passage to ensure he was alone, placed his right hand up against the wall under the candle sconce, feeling along the wall until his fingers found an indentation between two stones. He stuck his fingers into the crack, clasped the hidden handle, and gave it a gentle pull, opening the hidden doorway. Michael gently pushed the stone cantilever door and stepped forward as the door swung forward. Once inside, he located a similar indentation in the wall where he put his fingers in, and by repeating his previous motions he secured the door back to its original hidden position. It had been risky bringing the Taekyr Oogan back to the castle, but he had to hide him somewhere, and he couldn't chance taking him directly to Thaddeus.

Michael clasped his gloved hands behind his back as he strode purposefully through the passageway. The cold air did not chill him—nothing could cool the anger he felt toward this Taekyr. *What kind of an army are we going into battle with?* He shook his head at the memory of locating Oogan once his magical band was activated. He had half-hoped, no, he had been almost certain he would find the creature dead and rotting in a shallow grave on the Air Vessel's property. But to find him sheltered in a human barn stall like a common cow was certainly more than he could take.

Michael wrinkled his nose. The distasteful smell of the creature was closing in on him, causing him to draw shallow breaths in through his mouth. He moved deeper into the hidden room, moving from the antechamber to a smaller room. A bare candle in a bracket on the wall illuminated a small corner of the darkness, casting a faint light and shadows upon an array of encrusted, cast iron tools clad with wooden handles hung in a neat row. Some looked like large variations of kitchen knives, others a mix of pliers and fireplace pokers.

He had better be forthcoming with information. Michael smiled. *Or maybe not.* He selected a leather whip from the array on the wall. The soft, braided leather handle fit comfortably in his hand, and he examined the whip as if committing it to memory. The ends of the whip were frayed slightly and the ends tied with pieces of lead shot. It had been a while since Michael had used a cat o' nine tails on a prisoner. Thinking it would be wise to get in some practice extracting information from prisoners, he snapped the whip with a quick flick of his wrist, nodding approvingly at the echoing "crack" that reverberated all around him. He could hear a low whimper coming from the dark corner. Michael stepped into the center of the room and stared into the darkness of the whimpering corner.

"Oogan," Michael began softly, "you can make this a lot easier on yourself." Michael cracked the whip again. "Or," he continued as he gripped the long leather whip in his hand, "we could make this very difficult and, shall I mention, quite painful for you, and if there's time — we could fit in your brood too."

Michael took three large steps into the darkness, and with a great swoop of his arms wrapped the whip around Oogan's neck, twisting it tightly at the back of his head.

"If this is what I can do to you, imagine the pain I can inflict upon your brood."

Oogan turned a lighter shade of gray and sputtered as he struggled to breathe. Michael kicked a boot forward and hit Oogan in his soft underbelly, knocking him to the floor. He moaned in pain but said nothing, even though he knew that revealing what he knew would grant him reprieve from further punishment. Michael could see the cuts and bruises that Oogan bore as evidence of his handiwork, and he smiled at the memory of inflicting them. He brought a fist down hard on Oogan's right eye. It swelled immediately, blocking out the vision on that side. Michael was well-trained in torture and tactics of coercion. He knew that sometimes to extract information from prisoners it was necessary to appeal to their conscience. Judging from the look on Oogan's face when Michael mentioned his brood, it was obvious that he bore a very heavy conscience.

Michael strode back behind Oogan and lifted him off the floor. He whispered in almost a snarl, "I know you can withstand a great deal, Oogan. But remember where your true loyalties lie."

Michael released the whip from around Oogan's neck and walked to the far end of the room, returning with a bowl of water which he placed in front of Oogan. Oogan remained motionless, his good eye focused on Michael as he calmly pulled a wooden chair in front of him, the legs scraping as he it dragged across the floor. Michael sat down, placing his palms down on his thighs. He lifted a hand and motioned to Oogan to take a drink, and Oogan obediently bent down and lapped at the water, sparing an occasional upward glance toward Michael.

Michael waited until Oogan was sated and sat back down, his body weight resting on the claw-like tips of his tucked-in wings. His bulgy, wet eyes seemed even more protruding and moist than normal.

Michael smiled thinly at Oogan, his voice soft and gentle. "Your loyalties should be with your master and your brood. We have always been there for you, always looked after your needs." Michael leaned forward as Oogan cowered and shrunk farther into the corner. "They have confused you. I'm sure they treated you well and you were not harmed?"

Oogan nodded in reply.

"But you were captured by them, weren't you? I'm sure that they probably wanted to kill you at first. But it was probably easier for them to keep you alive. Then they would have tried to gain your trust and then use that trust to get information from you. Is this accurate?"

Oogan nodded again.

Michael rose from the chair and strode over to Oogan. Oogan shrank back against the stone wall.

"Ah, Oogan, this is my fault," Michael said, his head down, his voice dripping with sympathy. "I should have told you that we are at war and that the enemy would use such tactics if you were captured. I am to blame for this." Michael sighed heavily. "You are so young, and I perhaps expected too much from you."

Oogan cocked his head to one side and studied Michael carefully with his good eye. "No, master, it is I who have failed you," he croaked. "I have failed my brood."

"There, there," Michael crooned. He patted Oogan gently on the top of his rubbery gray head. "Hopefully no damage has been done."

Michael stepped back, turning away as he took a few paces toward the chair before halting and turning back to face Oogan.

"Will you tell me what you've told them?" Michael looked at Oogan, his face full of concern. "We can best protect ourselves if we know what they know. And it would really help if you could successfully fulfill your reconnaissance mission by providing information on 'The Four'. Why, I'm sure you would be given distinction for bravery, given that you endured and survived capture by the enemy." Michael smiled and awaited Oogan's response.

Oogan sighed. He had been given a job. He had to complete it.

"I'll tell you everything I know," Oogan croaked.

Michael grinned. His eyes looked frightening to Oogan.

"Excellent," he said, rubbing his hands together, as strode back and forth across the room. "Let's get started, then, shall we?"

***

Sara was sitting in her living room on the chair closest to the front window, peering aimlessly out at the yard as she stroked her cat, Frack, who had positioned himself on her lap the moment she had sat down. Even though he had almost knocked her coffee cup out of her other hand, she was grateful that at least someone, no, something wanted her company, even if it was blatant attention-whoring.

Sara stopped stroking the cat and stifled a yawn. She couldn't remember everyone leaving, or even going to bed. But she knew she had because she tossed and turned for hours until she had accepted that sleep was only going to continue to elude her. Instead, she got up and made coffee.

So Sara sat gazing out the window, sipping her cup of coffee, and watching the sun rise in the sky. She sighed deeply and gave Frack a scratch under the chin. Thoughts of Oogan would creep into her mind, and she couldn't help but wonder if he was okay. Part of her was worried that he was keeping silent and being mistreated, but she also wondered if he really didn't bond with her and took joy in being rescued. Either way, both scenarios hurt her. Looking out the window was her way of holding onto that last vestige of hope; perhaps Oogan would escape and return to her. Sara sipped her coffee. It settled in her stomach like a hard lump.

The sight of a pickup truck turning into her driveway pulled her thoughts from her vigil. The truck stopped behind hers in the driveway. *Ahh, Joe*, Sara thought. She stood and the cat leapt gracefully to the floor, tossing her an indignant look before jumping up and settling onto the sofa, wrapping his tail around him.

Sara opened the front door as Joe walked up the steps. She help the door open for him as he walked up the steps. She held the door open for him as he walked wordlessly into the living room.

"Coffee, Joe?" Sara waved her cup at him and smiled feebly. "It's strong, but still warm."

Joe stepped forward. "Yeah, sure, thanks."

Sara strode into the kitchen, opened the cupboard and pulled down a mug. Joe stepped behind her and slipped his arms around her waist and rested his chin against her shoulder.

"I was worried about you," Joe murmured in her ear, his dark hair brushing her cheek. He turned her around gently, his arms still around her waist. "Are you doing okay? Did you get much sleep?"

Sara lifted her arms up and wrapped them around his neck. He drew her toward him and held her, her head nestled into his chest, her body warm and soft against his. Sara pulled away slightly and lifted her head up. Their mouths met, and she kissed him deeply before gently pulling out of their embrace. She blushed slightly and wordlessly moved to pour coffee into a mug for him and refilled hers before guiding Joe into the living room. He sat down on the couch and she positioned herself beside him, snuggling under his arm.

"It was quiet here last night," Sara finally spoke as she cradled her cup in her hands. "I guess I wasn't used to it."

Joe turned to face her, his dark eyes fixed on hers. "I would have stayed if you had asked."

"Why didn't you ask me?" Sara countered; her blue eyes clear and alert.

Joe blushed. "Well, I....I...wasn't sure you would want me here if you were upset. And I didn't want you to think I would take advantage of that to stay over."

Sara laughed. "Do you think I would let you?"

Joe smiled. "Well, no, but I wouldn't want you to think that of me, that's all."

"So, where is this going?" Sara blurted out. She looked away, sipping her coffee.

"What?" Joe asked setting his cup on the side table. "Us?"

"Yeah," Sara said turning to face him. She set her cup down on the table beside his and leaned closer to Joe, her eyes level with his. "I don't mean marriage, kids, a house with a white picket fence. I just want to know if this relationship is going to move to the next level, or if we are just going to remain friends." Sara tossed her head and gently ran her hand down Joe's arm, and laid her hand to rest on his.

Joe grasped her hand and turned it over. He lifted her upright palm to his lips and kissed it gently.

"Sara, I care about you very much," Joe said softly, "and I would like to move this relationship to the next level. But with all that is going on right now, don't you think it's a good idea to wait until whatever it is we have to do is done?"

Sara bent her head down, tears flowing down her face. "What if we don't make it?" Sara whispered as she swiped at her face. "What if we lose?"

Joe lifted her chin up and pulled her face closer. "We—won't—lose," Joe said firmly. "You have trained us well. We will win."

Sara eyes scanned his face. "I want to believe it," she whispered, "and I want you."

Sara leaned forward and kissed Joe deeply, wrapping her arms around him, her fingers running through his soft dark hair. As she pulled away again, she raised him off the couch, her hand clasping his. Joe rose, and silently she led him into the bedroom.

***

Abby pulled her van into Sara's driveway at noon. William Walker was riding shotgun, his face hidden behind an armload of art supplies.

"You should have let me open the back," Abby said flatly rolling her eyes, sighing with indignation.

"And I said there was no point in goin' to all that fuss fer such a short drive." William's voice seemed slightly muffled by the pad of watercolor paper.

"Shouldn't we have called first?" William quickly changed the subject.

"No, no, I drop by here all the time, Sara doesn't mind—wait—hello," Abby spotted Joe's truck and pulled in behind it, cutting her ignition quickly.

"What 'hello'?" William said dropping the armload down so he could see out the window. He instantly spied Joe's truck.

"Hah!" He said triumphantly, a smug smile on his face. "See? We shoulda called first."

Abby got out of the van and came over to the passenger side and yanked open William's side. She grabbed his watercolor pad from him as he climbed out of the van.

"Fine, you win," Abby relented, a note of frustration in her voice. "We'll go down to the forest and I'll call her on my cell phone when we get there, okay? Besides, I have to check in with Dan."

Abby rummaged around in her coat pocket until her fingers grasped her phone. She speed-dialed Dan as they walked down the path toward the back of the barn.

"Damn! Voice mail." Abby paused briefly and then said, "Hi, Dan, it's me. William and I are at Sara's, so if you need me, you can get me on my cell. If not, I'll check in before we leave. Love you."

Abby shut the phone and stuffed it back into her pocket.

"He's a nice bloke, your Dan," William said casually.

"Yes, he is," Abby agreed.

"So what's he see in you?"

Abby sputtered and stopped in her tracks. She smiled salaciously and wiggled her eyebrows. "Must be because I'm so hot."

William chuckled. "Good answer."

He stopped at the edge of the forest and motioned to Abby for the paper. She handed it to him.

"I'm coming with you," Abby said, crossing her arms.

"Maybe later," William said as he stood near the trees. "This part I gotta to do on me own. The next part we'll do together."

"But what if you need help? We're supposed to be in pairs." Her dark eyes were looking redder, her arms still crossed over her chest. "Gabe said so, remember?"

"Look, I'll be careful, alright? And if I need yer help, I'll holler my head off." William gave her a pleading look. Abby nodded in resignation as William turned and walked into the forest.

Even though it had been dark the last time he had been in the woods, the river was easy for him to find. The draw of the water propelled him forward before he could even hear its constantly flowing water. It felt familiar. And safe. Almost like home. *Almost.*

William began his routine. He set up his paint box and scooped some water from the river. He set up a small easel by a rock not far from the river's edge. He stepped back and gave a satisfied look at the area he set up. *Perfect.*

William pulled off his coat and rolled up the sleeves of his flannel shirt. He crouched at the river's edge and gently brushed a finger across the surface of the water. It was hard for him to resist touching its rippling surface.

"Show me," he whispered.

And as he uttered the words, the water swirled and moved as colors played out across its surface. A view of a forest came into focus as well as a path. William picked up a brush and began painting frantically, keeping one eye on the surface of the water as he applied each brush stroke to the paper. A path. Some snow. More path. And then a stone object. William smiled. This was what he was waiting for. He painted frenetically, oblivious to everything but the swirling pictures in the river. When they stopped, he filled in the details as much as he possibly could.

No need to get too particular, Wills, he thought to himself. *It's not so much a painting as a road map.* William reluctantly packed up his paints and brushes and picked up the easel with the painting still attached. *Hopefully the others will know where to start*, William thought. He smiled proudly. *At least I know where it ends.*

William ambled back along the path toward the place where he was to reunite with Abby. As he reached the tree line, he paused for a moment and turned to face the forest once again. He stood silently, casting his gaze in all directions. *Coulda swore I heard whispering,* he thought. A chill ran through him. Shaking his head, he turned back and headed out of the forest.

Abby was leaning against the side of the barn waiting for William. She had been scanning the tree line, her eyes darting back and forth like a cat watching the birds, hoping one would drop to the ground. The sight of William emerging through the trees caused her to immediately stand up, as if she were assuming attention. She strode quickly over to William and reached out to take his paint box from his hand. Grateful for the lessening of his load, William released his grip on the handle. Abby glanced quickly at the easel and then immediately at William's face.

"Did you get what you needed?"

William nodded. He lifted the easel in an effort to turn it toward her, but Abby raised a hand to stop him.

"No, no," she said quickly. "It will probably be best for you to explain it to all of us in one shot," Abby suggested.

As she moved slowly down the path, she fell into step beside him, matching the cadence of his pace.

"Sara and Joe know this area much better than I do," she added. "We should hurry."

William looked at Abby as they neared the house. "Did ya already call Sara?" William gave her a skeptical look, as if he already knew the answer.

"Oh crap. No." Abby pushed the speed dial and talk buttons on her cell phone. After a brief moment, Abby spoke.

"Hi, Sara. It's Ab. How are you?" Without pausing she looked at William and gave him a wink. "Good. Well, William and I are practically at your front door. Now's not a bad time, is it? Okay, we'll wait here at the door for you, then. Bye."

Abby shut the phone and shoved it in her pocket as she started rocking back and forth on her heels in front of Sara's door. From the doorstep, they could hear people tromping heavy-footed across the living room floor and Sara's voice muttering something incomprehensible. William just stared at Abby as she calmly rocked back and forth on her heels. She turned to William and smiled.

"I guess maybe you were right. We probably should have called first. Whoops. Oh well."

William smiled thinly, but remained silent. Either Abby was a completely thoughtless friend or maybe this wasn't a common occurrence. But didn't Abby tell him that Joe was Sara's boyfriend? William shook his head. *Not my place, none of my business.*

William was jolted from his thoughts by the sound of the front door of Sara's home being pulled open. Sara stood in the doorway, fully dressed in faded jeans and a flannel shirt, her hair wrapped in a towel. Abby smiled and stepped into the house.

"William and I have been busy this morning. Well, mostly William, but he's got something to show us. Is that Joe's truck in the driveway?"

Abby set down the paint box and took off her coat and boots as she craned around looking for Joe.

"Uh, yeah," Sara stammered. "He's in the kitchen having coffee." Sara pulled the towel off her head and began squeezing the ends of her hair with the towel.

"Great!" Abby said enthusiastically as she pulled William into the kitchen, his arms wrapped carefully around the easel. "Let's go in the kitchen and grab a coffee while Sara fixes her hair. Then you can do your thing, okay?"

"Yeah, sure," William answered, unsure if she was being a smartass, referring to his contribution as "your thing." Not wanting to start a fight by asking, he silently followed Abby into the kitchen.

"Just help yourselves," Sara said loudly as she darted into the bathroom. "I just need to run a quick comb through my hair." She entered a room off the hallway and shut the door quickly behind her.

Abby strode into the kitchen, her eyes fixed on Joe, noting that his hair was rather damp looking. "Hey, Joe, how are you today?"

Abby smiled at him a grabbed a couple of mugs from the cupboard and filled them from the pot on the counter. She handed a mug to William, who was settling in a seat next to the easel set up in front of him.

"Uh, I'm doing okay," Joe responded as he diverted his eyes from Abby's penetrating stare.

"Good, good." Abby sipped at her coffee in a vain attempt to ignore the moment of awkward silence. Lucky for her, she didn't have to wait for long.

Sara strode back into the kitchen, her wet hair combed flat in a wetter version of her usual shoulder-length hairstyle. She swiftly sat down on a wooden chair between Joe and Abby. Joe avoided looking at her, and Sara ignored Abby's not-so-discreet knowing leer. Sara turned to face William.

"Did you go check things out?" Sara inquired politely.

William nodded.

"So, did the river yield any clues? What did you discover?" Sara was practically sitting on the edge of her chair, her eyes sparkling with anticipation.

William rose from his seat slowly and moved his easel so that it faced the table so that the others could see it more clearly.

"Well, it's not finished, but hopefully it will give us an idea where we have to go." William shifted uneasily as they "oohed" and "aahed" at the painting.

"This here," he said as he jabbed a gnarled finger at a drawing of a round stone well, "this is where we have to get to what cha call our main objective, if yeh will." William gave a jab to the path that led to it. "This is the path that leads to the well." William moved his finger down the painting to the lower left corner. "Down here is the entrance to the path. On one side of the path is a fence of some sort of wire. On the other side, there's a large boulder." William looked at the three faces intently staring at the painting. "Do any of ye know where this path starts?"

Sara jumped up. "Ooh! I do! I do!" Blushing, she sat back down on her chair, her face reddening slightly. "Sorry, I couldn't help myself. But I do know since it is on my property. It's less than a quarter mile east from the river."

William stood, waiting for them to say something. They remained silently staring at the painting. Sara had cocked her head to one side, her right eye closed as if she was trying to understand the perspective. William shook his head. Someone needed to take the lead. Didn't Gabe say they needed to move a little quicker? William cleared his throat and they all looked at him with expectation.

"So, when are we going?" William asked as he rubbed a hand over his eyes.

"How about now?" Joe offered quietly.

"Now?"

"Yeah, now," Abby chimed in. "Remember what Gabe said. We may not have the element of surprise if we don't figure it all out and act soon." Abby stood, as if ready to spring into action.

"Okay." Sara stood too, albeit with far less enthusiasm than Abby.

"Well, I'll bring the map," William said as he gently released the paper from the easel. "You bring a pencil and some paper," William said to Abby shortly.

"Why?" Abby demanded. "Why the paper? Why me?"

"We may need it to write a few things down."

"Like what?" Abby pressed, raising an eyebrow.

"I dunno, just things," William glared at in annoyance.

"Like what?" Abby repeated like a petulant preschooler.

"Just trust me, alright?"

"Yeah, yeah," Abby muttered. Sara handed her a pen and a spiral notebook.

As they stood in the doorway, Abby called Dan and left a message telling him they were changing locations. There was a change in the atmosphere in the room as they stood up, ready to face their first outing: their first common purpose since William's arrival in Harmon. It would be a trial run for the four of them, perhaps even a test of whether their abilities and training would be assets or hindrances. A surge of energy revitalized them and put all other thoughts and discomfort behind them. As Abby closed her phone, William announced loudly,

"Are we ready?" He looked at each of them in turn. Each nodded in assent, their eyes clear and bright with anticipation.

Sara and Abby smiled at each other before yelling in unison, "Let's go!"

CHAPTER 27

William and Abby deposited William's easel and paint box in Abby's van then fell immediately into step behind Sara and Joe as they meandered down the path leading to the barn and toward the forest beyond. Abby slowed her pace, and William matched his pace to her stride. He was busy scrutinizing his painting, his gray eyebrows furrowed, muttering incoherently under his breath. Abby didn't even bother to figure out what he was saying. It probably wasn't meant for her ears, and even if it were, she couldn't decipher his accent when he used such a low tone. Instead, she watched Sara and Joe intently. While they seemed reluctant to have any direct physical contact with each other, they still were walking rather close to each other and glancing at each other in an intimate way; smiling and speaking in hushed voices. *Why are they all doing that? Maybe I'm just going deaf.* Abby noted she could hear other noises, like the sounds of the birds in the trees— *boy, are they deafening*; their song rang more loudly now that she focused her full attention on them.

Abby stopped on the path and gazed into the branches of a maple tree, its branches bare except for the beginnings of little green buds. She looked at the figures moving in the canopy high above the maple. *Are those birds?* Somehow the shiver that went down her back told her that it was too early for the birds to be back.

"Whaddya lookin' at?" William demanded as he too stopped and gazed upward at the branches. Joe and Sara stopped and turned around to gaze upwards also, but Abby motioned at them.

"No, no, not to worry," Abby waved at them to continue. "Just looking at the birds."

Joe and Sara moved along the path ahead of them once more, and Abby and William followed silently behind. Once Sara and Joe arrived at the forest's edge, they paused and waited for William and Abby to catch up.

"Okay," Sara said, looking at William. We have to walk down along the line here until we reach your markers." Sara turned to Joe and Abby. "William and I will lead the way. You two follow us and keep your eyes open."

Joe and Abby both nodded as Sara and William followed a light trail, William clutching the painting/map in his gloved hands as he stumbled through some larger drifts of snow.

Abby eyed Joe, scrutinizing his expression for a hint of something that would give away what was going on. Joe caught Abby's stare, blushed and looked away. *Ah*, Abby thought, *something really good is going on. Good.* It had been a long time since Sara had anyone fun in her life. Abby smiled as she watched Sara talking with William as they walked. Sara was very animated, her arms moving about as she gesticulated rapidly with her hands, her face alight with a beaming smile. William was smiling too, laughing at the odd comment Sara would proffer. He was quite handsome when he smiled, Abby thought as she watched him chat with Sara. *I guess she really can bring out the best in people.* Abby sighed and clutched the spiral notebook she was carrying closer to her chest, wrapping her arms tightly around it. *I wonder why I always seem to bring out the worst.*

William and Sara had stopped a few feet ahead and Sara was waving her arms wildly above her head, making the hood of her winter jacket bob up and down behind her. Suppressing a grin, Abby followed Joe to catch up.

"There's the stone," Sara pointed at the rock, "and on the opposite side here is the wire fence." Sara turned to face William. "Can you lead us from here?"

William held the painting at arm's length, narrowed his eyes and scrutinized it one last time before he set his eyes upon the path laid out in front of him.

"Yeah, I think I can figger it out from here." William moved along the path slowly and deliberately. The icy ground crunched under every footfall and he had to wade through several drifts of snow. The bit of walking they did was arduous, but William was feeling rejuvenated instead of spent; he could feel the presence of the well—the call of the water guiding him.

The path wended through the forest to the east of the river. After what seemed to be an eternity the forest gave way to a clearing. In its center was a round stone well. The wooden posts that had held a small roof were still present, but the tiny roof that had once sheltered it had long since rotted away. William held up the painting for a final comparison. He only had one coin to offer, and he hadn't come all this way to bugger it all up. Satisfied that this was indeed the well, he rolled up the painting and handed it to Joe.

"Here, hold this for me." William motioned at Abby. "We need to get closer."

Abby nodded and pulled the pen out of the spine of the notebook she was clutching and stepped behind William as he bent down to peer into the murky depth of the well. Sara and Joe crept behind Abby but kept at a discreet distance. William walked to the well and fished around in his pocket until he grasped the coin given him by the Lady in the Lake. He cleared his throat and held the coin in his right hand he spoke.

"Spirit of the well, creature of the water. We four come to you fer guidance. Please accept this coin as tribute."

William closed his eyes and tossed the coin into the well. The sound of it hitting rocks on its descent and its contact with the water deep inside reverberated loudly, echoing all around them. The four of them waited and watched in silence.

Abby felt the hair on the back of her neck rise. She shuddered and looked at William, noticing that as he stood gazing down into the well, he shuddered also. A strange surge ran through, not just her, but everything around her. Abby looked to William for an answer, but much to her surprise he was staring at a vapory, bluish mist that seemed to have risen up from the well shaft. It was hovering in front of William, morphing into the shape of a young boy. He appeared liquid and vaporous at the same time. Abby felt herself drawn closer, as did Joe and Sara who had crept to within ten feet of the well. William motioned to Abby to get the pen ready, and she poised it over the paper as the sprite burst into song:

"There's no legend to tell the tale, no story handed down,
of when Man's welcome in our world was suddenly withdrawn.
The task falls heavily upon my song to sing of a time lost age,
before the barrier betwixt the realms was magically engaged.
Dark thoughts had risen upon the Feyland at time of man's unrest;
would their violence encompass us?
Man's actions were put to test.
It commenced with an unspoken thought, an underlying dread,
but soon the words were spoken and like a plague began to spread.
Would someday their skirmishes involve their fairy brothers?
Would they have to conquer them as they had conquered others?
The bond was tested mightily, still tension began to grow,
suspicion soon filled the air; their presence had to go.

A fairy troop took action, to drive the humans out,
their plan to make them fearful worked, indeed, without a doubt.
Soon men started fighting back, regardless of their fear,
the pressures began to take their toll—a war was drawing near.
And yet with all the turmoil, a couple hoped to wed,
a fairy maid and noble knight, that's what our folklore said,
To the Fairy Queen and Elthynne the pair went hand-in-hand;
to garner blessing of their union and a home in Feyland.
After hearing out the couple and the Elythynne members in turn,
the Queen raised her hand to speak—her face was grim and stern.
The couple stood united, confident in their bond;
a sense that something was amiss, they vowed to stand strong.
'Love is such a noble thing; it gives us strength and power,
but it is not enough to quell the unrest at this hour.
Our world is being threatened by man's violent, war-like ways;
preparations to seal our border are currently underway.
We cannot grant your union blessing in this land,
against man's inevitable invasion we must take a stand.
A fortnight from tomorrow a barrier will arise,
A veil to shroud our blessed world from prying human eyes.
You've little time together now to live in love's embrace,
so make the most, O Noble Knight, before you leave this place.'
Though her words rung sternly, the Queen she had a heart,
It was not of her intent to keep the pair apart.
In locations secret, doorways would be hidden.
Omphalos, as they are known, will place you where they're bidden.
But these allow short trips, a passing through the Veil,
those that harbor a greater ambition will set out only to fail.
Once the Veil was woven to keep the realms apart,
rebellion gripped the Feyland; their own war began to start.
Fairies that once stood side by side now took arms against each
other;
rebels that wished for peace with man, against their fairy brother.
The throes of chaos in the land was not confined to them,
war and plague were pandemic too, in the land of men.
The balance between the worlds had shifted, effecting myriad
turmoil,
but peace would finally be reclaimed after a hundred years of toil.
The stability of the barrier would occasionally be tested,
by not one hand, fairy or human, could its strength be bested.
But it is said the day will come when the barrier may fall,
And if it does the balance shift will wreak havoc on us all.

Four among the humans, a destiny to fulfill,
to contain the power of each element, vessels if you will.
A descendant of a noble line each will have to be,
to demonstrate their strength and power; to prevent dangerous
tragedy.
The first of the Four will rise in front, the Vessel of the Air,
she will glide above the ground, the wind upon her hair.
Crimson is the color that identifies her nature,
while calm her element appears to be, it can be ominous in nature.
The second will come from the right, a yellow blaze of fire,
the darkest element to control, it will often raise her ire.
Like a lion she must possess unbridled strength of spirit,
to learn to harness the power of the flame and not get lost within it.
From behind will appear the eldest of the Four,
although adorned in black his color range is more.
Water helps him channel his ability to see
events and certain happenings before they come to be.
From the left the fourth arrives, a figure bathed in white,
a man whose reason and his spirit are locked in bitter strife.
To mould the earth and harness the quakes the man must undertake,
to listen less to his head and let his spirit awake.
To the center they must converge; their paths now lie in tandem,
allies to fulfill their task, they must go hand-in-hand in.
Cooperation a vital key to keep the Veil drawn,
If they fail chaos will triumph – the balance will be gone."

With his final words the sprite dissipated into a fog that slipped
down into the dark abyss of the well, leaving behind the stunned silence
of the group and the sound of Abby's pen scribbling rapid notes in the
book mingling with the sound of water dripping off the stones and into
the well, echoing from within its depths.

When Abby finally managed to capture all the words on paper, she
slipped the pen back into the spiral spine of the notebook and lifted her
head up to see what was going on. She half expected, from the continued
silence, that the others had somehow been magically frozen in place.
They had, however, merely been stunned into silence by the magnitude
of the words in the Well Sprite's song.

William hadn't moved since he made the offering. He was staring
down into the well, perhaps searching the darkness for the sprite or a
vision. *Who knows what else he's doing now*, Abby thought. It was just
amazing to her that he was able to summon the water sprite at all. *Where
did he get that coin from?* She couldn't remember if he told them. Abby

was even more surprised to see that both Sara and Joe had crept closer to the well and were almost directly beside her, Sara clutching Joe's arm as they both stared mutely at the place where the Sprite had appeared.

I'm not going to be the one to break the silence, Abby thought determinedly. But it must have been quite a powerful sight to have rendered the others silent. *At least I got it all down on paper*; she mentally gave herself a pat on the back even though she was mildly disappointed. Abby looked around and admired how truly beautiful the place was. The sun was starting to peek out from between the clouds, and it felt warm – even warmer than she could remember it being the year before. Some of the thinner patches of snow were beginning to thaw, and she could see the little sprouts of grass peeking out from the dead leaves on the ground. And there was that sound again, whispering like before, but it seemed louder. Abby glanced up to the trees as she tried to follow the sound, but it was coming from all around them. The others appeared to notice too, and it roused them out of their collective silence.

Two little, fairy-like creatures darted out of the trees and began buzzing excitedly around the well. William shrunk back, startled and unsure of how to accept their presence. He relaxed almost at once when Abby said,

"Aren't those your little friends, Sara?"

"Yeah, they are," Sara answered with a smile toward them as they darted around Sara's head chattering like little birds. "I wonder what's up."

The little creatures hovered close to her ear and continued to speak rapidly. Sara's smile of welcome soon transformed to an expression of concern as the fairy folk flew up and out of sight.

"We have to hurry back," Sara spoke urgently as she turned to walk down the path. "They came to tell me that something was wrong at my place, that it appeared there may have been some intruders."

Joe stepped beside her quickly. "Are you sure they weren't talking about when Oogan was taken?"

"No, they definitely said an intruder *today*." Sara picked up the pace with Joe at her side following suit and Abby and William behind her attempting to keep up.

"Look, who knows what we may face today, okay?" Sara's eyes were dark. She was weary, but she raised her jaw in defiance. "If they're expecting a fight, they're gonna get one." Sara stopped and looked at them, her eyes boring into each of them in turn like blue lasers. "Be vigilant. And be prepared to fight."

They each nodded, and Sara smiled thinly as they muttered reassurances that they would do just that. Sara turned on her heel back to the path and continued forward at an almost maniacal pace, causing William and Abby to lag quite a distance behind. The walk back felt longer, even though they were each eager to talk about the Well Sprite's message and what it meant to them or what they would have to do next.

As Abby and William reached the edge of the forest, they caught a glimpse of Sara and Joe running toward the back of the barn; Sara was in the lead and running at a full sprint, yelling as she bolted forward. As she reached the door, Abby noticed a dark figure lying half-in, half-out of the barn door. Sara shrieked, scooped up the figure and ran into the barn with it. Joe held the door open for her and quickly followed her inside.

William reached out and squeezed Abby's arm, his fingers almost digging in to the flesh of her arm.

"That creature Sara is carryin' is hideous," William declared, his voice wavering slightly. "What the hell is it?"

Abby's expression remained impassive even though her heart sank into the pit of her stomach. While she wasn't one hundred percent sure, her gut confirmed her suspicion.

"That, William," she answered flatly, "was Oogan."

Abby pulled out her cell phone and speed dialed her house to check in with Dan at each change of location according to the plan. The answering machine took the call after the first ring.

Some system, she thought with annoyance as she waited for the beep. *Where the hell was he anyway?* She sighed, still annoyed and then heard the beep.

"Hi, Dan. It's me, your *wife*. Remember me? Anyway I'm calling to tell you we are back at Sara's, and I will leave another message when we leave." Abby flipped her phone shut and jammed it back in her pocket.

William was standing beside her, rocking back and forth on his heels, his hands jammed in his pockets.

"We can go in the barn," Abby suggested. "It's the only way we'll find out what's going on."

William looked at her, his eyes wide. "That creature, that's Oogan, right? Is it, ya know, tame?"

"Oogan, yeah, he's tame," Abby said flatly. "He's just hard to be around sometimes."

William continued to look at her as if unconvinced that Oogan was trustworthy.

"Look, he won't hurt us okay?" Abby said sharply. "He only likes Sara, and it's pretty obvious he doesn't care about the rest of us." Abby grabbed him by the arm. "Come on." She opened the barn door and pulled William in behind her.

Abby recognized Oogan's musky odor as soon as the door closed. Still strong, but it smelled slightly different than before. She walked further into the barn. *That sense of despair,* she noticed. *It's changed; still depressing and gloomy, but not as powerful. How strange.* Realizing she still had a death grip on William's arm she let go and smiled feebly at him. Abby led the way into the main area of the barn where the blanket had been laid out on the floor in front of the stall where Oogan's nest was located. Sara was kneeling over Oogan, and at her knees was an open first aid kit. Oogan was lying on the blanket with Joe on his other side.

Abby stepped closer. Oogan was in a bad way, he looked as if he was on the losing end of a fight. He appeared conscious but looked incapable of talking. His one eye was so grotesquely swollen it had completely shut. His face and lips seemed generally puffier, and he had some sort of dark liquid seeping from the corner of his mouth. His body was covered in many darker spots and cuts, some of which seemed to seep the same mucilaginous liquid. One of his wings was partially retracted, its thin, rubbery membrane torn from the tendon-like frame.

Sara was dabbing ointment onto his cuts with a cotton ball as Joe watched. William had come closer; he looked somewhat relieved that Oogan was not aware of his presence. Oogan moaned slightly as Sara continued to dab his wounds with ointment.

"Oogan, can you hear me?" Sara leaned closer to his face as his good eye fluttered open.

"Lady...Lady Sara," Oogan croaked, his voice weak and husky.

"Yes, Oogan, yes it's me," Sara answered. Sara bent closer, tucking a lock of hair behind her ear. "What happened to you? Why did you leave?"

Oogan tried to lift his head up. Sara motioned to Joe to help her as she put her arms under Oogan and lifted him upright. Joe steadied Oogan with one arm behind him and another in front, in case he teetered over either way. Though Oogan was unsteady and swayed slightly side-to-side, he was able to stand on his talons.

Sara put a bowl up to his mouth, and he eagerly lapped at the water it held. He nodded slightly to Sara, and she put the bowl down behind her.

"What happened to you, Oogan?" Sara asked softly as she reached out to stroke him lightly on the head.

"My master found me," Oogan said, his head drooping. "He took me away. I am sorry I broke my word to you."

Sara smiled slightly as she stroked his head. "It's okay; it's not your fault."

"He wanted me to tell him things. Things about you – all of you." Oogan's eyes glanced over to William. "But not you," he added. "I don't know you. But he does."

William's blue eyes widened and his cheeks flushed as he shrunk back. He gave Sara a panicked look but said nothing. Abby reached over and patted his arm reassuringly as Sara looked at Oogan again.

"Did he do this to you? Did your master harm you?"

"At first. I didn't want to tell, Lady Sara. I didn't want you to be hurt. But he wanted information. Something that would cause pain," Oogan looked at Abby, his open eye moist with what appeared to be tears.

Abby caught Oogan's glance, and a feeling of dread rose up from the pit of her stomach as nasty bile rose inside her. She gritted her teeth to fight the nausea that began to take hold as her stomach fluttered and tightened.

"Do you have something to tell Abby?" Sara inquired softly in a gently controlled tone.

"He wanted information. He wanted to know what was important to you. And I told him what I heard Abby say was most important to her."

Abby gasped in horror. "Dan," she whispered as she cut Oogan off in mid-sentence.

"I didn't want to hurt Abby either. I knew that would hurt you, too. I escaped to warn you. They are coming."

Abby looked at Sara, tears were streaming down her face. "Are they coming now?" Her voice was wavering as she tried to remain calm.

"No," Oogan croaked as he swayed. "They were preparing to leave as I left. But no one was here, and I fell down in the snow—,"

"I have to get home!" Abby screamed. "Now!"

Abby bolted for the door fumbling for her keys in her pocket. *How could I be so stupid? All the messages I left* – Abby's fingers pulled her keys from her pocket as she ran to her van.

"Wait!" Joe yelled. "You can't go alone!" Joe ran up to her and grabbed her arm. "What if they're still there Abby? What if there's more than one of them?" Joe looked at her, his dark eyes riveting on hers. "I'm coming with you."

Abby yanked her arm out of his grasp. "Then hurry the fuck up and get in the damn van!" she yelled as she opened the driver's side door and shoved the key in the ignition. Joe barely got his leg in and the door closed before she slammed the van into reverse and was peeling out of the driveway.

Abby flew down the road, her foot heavy on the pedal, her hands clutching the steering wheel so hard; her knuckles were white. She couldn't speak to Joe, even to tell him that she was glad he was with her. *I gotta get home* ran through her mind like some panicked Buddhist mantra. *Gotta get home.*

Abby slammed on the brakes and jerked the steering wheel to turn into her driveway. She pulled ahead and jerked to a stop, throwing the van into park, leaving it running as she jumped out.

The house looked the same as it always did. No sign of any activity at all. Dan's car was parked in its usual spot. The yard was empty. She moved quickly up to the porch. The storm door was ajar. Abby pushed it open. She could feel a weird sensation surge through her as she stepped through the threshold. Abby started to shake. *Just like at Sara's,* she thought as an icy chill ran through her.

"I'm right here, Abby," Joe's voice whispered from behind. "Do you want me to go first?"

Abby shook her head. She felt scared and angry. *This is my damn house,* she thought. *And I will protect it.* Abby walked through the porch and grabbed the handle of the interior door and gave it a light pull. *Unlocked,* she observed with growing anxiety. She pulled the door open with one hand and stepped quietly into the foyer. Behind her, Joe grabbed the door and entered the house behind her, closing the door soundlessly as Abby moved further into the house.

She glanced into the kitchen. Nothing. She stepped further into the hall and gently pushed open the bathroom door. Nothing. But the weird sensation was getting stronger. She could feel the hairs on her arms and the nape of her neck rise as the feeling grew stronger. Abby passed the dining table and stepped into the living room. As she headed toward the back of the sofa the feeling was intense, her senses screaming at her to take notice. She turned her head and looked down at the carpet in front of the sofa. A pair of feet wearing gray wool socks was sticking out on the floor in front of the couch. Abby cried out as she bolted around the couch and found Dan, lying fully dressed in jeans and a long-sleeve shirt lying face up on the floor. Abby kneeled down on the floor and cradled his head in her lap, desperate tears rolling down her cheeks.

"Dan! Wake up! Can you hear me! Wake up! Please!" Abby started crying hysterically. "Please, Dan, wake up!"

Joe kneeled down on the floor beside her.

"Please don't be dead!" Abby was weeping even harder, clutching Dan in her arms tightly.

Joe put his hand gently on her shoulder. "Abby," he spoke softly and firmly, "we have to get him some help now."

Joe lifted Dan's wrist and pressed his finger lightly against it, feeling a faint but steady pulse. Joe looked at Dan's chest. He was breathing, but it seemed to be rather shallow.

"Where's your phone?" Joe asked Abby.

"Kitchen counter." Abby cradled Dan in her arms as Joe stood and grabbed the phone from the counter. He brought it back over to the couch and handed her the phone.

"It's your house, Abby," Joe said softly. "You'd better make the call."

Abby nodded and dialed the phone.

"9-1-1. What is the nature of your emergency?"

"It's my husband. He's collapsed on the floor. I need an ambulance." Tears ran down her cheeks as she choked back sobs.

"An ambulance is being dispatched."

Abby couldn't remember if she said thank you or anything at all. All she could do was sit there, holding her husband with the hope that they would arrive in time to save him.

CHAPTER 28

Abby was sitting in an armchair at the side of the hospital bed. It was plain, leatherette, and functional; an average model that featured predominately in aging doctor's offices or hospital waiting rooms designed to be placed in any room regardless of décor; they are slightly more comfortable than a straight back chair, but easily disinfected with a swipe of a damp cloth and a spritz from spray bottle of antibacterial cleaner. It was just like everything else in the drab room: sterile and functional. Dan was lying half propped up and motionless in the bed, his chest rising and falling, giving the impression at first glance that he had just dozed off while reading a book. A more perceptive eye would notice that the bed was surrounded by various monitors and machines, each designed to monitor the vital signs of his body and emit periodic chirps, beeps, and alarms when whatever function it monitored changed, dropped drastically, or even failed. It all had been explained to her when Dan was admitted to the room, but she couldn't remember what it was they had said. Nothing any of them said made sense; it was as if all those medical people had been speaking in another language and underwater – she just couldn't hear and understand everything they told her. And she felt numb. Numb like she was in somebody else's life, like the whole situation was a scene in some soap opera on television. Who collapses into a coma for no reason? Abby wasn't about to offer up the possibility that he had been magically attacked. They would blame it on shock, the shock of discovering her husband on the floor. No, to tell the medical professionals what had really happened to Dan would guarantee her 48 hours in the sanitarium down the street for observation.

Abby leaned forward and squeezed Dan's hand. It was warm, but he didn't return the gesture. How many times had she held that hand and gotten a gentle squeeze in response? Abby swiped a tear off her cheek with her other hand, not daring to let go.

It's your fault, she told herself. She should never have dragged him into this, never should have mentioned him in front of Oogan—

Woulda, coulda, shoulda. She put her face down on their entwined hands.

The sound of footsteps in the doorway made Abby jump and she looked up to see Sara enter the room. Sara walked over to her and gave her a big hug. Abby felt comforted but moved quickly from Sara's embrace.

"Joe came back after the ambulance left and told us what happened," Sara spoke quietly as her gaze fell upon Dan.

"Do they have any idea what's wrong or what happened?"

Abby cleared her throat. "Well, I told them I got home and found him on the floor," Abby began, staring idly out the window. "But all they can determine for now is that he's in a coma. I think they plan to do more tests and continue monitoring him."

A nurse entered the room with a thermometer and a blood pressure cuff.

"I need to take some vitals," the nurse directed her comments to Abby but was shifting her gaze to Sara.

"Ab, want to go down to the cafeteria and get some coffee?" Sara asked; taking the hint the nurse was silently giving her.

"I don't want to leave him."

"He'll be okay. I need to do some blood draws too," the nurse stated as she started to place the blood pressure cuff on Dan. She turned and gave Abby a sympathetic look. "It's okay; he's in good hands here."

Sara raised her eyebrows expectantly. Abby pushed herself up and out of the chair. "I don't want to be gone too long," she murmured as she followed Sara out of the room.

Sara led the way to the elevator and they rode it down to the main floor, the only sound the hum of the elevator as it moved down the shaft and past several floors.

"This way," Sara said as they stepped off the elevator and into the hallway. Abby followed obediently and silently as they turned down another starkly bright corridor and entered the cafeteria. The brightness of the hallways and various passageways was a stark contrast to the bleakness Abby passed in the various rooms. How anyone could bear to be there day in and day out she couldn't imagine. Abby felt like every footstep was a chore; she continued to move forward, putting one foot in front of the other as she continued down the hallway, but she felt like her body was made of lead.

The main cafeteria was closed, but there was a small seating area and a cluster of vending machines available. Sara guided Abby to sit in a plastic chair at a table as she fed some one dollar bills into the coffee machine. Sara strode over to the table and placed a paper cup in front of Abby before sitting down in a plastic chair across the table from her.

"I can't vouch for its quality, but it's definitely hot and at least smells like coffee," Sara said as she took a tentative sip from her paper cup.

Abby sat there mutely, staring at the coffee with puffy, red eyes. Sara reached across the table and grabbed Abby's hand in hers. Startled, Abby looked at her despondently; her disheveled hair and red eyes gave her a slightly crazed appearance.

"Abby, I'm so sorry about Dan."

Abby nodded and looked down at her cup. "I can't do this anymore, Sara."

"Do you really mean that?" Sara gazed intently at her, her tone soft and clear.

"Yes. No. I don't know." Abby pulled her hand free and rose to her feet; she began to pace rapidly back and forth across the floor.

"My husband is in a coma and nobody knows why. He could die, God damn it!" Abby's voice was cracking and getting louder; tears were threatening to fall from her eyes.

"Or he could recover, Abby," Sara continued in her calm tone.

A rumbling sound came from outside and both women turned to face the window. The sky lit up with a flash of lightning, and they jumped slightly at the sound. The steady rain that had commenced earlier had increased in intensity and begun to pelt the windows in a heavy barrage.

"Things are getting worse, Abby," Sara said. "I believe Thaddeus planned this attack. He specifically designed it to intimidate you, to keep you out of the battle."

Abby crossed her arms in front of her chest. "Well, his plan really worked. I'm done. Through. Dan needs me, and I will be at his side."

Sara stood up and moved in front of Abby, halting her in her tracks. "Dan is a good man, and he deserves to have someone to be there beside him when he wakes up. But what if Thaddeus wins, Abby? Do you think when he conquers their world and ours that any of us or our loved ones will be safe? I really don't think we will be. No one will be safe. No one."

Abby stared out the window as tears ran down her already tear-stained face.

"I'm scared, Sara. I could lose him forever, just like I lost Callie." Abby shivered and clutched her arms around her. She felt like she had lost her world when her infant daughter died, and the pain had driven her inward with grief. If Dan hadn't been there, not only to share in her sorrow, but to give her a reason to continue on, she probably would have been destroyed by her heart ache. To even think of losing him was unbearable. What if she had to accept that Dan would never recover? She bit her lip to stop it from trembling.

"Abby, Dan wouldn't want you to give up without a fight. He supported you in this before; do you think he would change his mind now? Do you think he would let you give up?" Sara picked up her cup and took a couple more sips before tossing the paper cup into the garbage.

"I'm not going to pressure you, Abby, but you know we need you. You heard the Well Sprite's words. We have a destiny to fulfill, and we have to fight *together*. We are The Four. *Together*. There are no others that are sworn to this duty. Regardless of whether you come or not, the rest of us plan to fight. It's extremely possible we will not win without you. So you decide what you want to do—either you give up without a fight, or you join us and use it as an opportunity to exact vengeance for what happened to Dan."

Sara threw her purse strap over her shoulder and began to walk from the room. She paused at the doorway just as another rumble came from outside.

"Decide what you want to do, Abby. But do it soon—we are running out of time."

Sara swept out of the room. Abby stood at the window, watching the lightning cut across the sky while she listened to the sound of Sara's cowboy boots echoing down the hall.

***

William and Joe were sitting at the kitchen table at Sara's, an open pizza box on the table in front of them. Joe handed William a napkin and proceeded to tug a piece loose from the others, pulling lots of melted cheese along with it. He motioned to William to help himself, but William only looked at him in return.

"Are yeh sure we should be sittin' in Sara's house eatin' while she's gone?" William looked tired and worried.

Joe shrugged and swallowed a mouthful of pizza.

"Well, she did tell us to stick together and for us to be here when she got back," Joe said casually. "So we got pizza. Not a big deal. We'll just make sure we save her some." Joe finished his piece and fished another slice from the box.

William followed suit and set a slice down on the napkin in front of him, his eyes widened in realization.

"What about that Oogan character? Should we take him some pizza?"

William's lip rose as he spoke. Joe smiled. It was obvious that he had an interest in Oogan, even though he harbored an aversion to him.

"You don't have to worry about Oogan," Joe answered reassuringly. "I don't think he'd eat it anyway. Sara will probably take him a peanut butter and honey sandwich when she gets back. It's his favorite, so Sara says."

Joe looked at William waiting for his reaction. Keeping his expression neutral, William just nodded and picked up his slice of pizza. Joe could hear the rumblings of thunder in the distance, followed by the occasional flash of lightning. Joe could feel the earth calling to him— feel its beat, like a heart that was developing some weird type of arrhythmia. The beat was definitely wrong. *Very wrong.*

"What's the date today?" William's words were like a cold glass of water in his face, jolting him sharply from his thoughts.

"It's the 19th. March 19th," Joe answered absently. "Why?"

"Well, I'm starting to figger things out now, and they're starting to making a bit o' sense," William said taking a sip from a can of pop. "The Spring Equinox is tomorrow, March 20th." The Spring Equinox and the Autumnal Equinox in September are the two times a year that the day and night the same length." William took another bite from his pizza.

Joe stood up and opened Sara's fridge, pulling out another can of pop.

"Now, why would it matter if it was the Equinox?" Joe asked as he sat in his chair and opened his can of pop. "Why would it make a difference?"

"Well, here's my theory," William said, wiping his mouth with his napkin and taking a sip of his pop. "Magic closed the Veil, sealing Feyland from the human world, right? But the Equinoxes are natural happenstances. They occur because the earth moves closer to the sun in its orbital path. The day and night become of equal length. It's a natural time of balance. And maybe that's why we've bin called to fight. The Elements are using us as vessels to protect the natural order. The Elements work in harmony with nature; if the Veil falls and the balance between Feyland and our world is breached, maybe it'll have a devastating impact on the natural order. No more balance. That would be a very bad thing, am I right?"

Joe looked at William in awe and nodded. At first it didn't really seem to connect, to make sense, but he felt inside that William's theory did add up on some level. He opened his mouth to speak just as the front door flew open and Sara walked in. William and Joe both jumped. Sara shot them both a disgusted look.

"Geez, we're supposed to be getting ready for a fight, Dan's been attacked, and you two leave the front door unlocked?" William and Joe looked at each other sheepishly, but Sara quickly moved on.

"Alright, you guys are forgiven; you saved me some pizza."

Sara threw her coat on the couch and grabbed a piece of pizza from the box as she sat in a kitchen chair next to Joe. Joe got up and grabbed a can of pop from the fridge and set it on the table in front of Sara. She gave him a warm smile and muttered a muffled "thanks" between mouthfuls of pizza.

"So what have you two been talking about while I've been gone?" Sara reached for another slice.

"Well, William has this theory..." Joe started. He nodded to William. "You tell her."

"Er, okay." William gave Sara a condensed version of his "Equinox Theory" as Sara demolished another piece of pizza. Wiping her mouth, her expression grew stern. Her eyes seemed gray instead of their usual brilliant sapphire blue.

"That's tomorrow," Sara stated flatly, looking at a calendar on her kitchen wall. "That could be a problem."

"Why?" Both men chorused.

Joe gave her a confused look. "What's wrong?"

Sara took a sip of her pop and sighed. "Well, Abby's not sure she wants to fight. This thing with Dan has her scared, and rightly so." Sara looked at the two men. "We may have to go on without her."

But the Sprite said we have to work together!" William protested.

"I know."

"There's a big chance we will fail without her," Joe spoke quietly. Sara moved her hand on the table and laid it on top of hers.

"I know that too." Sara answered softly. "I told her the exact same thing. Maybe she will change her mind. But even if she does, I can't say she would do it by tomorrow. A lot has happened."

The three of them sat in silence, picking at congealed bits of cheese from the pizza and sipping from their cans of pop. While they all had a lot on their minds, each seemed reluctant to voice their thoughts or be the first to speak.

A knock at the door jolted each of them from their thoughts. Sara and Joe leapt from their seats as the front door opened and Abby walked in the door. Close behind her was Gabe, wearing a conical brown hat with a furred brim.

"My husband gets attacked in our home, and you guys leave the door unlocked? Geez, things really fall apart when I'm not here, don't they?"

Sara stared at Abby open-mouthed but silent. Joe raised a hand to his mouth to hide his smile.

"Not that I'm not grateful, but I'm curious. What made you change your mind?" Sara asked, wiping her fingertips on a paper napkin.

Abby poked her thumb toward Gabe. "This one here. We gotta make sure that we don't make him look bad, you know."

Gabe gave her a blank look. "I didn't do anythin'. I just ran into her on the way in the door."

"Then I guess I will just have to share my secret another time." Abby crossed her arms in front of her chest and lifted her chin defiantly. "Anyone got a problem with that?"

"Yeh come to stand and fight with us, Abby?" William spoke sharply, looking at her with one eyebrow raised.

"That depends, you old, wet blanket. Did you save me some 'Za?" Abby sauntered over to the table, snagged a piece of pizza and settled on a bar stool as she began stuffing the pizza into her mouth.

Sara, Joe, and William looked expectantly at Gabe, who was still waiting in the doorway.

"There's a piece here with your name on it," Sara offered, gesturing to the remaining slice of pizza in the box. Gabe wrinkled his nose in distaste.

"No thanks," Gabe said politely as he screwed up his face. "Looks like vomit on bannock to me."

Abby stuck her tongue out at him, but kept eating. Joe laughed, nodding in agreement.

"What brings you here, Gabe?" Joe asked as another flash of lightning lit up the sky.

"It's time," Gabe said. "The supporting forces are ready, but we need you to—,"

Abby cut in. "We're going in at dawn." She looked at their stunned expressions. "Anyone got a problem with that?"

Each of them shook their heads.

"Good," Abby raised her pizza to Gabe and he nodded in response.

"Just one thing, Gabe," William said. "How do we find this Omphalos thingy?"

Gabe smiled, his eyes disappearing under his beard. "You just go into the forest past the river. The forest will show you the way."

William raised an eyebrow. "You sure 'bout that?"

Gabe nodded. "I must go now and inform the Queen."

Gabe clasped his hand to his chest and drew his arm out to them. "Good tidin's on the 'morrow. See yeh victorious on the battlefield." He gave them a final salute and walked out the front door.

Sara looked at Abby. "I'm glad you're coming, Abby," she said softly, a weak smile on her face as she pushed her hair back out of her eyes. "Seriously, what made you change your mind?"

Abby looked at Sara and Sara could see the blazing fire inside her eyes. She had to catch herself so she wouldn't gasp aloud.

"Well, two things, really. One was Gabe told me that if you aren't winning a battle you change the rules of engagement. The other is something you said. I plan to go into battle tomorrow and exact my revenge on Thaddeus." The fire in her eyes blazed even brighter. "If I get hold of him, he'll wish he never screwed with me." Abby sat down on her stool again, like a bird on a perch.

"So, who's up for making a battle plan?" Abby asked.

Suddenly the room was filled with the chatter of them all speaking rapidly, each adding their own perspective, surprisingly with no dissension at all. *This plan is coming together*, Abby thought, the corner of her mouth lifting in a half smile. She grabbed a sheet of paper and started making notes as a flash and rumble filled the air. *Ready or not, we're going out there to fight.* No longer worried what the outcome would be, Abby felt proud of herself for taking a stand against Thaddeus and the tactics he employed to get what he wanted. And that, more than anything, made her feel she was making the right decision.

***

Gabe arrived at the castle well into the evening. He entered through a magically concealed doorway, one that the Queen herself had personally given him the key to when he was first promoted to Captain of the Guards. As he pocketed the key and strode up the stairs he tried to remember how long ago that was. *Perhaps it won't matter for much longer*, he thought darkly.

He made his way down a hall to a doorway at the top of the stairs. The Guard Royale, resplendent in their silver and blue uniforms were standing their usual watch as the Queen's personal advisor ushered him quietly into her private sitting room. The Queen was sitting at a desk in the corner writing something quickly. She waved him over with her free hand, and he swiftly moved in front of her, standing at attention.

When she set her pen down, he snapped his arm up in a sharp salute. She nodded her head regally and said, "Report."

Gabe sat down in the chair facing her desk. "The Four are prepared to attack, though the Fire Vessel wasn't sure that she would participate. Thaddeus had found her partner, and he is now in 'The Long Sleep'."

Queen Ezreanna gave him a concerned look. "Abby, is it?"

Gabe nodded.

"Is he in a safe location?"

"Yes, Yer Majesty."

"If we are victorious we will be able to help him. As long as he is kept safe, our people will be able to revive him."

Queen Ezreanna cast an eye out her window. The sky rumbled with the sound of distant thunder, but even as the lightning flashed across the sky, there was no sign whatsoever of rain. Ezreanna sighed. "Has it gotten this way in the human world too?"

Gabe nodded and she turned her attention back to the window.

"And what of their people, Gabe? Are they also in turmoil? Has the level of unrest escalated in their realm also?"

Gabe snorted. "They're humans. They spend so much time fightin' and pushin' each other it would be hard to notice any changes."

The Queen sighed. "How nice it must be to be blissfully ignorant of what is to come. Perhaps their ignorance is a blessing."

Gabe shifted uncomfortably in his seat. "It won't be so blissful if Thaddeus is successful."

Queen Ezreanna's expression changed. Her normally pale skin became red, her blue eyes blazed like an ice storm. "Have you so little faith in their abilities?"

Gabe stood quickly, bowing submissively to her. "On the contrary, Yer Majesty. I have great confidence in them. But I think Thaddeus has grown stronger, and I can't judge what I don't know."

"Well, that's certainly an honest answer." Queen Ezreanna stood, and Gabe was surprised to notice that she was clad in her uniform. Her long gray-blue jacket fell to just below her hips, and her trousers were bloused above her highly polished black boots. A thick silver belt around her waist held in place, on her left side, her sheathed sword and a pouch that contained magical weapons. She pulled open a desk drawer and drew out the knife that Gabe had brought her the night of the attack on Sara. Ezreanna cradled the knife in her hands as she gazed at the gemstones on its hilt with a sad look in her eyes. Her eyes quickly turned dark, and her expression turned stony with resolution as she tucked the knife into a holster strapped on her right thigh.

"You told them the signs are in place?"

"Not exactly. But they knew it was time. They will be arriving at dawn tomorrow."

"Are our troops ready?"

"Only the ones we are certain we can trust."

Ezreanna frowned. "I hope that's the majority of them."

"Yeh, fer the most part. But we're not utilizing the Taekyrs. I believe they're under the influence of Thaddeus."

"Poor creatures, it's not like they can help it, is it? They aren't very bright." Queen Ezreanna moved to another table where a map was laid out on its surface.

"Well, Gabe, it's time for you to do your day job."

Gabe moved to the map. Scrutinizing it briefly, he jabbed at the map, pointing a gnarled forefinger to a location. "This is where we should establish yer Field War Room," Gabe motioned to the map again. "This here is where we'll assemble our forces." Gabe looked at the Queen for approval.

"Where do you expect they'll launch their offensive?" Queen Ezreanna asked, drumming her fingers impatiently on the table.

Gabe indicated to another location on the map. "Here, but in the human realm." The Queen raised an eyebrow.

"I believe they will be following The Four into our realm. Of course, I probably could've had more information if I had taken Michael in for questioning."

"The Taekyr Captain?" Ezreanna queried. "I thought we had him under surveillance."

Gabe nodded. "He was, but he slipped away two days ago. We caught a lucky break though—his Taekyr spy returned to the Air Vessel, Sara, and he's being most cooperative."

"Good. We could use a bit of luck now." The Queen started to roll up maps and motioned to her advisor to gather various items at the table.

"I shall take my guard and head for the Field War Room. Ready the troops and meet us there. I want us to ride at the head of the army when dawn breaks."

"But what of the Elythynne, Yer Majesty? Shouldn't they be informed?" The Queen's advisor looked distressed.

"Several members of the Elythynne cannot be trusted. Have a herald send word to the Elythynne when dawn breaks. We shall see where their loyalties lie when the war begins." After she buckled on a thin silver chest plate of warded armor, Queen Ezreanna waved her advisor out of the room with a sweep of her hand and grabbed a silver gray peak hat from a nearby table and placed it upon her head.

"Let us be off to our duties, Gabe." The Queen bent down and clasped his hand in hers and gave it a firm shake. "I'll see you on the battlefield."

"Yes, Yer Majesty. Good hunting." Gabe bowed and saluted.

Queen Ezreanna returned the salute. "Also to you. And please, do come back in one piece."

CHAPTER 29

The smell of sage permeated the air as Joe moved from room to room, silently smudging each of them thoroughly before moving on to the next. He moved to the living room where Sara, William, and Abby had congregated and were watching him with interest. Once the room was smudged, a smoky haze hung in the air.

"Anyone want to smudge themselves before we go?" Joe asked.

"What will it do?" William asked as he moved closer.

"It's like a cleansing and a preparation. It helps to prepare us spiritually."

William looked uncomfortable. "How do you do it, then?"

"Like this," Joe set the abalone shell with the burning smudge stick on the table and bent down close to it, guiding the wisps of smoke up to his head and face and directing the smoke over his head, face and chest as if he were splashing and washing himself with water. He then stood up and held up the shell and the smudge stick in front of William. "I can hold it for you."

William bent slightly and mimicked Joe's movements. His movement was a little disjointed and jerky at first, but he soon relaxed as the smoke wafted over him.

"Thanks," William murmured as he stepped away and Abby moved forward and smudged.

Sara smudged last and gave Joe a long look after she was done. She looked as if she wanted to say something, but she gave him a weak smile instead. They stood together quietly for a moment before William's voice broke the silence.

"Shouldn't we stand in a circle or something?" His voice was low and somber.

"I think that's a great idea," Sara agreed. They stood together in a circle, tentatively clasping one another's hands.

Sara felt a surge go through her and wide-eyed, she looked up. *Whatever surged through me must also have surged through the others*, Sara guessed. They all bore similar expressions on their faces. Stunned silence filled the space within the circle, and it felt like their grips clenched a little tighter.

"Should we say something?" William asked as he shifted from side to side.

"Yeah, here come the Fantastic Four," Abby said with a laugh.

Sara laughed nervously too.

William shot Abby a dirty look. "That's not what I meant," he almost spat back at her.

"Take it easy!" Abby snapped.

"Well, knock it off then!" William retorted sharply.

Ignoring them both, Joe spoke firmly. "Here's to victory. Let's do this one for Dan."

"For Dan," the others repeated solemnly in unison.

Abby's eyes welled with tears. "Thank you," she forced out. "William?"

"Yeah?"

"I'm sorry."

"Forget it."

"Well, sunrise is at 5:47, and it's just 5:00 now, give or take a minute or two. Are you guys ready?" Sara looked at each of them in turn. They all nodded. "There's no turning back now. Let's go. Make sure you keep your eyes open."

Sara opened the door and walked out, zipping up her jacket as she walked down the path toward the forest.

It was still dark outside, though light was beginning to creep into the skyline: the night commencing its surrender to the light of day. Sara thought that Abby's plan of conducting the battle at dawn was ideal; at least they would be able to enter Feyland under cover of darkness, the only advantage they would have on unfamiliar ground.

"Should we have brought weapons?" William asked Sara in a hushed voice as they moved along the path.

"Did you miss the memo, William? We *are* the weapons," Abby said snidely as she walked past him on the path and moved in front of him.

"Remind me when this is over to drown her, will yeh?" William snapped at Joe.

"When this is over you can do what you like. I think I'm gonna take a nice vacation on a beach." Joe said. "Hey, Sara, you want to come?"

Sara looked over her shoulder at him and smiled. "Really?"

Joe nodded.

"I'd like that." Sara beamed.

The four of them stopped as they reached the forest's edge. Sara went to pull a flashlight out of her pocket, but Joe waved her hand away.

"Gabe said the forest would show us the way," he reminded her quietly.

They continued to move further into the forest in a tight group. Abby held her hands at the ready, her head swiveling in all directions for signs of anything out of the ordinary. Joe felt like his senses were hyper alert; the forest just sounded so much louder—as if he could hear the movement of every creature on the ground, in the trees, and in the air. And then he heard the whispering. At first it sounded like the wind whispering in the trees, except for the fact that there were actual words being spoken. He couldn't make out all the words, but some sounded strangely familiar –

The yelp of an animal caused all of them to jump in surprise, and Abby had to stifle her own mouth with her hand to stop from crying out. Or swearing. Joe turned to see a red tail fox standing on a slight rise on the path in the direction they were heading. Joe moved forward. He knew this fox. It was his fox, or, at least, the one he had seen so many times as of late. He moved forward, following its feather-duster-like tail as it moved forward and then stopped in what appeared to be an attempt to allow them to catch up. It ambled slowly along again each time they drew closer. The fox picked up the pace, moving to stand atop a hill off the path ahead of them. He was pacing and circling, yipping in a growling sort of way, and then it stopped abruptly, turning its snout to one direction, and positioned its body in a stance similar to one of a retriever pointing at a pheasant in the brush.

Joe strained to see exactly where and what the fox was pointing at and noticed that it was facing a large circle of trees with a clearing in their midst. The sound of the whispering voices seemed to be getting louder. *This is it, this is definitely it*, Joe thought. He moved closer to the trees, trying to move quietly as the frost-covered ground crunched underfoot. He could hear the whispering increase in volume as he moved closer to the trees.

Two of the trees were tall willows with long hanging branches that reached high and fell in cascades to the ground, each displaying green buds that would hold green leaves in the summer ahead. One tree, however, appeared dry; it was light in color, and had a large, scorched crack down the middle, as if it had been struck by lightning. It displayed no buds or other signs of life.

William looked around. "There's something missing here. I think this is the place..."

William's words ended abruptly as he stared at one of the other trees. A woman appeared within the trunk of the tree, her body moving and flowing outward, and as it did a gown formed along her curves. The gown was the color of the bark, darkened in spots similar to the scars on the trees and shadowy where the bark was thicker and older. The gown shifted and flowed along her body as if it was being blown by the wind on the tree, like the dress was alive and moving in tandem with the tree. The dryad's arms flowed down from the limbs, moving toward them with the grace of a ballerina, the movement just like the limbs of a willow tree being blown gently by the wind. The woman's skin was pale, within a shade or two of the tree's bark; her long hair flowed softly around her head, framing her delicate feminine face.

"They have come, sister, look! They have come! Join me in greeting them," she turned her head and addressed the tree beside her, her voice eager and trembling with excitement.

The Hamadryad in the other tree yawned and stretched her arms as looked at the four with mild curiosity. Her hair and skin was paler than her sister's, her limbs smaller and more spindly. She smiled shyly and nodded at them but did not speak.

"Is it time then? Are you in need of the Omphalos?" The first sister enquired.

"Yes," the four of them answered in unison.

"It is our job to protect it, and we three sisters have done so, since we were saplings." She motioned with her arm and stared at the dead tree across from her. "In the course of our duties our sister Delphia was murdered. I believe you are to stand against the One, the evil man who sanctioned her murder. We wish you good fortune in your battle. Our thoughts will be with you."

The Dryads spread their arms, and at once a huge stone appeared in the center of the grove, like a road appearing in the heat of the midday sun. It was a well-worn, chipped stone at least three feet in diameter. The surface of it and all around the base of it was inscribed with various symbols. Some looked to be Roman, though some could even have been Greek. Some of the symbols had probably never been seen by humans before now. William gasped. It was exactly how he had seen it in his vision. He turned quickly to face Sara.

"I've seen this before in one of my visions. We're going to be attacked—,"

As he spoke the words, the forest around them burst to life. *An ambush*, William thought. *He knew we would have to come here.*

Sara hopped two steps and instantly took flight into the air. "I got the aerial, you three cover the ground. And don't leave without me!"

Sara flew higher into the air and was accompanied by her two dragonfly-sized fairy friends, her constant companions in flight. Sara was flying toward what looked to be a head-on collision with a cloud of large bats.

William was busy ducking arrows that were flying at him from all directions. He scurried quickly for cover behind an oak tree as Abby started crafting fireballs between her hands. She tossed one overhand toward a dark shape off to the side of the rise where the fox had previously stood. The fireball collided with a moving dark shape, which shrieked and ran away in retreat, trailing fire in its wake. William watched as Joe bent down and uttered some words that caused the earth to crack, creating a rift between them and another attacking group: some humanoid and some hairy but shapeless creatures. William yelled to Abby and Joe.

"We have to get to the Omphalos while they are occupied!"

Abby and Joe followed William as they moved closer to the stone. They could hear Sara yelling in the distance, her form a whirling speck in the sky. *The lass can handle herself*, William thought. *We have to be ready; we have to do this right.*

William moved to the Omphalos and recognized the compass carved into the surface with each direction laid out.

"Abby, you need to be here," William said as he pointed to the south. Abby moved quickly into place and started to move her hands upward as if to touch the stone.

Instinctively, William yelled, "Don't touch it now! Wait for Sara!"

Abby jerked her hands back and nodded.

William pointed to Joe, but Joe was already moving into place at the north position. William nodded and moved into the west. From the east, Sara had jumped from her updraft and was running toward them at an incredible speed.

"Her feet are barely touching the ground," Abby whispered in awe as she watched her approach.

Joe cast a look over to the place where the fox had stood after guiding them to this place. He was startled to find a Native American man dressed in hides standing in its place. Joe couldn't help but notice that a pouch he was wearing bore the same unusual pattern as the one Floyd had given him. Surrounding the man was a group of much smaller men clad in clothes bearing the same distinct pattern. Joe recognized them from his vision. *The Mae Mae Quay Shewok.* The taller man standing with them bore an uncanny resemblance to his father. He looked almost like Joe remembered his father, just older, and perhaps a little sadder-looking too.

"Okay, I'm here. Ready?" Joe turned toward Sara's voice as she bounded over to the stone, breathless from her run.

Joe turned back to look at the group again to search out the man he thought was his father, but the fox stood there once more. The diminutive warriors were screaming in defiance, charging toward a group of creatures heading toward them, their spears and arrows pointing towards the advancing enemy.

"Joe! You ready, Joe?" The sound of William's voice made him turn toward the stone Omphalos once more.

"Uh, yeah. Yeah. I'm ready."

"Okay, everyone!" Sara said excitedly. "On the count of four. Together – 1, 2, 3, 4....now!"

Simultaneously, they all placed their hands on the cold stone slab. William thought he would feel a slight surge or pull, but he felt nothing. In fact, apart from the sky changing, the forest around them looked virtually unchanged.

"Are we here?" William asked, turning his head around and around. Nothing in the surrounding area looked much different or any more familiar to him. On closer inspection, he did notice that there was no sign of snow, or any evidence of it upon the ground. There wasn't even a hint of frost on the ground. They were still in a clearing in a forest, but God only knows where. He started to feel like he was being watched, as if an ambush was waiting for them to arrive.

Joe looked around. He knew what to do. He knew the answer on which way to go. He lifted his hands from the stone and walked forward to the edge of the trees.

"Where are you going?" Sara said, trotting along behind as he strode purposefully ahead.

"This way," Joe said calmly as he continued forth.

"Why?"

"Because we're supposed to, that's why."

"Why?" Sara persisted.

"I'm looking for—,"Joe's voice trailed off as he reached a pasture of long grass. Up ahead in the tall grass were large, dark brown figures. Some were stationary; some were ambling through the grass.

"What the bloody hell are those?" William stood stock still, his blue eyes threatening to pop out of his eye sockets.

Joe smiled. "Buffalo. We have to follow the buffalo."

"Why?" William asked, looking uncomfortably at the large, slow moving creatures.

"Why do we do anything?" Joe asked. "You know the answer: because we're supposed to."

"They won't attack us, will they?" William eyes their massive forms warily.

Joe chuckled. "No, William, I think they're on our side."

Abby stomped forward, her hands on her hips. "Are you two done? Can we go now?"

William nodded and made a face at her. Ignoring him, Abby turned to Joe as they followed the herd of buffalo as they moved across the plain and toward a river.

"How far, Joe? Any idea?" Abby asked as she scanned the area for threats.

"I don't know, Ab," Joe said, "as far as we have to."

"Hey, guys, wait!" Sara blurted. "I could scout ahead, you know, do some aerial reconnaissance and let you know what's in front of us."

"Do you think that's a good idea, Sara?" Abby asked, a serious look on her face. "The enemy may do the same thing. What if you're ambushed?"

"I'm willing to risk it," Sara said simply. She turned to William and Joe. "What do you two think?"

William nodded in agreement.

"Just be careful. And don't go too far," Joe cautioned.

"Yes, Mom," Sara mocked. She blew him a kiss and rose up on the wind, her two friends at her side and as she flew upward and out of sight.

"I can't see her, can you see her?" Abby pulled anxiously at Joe's arms.

Joe patted Abby's hand reassuringly. "If we can't see her, maybe Thaddeus can't either."

"She better save that bastard for me," Abby snarled, the heat rising in her hands.

Joe grabbed Abby's hands. Clasping them together he looked her straight in the eye.

"Take it easy, okay?" If you set this grass on fire, all of us will burn up with it."

"All the more reason to get the hell out of here," Abby said shrilly. "It's starting to creep me out." Abby gave a little shudder. William moved closer to her and kept his eyes scanning the area.

Joe focused again on the buffalo. They seemed to be moving quicker now. *Do they know we are following them?*

William could feel the pull inside him. "Water," he whispered.

"Yeah, I'm getting thirsty too," Abby said, swallowing hard.

"No, I'm not thirsty. It's water. I feel water nearby." William held his hand up to his eyes and searched the area. *Close, so close.* It felt so familiar, so inviting…

A crash in the grass behind them caused the three of them to jump into a huddle.

Sara popped up out of the grass, wiping the dirt off her jeans and jacket.

"Sorry 'bout that," she said sheepishly. "I guess the grass made me overestimate my landing, and I fell on my—,"

"What did you see up ahead?" William asked eagerly. "Water, a pond?"

Sara smiled. "Yeah, a little lake or river or something. But on the other side is an army."

The other three looked alarmed. Sara caught their glances and tried to assuage their fears. "I saw Gabe down there. I think they are allies."

"How far away is it?" William asked as he stopped walking briefly. He bent over slightly, bracing his hands on his thighs for support. His knees were killing him too, but he wasn't going to ask them to slow down. He would rest later, when everything was over.

"Hey, Sara," Abby said, her voice cloyingly sweet. "Do you think you could give us a ride?"

* * *

William waited at the side of the river at the base of a large oak tree. Sara had been more than eager to give them a ride, but she was only willing to take them one at a time. "Don't want to drop anybody," she had said. William was grateful she had taken him first. It felt good to just sit down, stretch his legs out, and rest for a while. He felt guilty—he had done so little when they were attacked, and yet his body felt as if it waged a hundred battles. But now he was near the water, and its proximity made him feel safe and a little rejuvenated. William slipped his hand into the water to scoop up a handful to drink. He couldn't help but let his hand linger for a moment under its surface; a pang of loneliness suddenly surged through him.

"Rhysdale," he whispered. "Where are you when I need you?"

The water started to ripple and churn and the touch of familiar cool fingers against his made him forget about his aches and pains and his worries about the unknown future ahead of him. He lifted his arm up and guided the blue body and familiar red hair up to the surface and onto the bank beside him.

"Rhysdale," William breathed as tears silently streamed down his face.

Rhysdale clutched his hand and sat on the bank, her legs dangling in the water. She pressed her mouth to his, kissing him deeply until she pulled away and looked at him with misty eyes.

"William," she said in alarm. "Are you not happy to see me?"

William swallowed hard, trying to regain some composure.

"O' course I'm extremely happy to see yeh. It's just—I didn't realize until right this moment how much I missed home. And you."

Rhysdale wrapped her arms around him and gently pressed his head onto her shoulder. William sighed. Her skin felt cool against his cheek, her hair smelled like fragrant lilies. She felt so comfortable and familiar. He clutched her tightly to him, reluctant to let her go, but released her when he remembered that Sara would soon be back with one of the others. Rhysdale pulled gently from his embrace.

"The others are here?" Rhysdale examined him carefully, her green eyes bright and clear. "Are you prepared for war?"

"Well, we're ready for something," William answered.

"The Queen's army is assembled on the other side of the river," Rhysdale said. She tossed her head, her hair gently cascading around her face. "I believe they are awaiting your arrival."

"We'll be there soon enough," William said. "Have you any idea what is going to happen?"

Rhysdale looked at William with interest. "It is believed that Thaddeus will come through the Veil. He was banished from Feyland not long after the Veil was put in place. He started an uprising—,"

William cut in. "Yeah, I heard about that. Those that wanted to keep the two worlds together sided with him."

"Yes, but Thaddeus planned not only overthrow the Queen and replace her as a King in Feyland, but also to rule the human world as well. If he comes through the Veil and defeats our armies and the vessels, both worlds will fall under the rule of a malevolent tyrant."

Rhysdale looked toward sky behind William just as Sara landed on the ground lightly on her feet, while Abby crashed into a thicket of shrubs. Abby cursed as she tried to extricate herself.

"I told you to be careful landing," Sara smirked. "It does take some practice."

Abby cursed again and continued to pull herself out of the bush as Sara turned to William.

"I've got to go back and get Joe. Be right back." Sara caught sight of Rhysdale, but showed no sign of surprise at seeing a beautiful, blue redhead sitting beside William. "Oh, hello," Sara waved at her as she lit into the sky again and moved quickly out of sight.

"They'll see her moving in the air soon enough," Rhysdale said quietly. "You'll need to move quickly to get across the river." She slipped back into the water. "I will go look for a water craft to carry you across the river." Rhysdale leaned forward and pressed her lips gently on his cheek.

"I will return soonest," Rhysdale said and slipped under the surface of the water.

William watched as the ripples slowly disappeared and the water became still. William looked up; it was getting closer to first light. *Sara had better hurry back*, he thought anxious. *We're running out of time if we are to attack at sunrise.*

Sara appeared almost instantly and set Joe down gently next to William under the tree just as Abby stumbled out of the undergrowth, her jeans dirty and a tear in the sleeve of her jacket.

"How come you let Joe down so easy?" Abby demanded, noting that Joe didn't have any tears in his clothes.

"Well, Joe listened to the instructions properly," Sara stated simply.

"Where did your friend go, William?" Sara inquired politely, cutting off another one of Abby's streams of off-color commentary.

"She went to see if she could get us a ride across the river."

Joe raised an eyebrow at William.

"She's okay, we can trust her." William looked down at his legs and then up at Joe. "I've known her a long time. Since the first time I ever painted a vision. She's one of the only people I trust."

Joe looked at William and smiled. "Then that's good enough for us."

Both Abby and Sara nodded in agreement.

Sara moved along the bank under cover of the bulrushes that sprouted up out of the water on the river's edge. She motioned for Abby and Joe to follow, and they crept along the path until they were beside Sara, who was crouched down and peering through a break in the reeds.

"See there," Sara spoke in a low voice as she motioned to the opposite bank of the river. "If you look through here, you can just barely see the army. There's a tent there too, a little off in the distance. It looks important, doesn't it?"

Abby and Joe both teetered forward as they crouched, bent over, attempting to catch a glimpse of the soldiers and the tent. There appeared to be hundreds of soldiers, from what movement Abby could actually see as the sun was beginning to rise on the edge of the horizon. The tent Sara pointed out did look quite impressive—its silver and blue colors complete with matching pennants and its officious look was obvious to the four of them. Some very important people were probably inside that tent. Abby was getting impatient and began to pace. This was no time to be speculating—this was the time for action, something they had been training for. And sunrise was fast approaching.

"Sara, we should go," Abby said as she remained in her crouched position. "We have to be there at sunrise—,"

"Yes, I know." Sara sighed in resignation as she started to head back to the tree where they had left William.

Sara stood near the tree and turned around in a full circle scanning the area. She could have sworn he was sitting here under the tree while they went upriver.

"Abby, Joe," Sara spoke, her voice a little higher than usual. "William was here, wasn't he?"

Abby and Joe both nodded.

Sara stepped to the edge of the river. She looked downriver but didn't see him. Sara looked upriver and saw a small rowboat with a solitary passenger moving silently away as if invisibly propelled. Sara pointed, too shocked to say anything. Abby and Joe followed her stare.

"WHERE THE HELL IS HE GOING?" Abby bellowed. "HE'S LEAVING WITHOUT US!"

Abby looked at Joe as if she expected him to give her an answer, an explanation, anything to show William wasn't abandoning them before the start of the battle. Abby sat abruptly on the bank, her eyes riveted on the small boat as it moved away. She felt numb.

"I trusted him," she whispered, "and I was almost starting to like him too."

Joe sat down beside Abby on one side, and Sara sat down at her other side. They both put a comforting arm around her.

"Have a little faith, Abby," Joe said quietly. "Not everything is always as it appears. Maybe he'll send the boat back for us, like Sara did giving us rides."

The rumbles in the sky were becoming more frequent and lightning flashed, cutting bright slashes across the sky.

"I didn't think he would abandon us," Sara said simply as she watched the sky and river.

The approach of dawn was imminent, but the light in the sky seemed to be going backward now instead of forward in time. With each clap of thunder the sky drew darker, the darkness only brightened by the ever more frequent thunder. And then it went still; the type of stillness that people describe experiencing just before the onset of a devastating storm, tornado or hurricane. The stillness brought with it a weird sickly sense, like the sensation they had experienced when they had been in Sara's barn after the attack on Oogan...

Abby couldn't breathe. She started to gasp for air. Her chest felt constricted, like she was fighting with a boa constrictor to breathe. She fought against the overwhelming anxiety that she felt, which was similar to the anxiety she endured when she had attacks of claustrophobia. Her chest tightened, and it hurt just to breathe, compounding her heightened sense of panic over being trapped on the wrong side of the river. And she knew, no, she could sense, that something bad was about to go down. Abby kneeled down, her eyes wild with fear as she stared straight ahead and tried to gulp in as much air as she could to fill her screaming lungs.

Joe knelt down beside her. "Slowly, Abby. Breathe slowly. Breathe in your mouth, and out your nose."

Joe watched Abby with concern in his eyes and she stared at him, her dark eyes still as big as marbles and tried to do what Joe instructed. At first it made her head swim with dizziness, but it gradually began to have a calming effect on her.

"We...we have to get across the river..."

Abby gasped as she continued to breathe according to Joe's instructions. "Don't you two feel it?"

Joe looked at Sara who was still staring down the river, watching the tiny speck of a boat disappear from view. Sara turned, her eyes scanning over the fluffy tops of the bulrushes. She was standing tall, her blue eyes sharp, her body positioned in such an alert stance, she reminded Joe of a cat ready to pounce.

"I feel it too," Sara said quietly. "I know they're here—it's as if they're waiting for us to move before they strike—damn it, William! Where the hell have you gone?"

***

William was in the boat, which was moving at break-neck speed up the river. Rhysdale would not stop even after he had figured out she had no intention of taking him across the river to the still amassing army.

The others will think I've turned tail and run, William thought sadly. *The first group of people who've ever made me feel like I belonged, and now they probably think I'm abandoning them like a bloody coward. People I had something in common with.* William shook his head. *How could she do this to me?*

An overwhelming rage rushed over him. *She was the one who told me to seek out other water creatures. She was the one who urged me to treat this ability as a gift and not a curse. She was the one who convinced me to follow this uncertain path, and now she's taking me away?*

William leaned over the side of the boat and stuck his hand in the water.

If you don't stop this boat immediately and give me some explanation he thought as loudly and as angrily as he could, *I'll flip the bloody boat and drown meself. And if I can get my hands on you, I'll take yeh down with me!*

Instantly, the boat slowed to almost a creep and veered off on an angle toward the bank, still on the opposite side of the amassing soldiers they had long since passed. The boat rode up slightly on the gravelly edge and William clambered out, moving to the side of the boat and waiting there for Rhysdale to appear. After a brief moment, Rhysdale's head slowly emerged from the water and she reached over and lifted herself slightly out of the water, half-sitting, half reclining on a sandy spot near William. As was her usual custom, she was still partially submerged in the water. She looked up at William, her eyes more liquid than the river she rose from. Her head was slightly bowed and she was quietly staring at William.

"What were yeh thinkin'?" William blurted out. "What's going on? And if somethin' is going on, why won't you tell me?" William could sense her confusion, but it baffled him too.

Rhysdale looked at William and closed her eyes, causing tears to flood down her blue cheeks in iridescent trails. She opened her eyes again and fixed her gaze on his.

"You are mortal," she whispered.

William didn't understand. "I've always been mortal," he said gruffly. "What's that got to do with anythin'?"

"If there's a battle, you could die. You could lose your precious life."

"It's a possibility, Rhysdale. But I'm prepared to fight and die. There's always a chance I will survive too. Nothing is certain. Not even death." William looked at her, hoping his words would calm her, ease the fear she seemed to have.

"I don't want you to die, William," Rhysdale swiped at the tears falling from her eyes. "He told me if I kept you from the battle, that you would be spared. And when the Veil is lifted, we can live here together."

William felt the blood in his veins run cold. It felt as if it all ran to his ears, causing a thumping noise to muffle his hearing, but soon realized that the noise in his ears was the jack-rabbit-like beating of his heart. Everything instantly felt out of control and cold.

"Who are you talking about?" William asked cautiously.

"Thaddeus," Rhysdale answered softly. "He promised you would be safe, as long as you did not join the fight."

William bit his lip to keep from screaming at her. "How long have you known me, Rhysdale?" William asked calmly.

"Several decades," she answered.

"In that time, have I ever lied to you or misled you in any way?"

"I don't believe so, no."

"Do you trust me?"

"Implicitly," she answered immediately.

"Rhysdale, you have to trust me now. Thaddeus has lied to you. He used you to lure me away from the others so he can defeat and kill them. Then, he will ensure that the threat of the Four is completely gone by killin' me. Then, he will probably kill you too." William leaned over and held her hands in his. Her long slender fingers quickly entwined with his.

"I am grateful that yeh care fer me and want me to be safe. But yeh have to trust me, not him. This fight must be won at all costs; otherwise both our worlds will be ruined." William lifted one hand up and raised her chin gently so that their eyes met.

"We could go somewhere else, we could hide." She pleaded with tears in her eyes. "Please."

"Rhysdale, no. We can't allow millions teh suffer so we can be together. We have to do the right thing. Please, please help me in this. If we are meant to be together, then we'll find a way. But it has to be the right way. We both have teh be able teh live with the consequences of our actions."

William looked at her as she brushed more tears from her face and lifted her chin up proudly. "I will stand with you, William, no matter what happens."

She tilted her head toward his and gave him a kiss on the mouth, her mouth slightly open as she lingered close to him.

A crack of thunder broke them apart and William looked downriver and saw the flash of lights and a red glow in the sky. The earth seemed to move slightly as he sat on the ground.

"Thaddeus appears to have found your friends," Rhysdale said as she watched the glow surge brighter.

William stood and gave the boat a push with his foot and then hopped into it as it drifted free from the shore.

"We have to go back." William said as Rhysdale slipped into the water.

"I'll get you there quickly." Rhysdale leapt into the water and disappeared under its surface.

The boat picked up speed immediately and the prow raised slightly out of the water as it moved back toward the place the others had been, traveling at twice its previous speed.

"I hope we make it in time," William whispered as the boat sped downriver, thunder and flashes of light filling the sky overhead.

William smiled. *If we get there in time, I just might have a surprise for Thaddeus. Yep, a really big surprise.*

CHAPTER 30

William could see the riverbank where he had left Abby, Joe, and Sara. The patch of land was now an explosion of activity: grunts, shrieks, howls, and even screams choroused in the air, and the chaos involved an assortment of dwarf-like creatures running in multiple directions. The entire area was cast in a red glow and an acrid-smelling smoke reminiscent of cordite hung suspended in the air. In the center of the melee of activity was a tall mound of earth, one that William knew had not been there before.

The mound rose twenty feet straight up in the air, and at its peak Joe, Sara, and Abby were looking down like they were termites fiercely guarding their nest and territory from marauding invaders. And while they were not actually defending their territory, they were, in a rather bizarre way, playing a carefully orchestrated King of the Hill game. They were doing their best to keep to the higher ground and not get knocked down from their lofty peak into the amassing enemy troops below. While William looked on, Sara sent a gust of wind downward, forcing the soldiers to retreat a few feet while Abby casually chucked random fireballs down into their midst, sending the soldiers on her side of the mound scurrying for cover behind trees to shield themselves from the oncoming flames. After the fireballs dissipated and the soldiers deemed it was safe, they cautiously emerged from behind the shelter of the trees to mount retaliatory strikes by hurling arrows, spears, and even rocks. Joe countered their attacks by lifting the mound higher, which aided in deflecting the striking weapons away from them as the weapons, and rocks harmlessly embedded into the soil below them.

Perfect, William thought as the boat slowed and Rhysdale moved to the opposite side of the boat, her head bobbing just above the surface as she looked at William, awaiting instructions.

Hang on to the side of the boat and hold on tight, William thought at Rhysdale as he thrust his arm over the side and into the water. Closing his eyes, he envisioned a large waterspout forming in front of him.

When he opened his eyes it was as if his thoughts materialized in front of him. He glimpsed a swirling vortex of water taking shape in the water beside him. The boat began to shift and turn as the water churned around it, the boat barely evading capture in the spinning whirlpool. With a motion of his hand, William directed the water higher and as it rose upward, it gained strength and momentum, swirling even faster until it formed into a very tall, fast-moving waterspout. William directed it forward toward the base of the mound as it dashed upon the shore. It wended its way inland as it swirled and spun up and over the river bank. A group of soldiers saw it approach and, panic-stricken, ran screaming in retreat into the long grass and surrounding forest as fast as their legs could carry them. The others, who turned only at the sounds of the screams of their retreating comrades, recognized the danger too late and were caught in the swirling motion of the waterspout, disappearing within its depths as it moved further inland.

With a flick of his wrist William directed a wave toward the shore, positioning the boat at the base of the earthen mound, and with another motion he raised the height of the wave up to the same level as the mound. He could hear the yells of some of the soldiers as they regrouped once again and assembled for another series of attacks.

William stood up in the boat. "Abby, Joe, Sara, get in the boat now! They're bloody well coming back. Hurry!" William waved frantically as Abby leapt smoothly from the mound and landed cat-like into the boat. Joe and Sara leapt hand-in-hand behind her.

"Quick, everyone, sit down and hold on!" William yelled as he sat back down. He looked over and nodded to Rhysdale who was still clinging to the side of the boat. William made the wave ebb back away from shore, and the boat glided easily back onto the river just as the regrouped soldiers burst through the grass.

Rhysdale slipped wordlessly under the water and, unseen by the others, led the boat downriver and toward the bank on the opposite side. Abby looked at William, her dark eyes narrowed as she placed a hand on her hip.

"Where the hell did you go, anyway?" she demanded.

The fire was blazing in her eyes, but William didn't care. He felt his own anger rising at the implication hidden underneath her question.

"What the hell does it matter now, anyway?" William bellowed, his ruddy face growing redder. "I'm back now."

Abby and William were staring hard at each other.

It's like watching two cats staring each other down, Joe thought as he quietly observed them. *No matter who wins, there's gonna be a fight.*

"Well, your timing couldn't have been better," Sara chirped cheerfully, attempting to smile at Abby and William.

Sara's smile vanished as she looked to the sky, and a frown came to her face when she looked ahead as they approached the opposite bank. She took in the sight of the mass of soldiers. These soldiers were different than the ones that had ambushed them. There were many different groups of soldiers milling in organized groupings. One group looked like humans but had large, prominent eyes. They appeared battle-ready in their functional armor and helms; each one carried a large shield at one side and a sword at the other. They stood out from the other types of soldiers, mostly because they were so much taller than the other formations of soldiers.

"Um, Sara?" Joe tapped her lightly on the arm. His eyes were tracking a company of soldiers that were pointing in their direction and making their way toward a beached and empty longboat. "How do we know these soldiers know who we are and that we are their allies?" Joe noticed that they were pushing the longboat out into the water, their personal armaments visible at their sides as they worked a series of oars.

"Ooh, good point, Joe!" Sara said as she too spied the longboat heading toward them. "Should we send a sign or something?"

"How?" Abby asked as she moved her hands up out of the boat.

"I dunno. Throw a fireball into the air or something," Sara suggested.

Abby nodded and placed her hands slightly apart until a baseball-size fireball formed between her hands. She tossed it in the direction of the longboat, and it struck the water with a hiss just short of the prow. A few of the soldiers, yelled in surprise.

"No! Not at them!" Sara yelled in frustration.

The soldiers in the longboat started rowing more vigorously, quickly closing the space between the two boats.

"Well, now what, then?" Abby asked impatiently.

"William, do something!" Sara yelled.

William waved his hand in a sweeping motion, and a gentle but large wave lifted the longboat on its crest, pushing it softly up onto the riverbank a few feet away from where it had started. The soldiers yelled in surprise and shock as they leapt from the boat and onto the shore.

"Well, that worked," Abby said to William in a half-hearted way. "Now what?"

"Hey, Sara," Joe spoke quietly, "can you pass a message, you know, on the wind?"

Sara looked at Joe with amazement. "I've never tried that. Do you think it'll work?"

"Try and we'll find out," Joe said simply.

Sara scanned the shoreline once again. *Surely someone is aware we're coming.* Sara's eyes rested on a diminutive man on the shore. He was wearing what appeared to be some odd type of military fatigues; olive green trousers, a vest, and an odd-shaped helmet that looked rather like a stainless steel salad bowl she owned. The face that was barely visible under the helmet was almost completely covered by a wild gray and silver beard. Sara smiled. *Gabe.* She would try to send a message to him.

"Gabe, we are approaching in a boat from across the river. Please stand down your soldiers so that we may approach safely." Sara spoke in a normal, soft tone.

She moved her hand, as she imagined capturing her words in a comic strip bubble and then blew gently. Her breath generated a gentle breeze, rippling the water in front of the boat as it moved forward. Then stillness settled in once more; the only sound audible was that of the water gently slapping at the side of the boat. Sara watched Gabe, waiting to see if the message conveyed to him.

"Has it worked?" Joe asked softly, watching her and trying to follow her eyes.

"I dunno." Sara ran a hand through her hair pensively. "Like I said, I've never done that before."

No sooner had the words come out of her mouth, she waved a hand at the others. "Wait!" She said abruptly, standing up in the boat.

Gabe had turned his head slightly to one side, his back ramrod straight. He looked off into the distance, but remained unwaveringly still. He walked a couple of paces along the riverbank and then turned on his heel to face the water. He held a hand up to his helmet brim and scanned the horizon. As he laid eyes upon their boat, he lifted his arm out, pointed at them, and gave them an acknowledging wave.

Sara jumped up and smiled broadly as she waved enthusiastically in return. "He's seen us! He's seen us!" Sara yelled excitedly as she bobbed up and down on the boat.

"Hey, watch it!" William cautioned, his hands clutching the sides. "You'll send us all into the drink!"

Abby raised an eyebrow, a sarcastic smile on her face. "What are you afraid of? You're the Water Vessel."

"Maybe I'm just makin' sure yer pilot light doesn't get snuffed out," William retorted a little too sweetly, a thin smile on his face.

"You're too kind," Abby replied, mimicking his tone and rolling her eyes.

The sound of a trumpet bleating filled the air. Its herald appeared to be a signal of some sort, and crowds of fairy folk, soldiers and civilian alike, thronged to stand in a line along the riverbank. As their boat floated closer, applause and cheers greeted them. Sara beamed at the large mass of bodies that filed alongside while Joe, Abby, and William smiled nervously in response.

The boat was almost touching the sandy shoal when Abby was hit with the sudden realization that the storm cloud had passed and the sun was rising in the sky. Her heart gave a little leap. It was sunrise. It was *time*. And suddenly everything felt wrong. Her head began to hurt; her stomach was full of butterflies trying to take flight from her body. And then that *feeling*. She felt panicky, but she had to do something. *Now*.

"Get out of the boat! Now!" Abby screamed hysterically. Sara, Joe, and William leapt over the side of the boat and into the knee-deep water. But Abby felt her body become heavy; it wasn't responding as quickly as her brain was moving. It was like she was suddenly moving in slow motion as she turned around and instinctively searched the sky. She saw the sun slowly rising upon the horizon; she felt its glowing warmth upon her face. Then she felt pain. Hot, paralyzing, burning pain—pain so intense that it spread through her as she was lifted out of the boat and thrown through the air across the shore. She heard a loud snap and felt her body impact with something hard, and she slid down it; her back leaned against the tree she hit as she landed in a slumped sitting position upon the ground. She could hear screams all around her; people were running in every direction attempting to escape whatever force it was that threw her. Abby was dazed and couldn't focus, but she felt compelled to watch the chaos that had erupted as if it was a television drama being played out in front of her. She could see people running blindly in all directions and occasional bright flashes of light that materialized in mid-air in front of her eyes, but she was powerless to stop it and still too stunned to move or call out in warning. The intensity of the bright light made her feel dizzy and nauseated. She leaned over and threw up. She closed her eyes and tried to steady herself, but her head hurt even more and the colors got more intense, exploding vividly inside her eyelids.

Abby leaned her head back against the tree and opened her eyes again. She raised her hands up to her stomach; maybe that would ease the nausea? Her abdomen was painful and wet to the touch. *Can't be water*, she thought. *Too warm*. Abby knew she'd been hurt, but she wasn't going to look at it. *If you look at it*, she reasoned, *it will only hurt more. I'm just gonna sit here and rest a little bit.*

Abby closed her eyes and let the darkness push the loud, bright colors out of her head and into oblivion.

***

William instinctively moved out of the boat and into the water when Abby yelled, though the thought had, for a split second, passed through his head as to why he should listen to that bossy cow. William had frozen in horror when he realized it was Abby who was tossed through the air like a rag doll. He heard her land with a sickening crunch against the tree where she still lay motionless. William realized that the warning she called out to them had drawn the attention of the enemy and made her a target.

Don't be dead. Please don't be dead, he kept repeating over and over in his head.

William caught sight of a man, not much younger than him, descending from the sky.

That's him. That's that Thaddeus guy, William thought as the man landed on the ground nearest the water's edge. William looked over at Sara and Joe.

"You two, run! Get outta here!" he pleaded urgently. "I'll hold him off! Please, just get outta here!" William got behind them both and started shoving them out of the water and toward the shore.

Sara turned and faced William. "No. We're not leaving without you."

"You're no good dead, are yeh? Let's not make this too easy fer him."

Sara clutched his arm in desperation, tears running down her face.

William pulled her hand off and continued pushing her away. "We haven't lost yet. We're just separating. I'll catch you up. Now be off!"

William gave her one final push as Joe grabbed her hand. They ran together into the throng of people and were enveloped in the chaos of the crowd.

William watched as they disappeared and then turned to see a lone Thaddeus making his way toward him. Thaddeus did look imposing. His gray hair and steel blue eyes looked lethal: they looked as if they were lit by an internal magical fire, and an evil one at that. His gray drover-style coat fluttered behind him as he calmly moved forward.

Get close, William thought angrily. *Why the hell should I come to you?*

Thaddeus was only a few feet from William when he stopped. He stared at him, and a mixture of revulsion and curiosity played across his face.

"You disappoint me, Walker," Thaddeus drawled calmly as he stood eyeing William with contempt.

"How so?" William asked in surprise, hoping to stall for time.

Thaddeus stuck his hands in his pockets as if searching for something within their contents.

"You had a free pass. A get-out-of-jail-free card. No problems. But you had to be a good guy, didn't you? Had to be a hero, didn't you, William?" Thaddeus' eyes narrowed. "Well, it's too late now. I hope that you realize what you've done."

Rhysdale slipped up out of the water and stood defiantly in the knee-deep water directly in front of Thaddeus. William was shocked and surprised. He had never seen her stand before. He had never even given a thought as to whether she could or not. She spread her thin, blue-skinned arms out to her side to block Thaddeus from William.

Thaddeus threw back his head and laughed. "Do you think you have the ability to stop me, Undine?" Thaddeus looked at her with a contemptuous sneer. "You have certainly made the transition from ally to enemy rather quickly. Does your friend know how involved you were in all of this?"

Thaddeus looked at William, waiting for his reaction. William felt powerless to move or even to speak.

"William knows I did not want him harmed," Rhysdale replied, holding her ground. "My intentions were pure, unlike yours."

Thaddeus moved a step forward, closing the gap between them. Rhysdale did not move, she continued to glare at him in defiance.

"Still, you chose to assist me, didn't you? As long as you could have the one thing you desired. Do you think I will allow you to betray me and have your reward?"

Rhysdale turned to face William. "William, flee quickly! Now!" she yelled over her shoulder as Thaddeus moved his hand quickly to her abdomen, lifting her slightly up in the air. It wasn't until Rhysdale dropped limply into the water and Thaddeus pulled his hand away that William saw he had a blood-drenched dagger in his hand.

William felt rage and sorrow explode within him. He lifted his hands and the water churned all around him. Waves taller than Thaddeus began to push at him, knocking him down. William moved forward and clasped Rhysdale under each arm and, summoning all the strength he could muster from his protesting body, pulled her away as another water spout began to form. It swirled in front of him and caught Thaddeus, twisting and pulling him up into the air as it pulled away from the riverbank and made its way farther downriver with Thaddeus caught in its depths.

That should buy a few minutes, William thought as he continued to pull Rhysdale's limp form up onto the riverbank, ensuring that the soles of her dainty bare feet still maintained contact with the water.

William set Rhysdale down on her back and lay down beside her, gently pushing her red hair back from the soft blue skin of her face. Her color was changing, as if it was draining out of her, making her skin paler and thinner. William looked to her stomach, and through the gash in her iridescent green dress he saw a large knife wound; blood still pulsing rhythmically out of her body. He was surprised that, though she was such a pale blue color, her blood was so vividly red. It had already begun to stain the water around her faintly pink.

William removed his wet jacket and folded it up, placing it under her head. He quickly tore a sleeve off his shirt, folded it up, and pressed it against her wound. Rhysdale gasped and lifted her hand up to her belly, her hand touching his. Her eyes fluttered open and she smiled at William.

"Forgive me," she gasped; her voice feeble and faint.

"O' course I do," William responded, choking back the tears that were threatening to break the brave façade he hoped to maintain.

Rhysdale pushed his hand away and pressed down on the cloth on her belly with a delicate hand.

"You must go," Rhysdale whispered, "you must do what you are supposed to do."

"I can't leave you like this," William said sadly. He could sense that if he left, she would die alone on this beach.

"I can call for help," Rhysdale spoke with more effort. "But you must go on."

"I...I love you...," William whispered as his voice broke away.

He wanted to say more, that he always loved her but didn't want to risk losing his best friend, that he thought she was too good for him, and that she deserved someone better, someone younger, someone sweeter, not him. He fought his emotions as he kneeled beside her in the water. He began to feel that strange feeling he felt before, and he could see a dark cloud forming and moving on the horizon once again, the same eerie red aura surrounding it.

"Go now," Rhysdale urged. "Win this for me too," she whispered as she closed her eyes.

William stood up and moved a few feet away, but he hesitated and turned to look at her once more. She lay so still on the sand, her red hair splayed around her head like a radiant halo, her body so beautiful and still, surrounded by the pink, blood-tinged water. Even though chaotic noises permeated the air all around him, the moment was silent and somber. He had to remember her, remember her just like this, just in case.....

William shook the thought from his head. *No, no time to think of that now, but where to go?* William looked forward and saw Abby still sitting slumped forward, her back up against the tree where she had landed, her brown hair hanging over her face, and her head hung down. William kneeled down in front of her and gently pushed her hair out of her eyes before tucking it carefully behind her ears. Her eyelids fluttered as she opened her eyes, squinting in an attempt to get him into focus.

"Hey," Abby said feebly. Her pupils were as big as marbles. "I got such a headache. My side hurts too." Her head bobbed as she tried to focus her eyes once more. "I think I'm dying."

William grabbed her arm and threw it over his shoulder and cautiously began to stand.

"Don't be so damned dramatic, hothead. Yeh aren't gonna die. We're gonna win, isn't that what yeh said?" William began to move forward a couple steps, supporting Abby with his left arm. He draped her right arm over his shoulder.

"Yeah, gonna win," Abby echoed hollowly as she gingerly stepped forward.

Thaddeus will be back soon, William thought. *And we gotta find Sara and Joe.* William looked up and finally saw the surrounding area as if for the first time. He was amazed to hear yells and war cries resound in the air; the sound of swords crashing together and the zing of arrows as they left their bows. Tiny creatures appeared in clouds in the air like swarms of killer bees battling for supremacy. Bodies lay scattered on the ground as fierce battles continued on the field and in the sky around them, the soldiers oblivious to their presence. It was almost as if they were invisible.

Gotta find Joe and Sara, William thought. *I wonder where the hell they've gone off to?*

"Hey, Abby, where do you think Joe and Sara went?" William hoped the question would help her stay conscious and maybe focus on their mission.

Abby sighed as she stumbled forward. "Well...whenever I go someplace...unfamiliar, I look for familiar faces. That help?" Abby's head rolled slightly as she continued to propel her feet slowly forward.

William nodded. "Yeah, that helped. Thanks," he answered in what he hoped was a cheerful tone. William looked around the battlefield.

Now all I have to do now is find Gabe. Yeah, sure, that'll be easy. William tightened his grip on Abby's waist and shook his head. *Yeah, easier said than done.*

***

Sara and Joe ran hand-in-hand through the chaotic crowd searching for Gabe. *He'll know what to do,* Sara thought. Recalling the sight of Abby flying through the air, she shuddered. *Is Abby dead? And what about William?* Sara wasn't sure if he was still locked in mortal combat or taking the worst in a deadly fight. Sara felt guilty knowing that she was the only one that had ever fought Thaddeus and won, but now was running from him and leaving her friends to stand alone. And Abby had warned them…and it cost her.

Sara stopped abruptly, her sudden stop pulling Joe back hard and almost knocking him off his feet.

"What's up?" Joe asked as he moved to her side.

Sara looked around and observed the battles. All around her were various fairy folk in battle, and, not really knowing the soldiers, she was finding it was extremely hard to tell who was winning. The air was filled with so many flying creatures it appeared that swarms of locusts and dragonflies were at war. Bodies littered the ground, and those still fighting stepped over or around the corpses and wounded as they continued to fight. The sound of cannons echoed in the distance, the flash from the barrels illuminating the dull sky.

As Sara continued to look ahead, she could see the blue and silver tent she had noticed before situated up on the hill crest. Sara pointed it out to Joe.

"That looks like a command center of some sort," Sara spoke as she continued to point in its direction. "If we get there, we have a chance of finding Gabe and figuring out our next steps."

Joe looked at Sara and rubbed his chin in contemplation. "But what if it's a command center for the bad guys?"

"Then we take it out. You okay with that?"

"Sure," Joe shrugged. Sara grabbed his hand once again and increased her stride as Joe fell easily into the rhythm of her pace.

***

"No, I gotta rest, I gotta close my eyes," Abby said as she feebly fought to extricate herself from William's steadying grip. William further tightened his grip on her waist and shoulder and Abby howled in protest.

"Yeh can't rest yet, okay?" William tried to make eye contact with her but her head bobbed back and forth too much. "I'll let yeh know when we can rest, okay?"

Abby's head rolled over next to his face. "Okay," was all she managed to gasp out as she stopped struggling against his grasp.

A very short man appeared on the path in front of them. William stopped and tightened his hold on Abby, drawing another gasp of protest from her. The diminutive man looked similar to Gabe in size and build, but he was clean-shaven, neat in appearance, and clad in a rather severe dark-colored uniform.

"Whaddya want?" William snapped at him, his eyes narrowing under his bushy, gray eyebrows.

"I have been sent to search for you," the man replied coolly. "Are you not two of the vessels?"

William eyed him suspiciously. "Who wants teh know?" he demanded. He hoped Abby had some fight left in her in case they had to flee.

Abby lifted her head and sniffed the air. She wrinkled her nose in distaste.

"You smell familiar," Abby said faintly as she tried to pull herself up. She slumped back against William, sweat beading on her brow.

"Yes, I probably do," Michael agreed calmly. "I work with Gabe at the castle, and I'm here to escort you both to him."

William stayed rooted to the spot, unconvinced. "Where are the others, then?"

Michael smiled. "Gabe has already found them. I was sent to locate you two. How very fortunate for all of us that I have located you and that you are safe." Michael smiled at both of them and clasped his hands together.

"Well, we must get you four together, so let's be on our way, shall we?" Michael turned and gestured forward for them to start moving along the path.

William and Abby looked at each other and shrugged. *Something don't seem right about this guy*, William thought as he eyed Michael's back warily. And he did smell familiar to him too, but in an odd sort of way. *This guy's not tellin' us the truth*, William thought as he pulled Abby along. Reluctantly, he decided to follow him for now. *If he's not who he says*, William decided, *I'll let her fry his ass.*

William smiled and hoped once again that the hothead still had a few good ones left in her.

* * *

Queen Ezreanna scrutinized the map laid out on the low table in front of her. The map was filled with models of sections that designated areas of troop placement on the ground as well as a floating section that showed aerial troops. She frowned, noting a large section of red models had appeared to be pushing through the middle of her blue troops. A rather large Minotaur with impressive horns stood on the opposite side of the table, peering down as she waved her hand in a sweeping motion. Several of the blue models she gestured toward moved from one side of the table into position in front of the mass of red models. The shadow cast from the Minotaur's body made a great many of the figures difficult to see.

"We need to fortify this flank. Enemy troops have broken through our line. Can you move reinforcements there immediately, General?"

The Minotaur general stood to attention. His large bull head seemed oversized and out of proportion to his uniform-clad body.

"I will move them immediately, Your Highness." The general replied officiously as he bowed deeply. "We are taking heavy casualties. I can divert troops from the castle."

"Then do it," the Queen ordered swiftly. "The castle is no good to us if we are defeated." Ezreanna sighed and put a hand to the dagger on her thigh.

The General nodded. "We will do our best to ensure that is not the outcome, Your Highness."

"Good. You have your orders," the Queen said dismissively with a thin smile as the general saluted and disappeared behind the tent door flap.

Ezreanna pulled off her hat and ran her fingers through her hair. *Gabe is taking too long, something's gone wrong.* She could feel it like the pull of a magnet. And where were his charges? She knew they had arrived, a messenger had conveyed the information to her. But she also learned just as quickly that with their arrival Thaddeus had also entered Feyland and that his army had launched its attack.

Ezreanna could feel his presence. She shook with indignant anger.

"Are you feeling well, Your Majesty?"

Ezreanna turned toward the voice. She smiled at the elderly Sage who had risen from his chair and stood behind her. She had been so lost in her thoughts she had forgotten he was even present.

"Forgive me, Master Sage. I am rather distracted."

"Please do not feel that you are alone in this. We Sages also feel the changes in the air. The Veil has been breached in its most fragile state. And now this war—," his voice trailed off as his wide eyes appeared to focus on something off in the distance. He quickly caught himself and looked at her once more. "Well, it seems all so familiar, doesn't it? As if history is attempting to repeat itself yet again."

"Indeed," the Queen answered as she kept her eyes on the doorway.

But this time it must be finished, she reminded herself. *I just hope I don't fail...*

* * *

The scout's words continued to ring in Gabe's ears as he ran through the forest. "Yeah, I seen two o' them running from the boat after one o' them was thrown through the air. The other one stayed in the water, but I dunno what happened to him. I got scared and ran."

Gabe had calmed the young man down and sent him back to his unit. And now he was trying to trace their steps and locate them and find out what happened to the others. Gabe was positive it was Joe and Sara who had run off together, and he had no doubt that they would be searching for him. The battle loomed on all around him as he navigated his way through the mass of bodies and casualties.

Gabe stopped and surveyed the area. From where he was standing he could see the Queen's tent on the rise just up ahead. Half a mile ahead of him he saw a sudden gust of wind pick up and toss several soldiers through the air. A rumble in the ground started, and Gabe grabbed onto the nearest tree for support. The tremors shook the ground but stopped as quickly as they came. Flashes of lightning pierced the sky and thunderclaps fill the air. *The signs*, Gabe thought as he picked up the pace. Sara and Joe were ahead of him, of that he was certain. But the increase in the storms could only mean the Veil was weakening even further. Gabe caught a glimpse of a tall blonde woman and a taller dark-haired man heading for the Queen's tent. Gabe broke into a run. He knew he might not get there in time to make introductions, but hoped he would arrive before either of them did anything stupid. Gabe ran full out. He narrowed the gap considerably and was pleased that at his age and stature he could run faster than most humans. Stopping to catch his breath, Gabe yelled, "Oi! Sara, Joe!"

Sara stopped and spun around. She smiled as she laid eyes upon Gabe and ran up to him, kneeled down, and gave him a hug. Gabe blushed and pulled out of her embrace. "What's that fer?" he tried to growl at her.

Sara smiled and stood up. "I'm so relieved to see you." She looked at the tent only a few feet away. "Should we go in there, then?"

Gabe looked at Sara and Joe and nodded solemnly. "Yeah, I think it's time for yeh both teh meet the Queen."

Sara gasped and began to smooth her hair with her hands as Joe approached the tent.

"Ladies first," Joe smiled at her and motioned for her to lead the way.

Straightening up, Sara smiled, took a deep breath, and stepped past the guards that Gabe had motioned to. Pushing back the tent flaps, Sara squared her shoulders and entered, trailed by Joe and Gabe.

CHAPTER 31

William half-carried Abby as they moved carefully over fallen logs and through thick underbrush. Minutes passed like hours as they trudged purposefully through the dense woods. It hardly seemed possible that this morning had started out as a cold winter day in Michigan. *Was that really only a few hours ago?* William shook the thought from his head as beads of sweat formed and trickled down his face and neck. The rattle of thunder and the occasional flash of lightning startled him and kept him on edge. The air felt thick from the humidity and, coupled with the added burden of toting Abby around, made him feel the strain of exertion. He silently reminisced about how cool and clear the river was. He had such a thirst, but there was no way to quench it.

William was getting an odd feeling about the man leading them. He had said he was taking them to Gabe and the others, but William could hardly help but notice that they had moved away from the battle and not through it. William casually glanced around, taking measure of his surroundings in the forest they were now deep in the midst of. The silence indicated that there wasn't a single creature around at all—not even birds were present in the trees or in the air. *How odd.* William looked down at Abby's face. Her eyes were closed, she was breathing very shallow, her complexion wan and waxy. She was fading in and out of consciousness, occasionally whispering something incoherent. William wasn't even sure she was trying to speak to him, but he still moved closer to her when she spoke, in case she did say something he could understand.

"This way. Up here," Michael spoke, his voice cool and controlled. He gestured to an opening in a rock formation up ahead.

William scrutinized him carefully. "What's that? Are we meeting Gabe there?"

Michael smiled. "No. I thought it would be a safe place to take a short rest." Michael patted a pouch on his belt. "I have some medicine that may help your friend." He patted his other side where a canteen of water hung. "I thought you may also wish to have a rest and a cool drink."

William nodded and continued toward the opening in the rock. *A cave*, he thought as he neared its entrance. *Is this some sort of trap?*

William tried to peer inside without stepping past the entrance. He felt edgy, like someone was staring holes in his back. He half turned and caught Michael eyeing him carefully.

"Is there anything wrong?" Michael asked, stepping forward.

"Uh, could yeh check if there are any animals in there?" William asked, hoping he wouldn't sound distrustful. "I don't want to set her down if something could harm her."

"Of course."

Michael strode deep into the cave and William looked around its perimeter cautiously.

Not a soul around, he thought as his gaze turned toward the sky. It was getting darker, almost as if it was close to sunset. Had that much time passed already? He had thought it was only mid-day at his best guess, but perhaps time moved differently here.

Michael stepped out of the darkness of the cave. "Nothing to report," he noted cheerfully. "It's all clear."

Michael looked up and half-frowned as a flash of lightning streaked across the ever-darkening sky accompanied by a clap of thunder. "It's getting worse, isn't it? We need to get you two to work soon. Come on; let me help you get her into the cave." Michael moved to Abby's side, but William pulled her closer.

"It's okay. I got her." William said as he moved Abby just inside the mouth of the cave. It was so deep and dark that William couldn't see the back of the cave. The ground inside was partially covered in a soft bed of moss, and William carefully clutched Abby as he bent down and kneeled upon the ground. He gasped as his knees screamed in protest, but he kept his grip and then gently laid her down on her back.

Michael stepped beside him and offered the canteen. William lifted Abby's head and pressed it to her lips. Abby took a small sip without opening her eyes and then turned her head away. William placed her back on the ground and took a few sips before he handed it back to Michael.

"Thanks." He said, managing a weak smile.

"You're welcome." Michael replied as he set the canteen down. Michael removed the pouch from his belt and pulled out some herbs and a cloth bandage. He carefully poured some water on the bandage and spread it out on his leg. He selected a couple of bundles of herbs and crushed them carefully between his hands, letting them fall onto the bandage. Michael turned and handed William another cloth bandage and the canteen once more.

"You may want to clean the wound first."

William poured some water on the bandage and moved toward the gash in Abby's side. Covered with dried blood, it didn't look too bad, but once he dabbed at it carefully with the wet cloth and removed the blood and dirt, it looked to be a very deep and open puncture wound, like she had been pierced with a bayonet. Whatever impaled her looked as though it went straight through, missing her vital organs. It most likely happened when Abby hit the tree. A broken branch must have caused it, William deduced, remembering how forcefully she was flung through the air. William grimaced at the raw wound, but quickly tried to show a more clinical detachment as Michael moved to place the bandage he prepared onto Abby's wound. William caught him by the wrist.

"I'll do it." William said as Michael handed it to him. The herbs appeared to have emulsified and William raised a skeptical eyebrow.

"Just place it down upon the wound." Michael instructed. "Apply gentle pressure."

With shaking hands, William placed the bandage on Abby. It made him feel sad to see her so vulnerable. It was disturbing, and he found it oddly unnerving.

"You are a very good friend to her," Michael spoke, breaking the silence. He sighed as he pulled a vial and a tin cup out of his pouch. "I used to have a good friend once." Michael said as he poured some of the contents of the vial into the cup and added some water from the canteen. He handed the cup to William, who grasped it with one hand as he continued to press the bandage on Abby.

"And what happened to yer friend, then?" William said quietly, still watching Abby.

"Well, my friend and I had a difference of opinion," Michael said as he stowed his herbs back in his pouch and attached it back to his belt. "We both felt strongly that we were right and that our beliefs were worth fighting for." Michael sighed and took a sip from his canteen.

"I betrayed him." Michael said softly. "I stood up for what I believed in. Perhaps it was wrong; who's to say? But I do regret the loss of my friend... I regret it every day of my life."

William looked at the tin cup in his hand. "What this fer, then?"

"It's an elixir. It will help you to regain your strength. Drink." Michael urged him with a wave of his hand.

"Are yeh tryin' teh kill me?" William blurted out as he stared evenly at Michael, holding the cup away from him.

Michael laughed and took the cup from him, drank a large swallow, and gave it back to William. Satisfied, William tossed back the contents of the cup in one gulp and handed the cup back to Michael with a nod. William felt a warm surge run through him. It felt good. All his aches and twinges disappeared, his joints no longer hurt, and he felt a surge of energy run through him. He suddenly felt as if he could achieve the impossible. He smiled gratefully at Michael.

"Amazin'," was all William could say. Michael nodded.

Abby began to stir; her eyes flew open and she gulped in air as if she was breathing it for the first time.

"You can remove that bandage now." Michael said. William gently lifted it back and was shocked to find that the wound had knit itself together, leaving only a rather angry-looking red line across Abby's side where the open gash had been. William's jaw dropped, but he recovered quickly and lifted Abby up into a sitting position.

Michael handed her the canteen. Abby looked toward William for reassurance and drank only after William nodded his approval. After taking several swallows, she looked at Michael and then to William.

"I feel better," Abby stated as she looked at William in astonishment. "What are we doing next?"

William smiled as he looked at her. "I guess we're headin' out?"

He looked at Michael for approval.

Michael nodded. "If you're both ready, let's continue our journey."

Abby leapt to her feet and dusted off her pants. "Yeah, let's get going," Abby said impatiently. "We don't want to miss anything, do we?" She strode out of the cave, William following her in her wake.

Michael lingered in the cave for a moment. He sighed gently. "Yes, it's time to revisit an old friend." Michael put his canteen back on his belt and walked out of the cave, hoping the dark sky wasn't a harbinger of things to come.

***

Thaddeus strode through the battlefield, an observer to the fighting that was going on all around him. The clang of swords, the sounds of cannon fire mingling with the intermittent sounds of thunder rang through the air. The smoke and smell of gun powder and fire hung acridly in the air, as did the coppery, metallic smell of blood that had been drawn and spilled; the sight of it was omnipresent on the battlefield. Thaddeus folded his hands behind him as he continued his stroll, stepping casually over the bodies that littered the ground. His troops had breached this flank successfully and appeared to have encountered only token resistance and taken fewer casualties. Thaddeus frowned slightly.

He knew from experience that the majority of troops had already fallen back to cover more vital positions. He smiled widely, thinking how perfectly advantageous it was to have had the same military training as the Queen. *Our father was the best*, he thought to himself. *Too bad he limited my potential.*

A clap of thunder rang through the air as a purple bolt of lightning illuminated the sky.

Thaddeus looked up and silently wondered where Michael was. *Stick to the plan*, he thought as he gazed toward the hills. So far, with the exception of the loss of the Water Vessel and Michael's unexpected disappearance, the plan was working well. "They cannot succeed if there are only three," he whispered. The ground rumbled and shook. Thaddeus smiled. The Veil was coming undone.

"Soon, soon," he whispered with satisfaction as he clasped his hands together in front of him. "Soon, two worlds will be one. And I will take my place as its leader."

Thaddeus rubbed his hands and followed the path away from the battle, following the river upstream.

***

Sara stood inside the blue and silver tent trying to take in every object that surrounded her. Everything was so luxurious and plush; she had a hard time believing it was an operational headquarters and not some fancy tent that royalty would use when they went camping. The candelabras, the beautiful watered-silk-upholstered wing-back chairs—she didn't have furniture this nice in her home. Sensing her head was swiveling around too much, she tried to look at the Queen, attempting, with great effort, not to appear as if she was staring. The Queen caught Sara's eye and smiled warmly, but Sara could only smile back and then avert her eyes, a red flush creeping into her cheeks.

"Do you know where the others are?" Queen Ezreanna directed the question to Joe.

Joe stood straight, a look of concern across his face. "William urged us to go on without him. I don't know what happened to him. After Thaddeus attacked Abby, everything happened so fast—,"

"Abby, she is the Fire Vessel?" Queen Ezreanna interrupted.

"Aye," Gabe cut in, as he stepped forward. "She was badly injured in the attack. I sent a scout to search for them or any news of them, but it may take a few hours, Your Highness." Gabe bowed deeply. Queen Ezreanna acknowledged him with a nod.

"A few hours may be far too late." The Queen said as she turned her attention back to the map board. A wave of her hand caused the troop movement pieces to illuminate.

"Thaddeus has already captured ground here and has broken through the flank here." She motioned with her right index finger. "The time is coming for the vessels to make a stand." The Queen folded her arms across her chest. "I can provide military cover for you; ensure that the only battle you will fight today is the one that fate has reserved for you. But I am at a loss as to where that is, and I am not sure if two of you can succeed in a battle that is intended for all four of you."

Sara cast Joe an anxious look. He held her gaze and nodded solemnly. Gabe stepped quickly out of the tent as Sara stepped closer to the Queen.

She's so strong and beautiful, Sara thought as she gazed at the Queen. Sara sensed an underlying sadness as she returned her attention to the battlefield model. Aware that Sara was once again observing her, the Queen tilted her head upward to meet her eyes. Sara cleared her throat.

"We will do what we can with what we have, Your Majesty." Sara spoke softly but firmly, hoping she sounded encouraging. "We will do our best to see that we fight as hard as we can."

The Queen smiled politely and gave Sara's shoulder a gentle squeeze. "Thank you, Lady Sara." She said softly. "Very well, then. How should we plot our next move?" The Queen stood at the edge of the map board quietly surveying it, as Sara and Joe stood quietly scrutinizing it in deep contemplation. The near reverent silence was broken as Gabe barged back into the tent, causing the flaps to flail wildly about in his wake.

"Your Majesty," Gabe rushed toward the Queen, upsetting a stool in his path. "I have news of the other two vessels."

"Report!" The Queen ordered, as Sara and Joe pressed closer.

"A scout saw them on the other side of the mountain. Both of them are fine, and they appear to be heading toward the river."

Smiling, Sara grabbed Joe's arm and sighed with apparent relief. Joe smiled and patted her hand reassuringly.

"Yes, of course!" Queen Ezreanna burst out. "They must be heading to the Temple of the Elemental Spirits. That is where they must go. It appears that this has to go full circle." The Queen smiled knowingly, oblivious to the looks of confusion on Sara and Joe's faces. They looked at Gabe, eyebrows raised.

"It's where it all began." Gabe offered as way of an explanation. "The magic teh weave the Veil was cast at the Temple. It stands teh reason that it would be the place to go."

Gabe looked at the Queen. "Before we depart, I must warn yeh that the scout reported that the two vessels are not alone; they are accompanied by another. Whatever we do, we must ensure we don't walk into a trap. Remember, eyes wide open."

"Agreed." Queen Ezreanna concurred as she reached for her hat. She cast a glance toward Sara and Joe, and both of them nodded in agreement. She watched them and saw Sara stumble slightly forward, clutching Joe's arm for support. He reach for her and grasped her arm with his other hand, the expression on his face seemed to mirror hers.

"Joe," Sara spoke softly, as if struggling to speak, "I felt so…,"

"I know." Joe answered, his voice faltering slightly. "I felt it too." They both stood there as if frozen on the spot, staring like they were both caught in some kind of trance. A huge crack of lightning resounded through the air and all of them jumped in surprise. The sound appeared to jolt Joe and Sara back from their reverie as the tent started to darken.

"Darkness is falling." Gabe said as he peered outside the tent, a gust of wind slipped through the open flap and rustled papers on the Queen's table.

"We must hurry." The Queen spoke. She stood in front of Joe and Sara. "We will follow you, ensure you are kept safe, and, if necessary, provide a diversion. Is that acceptable?"

Sara and Joe nodded in agreement.

"How do you plan to get there? Do you need assistance?" Ezreanna looked at Sara and Joe with concern.

Sara laughed lightly. "I believe we will take to the sky."

"Do you need Gabe to accompany you and show you the way?"

Sara and Joe shook their heads. "No." Sara answered calmly. "I can just tell where we are meant to go."

Joe looked at Sara, nodding in agreement. "I feel it too. It's like a magnet, drawing me toward it."

"Yes." Sara agreed smiling.

"Well, we will not hinder you any longer. Go safely into the sky, Lady Sara and Sir Joe. We shall see you soon enough." The Queen smiled at them as Sara gave a polite bow and pulled Joe gently by the hand and out of the tent.

They stood outside for a moment, watching the lightning dart across the dark sky. The sky was oddly beautiful and yet strangely ominous and disturbing. It was dark, but not quite as dark as the dead of night.

"It's like the sky before an eclipse." Joe muttered as he gave the ever-darkening sky an appraising look. He gave Sara's hand a squeeze, and she gave a gentle, confirmatory squeeze back.

"Ready?" Sara asked as she slipped an arm about Joe's waist.

"I'm not about to go back, that's for sure." Joe said firmly, a smile half raised on his lips.

"Glad to hear it. On three! One, two, three!"

As they rose into the sky, Sara's two little companions appeared and twittered above her head as they rose higher into the sky. Joe could hear them, but they sounded like hummingbirds hovering at a feeder, their chatter sounded like fingers rapidly tapping the high keys on a piano. Yet Sara nodded and smiled and answered them in response. Joe was amazed that she could understand them. A flash of lightning passed over his head and he jumped slightly. He mused about how ironic it would be to come this far only to be struck and killed by lightning.

Joe laughed softly to himself. 'Somehow, I don't think we'd get off so easily."

"What was that?" Sara asked.

"Oh, nothing."

Joe felt the odd pulling drawing sensation start in his stomach and he looked down. Below them on the ground was a pasture and in its center was a large stone circle.

"Sara! Down there!" Joe pointed frantically.

Sara nodded. "I know. I can feel it too." She motioned to the little iridescent beings close to her head. "They also told me. I'm taking us down." Sara slowed and began to descend gradually. Joe's ears popped, and the air gradually got warmer as they descended into the pasture.

Joe looked ahead and caught a glimpse of large figures moving toward them as they softly touched down onto the ground. Sara clutched Joe's arm.

"I think we're being surrounded," Sara whispered frantically in his ear.

Joe held up a hand motioning her to be silent. As his eyes adjusted, he breathed a sigh of relief. They were being surrounded, but he knew it was safe.

"Sara, it's okay." He whispered back, patting her hand reassuringly. "It's the buffalo; I think they are leading the way."

Sara breathed a sigh of relief. The herd advanced slowly into a circle and quietly surrounded them as they continued to move forward, keeping Joe and Sara safely in their midst. As they advanced, Sara and Joe could see the temple coming into view. It looked like something out of a storybook of myths, something neither of them had ever seen. Sara rather thought it was very much an architectural hybrid of Stonehenge and an ancient Greek temple. Large vertical stones rose high into the sky, each at least four feet in diameter and 20 feet high. The stones were arranged in a circle, each with a couple of feet space between them. At four points large horizontal stones capped the upright stones. The capstones were at least as thick as the standing stones, but probably only half as long by her estimation. Each of the four prominent stones had a symbol carved in the center, and all the upright stones had numerous carvings upon their surfaces. Two marble, ionic columns stood at what appeared to be the entrance.

As they neared the temple, the buffalo herd parted and then slowly melted away, leaving Joe and Sara standing in front of what was obviously the temple entrance. Joe turned back and looked at the herd as they ambled back down to the opposite end of the pasture.

"Meegwetch." Joe murmured softly in gratitude as he bowed his head. He watched them for a moment and turned his attention back to Sara, who was delicately tracing a carving in a stone with her finger.

"Look, Joe, it's a spiral." Sara's voice was low. "There must be thousands of them all over these stones."

Joe looked up at the capstone above their heads. The symbol $\approx$ was in the center.

"Water." Joe said simply.

"What?"

"Water." Joe grabbed Sara's hand and looked up the symbol. "It represents Water. Let's look at the others."

They walked quietly around the circle, gazing at each of the capstones and the symbols, finding one for each of the elements. Joe's heart raced as he looked at the Earth symbol, and Sara jumped with excitement when she spotted the Air symbol. Joe reached into his pocket and drew out a pouch of tobacco. He grabbed a handful and laid down little piles on the ground at each of the capstone points.

Joe marveled at the immense stature of the temple. This was the place where the Queen said it all began. And now he was here. *Full circle. Things have to come full circle, isn't that what everyone says?* Joe slipped an arm around Sara's shoulder and she moved closer, slipping her arm about his waist as she nestled her head against his shoulder. As they stood there together in silent awe, a sense of calm washed over them. Sara looked up at Joe and he smiled.

It would be okay, they would be alright. And in their silent exchange they both understood they would do their best, and whatever the outcome, it would be enough.

***

"Abby, wait!" William yelled at her back as she continued stomping through the woods. William could hardly believe the recovery she had made. Only hours before she had been concussed, low on blood, and certainly close to death, but now she was revitalized and stronger and as bitchy and bossy as ever.

"Well, hurry up, then!" Abby yelled impatiently. She had stopped and turned to face him, her arms across her chest, tapping her foot rhythmically on the ground.

And more pissed off too, William thought shaking his head. He had hardly thought it possible. A hand on his arm caused him to jump slightly.

"You alright, William?" Michael inquired politely.

"Yeah, alright." William muttered. "She's just running me through my paces. Not to worry."

William increased his stride and caught up to Abby who was still rooted to the spot. She was looking all around her as if looking for something familiar. She pointed to a break in the trees.

"See that?" Abby waited for William to nod. "That's the river. I believe we are much farther upstream. We have to go this way." Abby pointed ahead and a little to the right. "That's where we have to go."

"How are yeh so sure?" William asked.

"Don't you feel it? It's like a pull inside." She looked at William waiting for a response.

Geez, he thought. He did feel something too, but he attributed it to the elixir Michael had given him. Now that Abby mentioned it, he noticed it even more. It seemed much stronger, now that he identified it. A tugging pull in that direction, emanating from deep inside his core.

"Yeah," he whispered, looking at her. "I do feel it."

They both looked up at the uncannily dark sky. Not a cloud or a star within it. It felt as if everything was going to be enveloped in a large dark void. William shuddered. Abby put her hand on his arm.

"Look," she said, her voice cracking slightly, "I'm sorry if I'm acting pissed off and in a hurry. The fact is I *am* pissed off. I'm pissed off at what happened to Dan. I'm pissed off I got caught off guard and knocked on my ass. And now I'm pissed off enough to be ready for this fight." Abby sighed and moved her hand to his, giving it a gentle squeeze. "Thanks for sticking by me. I really do appreciate what you've done for me."

William smiled and nodded.

"Now, let's go kick some ass, okay?" And without waiting for him to respond, Abby plowed through the woods, pulling William by the hand as Michael followed silently in their wake.

William was mildly surprised at how well he was able to keep pace, even though Abby still had a death grip on his hand and exerted a little motivating pressure when he, in her eyes, lagged behind. And William dutifully followed without having to catch his breath or stop to give his aching joints a break. In fact, he felt no pain, just an odd energy and exhilaration. He felt so full of energy that he almost expected he was vibrating.

"Look, here!" Abby spoke excitedly, pushing back the saplings in front of her to reveal a grassy field. The river ran parallel to the field, and up ahead, jutting up on the horizon, there appeared to be a stone structure. It stood alone, beckoning like a lighthouse to a ship lost at sea.

"That's it!" Abby said triumphantly. She turned to Michael. "What is that place?"

Michael cleared his throat. "It is an old temple, The Temple of the Elemental Spirits; the place where the Veil was woven a long, long time ago." Michael stroked his chin as he stared at the structure in the distance as if chasing some long forgotten memory.

"What the...," Abby said in startled surprise as a herd of grazing buffalo wandered over to the tree line.

"Don't be afraid." Michael said calmly. "They are the guardians of this area. It is a very special and sacred place. They helped to weave the magic that created the Veil."

"Buffalo?" Abby said incredulously, her eyes wide as she stared at the herd. "But they don't even speak!"

"They don't need to." Michael said simply. "Besides, talking is an overrated quality. Listening is a much more important one."

The snort of a nearby buffalo made Abby jump slightly. Michael smiled.

"I think that one agrees with yeh." William said chuckling.

Michael smiled. "I believe they will escort you to the temple. I wish good luck to you. I enjoyed traveling with both of you."

William's eyes narrowed. "Aren't yeh coming with us?"

Michael shook his head. "I will make sure you are protected, and I will watch the area for any signs of trouble."

The sky darkened again as a rumble and flash of light filled the air.

"You must go quickly." Michael urged, pushing them amid the buffalo. "Go, make haste!" And then he disappeared into a thicket of trees.

"That was...abrupt." Abby said as she pulled William along again.

The herd surrounded them at all sides and moved at a comfortable pace, leaving William and Abby plenty of room to walk freely as they moved toward the temple. William felt safe within the herd. Such large creatures; it was hard for him to wrap his mind around the fact that they could emanate such a feeling of calm. *Serenity, that's what it is. How extraordinary.*

"Hey, William," Abby said, quietly staring ahead. "Buffalo are pretty cool."

"Yeah," William replied. "Couldn't have said it better myself."

As they moved nearer, William was awestruck by the immense stature of the temple. It shared some similarities with Stonehenge, but somehow different in a way he couldn't quite put his finger on.

William stopped suddenly, and, not realizing Abby still had a grip on his hand, almost pulled her backward off her feet.

"Geez, William! What the…," Abby started. William put a finger up to his lips and pointed toward the temple. A dark figure was walking slowly around the perimeter. Abby gasped in shock but said nothing and continued to watch the temple. Then another figure appeared and stood beside the first. Abby sighed in relief. She'd recognize that blonde hair anywhere.

"It's them, William! It's Joe and Sara! Come on, let's hurry!" Abby tugged William and started to run toward the temple, the herd of buffalo quietly parting in front of them to let them pass. Abby couldn't believe it. *We found them!*

Sara turned to face them as Abby ran into view. She squealed with delight and wrapped Abby in a warm hug.

"Abby, you're okay! We were so worried. Thank goodness you're safe."

Sara let Abby go as William shook hands with Joe.

"Well, actually, it's thanks to William." Abby said, grasping a blushing William by the shoulder. "He took care of me and kept me safe."

Sara gave William a big bear hug.

"Well, I'm not completely responsible, that Michael fellow healed yeh—,"

"Who's Michael?" Sara asked casually, looking past Abby and William.

William shrugged. "I dunno exactly. Some fella; said that he worked at the castle with Gabe. Said Gabe sent him to find us."

Joe and Sara exchanged nervous glances.

"Uh, where's he now?" Joe asked, looking around. "We'd like to thank him."

"He said he had to go." William answered. "He said something about making sure we weren't attacked."

Abby stood still, staring ahead, running her hand through her hair. Suddenly, her eyes widened. "I remember that smell, William. Remember how he smelled familiar?"

"Yeah," William said staring at Abby with wide eyes.

"He smelled like Oogan. The same goddamn stink." Abby went white. "Holy shit!" Abby swayed and William caught her by the arm. She felt the same feeling, the same change in the area as she had back at the river before the attack. She shrank into William's hold, gripping his arm tightly.

"Ya stay with us, okay?" William admonished.

Abby nodded wordlessly and looked around wildly, as if waiting for another attack from the sky, which had been remarkably calm since they arrived.

Joe cut into the silence. "Abby, William, you gotta check this place out. Come see."

Joe and Sara led them around the outside of the temple, pointing out the capstones and the elemental symbols on each of them. They entered the temple together and stood in the center, awestruck at the enormity and the history of the temple.

"Look at this symbol." Abby pointed to a carved symbol on a flat stone inside. "It's Mayan."

"How'd ya know that?" William asked surprised.

"I went to Mexico once and toured some ruins." Abby said matter-of-factly.

"Are there any Native North American symbols?" William asked Joe.

"I'm sure there are a few symbols, but in general, my people didn't have a written language. Our culture is based on an oral tradition." Joe replied.

"Oh, I didn't know that." William stammered. He turned his attention to some other stones. They all appeared to be etched with various symbols, a lot of spirals, but also a few that seemed to be from a great many cultures.

"Let's go back outside." Sara said as they all converged in the center.

"Why?" Abby asked, staring at her.

"Well, the Queen said she would send troops to aid us—she's probably going to arrive soon." Sara replied, straightening her jacket.

William looked down at his shirt and realized it was dirty and missing a sleeve. He was unsure if he should tear off the remaining sleeve or just meet the Queen as he was. *Good enough for me*, he decided.

As they stepped outside, they paused to gaze up at the sky which had become a dark purple color and was oddly quiet and still. Off in the distance, a red aura glowed and filled the sky as the sound of something large approaching echoed in the air.

Gabe appeared in front of them, causing Abby and William to jump suddenly.

"Gabe! You scared the shit outta me!" Abby yelled at him. Stifling a laugh she asked, "What's the hell is that on top of your head?"

Gabe rolled his eyes and pushed the helmet down harder on his head. "Ain't cha ever seen a helmet before?"

Biting her lip to hold back a smile, Abby shook her head and looked away.

"Well, yeh have now." Gabe looked at William, his eyes narrow. "Survived alright, did yeh, Walker?"

"Yeah, I suppose." William answered indifferently.

"Heard ya had a travelin' companion," Gabe asked, his eyes almost boring holes in William.

"Yeah, a guy who said he worked at the castle with yeh. Said his name was—,"

"Commander!" A voice cut William off as a young scout hastily stood in front of Gabe.

"Yeah, what is it?" Gabe said gruffly.

"Her Majesty and her guard are on their way. She said to relay to you that all is in place. I am here to await your instructions." The young scout stood at attention but was sneaking sidelong glances at Joe, Sara, Abby, and William.

"Please relay that we are ready. She may approach when ready."

The scout snapped his hand up in a smart salute. "Very good, sir!" He quickly bolted out of sight.

"Idiot," Gabe muttered, "didn't even give me a chance to tell him you never salute in the field. It'll get someone killed—AARGH!"

Gabe was unable to complete his sentence, as he was lifted high into the sky, pulled backward by some unseen force.

"Not this time!" Sara yelled. Sara hopped up on a gust of wind and directed a change in its direction, halting Gabe in mid-air and pulling him toward her, catching him about the waist. She quickly alit on the ground and set Gabe down gently. Red-faced, he mumbled a barely audible "thank yeh".

But then was no time for chatter. The sky surrounding them turned a ruby red hue. Abby felt her insides turn to jelly. She didn't want to hurt, didn't want to die. And suddenly her thoughts turned to Dan, lying motionless in the hospital, unable to speak, to touch, or even to hold her. She recovered from her attack. Would Dan? Would he ever be the same? Anger welled up inside her. She felt the Fire light within her.

Use it, feel it, a voice inside her called, as she felt a pull once again inside her. Calmly, she walked inside the temple and stood directly under the capstone that called her, the one etched with the Fire symbols. She surrendered to the pull that brought her to this place.

"I am here," she declared. "Give me strength."

Sara, Joe, and William looked at Abby. Gabe nodded to them, and they quickly walked to the capstone that represented their Elements. As they took their places, the Queen arrived with her Royal Guard and hurriedly entered the temple. She watched in silence as each of the vessels took their place within the temple under their respective capstone in silent reverence.

"Has it begun?" Queen Ezreanna enquired softly as she looked at Gabe. Gabe nodded. The red hue in the sky flashed brightly. Thaddeus appeared in front of Gabe and the Queen in the archway that served as the temple entrance. The clamor of soldiers fighting came from behind them.

"Indeed, it has begun." Thaddeus said, his eyes wild, his smile wide. "And I intend to stop them and destroy the Veil once and for all."

Thaddeus moved toward Gabe. "But first, I plan to get rid of you. These four couldn't have survived without your help." Thaddeus pulled a knife from his belt and stepped closer. Gabe pulled a sword from his scabbard.

"You'll get a fight, yeh bastard," Gabe spat angrily as he rushed forward. The clang of steel rang through the air as Gabe and Thaddeus crossed blades. Gabe sliced Thaddeus across the hand and he howled in rage, raising his knife higher and quicker with each motion. Thaddeus gained the upper ground and, sticking out his foot, tripped Gabe and sent him tumbling flat on his back, his sword flying from his grip. Gabe closed his eyes.

Goddess, let it be quick, he prayed as Thaddeus loomed over him. A yell of surprise caused Gabe to open his eyes, and he was shocked to find Thaddeus was no longer looming over him, but grappling with Michael on the ground. Outside, screams from soldiers behind him made him turn around in surprise. Through the gaps in the stones, Gabe could see Thaddeus' men running in retreat as a flock of Taekyrs flew over the open sky of the temple toward the group of enemy soldiers, throwing rocks and swooping down on them. Some of Thaddeus' soldiers were laying down their weapons and surrendering, while others ran shrieking into the woods.

Good old Oogan, Gabe thought, chuckling to himself. Gabe turned his attention back to the two men scuffling on the ground.

"Traitor!" Thaddeus growled. "How dare you betray me!" His voice was filled with venom. "You could've been second-in-command under my rule! And you've tossed it all away!"

Michael struggled to keep the knife from his throat. "I was misguided to follow you. You'll never rule, and I'll never let you harm Gabe or anyone anymore, you crazy son of a bitch." Michael lunged for the knife, but Thaddeus was quicker. He plunged the knife into

Michael's chest. Michael's face went blank and Thaddeus easily tossed his limp body aside.

"Now, sister, it is your turn." Thaddeus gripped his knife in his hand as he advanced toward her. Queen Ezreanna tossed her hat aside and pulled the knife from her thigh and crouched down like a tigress ready to strike. None of their magic would work here in this holy place, the heart of all old magic. At least they would have an even playing field.

"Yes, brother, it is time," she whispered, turning the knife in her hand.

Suddenly, all activity around them ceased. The sounds of the melee outside the temple caused by the Taekyrs attack ceased. Gabe looked upward. The Taekyrs were still in the air, but were frozen in place, as were the soldiers on the battlefield. Everything and everyone outside the Temple was frozen, as if they were in a movie that was paused upon the screen. Gabe looked over at the Queen and Thaddeus. They were still moving, circling each other like a snake and a mongoose ready to fight. He glanced back inside the temple and noticed that The Four had turned, each of them facing the core of the Temple, each rooted firmly to the ground with arms extended out to their sides. They all wore peaceful, beatific expressions on their faces. A bright white light was radiating from the center of the temple, filling the sky, erasing the red hue that had hung there only moments ago.

"We are the Elements." The Four spoke in unison. "Earth, Water, Air, and Fire. Through the strength of our power, the Veil has been restored. The Veil will remain in place."

"NO!" Thaddeus screamed with rage. He looked at the Queen, his face contorted with rage, his eyes dark and angry. "I will still destroy you!" He screamed, lunging at Queen Ezreanna.

She dodged sideways and deflected a blow with her arm. Lifting her leg, she kicked him hard in the ribs. Clutching his side, he bent down and grabbed her ankle, pulling her down. Swiftly, she kicked Thaddeus in the face with her other foot and then rolled away, pushing herself upright. Thaddeus jumped on her back. Quickly, she bent down and flung him off her. He landed hard on his back on the ground in front of her. Without hesitating or missing a beat, she swiftly plunged her dagger into his chest. Thaddeus sagged into the ground.

Queen Ezreanna bent over gasping, the palms of her hands braced on her thighs as she gulped in air.

"Are you alright, Your Majesty?"

I just killed my brother. The Queen nodded wordlessly and motioned to where Michael was lying prone on the ground. Gabe nodded and knelt down on the ground beside him. Michael's breathing was shallow and blood still seeped from his wound. Gabe struggled to open the medical pouch on Michael's belt, but Michael's hand came up and gently caught his wrist.

"It's too late," he whispered.

"Why did yeh save me?" Gabe asked quietly, staring into Michael's eyes.

"Because it was the right time to do the right thing. I'm sorry for ever betraying you, my dear old friend. I have missed your company."

Gabe wiped a tear from his eyes. "And I've missed yers."

"Forgive me," Michael gasped, clutching his wound with one hand.

Gabe nodded. "Aye, yeh. I forgive yeh."

Michael smiled and closed his eyes. Gabe set his lifeless hand down gently across his body and stood up.

Queen Ezreanna stepped toward him and turned to face The Four, who were still standing stock still and emanating a luminous white light.

"What of them now that Thaddeus is dead? Isn't their task over..."

The Queen screamed shrilly as Thaddeus rose up, pulling the knife from his chest, and lurched toward her. The Four moved toward him as if they were one, and as one they spoke. "The enemy must be destroyed. Harmony and balance must be restored."

A white light rose from each of them, like four ethereal knife blades, piercing into Thaddeus and filling him, the excess light escaping through his eye sockets and mouth. Without warning, he burst apart into a hail of crystals that scattered on the wind like thousands of luminous snowflakes. And as instantly as they appeared, they disappeared, carried away on the wind that left as fast as it came. Thaddeus was gone.

The white light from the Temple gradually dimmed before dissipating; the Taekyrs in the air were once again in flight, though they appeared slightly confused as to which direction they were to fly. The soldiers on the ground also were disoriented, but Gabe quickly had his soldiers round up Thaddeus' men to escort them back to the village.

Sara, Joe, Abby, and William looked around in amazement.

"Are you well?" The Queen inquired politely. Even though they too were disoriented, they each nodded in assent.

"Is it over?" William asked cautiously.

"Yes, I believe so. For now," the Queen answered simply.

Abby spotted the body of Michael on the ground and nudged William. He put his arm around her as she wiped a tear from her eye.

"What happened to him?" Abby whispered as tears streamed down her face.

Gabe swallowed hard. "He was a good friend. He stood up and fought for what he believed in. Yeah, he was a good friend."

Abby and William glanced at each other solemnly.

"Ensure that a litter arrives for Michael," Queen Ezreanna instructed Gabe. "He will be taken back to the castle for a proper burial." The Queen turned to face Sara, Joe, Abby, and William.

"Come, we will all return to the castle, have some food, and rest." She turned quickly and led the way. The four of them paused and gazed up at the sky for a moment. Gone were the eerie red glow and the dark purple expanse. The night sky was clear and filled with stars, and a bright crescent moon hung in the sky above them.

Sara smiled as William fumbled attempting to tear off his remaining sleeve. She laid a hand on his arm. "Let it be 'til morning."

William shrugged and nodded as the four of them walked toward the lights on the horizon.

***

The sun was low in the morning sky as Abby sat on a bench in the courtyard, sipping a cup of coffee. The sun felt warm on her skin and the sounds of the birds chirping happily in the trees was soothing. It was a beautiful place, one that she hoped she could visit again. And she could visit again; Queen Ezreanna had told them were would be welcome as honored guests any time they wished to visit. She could imagine visiting the village, taking in the shops—she could see that it would be a rather pleasant place to get away from it all...as long as there was no war to fight.

Abby smiled and sipped her coffee. *Yeah, I could handle that.*

The sight of Sara entering the courtyard made her sit up and try to catch her eye. As Sara turned her head, Abby gave her a little wave. Sara smiled and waved back as she strode over to the stone bench. Abby saw that Joe and William were following behind her.

"Morning, Sara," Abby smiled as she sipped her coffee. "What have you been up to?"

Sara plopped down beside her on the bench. Abby noticed she was wearing a white long-sleeve tunic and a blue cotton skirt and sandals on her feet.

"Nice clothes," Abby said complementing Sara on her appearance. Abby eyed Joe and William. They too had changed clothes and were wearing white tunic shirts. Only William had changed his trousers. Abby smiled. Joe always did prefer to wear jeans.

"You could've changed too, Abby," Sara said casually, her eyes appraising Abby's clothing. "They are very hospitable here."

Abby shrugged as she looked down at her torn and bloodied clothes. "Yeah, I know. But I'm in a bit of a hurry. I was just going to finish my coffee and then head back." Abby put her hand in her pocket and pulled out a small glass vial. "I've got to deliver this," she spoke quietly. "It's for Dan. Queen Ezreanna said if I give it to him, he'll make an almost full recovery." She hurriedly tucked it deep into her pocket. Abby looked at William who was standing beside Joe.

"What are your plans, William?" Abby inquired tentatively.

"Well....I intend to stay here for a few days," William stammered, looking down at his feet as he nervously shuffled from one foot to the other. "My friend is recovering, and I want to spend some time with her."

Joe stepped forward. "Sara and I are gonna stay for a few days too," Joe added smiling at Abby. "The Queen said we could stay, and I don't have to be at work for a few days—,"

"Yeah, and we can spend some time with Oogan too," Sara cut in excitedly. Joe rolled his eyes but said nothing.

Abby laughed loudly.

"He was there in the end, wasn't he?" Sara beamed proudly. "I knew he wasn't bad, didn't I say so? Anyway, the Queen said he could visit me too whenever he wants. Isn't that great?"

Abby smiled. "Yeah, I guess it's great. Say hi to him for me."

Sara's jaw dropped. "Really?"

"Yeah, really," Abby replied, surprised that she actually meant it.

"If you want, he can visit you too," Sara offered.

Abby raised an eyebrow. "Don't push it, okay?"

"Yeah, okay," Sara said smiling.

Abby sipped her coffee and gazed absently out at the garden in front of her. The scent of the brilliantly-colored flowers was pervasive and almost intoxicating. "You know, I spoke with Queen Ezreanna this morning," Abby said quietly. "She told me that we are the first of the four vessels to all survive after being called upon," Abby surveyed the others, trying to gauge their reactions, but they stood resolute, their eyes fixed on her.

"No one here really knows what will happen with us, you know. It's not known if we will keep our abilities, lose them, or if they will gradually fade with time. We are entering uncharted territory." Abby stood, setting her mug down on a nearby table. "I do know that we are linked together, whether it is divine force or some weird kind of *espirit de corps*. I do hope that no matter where we each end up, we still stay close."

Sara stepped forward. "You know you'll see me when I get back," she said as she gave her a big hug.

Joe stepped forward and hugged her gently too. "Give Dan our best...we'll see you both soon."

Abby nodded and pulled away gently. She stood in front of William, who was trying hard to hold back tears that were already streaming down his cheeks.

Abby smiled. "You really are a Water Vessel, aren't you?" She gave him a big hug. "Thank you," she whispered in his ear as she gently kissed his wet cheek.

"I'll...I'll see yeh soon, hothead," William said, his voice choked up.

Abby smiled warmly. "I know." She turned toward the gate. "I gotta get going."

Sara walked beside her as she approached the gate. "We'll walk you to the stone."

Abby nodded in agreement as they all strode out the gate and into the woods that kept the Omphalos hidden. As they approached the stone, Abby stopped abruptly.

"What?" Sara asked, looking at her with confusion.

Abby crouched down and pointed to a bush ahead that was rustling. She crept up silently and stood directly in front of it. As she bent down to examine it, a group of four children burst out of the bush laughing and giggling as they ran in play.

"Hey, wait!" Sara yelled at them.

It was strange to see children playing, oblivious to all the fighting and danger that had been so prevalent yesterday. Wasn't that really what the fighting was for? Protecting the innocent and keeping them safe? Abby watched the children as they ran, stifling the yawn that was trying to escape. The children kept running, all except for one petite little girl with long dark-brown hair. She stopped and turned to look at them, her brown eyes wide with curiosity. She stood silently, staring coolly at Sara, Joe, and William. Her eyes then locked on Abby, and she stared at her for the longest time. Abby couldn't help but stare back, powerless to even speak. Suddenly, an odd chattering voice broke the silence, and the child turned and dashed into the forest, her brown hair trailing loosely behind her. Abby felt dazed and suddenly exhausted. But she still had to go. Sara was still watching the little girl's departure.

"You okay, Sara?" Abby asked as Sara's head swung around.

"Abby, didn't you think that little girl...," Sara stammered, unable to complete her sentence. Joe caught her arm and shook his head.

Abby stared at the stone, eager to get back and give the potion to Dan.

"Um, yeah, cute kid," Abby replied casually. "You three stay safe, and I'll see you all soon."

Sara, Joe, and William nodded and waved as Abby placed her hands on the Omphalos and disappeared. The three of them stood solemnly together for a brief moment, each of them knowing it was not the end, but merely a respite. They knew the possibility existed that they were still endowed with their abilities, and each of them knew they were sworn to do whatever was within their means to protect their world and Feyland. The future was going to be a challenge, a journey into uncharted territory—one that they knew they would have to, once more, face together as The Four.

ABOUT THE AUTHOR

Lenore has always been passionate about writing from an early age. Her first book, *Good Luck, Bad Luck*, is still a family favorite.
Lenore is a free-lance writer and former staff writer for the *Emmett Village News*, where she was known locally for her monthly articles.
Lenore's passion also extends into the art world, where she likes to create in pencil, pen and ink, metalsmithing, and mixed media. She was the president of the Richmond Area Art Association for many years. During her tenure she was dedicated to exposing the community to local artists through art exhibitions, thereby generating interest in the visual arts.
Lenore served in the armed forces and held the highest rank of sergeant. She currently lives in Michigan with her family: her husband, Dan, her two sons, Hunter and Archer, and a few too many cats.
Lenore loves to hear from her readers, friends, and family and often makes them characters.
You can follow *The Four Sworn* at:
www.thefoursworn.com
or on Facebook at:
https://www.facebook.com/TheFourSworn

www.ingramcontent.com/pod-product-compliance
Lightning Source LLC
Chambersburg PA
CBHW071445170626
46811CB00007B/2483